Priscilla

To Benita,

Priscilla

Engaging in the Game of Politics

All the best,

M. Simms Maddox

07/21/2018

DR. M.J. SIMMS-MADDOX

Priscilla

Copyright © 2016 by Dr. M.J. Simms-Maddox

Published by:
M.J. Simms-Maddox, Inc.
www.mjsimmsmaddoxinc.com

Publishing consultant:
Professional Woman Publishing, LLC.
www.pwnbooks.com

PWN

ISBN: 978-0-578-17899-8

*To the loving memory of my father,
the Reverend John Wesley Simms.*

Acknowledgments

Some time ago I experienced a series of recurring dreams about a conversation that I had with my father, himself a great storyteller. It had not been a bad conversation, rather one in which a loving father shares precious thoughts about his life and his hopes for his beloved daughter. While penning my recollections about that conversation, I began recalling many earlier experiences, particularly my tenure as a legislative aide in the Ohio Senate in the early 1980s. Thus began the Priscilla trilogy.

Three of my former instructors at Livingstone College—Albert Clayton Boothby, Abna Aggrey Lancaster and Karen Rawling—believed that I had "a way with words;" and former classmates and longtime friends Cathy Bracket Dover and Ada Mae White Taylor encouraged me "to write a book" in the first place. Two other friends, Katie Cohen and Lavon Taylor, might be amused to see characters resembling our friendship.

I also was inspired by my siblings: John Simms, Jr., Sharon K. Dixon Dewberry (who died shortly after this story was written), Coleen C. Nelson (a published author of children's books), H. Paulette Simms and Jina L. Simms-McGriff, respectively.

However, my greatest inspiration to write stems from my mother, Hazel B. Owens Simms, who also happens to be our family's first published author.

Editor Lee Titus Elliott performed substantial editing and copyediting of my original work. Laurie Devine helped me to further develop my characters. Livingstone College colleagues Michael D. Connor and Donna Girouard provided thoughtful insight near the end of this endeavor; and to my darling husband Odinga for his moral support and for his tremendous tolerance during our loss of quality time together, I am deeply grateful.

It is also important to point out that there is no inner circle in the Ohio Democratic Party called "the Collective Force," I made up that, too.

Notwithstanding, any sayings such as the one about lawmakers always thinking of ways to retain majority party control of their respective legislative chambers are based on my own understanding as a political scientist.

Contents

CHAPTER 1

Teaching, a Noble Profession

August 14, 1978
Tallahassee, Florida

"Folks," said the captain over the PA system, "we're circling over Leon County and will be landing in Tallahassee in a few minutes."

As Priscilla J. Austin felt the huge airliner descend for landing, the captain continued: "Just ahead of us is the capitol. Those of you on the left side of the cabin can see the new twin State Legislative Towers—next to that shiny gold dome, the original Florida Statehouse."

Priscilla peered out her window aboard her Eastern Airlines flight and thought: *You have got to be kidding me. This is the state's capital? And this is all there is? Just two state office towers and the original capitol and a patchwork of drab-colored buildings scattered about? And that's odd ... the city is laid out in the shape of a T. Surely the city's growth wasn't arranged to spell out its initial from the air."*

The captain went on: "Historically, Leon County has had the largest concentration of plantations in the South. Look, you can see quite a few of them. Tallahassee itself is home to the Apalachee Indian tribe, and *two* nationally recognized college football teams. Any Seminoles and Rattlers onboard?" His message was followed by cheers and clapping.

Priscilla was unimpressed by the enthusiasm of the sports fans because she had expected to see a big city like Buffalo, Cleveland, Columbus, maybe even a little like New York. Where were the clusters of bridges and buildings in all shapes and sizes, roadways radiating from the city center, backed-up traffic? And skyscrapers? Where are the skyscrapers? Instead she saw sprawling groves of tall pines, pockets of lakes, small oval-shaped fish ponds, church steeples here and there, and a smattering of neighborhoods and gashes of red clay littered with heavy construction equipment.

She stared at the red dirt. *It's everywhere, Lots and lots of red dirt. And all those pine trees. This is like flying into the islands. Everything's so open and flat.*

As she peered out her window, she remembered that, nearly a decade ago, her father had accompanied her on her first flight ever as she commenced her undergraduate studies at the church-sponsored Livingstone College in Salisbury, North Carolina. They had flown to the Charlotte Douglas International Airport on Allegheny Airlines, rented a red Corvette and driven to the nearby college campus. Along the way they had driven past rows upon rows of pine trees, so Priscilla had asked, "Daddy, why're you dumping me off in the backwoods of this state?"

But for this trip, her father had driven her nearly ninety miles north of their hometown of Prendergast, New York to the Buffalo Niagara International Airport where he had bid her farewell and where she alone had boarded the Eastern Airlines flight.

Priscilla was a daughter who had been raised like a son, and she had been raised to do that which had pleased her parents. Strongly bound to her father, she was about to commence a career as a college professor, something that she knew pleased him.

"Fasten your seatbelts, folks."

In its final descent, Priscilla felt the airliner swoop down amid a cluster of pines. In a few seconds, she saw the pines sweep by her as the plane braked with a roar, bounced twice on the tarmac and then rolled to a deafening stop.

Priscilla moved into the aisle along with the other passengers. Carrying her shoulder bag and the new, buttery-leather attaché case—which had been a going-away gift from her parents—she stepped out of the cool airliner, down the steps and onto the tarmac, emerging into a sunset as hot as an August noon against her face. Almost immediately, the humidity hit her. She felt sweat drops on her forehead. Just ahead of her, a small child wailed in misery on a father's shoulder. A pair of older women, about her mother's age but darker-complexioned, church ladies by the looks of their flowered dresses and hats—*Hats!*—took tiny paper funeral home fans out of their purses and began flicking them across their faces.

Inside the terminal, she was met with high-pitched screeching voices. "Hi, y'all! Welcome to Tall-a-hass-ee!"

It was in that moment that Priscilla got a glimmering of what it might mean to follow her father's dream of how to live her life. OK, with eyes open wide she was joining what he always called "the noble profession of teaching," and at the university level, as an assistant professor at Florida A&M University (FAMU), one of the most prestigious, public, historic black institutions of higher learning in the country. She had mostly finished her doctorate and had thought she was on board with carving out a respectable station in life here in Florida's capital city. But her Daddy had compared Tallahassee to the life she had enjoyed growing up in the relatively small but sophisticated upstate New York town of Prendergast.

As it so happened, Priscilla's father—the Reverend James Nelson Austin, was acutely aware that, although his daughter was a self-assured, strong-willed and enterprising young woman, she had yet to develop a sophisticated outlook on life. That—as she approached her twenty-fifth birthday—Priscilla, more than any of her other siblings, had yet to come into her own; she was still living and doing things that pleased her parents, rather than herself. So, while Priscilla compared the obvious similarities between Salisbury and Tallahassee—not with Prendergast, for in her mind, no other place compared with her beloved Prendergast—the good reverend had determined that it was time for her to experience life of a higher order, one in which he might not be there for her, one in which she would have to fend for herself. Besides, he himself was experiencing something that had caused him to act more deliberately than once anticipated. He so wanted for Priscilla to come into her own. Poor Priscilla, she had no idea that she was not only still being groomed by her father, but that she was also commencing a journey that would lead to a sea of change in her life. Why, even the good reverend could not have predicted what would happen.

Priscilla squared her shoulders and straightened the fitted jacket of her classic, pale blue linen suit. Maybe Tallahassee was too hot and humid, and from the air it had not looked like much. But no one knew her here. She would create a new life for herself, and she would be happy. Two thoughts cheered her: She was her father's daughter. And as a modern, educated black woman, she was equal to whatever would come her way in Florida's capital city.

Whether those two inspiring thoughts contained the seeds of conflict or not, she stepped smartly ahead into the new life that she was sure she would make into a success.

Only a few days after her arrival, Dean Lionel Newsome seemed as welcoming as a favorite uncle. He had called her into his office, sat her down, and was far more solicitous than any academic officer she had previously encountered in her undergraduate years at Livingstone or in her graduate school at *The* Ohio State University.

He liked the way she looked: handsome rather than pretty, conservative tailored clothes, dignified beyond her years, perhaps a little aloof—but in his opinion, that was a good thing especially in a young professor who had to exercise authority over students not much younger than she was. As to skin color, Priscilla was what people in his Mississippi hometown called "redbone." But she was not "red," rather fair-complexioned of mixed race—black American mixed with British on her father's side and Irish on her mother's. Moreover, she would be the first to boast of Choctaw on her father's side and, as she had indicated in her application, Cherokee on her mother's as well.

Priscilla settled back into her chair in the dean's private office and basked in his attention. She put the personal welcome to a junior faculty member down to what must be the family feeling of a historic Black university. Besides, she had always been her Daddy's favorite. She was accustomed to preferred treatment by a male authority figure. But it felt good to be here in this job, which apart from a short interval back home in Prendergast as a systems analyst—computer programmer was more like it—was the first full-time employment she had acquired on her own and away from the direct influence of her father.

Dean Newsome—well-groomed, in his late sixties and stoic in demeanor—had begun by noting how pleased his Department of Political Science was to have her teaching in her specialty, American Politics with a concentration in State Legislative Politics. Priscilla was aware how unusual it was at small universities for new and junior faculty to teach in their specialty, but FAMU was no small university. The university boasted a current enrollment of over three thousand students along with several highly acclaimed graduate-level programs. It was the largest of the historically black colleges and universities (HBCU). Moreover, Priscilla was aware how keenly those HBCUs competed for the best, brightest and most ambitious academics with doctorates—or, in Priscilla's case, near-completed doctorates. The head of the recruiting team who had offered her this position had said how lucky they were, in particular, to get a *woman* with her demographics and credentials.

"At FAMU," the dean was telling her, "the path to tenure is simple. In your case Ms. Austin, complete your doctoral dissertation, produce a good measure of research and publish some of your work."

Welcome to academe, ole girl, she thought.

But there were no surprises in his formula for success. That pathway was the same in colleges and universities all over the country.

But what the dean said next was not what she had expected.

His intention, Dean Newsome said, was not to pry or intrude, but to bond with this "newly hired young professor," as he had put it. "Enough about your future, now," he paused. Then, "I see you grew up in Upstate New York. But where are your folks from?"

Priscilla smiled. Obviously now the dean was chit-chatting. In a moment the meeting would be over and she would get on with her new life. "Mississippi."

"Really?" The dean leaned forward. "Where 'bouts? I'm from Canton."

"You don't say." Priscilla frowned. She had not known they shared a Mississippi connection. Her father was from Canton, and the place was not big. Her whole family, on several summer vacations, had visited kinfolks there. It had always been quite the experience, there in the Deep South. Never had she been so grateful that she grew up in Prendergast, New York, as when she had experienced Mississippi. A thought flickered, but she quickly dismissed it. The dean could not know her father. *I know I didn't slip and say Daddy's name. Nor did I say he was from Canton.* Yet as the dean digressed with some story about his folks back there in Canton, Priscilla wondered if it were possible after all that her father, a Methodist minister who was—in his way, as political as any representative in any legislature, was a personal acquaintance of her dean. *Had Daddy had anything to do with this faculty appointment? Nah*, she thought, *oh no.* She was a double minority: black and female. Her academic credentials were outstanding. She was presently completing what would eventually be the first of two different dissertations. This one was a nationwide study of black state lawmakers. And although she did not know it at the time, she would later examine the political attitudes and behavior of black college students. The recruiter had said they were lucky to get her.

Priscilla dismissed her suspicion. The dean was being friendly and welcoming. He had found a mutual connection and was honoring it. She would be gracious enough to accept that connection. And she herself was, just like her father, naturally astute when it came to politics, which were all about relationships. She had innately understood that it was one thing to *make* connections, but another to *have* them. Even in college Priscilla had begun to grasp how small the world was and that people really were connected; it made them seem very close, somehow. She listened as the dean acknowledged familiarity with some of the other families in the small rural town of Canton. So what if the dean had some distant acquaintance with her father. Priscilla relaxed, remembering the many gifts she had received from the father she had always admired. Back when she was only a teenager, she remembered his telling her: "Priscilla, you are blessed with many talents, among them being the ability to persuade others. Use your talents wisely." At the time, she had not realized the significance of his instruction. Her father himself had always been politically active, especially as a minor but steadfast minister in the civil rights movement, and he had primed her to follow his footsteps. So it was that nobody had been surprised at her decision to study political science in college and eventually pursue a doctorate in that discipline. But aside from a legislative internship, Priscilla had never seemed eager to go into politics herself.

The dean was showing her to the door and shaking her hand. They both were smiling. Priscilla could hardly wait to write her father about how connected they all were to that little Mississippi Delta town.

There was much more to write home about than a distant connection between her academic dean and her father's family.

Priscilla took pride in her letter-writing to family and friends. Everything—even the address of her new townhouse—was so fresh and new that she had to share it with those back home. Apalachee Parkway—"derived," she wrote, "from the American Indian Apalachi tribe"—was the main thoroughfare to the capitol and the new state office twin towers. She wrote in plain language and in conversational mode, and she employed the descriptive and literary motives of the moment. Mostly, though, she wrote as if she had a captive audience. "Colorful flora, giant cacti and palm trees, not pines, adorn the grounds of this new housing complex," she wrote about her new neighborhood. "Clusters of Spanish moss complement the landscape and dangle amid the dense woods that adjoin the old narrow roadways. But you don't want to have car trouble around here, definitely not at night, because that's when the eerie effects of such exoticism are most apparent."

Yet she was not so rhapsodic a few days after she had moved into her new home, when she rushed to the manager's office to report an emergency. "There're these really big ghastly bugs swarming all over the place!"

"Sure, honey," drawled the manager, not bothering to look up from his newspaper. "What'd you expect? This is, after all, Flawreeda. I'll give ya the name of an exterminator. Here ya go. Give 'em a call."

Priscilla cringed at the mere mention of the word "exterminator." Never before had she had occasion to use the term. Now, she required the services of a bug killer! *Yuck.*

Several weeks later, she experienced another problem. "My menstrual cycle is out of sorts, and I've been bleeding profusely," Priscilla said to the nurse who answered the phone at her doctor's office. She had also, she said, been burnt to a bronze crisp while sunbathing by the pool at her townhouse complex. Her body ached to the touch.

Later, the doctor cautioned her. "This is the South. The semitropical South, at that. Your body needs time to adjust to this climate, especially to our heat and humidity. Stay out of the sun as much as possible. Lying around the pool unprotected from direct sunlight isn't good for you. This is, after all, Flawreeda."

Why, she fumed to herself, *do these people talk to me like I don't understand them or know where I am? This isn't a foreign country. This is America. And they talk so slowly, sort of . . . like I don't understand English.*

But she had to admit she had probably had too much of this powerful Florida sun. She had spent too much time wading in the pool and lobbing tennis balls whenever she felt like it—often without sunscreen. In the doctor's office, as she was getting dressed after his examination,

Priscilla took a good look at her arms and legs. She was one of the relatively fair, though not the fairest-complexioned, of the five Austin sisters and brother, who varied in color from a striking ebony hue to white. What they all had in common were high cheekbones inherited from their mother's Cherokee grandmother. Growing up, all of them had been conscious of the lightness or darkness of their individual skin tones. But their father had taught them not to dwell on skin color, and that they must never discriminate or mistreat someone because of the way they looked—especially their color. Even so, Priscilla had always been aware that lighter complexioned people fared better in society.

Again she stared at how her skin had darkened in the Florida sun. She laughed. She liked it darker. She was none too thrilled to discover, however, that burned skin hurt. She had assumed, incorrectly, that since she was black, the sun would not bother her, any more than the native speech patterns. But it did not take long for her to become accustomed to that piercing Southern accent and that slow Southern speech. Or sunscreen.

It was not long, too, before she hosted her first guests.

Only a few days after she moved into her townhouse, her father Nelson and his fishing companion, Oscar, arrived with Priscilla's car, a 1976 crimson-and-metallic-gray Mustang hitched to Oscar's old double-gas-tank truck. Nelson had offered "to do this small favor" of towing her car to her doorstep "to make your transition a smooth one." At the time, Priscilla had never wondered if this trip was more to check up on her than to fish, as her father and Oscar insisted, their favorite watering holes along the Eastern Seaboard to the Gulf.

In anticipation of their arrival, Priscilla had kept watch from the veranda of her second-story bedroom, so before the men had even unhitched her car, she had run out to the parking lot to greet them. Like a child, she had urged, "Come on in and check out my new place." But she was unprepared for what seemed to her to be their lack of interest. The two men fussed with the car and then their luggage. Finally, to appease his daughter, Nelson went upstairs and rushed through the dwelling as if he were searching for something he was unable to find.

"Ah, nice," he finally said. "Really nice, Priscilla."

She could have sworn, before he averted his head from her, that she saw a pool of tears fill his eyes. She was puzzled, however, when he showed little interest in the décor of her townhouse—and definitely disappointed when, a few moments later, he and Oscar said they were off to do some fishing.

But before he left, Nelson took his daughter's expectant face between his hands. "I am so pleased that you have found reasonably secure and decent living quarters," he said. Then he leaned down and kissed Priscilla on her cheek. "Sorry, kiddo, but we've got to get moving. Those fish aren't exactly waiting on us."

Priscilla clung to him. "Oh, come on, Daddy. You guys didn't come this far to rush right off. At least let me prepare you some lunch."

Oscar accepted her offer almost immediately. "Nelson, an hour or so won't hurt."

As her father wiped his eyes, he sat down at the head of her table, and Priscilla saw his tears and recognized them for what they were. It was not that he did not want to spend any time with her. She knew her Daddy. He was overwhelmed to see that she had settled in to her new life so well. Although, of course, he would be the first to see that as a result of his tutelage, Priscilla had developed into an independent woman right before his very eyes.

One of the first clouds in that bright Florida sky came when Priscilla least expected it: her first day of classes. In graduate school at Ohio State, she had been a teaching assistant (TA) and had lectured many undergraduate sessions, especially the large introductory classes. Everyone, her father included, had always told her she was a natural-born teacher; and so it was that she had settled into the Political Department at FAMU, too, with nary a problem. Her office on the second floor of Tucker Hall, with the other social and behavioral sciences professors, had already become her professional nest.

She had been confident, too, on her way to the first day of classes. It was customary for the newest member of the FAMU faculty to teach the introductory classes, each with an average enrollment of one hundred and fifty to two hundred students. With her experience as a TA at Ohio State as her framework, Priscilla was familiar with similar class sizes and well-prepared for her new assignment.

Priscilla followed the traditional style of lecturing. Before each class, she would enter the lecture hall, nod at her students, step up on the platform and commence writing notes on the chalkboard. The late seventies was a generation before the digital era.

But this first morning at FAMU, just as she was ready to begin her lecture on the Watergate Scandal and the Vietnam War, she heard the whispers and saw the students' expressions of amazement even before she had turned to the chalkboard.

"Surely she's not the professor," one student muttered.

"No, she's too young," another answered.

"Must be a TA," guessed another. "That's all we ever get—teaching assistants."

Priscilla had just decided to ignore those comments and had written "Watergate" on the chalkboard, when the harsh masculine voice of a student rang out in the lecture hall.

"What can *you* possibly tell *me* about Watergate or Vietnam, *young lady*? Not only am I older than you. I was there. I served in Nam. Besides," the veteran shouted, "how *old* are you anyway?"

The whole lecture hall went silent. Neither Priscilla nor the other students seemed to know how to react. Priscilla looked the veteran over. He was wearing camouflage, and it seemed he thought she was enemy with whom he was at war. *He's fuming*, Priscilla thought. *Not a bad-looking fellow. But I've got to work this one carefully. Should I let this go and make nice with him?* But he seemed to her a bully, and maybe she should begin her teaching by drawing the line at what she would accept and what she would not. She was aware that some folks at her undergraduate and graduate school had criticized her for being aloof. But she took pride in being her father's daughter, and Nelson had taught her that being upright was right even if it was not popular. *Maybe this vet—and the other students, too—won't like me so much, but I've got to draw the line right here, and* now, she decided.

Still she hesitated for another instant of reflection. FAMU was *not* Ohio State or any other mega-campus. Already she had noticed that the friendly campus ambience seemed to reward a personal style of teaching and interaction with the students. But—again, another lesson imparted from her father—standards were standards. She was a professor, not the social director on a cruise ship. Ideas were what inspired her, rather than interactions with people. Her mission in Tallahassee was to become a first-rate college professor, nothing more, and she would keep her mind on that goal. Priscilla took a deep breath. Finally, there was the unspoken fact that she was not only a young professor but a female one. Priscilla's adoption of the new-age feminism made her even less likely to bend to the heckler in her class.

She was a picture of relaxed authority as she stepped out from behind the lectern. She briefly described her educational background, adding that, "like most other interested people," she "had followed the Congressional hearings on television and had read about incidents related to the war and the scandal in the newspapers." Then she walked toward center stage, looked up at the students in the inclined section in the rear of the hall and said, "My own father is a staunch Republican, poor fellow. And he was distraught over the horrible debacle, especially with President Nixon's subsequent resignation for his *abuse of power*."

Then, with the stride of a seasoned public speaker and with a little bit of what her sisters had often teased her was her Bette Davis kind of moxie, Priscilla locked into the gaze of her aggressor. "Now about my age ..." She paused. Sometimes in the past, Priscilla had bumped up her age a notch or two, acutely aware that college students held greater respect for older, more seasoned professors. In fact, some students openly challenged, even outright disrespected, young or new professors—one of the ordeals of teaching at the college or university level. *Oh, well*, she thought. She was what she was. She would tell the truth. "Though it's frankly irrelevant to my employment here, I'm twenty-five years old."

She let that sink in, and then chose to ignore the muffled snickers before she continued. "The law says, 'Though shall not discriminate on the basis of race, creed, color, national origin, age, gender, and a few other variables.'" Again she paused. "And, oh yeah, I realize I might not *look* the stereotypical role of a professor—at least not of the type you maybe had when you first started college. But in this at least, Bob Dylan was right. Some things in this society really are changing. After all, isn't that why you and the others are here—to improve your lot and do a little better than the previous generations?"

Priscilla smartly turned back to the chalkboard but then hesitated and faced the class again as though she had forgotten something. This time she spoke directly to the veteran who had challenged her. "Just one more thing. I have an older brother, about your age, who also served in the army in Nam, just like you did. Plus I have two sisters—career soldiers—serving in Uncle Sam's Air Force and Navy. You're not the only one with experience of Vietnam." She nodded in finality. "Now ... shall I continue with the class?"

She waited while the students opened their notebooks. And then, in earnest, she got down to the business of her new life as a college professor.

CHAPTER 2

Not From 'Round These Parts

Priscilla was in a fairly good mood as she headed home from church that next Sunday, only a few days after her encounter with the angry veteran in her American Politics class. As a lifelong member of the African Methodist Episcopal Zion denomination, she had asked some of her new colleagues whether there were any such churches in Tallahassee. They had told her there was one AME Church, Macedonia, but no AME Zion Churches. *Close enough*, she had thought. She had already determined that Sunday going-to-church visits would be one of her regular weekend rituals. As a preacher's daughter, she and the rest of her family had rarely missed a Sunday in the pews. She had dressed this morning in one of her favorite tailored suits, the double-breasted black linen one with a fine white silk blouse that her mother had helped her choose at Prendergast's finest ladies' salon. No hat, of course. Priscilla went to church most Sundays, but she never had been and never would be one to wear a big floppy hat just to praise the Lord.

As she cruised along what she supposed was the way home in her sleek Mustang, Priscilla reckoned she already had set a pattern of a rather regimented life: campus, church and occasional visits to the shopping mall near her home. *Nothing wrong with setting a positive ritual,* she told herself. She meant to be a success, and her Daddy had always impressed upon her that a disciplined life was a successful life. She told herself she was already well on the way to doing just that. Finding a welcoming church community was certainly a step in the right direction. So far her experiences at her new church had been positive. Located near the university and close to downtown, the congregants were primarily professionals—college professors, and even a congressman. Every time she went, she was pleased to recognize a few faces she had seen around the campus. Then, this morning, when she lingered after the service, the pastor had told her that he had been a FAMU alumnus. He had even once been a drum major for the nationally acclaimed Marching One Hundred Band, which he said—with a pride that still resonated after all those years—had often been invited to participate in presidential inaugural parades in Washington, D.C.

Yet as she drove along, Priscilla, engrossed in remembering how at home she had felt at church, suddenly realized she was in a neighborhood wholly unfamiliar to her. Had she somehow missed her turn? She concentrated on getting her bearings. But just after crossing Miccosukee Boulevard, she noticed how seedy the houses and stores had become. This was a side of Tallahassee she had not seen before. Her own neighborhood, a new development on the outskirts of the city, seemed part of another world. She passed a large cinderblock apartment building with shattered windows and tattered clothes hanging from railings. Row upon row of identical, rectangular-shaped, bland-colored houses ran along the street. She wondered where the grass was, and thought: *I could never live in a place like this!*

She passed an unattractive sign in huge block letters that read: CHIPLEY SQUARE HOUSING PROJECT, and realized that back home there were no such "projects". Nor had she ever known anyone who resided in such housing. Everybody she had ever really known lived in a house, a townhouse, an apartment complex or even a mansion—nothing government-owned. She recalled recent letters she had written to family and friends about the clusters of Spanish moss that dangled amid the dense woods near her home. *No such scene in this neck of the woods.*

Then another thought: *I have no idea where I am.*

She felt her blood pressure escalate. *I'm lost! But at least it's not at night!*

As she drove, her eyes wandered off the road, looking for possible sources of help. People meandering down the sidewalk wore shorts, cut-off jeans, sandals or bare feet. A few women were clad in loose-fitting blouses and short skirts or shorts. Nobody was dressed up like she was, fresh from church. Priscilla saw several old cars that looked as if they had not been moved for a while, including a rusty black Cadillac without tires, mounted on blocks. She watched as an old Dodge van, filled with children, clattered past in the other lane. From her rearview mirror, she noticed plumes of gray smoke billowing from its tailpipe.

Then suddenly, as she was about to pass through the intersection at Chipley Square, she felt a massive crush against her left side. Instinctively, she covered her face. A moment later, she lost consciousness.

Later, when she read the police report, she learned that immediately after the collision, some people from the neighborhood had approached the crash. Two women who had witnessed the crash told police they had seen fumes rising from the Mustang's floor. Since the driver's side of the car had been severely damaged, the women had pulled open the passenger door. Then one of them—Monica Ratcliff, according to the police report—had climbed into the car, tossed out some of the broken glass through what had been the windshield and unlatched Priscilla's seatbelt. Somehow she had managed to wedge herself behind the driver's seat and lift Priscilla to the other seat. Since Priscilla was unconscious, Monica had needed her friend's help in getting the driver out of the vehicle. They had even collected Priscilla's purse and some of her other belongings from the floor. They had carried Priscilla out of harm's way, gently placed her on the ground and even picked particles of glass from her hair and from her forearms. "She sure ain't from 'round here," one of the women had told the police. According to the emergency medical team—which soon arrived with an ambulance—it had been thought that Priscilla had been badly bruised but had escaped broken bones or major lacerations.

When she awakened awhile later in the emergency room at the Tallahassee General Hospital, Priscilla had no idea what had happened after she blacked out. She had not even remembered the ride in the ambulance. Her first conscious thought had been annoyance that strangers were touching her, and in such a tiny room.

One woman, who kept identifying herself as a paramedic, had repeatedly asked Priscilla the name of her insurance provider. But Priscilla had still been too dazed to respond. Later she remembered frowning at one young man in uniform as he took her pulse, while another intern checked her blood pressure. By then, they had found her identification cards in her purse and were calling her by name. And she did have some vague recollection of staff marveling that, apart from some scrapes and bruises, she had sustained no major physical injuries. As the medical team continued to check her out, Priscilla had come to enough to gaze at the walls and ceiling and pray that all this was just a bad dream.

She was relieved when the attending physician, a tall, slim woman of forty, stood beside her bed. "Folks, I'll take it from here," she told the other staff. "Hello, Ms. Austin. I'm Dr. Anita Tousse."

Priscilla took one look at the doctor and blurted out, "I could be dead!" She took a deep breath. She had no idea how she looked now or after the accident. She was oblivious to the fact that her hands and arms had already been cleaned and bandaged. She learned later that her face had nicks and scratches, but no major lacerations. "And I don't even think that guy who was in here before you even checked to see how I was doing."

"I'm sorry to hear that, Ms. Austin," the doctor said. As she pressed down on her lower abdomen and other parts of Priscilla's body, she kept asking: "Can you feel anything I'm doing? How about this? Are you experiencing any pain?"

"My entire left side is throbbing. And I'm a little light-headed."

Dr. Tousse nodded. "I understand from the paramedics that you lost consciousness for a while. And there seems to be a little gap between what you recall and what some of the witnesses saw." The doctor continued checking for any signs of pain. "Apparently, some of what happened has eluded you. But I'm certain you've sustained a concussion."

Dr. Tousse had more bad news. She thought it best, before even considering releasing Priscilla, to take a Magnetic Resonance Imaging (MRI).

Priscilla whitened. One of her aunts back in Indianapolis had endured one of those tests, and Priscilla, who was claustrophobic, had assured herself then that she would never consent to let herself endure being moved slowly through some gigantic tube of an X-ray. But it seemed she was not to have the luxury of choice. Before long, she was supine—facing the underbelly of an enormous machine—and being instructed not to move. Priscilla, as she felt herself being rolled slowly, oh too slowly, along, thought she would die of fear. She considered how first she had been forced to reconcile to the fact that she had been in a bad car accident, then to the fact that she was in the hospital. *Now this!* She wished the doctor had spent more time preparing her for what was to happen, especially the loud tapping sound which continued and continued. As her body rode back and forth through the tube, she wondered: *What's that horrible sound? Is the darn machine broken?* Her head ached. She was nauseated. Her muscles tightened. She balled up her fists. She closed her eyes. Her body trembled. Beads of sweat rolled down her face, neck and arms. *This cannot be happening to me!*

As the machine's motions increased, Priscilla's body shook.

The technician's voice boomed at her: "Try to be still."

Priscilla wanted to curse at the man. *Can't he see I'm uncomfortable in this darn contraption? Get me out of here!* Yet somehow she managed to endure the MRI.

Back in her room, two new faces greeted her. A young black police officer introduced himself and his partner. "Well, Ms. Austin, I'm Officer Marvin Lancaster and this here's Detective Lance Sommers."

The detective started the questions. "Do you recall *why* you're here and *what* exactly happened to you?"

Still somewhat shaken from that traumatic MRI, Priscilla fixed her eyes suspiciously on the detective. Instead, she directed her answer to Officer Lancaster. "Yes, Officer, I remember." She wondered why a detective had come to the hospital to investigate what she assumed was a simple car accident. What she found out later was that the driver of the other car was a known narcotics dealer. The detective apparently had been trying to assess whether she had any connection to that driver before the crash. Little did she know it, but it had been to her advantage that, according to the hospital personnel, the uninjured driver of the Pontiac which had hit her had not even checked to see how she was doing.

Priscilla patiently told her story. "I was driving home from church," she began. Then she described realizing she was lost in a part of the city she had never seen. Her account of the actual accident was brief. "I remember a massive crash, or crunch of sorts on my left side ... covering my face, feeling like I was in a whirlpool and then slamming down hard to the ground. That's about all I honestly remember. I don't even know how I got out of my car or to the hospital."

The officers exchanged a knowing look.

Detective Sommers nodded. "That fits what we've heard." Then, "Ma'am, you're not from 'round these parts, are you?"

"No, Detective, I'm not 'from 'round these parts.'" Priscilla was lying down, or she might have drawn herself up to full height. "I am from Prendergast, New York. And I am on the faculty at FAMU. And I have *never* even been in an accident before, not to mention one in which I had a near-death experience."

After Priscilla stopped talking, the detective shared with her the "several consistent accounts of the accident" that had already been provided by Monica Ratcliff and the other woman who had rescued her from her wrecked car. The two witnesses were residents of the Chipley Square Housing Project and were both on welfare. They had not only confirmed Priscilla's account of the accident but had also done so with greater clarity and much more detail. They had acknowledged that they had pulled Priscilla out of her car and called the police and an ambulance. "The driver of the other car was speeding," Monica had told the officers, "and ran straight through that stop sign. And no, he didn't even come back to see what'd happened to that girl."

As it turned out, the police officers had merely wanted to get Priscilla's side of the story, "for the record." They told Priscilla they were satisfied that she had not known the other driver and that there were no contradictions in the various accounts of the accident. Officer

Lancaster added that since there were no signs of any kind of skid marks on either side of the intersection, their findings were that the other driver had neither stopped nor yielded at the stop sign.

As the policemen concluded their visit, Dr. Tousse was back again. This time she perched on the side of Priscilla's bed and told her the most significant result they already had from their testing. Priscilla would have to consult with her own doctor about this, but the emergency room physician said it looked like she might have a condition called "benign positional vertigo." As Dr. Tousse explained it, this was a rare but incurable condition that Priscilla sustained in the accident. "In layman's terms," the doctor said, "the impact of the collision joggled your brain." What this meant, she added, was that if Priscilla tilted her head a certain way, her equilibrium would be thrown out of balance and she would feel faint and dizzy, as if floating in an ocean. She offered to show Priscilla exercises to alleviate some of the discomfort. "But," the doctor concluded regrettably, "unfortunately, there is no cure for benign positional vertigo. It's something you'll just have to learn to live with."

"Oh, dear me," Priscilla whispered to herself. Of course she would seek a second opinion. This doctor seemed nice, but her diagnosis was not what Priscilla had wanted to hear.

Priscilla nodded when the doctor said they would be keeping her in the hospital overnight for observation. Today had been much more than she bargained for.

Priscilla took a taxi home the next morning from the hospital and then arranged for her insurance agent to assess her car's damage at the garage where it had been towed. Later she called Dean Newsome and her department head at the university to inform them of the accident. She skipped supper and dropped, exhausted and fully clothed, onto her bed. She slept soundly until daybreak. She later found out that her colleagues at school had heard about the accident on the evening news and were therefore relieved to learn of her "satisfactory status".

Priscilla downplayed the seriousness of the accident when she finally called home the next day. "Well, folks, I was in a little fender bender, but I didn't suffer any major injury," she told her father and then her mother and her brother and two of her sisters, who all had been at their parents' home in Prendergast. She told them she was "just a little shaken up, but I'm all right" and "enjoying a few days out of the office to rest up." Priscilla had consciously used the kind of language she had always heard from her father whenever he had found it difficult to share with his family the true extent of any unpleasant circumstances. She was definitely her father's daughter.

It was another three days before she saw the damage to that Mustang she had always loved. Priscilla was surprised how banged up it was on the driver's side. It looked like a total wreck, there in the parking lot of a service station where it had been towed. She shook her head, for the first time aware of how fortunate she had been. The crumpled driver's door had been bent inward almost to the center of the car. If it had bent inward just a couple of inches more toward the windshield, she would have been decapitated. *Oh my*, she thought. Dr. Tousse, as well as Monica and the other woman who had rescued her from the crash, had been correct in describing her survival as a miracle.

She had more surprises in store for her when she read the full police report. She learned that all the statements from the witnesses had been consistent, but that Monica Ratcliff's had been the most thorough:

> Around one-thirty Sunday afternoon, most of my neighbors and I in the Chipley Square Housing Project were outside in our yards or visiting with neighbors, and some of our children played in the street in front of our homes. We were having a fish fry and enjoying the day. But we couldn't help but notice that girl driving through our neighborhood. She drove a nice-looking silver-metallic Mustang. Sort of reddish color for the interior. There was a FAMU decal on her windshield. From my yard, I could tell she didn't look like she was from 'round here.

As the girl drove down Horah Street, we could hear the driver of the Pontiac approaching the intersection at Chipley and Horah. We heard the roar of his engine because he was speeding, so some of us realized that what eventually happened was going to happen anyway.

The girl in the Mustang had the right-of-way on Horah Street; the driver of the Pontiac had a stop sign on Chipley at the intersection of Horah. But just as the girl in the Mustang was about to drive across Chipley, the driver of the Pontiac sped through the stop. Just like that he did. That man had no intention of stopping, and that poor girl never even saw him coming. The two cars collided; the Pontiac had rammed into the driver's side of the Mustang. Then, on impact, the Mustang rose up off the ground midair, twirled around, and plummeted back down onto the curb in the opposite direction it was driven from.

Some of us ran over to examine the situation. It was a horrible scene. We just knew that girl was dead and all mangled up, but she wasn't. It all happened so quickly, but at the time, it seemed much longer. Then we rescued her from the accident.

Reading that report, Priscilla realized that she had been doubly saved by this woman: first at the scene of the accident, when she had saved her life. And second, afterwards, when her details about the accident had convinced the police and the insurance company that she was not at fault for the accident. Priscilla received the fruits of that last factor when, later that week, her insurance agent said her Mustang had been totaled and she would be compensated for not only her injuries but also with another car of her choosing. Priscilla was satisfied at that settlement. She had loved that car and decided to replace it with an exact replica: metallic gray with crimson interior—the Buckeye colors.

But she knew she had one more reckoning to tend to.

She drove a rental car out to the Chipley Square Housing Project to give heartfelt thanks to Monica and the other woman who had rescued her from the accident. However, the more dented and battered doors she knocked on in the vast and gloomy complex, the more dented and battered doors that shut in her face.

Priscilla kept yelling through each door that kept shutting her out: "I just want to thank the women who helped me out of that wreck." But she did not understand that, as far as Monica and the other woman were concerned, the day of the accident was *over*—and they neither desired nor required Priscilla's self-serving gratitude and patronizing posture for any affirmation of their deeds. To them, today was just another day further from the accident, and the likes of Priscilla J. Austin had been unwelcomed then, and were unwelcome now.

CHAPTER 3

Nelson's Mysterious Request

June 5 – July 21, 1980
Trinidad-Tobago

Priscilla squinted into the lens of her camera, careful to keep the brilliant West Indian sun at her back. *Beautiful shot*, she told herself. Again and again she snapped the graceful boat, the turquoise sea and the frolicking people—wanting to save the images of this perfect morning on this perfect island for posterity.

Life, she reflected, *was good*. She could hardly believe that she had finished two years at FAMU. Two good years. She liked teaching, and she liked her school. But she asked herself: *Do I love it?*

Priscilla sighed. *Maybe so, maybe not*. She was not used to feeling ambivalent like this. She was an absolute kind of girl. Her father's daughter. Nelson had always been most definite about everything.

But Priscilla had made the right decision when she had volunteered to accompany six graduate students from the Department of Political Science to the University of the West Indies in Trinidad-Tobago, where she was spending the greater part of her summer. During leisure time, like this morning, she often ventured off on her own. She and some avid amateur deep-sea divers had arrived at the docks off the Gulf of Parnia where they had waded in the water and were waiting for their signal to embark.

Priscilla clicked her camera again. Then, when one of the divers introduced himself and offered to take her picture, she smiled at this young man who said he was Roshan Patel.

He was good-looking: small, almost delicate of frame. He told her that he was a graduate student majoring in engineering in Toronto and was home in Trinidad-Tobago for the summer. She was surprised to learn that many East Indians resided in Trinidad-Tobago. There was time for her to note that she liked the affable way he had about him. But her mind was on the boat ride and diving.

Someone yelled out, "They're calling us to come aboard." The amateur divers, including Priscilla, all ran toward the boat in glee. They were jubilant during the short ride over to the reefs. As soon as the captain gave the order for his men to drop anchor, Priscilla leapt into the sea with Roshan and the others.

This was not her first dive. Shortly after she first arrived at Port of Spain, she had discovered she had more of a taste for the adventure on outings that require heavy diving gear than for the sedate little trips on the glass-bottom boats that so many tourists preferred. But what had lured her into her first dive had been the sight of lightly-clad locals cavorting onboard an old weathered vessel. She had also observed that none of the divers onboard that particular vessel wore the heavy diving gear. And so she had chosen that boat. When she went on board to have a closer look she had been delighted at how friendly the men were to her. So she had joined their tour and absolutely loved it. She supposed, looking back on that first dive, that she had been especially drawn to how free they seemed to be. She had liked that the men wore shorts and the women rolled up their shorts and pants and took off their tops, exposing their bras or bikini tops, and so she had done the same. She had long remembered the feel of the sun on her bare skin. She had not, she remembered assuring herself, come all the way to Trinidad-Tobago to behave as if she were in a nunnery of sorts.

Four weeks later, after she had returned to her home in Tallahassee, Priscilla sat at her desk at FAMU and looked at the letter she had drafted to Dean Newsome to "request a leave of absence to acquire some teaching experience at the University of the West Indies' Trinidad campus." Should she send this or not?

As she contemplated what to do with the letter, her mind drifted back to those happy times when she had not been on duty with her students. She particularly remembered the morning that she had met Roshan: how she had removed her T-shirt, rolled up her safari shorts and jumped aboard that diving boat.

Once the boat was out a distance, she, along with the other divers, had leaped into the magnificent, inviting water. Sitting motionless at her desk in Tucker Hall, chills ran across her body as she remembered how she had grabbed hold of the ankles of one of the experienced divers and glided through the depths of the Caribbean Sea. The locals had told her later that they had all learned to dive in exactly that way, by simply hanging onto the ankles of a veteran diver.

From that memory, Priscilla had gone on to another that was more personal, and dearer to her. She remembered the night she and Roshan had strolled along the beach, embraced and then fallen down on the wet sand and tumbled about …

"Well," she had written in her journal the next morning: "we did it."

But Priscilla sighed and put the draft of the letter away. That particular passionate trip down memory lane did not leave her any closer to a decision on whether to request the leave of absence from FAMU.

Still later in the summer, back from a quick trip home to Prendergast before the fall semester was to begin, Priscilla was enthusiastic as she told her father about the wonders of her time in the Caribbean. Her mother was visiting one of her older daughters, so on this particular evening it was just Priscilla and her father looking at her photographs of the beautiful coral reefs, the variety of marine life and some of the local divers.

Priscilla pointed to one of her favorites. "Just look at the multicolored and oddly shaped fishes and the creepy, crawling eels! They reminded me of snakes the way they slithered about."

"My girl is still afraid of snakes, I see." Nelson smiled. "But I never knew you were so adventurous. My goodness, Priscilla, where'd you get the nerve for such activity?"

Priscilla was too caught up in telling her story to answer his question. "I really liked seeing the octopuses. Or is that octopi? Whatever! They don't mingle much with the other creatures. They just hang around the bottom of the ocean and come to the surface only when necessary." Animated, she attempted to demonstrate their sucker-clad arms as they swirled about the depths of the ocean. "Unlike all the other creatures, only the octopuses have those long extensions, which they use to snare their prey."

Nelson seemed amused at his daughter's carefree taste for adventure. "Girl, when did you learn to swim well enough to go into such deep waters?"

"Oh, Daddy, you don't need to be a good swimmer to venture into salt water. You mostly float around anyway. And man alive, did I have fun!"

It was left to her mother, during a long-distance phone call, to ask the question Nelson had not raised. As she listened to Priscilla telling her about taking off her blouse and swimming in her bra, her mother seemed shocked. "You went into the ocean *and* took pictures in your bra? What were you thinking? And all those men hanging around you?"

"Oh, Momma!" Priscilla rolled her eyes. "That's just the way life is there."

Back home in Tallahassee, during the final week of that languorous Caribbean summer, Priscilla stepped onto the veranda off her bedroom. She basked in the glow of sunlight. For once, she hardly noticed the heavy heat and dense humidity.

Rapt, she considered how well she had adjusted to the drastic change in climate and her new lifestyle. Just last week, she had finally bowed to the inevitable and instructed her hair stylist to cut off her long curls and give her a short Afro. She ran her fingers through her hair and felt so free. Not for her—not anymore—the careful permanents to tame her hair into something it had never been intended to be. No more would her locks be tormented by the humidity. Her hair was au naturel, and she loved it!

Priscilla stepped to the railing of her veranda and shouted: "Who would've thought I'd make it this far, that I'd make it on my own? Surely the gods countenanced all this. Thank you, thank you and thank you."

She did not care whether anyone within hearing range might call her mad. She was so happy, and that was all that mattered. But Priscilla was a realist, and she knew she was not risking so much with her theatrics. It was midday, so most of her neighbors were at work.

She laughed out loud in sheer joy.

And then she heard the telephone ring in her bedroom. *Wrong number.* She was not expecting any calls. *Who could that be?*

She walked back inside to the nightstand and picked up the receiver. Unprepared for the call, she hesitated for a few seconds, and then asked, "Hello?"

"Priscilla, this is your father."

She grinned at the familiar, and so pleasant, carefully modulated tone. As if Arthur Ashe, her favorite tennis player, had scored a difficult point, Priscilla yelled out gleefully. "Wow, Daddy, is that you? What a heck of a surprise! Are you trying to give me a heart attack in the middle of the day, or what? Is everything all right? My goodness, I'm ranting. What's going on? Why're you calling at this odd time?"

For her whole adult life, Nelson had been unsuccessful in persuading her to address him as "Father" or "Reverend." "'You're a young woman now,'" he had told her on her twenty-first birthday. "Calling me 'Daddy' is a little inappropriate, don't you think? Call me 'Father' or 'Reverend.'" But Priscilla never heeded her father's advice. The Reverend James Nelson Austin was her "Daddy." Eventually, even he came to accept her habit.

He cleared his throat. "Well, uh, you know, I thought I was better prepared than this. Give me a moment, will you, Priscilla?" Then, quickly, he seemed to revert to small talk. "How're you doing? Things going okay for you at the university?"

As she listened to her father struggling to the point of his call, Priscilla had a picture-perfect image of exactly how he looked at this moment. Nelson stood slightly less than six feet in height, was of average weight and was light brown in complexion. His close-cut hair receded from his forehead. He cultivated an impressive moustache, which he trimmed and tweaked with pride each morning. Since he was always in the best of health and appearance, most people who saw him assumed he was in his mid-to-late fifties. But he was nearly seventy years old.

Still excited by the sound of her father's voice, Priscilla said in rapid succession, "Yeah, yeah, my job's going fine, just fine. I've been working on what I still have to do with that dissertation, and that's coming along. And classes start next week." She considered, and then instantly rejected, mentioning the possibility of sending in that application to teach this winter in the West Indies. Her "Daddy" might not approve. She laughed out loud. "Say, Daddy, you still wearing those Groucho Marx knockoffs? Or did you finally breakdown and buy some new ones?"

There was a pause. "What's that? Oh, I see, you're making fun of my glasses again. No, I still wear the same ones." Another pause.

Priscilla frowned. It was not like her Daddy to have difficulty with words.

"Look," he finally said. "Priscilla … I realize this call is a little out of the ordinary. But I need to discuss something very important with you."

By then Priscilla had paced to the living room and plopped down on her sofa. She dropped her legs over one of its arms and hunched over the phone. "Okay, Daddy," she said, "I'm listening." She knew how proud her father was, and how rare that he was, in essence asking for her support. But it was not exactly in her nature to be cognizant of the feelings of her father, or anyone else, for that matter. But she was flattered that it seemed he had turned to her for something that was "very important" to him.

"Take your time, Daddy."

Nelson continued. "I went to the doctor the other day and found out I have 'a touch of sugar.' Now, don't go getting alarmed or anything. It's only a 'touch of sugar.'"

Priscilla was well aware that a black metaphor for diabetes is "touch of sugar." But her father had never been a diabetic, and it did not run in his family. As she listened to him talking about being on a special low-salt diet and "eating bland foods like poached eggs," she recalled, however, that he did have high blood pressure. But the diet that he was describing to her sounded more suitable for patients with hypertension than for those with diabetes.

As she pondered what he was saying—and maybe not saying, she heard what seemed his subtly changing the subject.

"You know," he said, "it's actually your mother I want to talk to you about. I suppose you know how much I love her. And, right now, I need her here with me."

Surprised, Priscilla interrupted him. Just a short while ago, during her own late summer visit home, her father had explained her mother's absence in California as having something to do with their eldest daughter Ellen. But Priscilla had thought her mother would have returned by now. "So Mom's not back yet?"

"Nah, she's not made it back 'yet.'" There was a long pause before, lamely, her father went back to his dietary needs. "You see, Priscilla, the doctor has put me on a strict diet, and I need your mom home to help me to do it right."

Again there was a silence. As Priscilla tried to make sense of what her father was saying, the silence built. She felt a surge of pity, mixed with anxiety. But she did not know what to say or do. Her father had never sounded like this before. Maybe, she thought, the best thing she could do was give him a chance to collect himself. And it occurred to her that he had not yet told her everything she might need to know. Was he hiding something? About his illness? About his relationship with her mother?

31

To Priscilla's relief, Nelson abruptly ended his silence. "Priscilla, I need for you to call your mom. Explain all this to her and encourage her to come back home. If you call Liza, she'll listen to *you*, Priscilla."

Hearing that "*you*," Priscilla became fully aware that her "Daddy" was invoking their special bond. She had always been and still was his favorite. He was using that bond to persuade her to call her mother on his behalf.

Priscilla leaned her head back on the arm of the couch and considered. She had grown up thinking that her parents and her brother and sisters were a big, happy, blended family. Nelson and Liza were Priscilla's biological parents, and the two of them had also spawned two other daughters—Helen and Camille. In addition, Nelson had a son, Nelson, Jr., from his first marriage—who was not only the eldest sibling but the only male; and, Liza had two older daughters—Ellen and Harriet—from a previous marriage, as well. As it so happened, Liza had been on an extended visit this summer with Ellen in San Francisco. But Priscilla had heard the speculations from her other sisters that this time what the visit was really about was Liza leaving Nelson.

Her father was talking again about his diet, but Priscilla was so lost in thought that she hardly heard his words, only a vulnerability in his voice that she had never before heard. For maybe the first time in her life, she heard what could have been uncertainly—or was it humility?—in the timbre of his voice. As she listened, it seemed her Daddy was casting aside his usual pride and revealing his frailty as never before.

She wondered, *What the devil is really going on?* She thought about how odd it was that he had called midday, not in the evening or on the weekend, which was her family's customary practice. Instinctively, she knew, *something's not right.* Then she gasped because an intuition swept over her. Just as she had finally made a go of her life, her father was about to ask her to put her life on hold.

She reacted before she thought any of this over. Her fearful voice rose as she cut into his inane discussion of eggs and butter. "But Daddy, if Momma doesn't want to be with you, why's it that you want to be with her? Just let her go, and move on." Later, when she thought back on this conversation, she wondered if maybe she might have been more

32

sympathetic. But she was twenty-seven years old, and her life experience had taught her to be successful, ambitious and perhaps a bit selfish. Never before had she consciously set about to be sympathetic to the needs of another, even the needs of the person she loved most in the world. Her philosophy was, "Find a way to get over the hurt and move on."

And so she continued to lash out. "And another thing, Daddy ... Why did you call me? Why couldn't you've called Momma yourself? Or, for that matter, why not ask Ellen or Harriet or one of the others? Why me?" Once spoken, Priscilla could not take the words back.

But the mild-mannered Nelson said, "I expected you'd say something like that. You sound just like your mother. You see, Priscilla, you have some of Liza's traits and some of mine, and I know you don't want to hear how I feel about her, and how I want her here with me." Then Nelson summed it up. "All I'm asking you to do is 'make the call.' Your mother will listen to *you*, Priscilla."

Another silence fell, and Priscilla thought the only thing left to say in this conversation was 'goodbye.' But she was wrong.

Nelson hesitated again before finally speaking the words that would resonate with Priscilla for years: "Priscilla, there is one more thing I need from you. I need for you to move a little closer to home. Some *things* are happening here, and it would be good if you were nearby to help out."

Air escaped her lungs to the cadence of her father's words. Why the telephone did not slip from her palm was a mystery to her. *Okay, now,* she thought, *what's he not telling me? Why the strained secrecy?* But Priscilla could not quite form those words. Her lips would not move. For a long moment, Priscilla remained uncharacteristically silent.

"Child," Nelson finally said, "I realize that all this is a little sudden and unexpected, and that I'm asking a lot of you. But I really do need for you to do these two favors for your ole man." Relieved that he had finally said what he had to say, Nelson breathed out such a vast sigh of relief that to his daughter it sounded like wind rippling through the phone line.

Priscilla could not see but *felt* tears in her father's eyes. And somehow she knew that her father, too, could see and feel her stunned,

PRISCILLA

red-faced reaction. For all her twenty-seven years, they had shoul-
dered each other's burdens, absorbed each other's pain and frustrations
and, yes, shared whatever happiness each other's accomplishments had
brought them.

Priscilla was finally able to think coherent thoughts. *Daddy really
does want me to put my life on hold. Pick up stakes just before the semester
starts. But why? For what? What exactly is going on?*

She was now acutely aware that her Daddy had been speaking of
something more serious than a lover's quarrel with her mother. Her
throat ached from words she had spoken and those she had not. She
wanted to cry.

But instead she sounded angry. That was just the way she was. That
was the way Nelson had raised her to be.

"But Daddy, it's only been two years since I took this job in the
first place. And I moved here because *you* wanted me to. Remember,
Daddy? Don't you remember I came here primarily because *you* wanted
me to take this job? Now, without telling me much about your reasons,
you want me to move back, 'closer to home?'"

In some part of herself she was aware that her anger must be piercing her father's very being. But while that thoughtful part of herself
was trying to figure out what was *really* going on, she continued to
give voice to her frustration.

"My goodness, Daddy, something's the matter and you're only
giving me part of the story. I don't like this. I don't like this one bit!"
Priscilla pouted like a child.

But then she wiped the mucous dripping from her nose with the
backside of her forearm, cleared her throat and relented, as she knew she
would. "OK, Daddy, I'll call Mom, and I'll move back 'closer to home.'"

Still, she felt a need to get her jabs in. "But I gotta hand it to
you, Daddy. When you ask a favor, you know how to go for the big
ones. Especially the second favor." Of course she knew he could not
see her, but to console herself at least she faked a smile. She stood up,
rummaged in a drawer for the pack of cigarettes that she kept for an
occasional smoke. She lit one, and her eyes rose to the framed portrait
of the female matador on the wall. Her smile widened.

34

Her confidence restored, she picked up the receiver and spoke into it. "Daddy, give me a few days to think this through and make some things happen."

Business out of the way, their conversation ebbed to updates about her brother and sisters. After Priscilla hung up the phone, she sighed. In her heart she had already known that her plans to return to the West Indies had only been a dream. Again she sighed.

She gave the telephone another look. Should she call her mother straightaway? She had never been anywhere near as close to her mother as to her father. She supposed she never thought the two of them had much in common. As far back as she could remember, Liza had relied on Nelson for security, reputation and livelihood. But later, when Priscilla was near the end of high school and had begun to fancy herself a feminist, she had warmed to her mother telling her and her sisters to learn to be independent. "Get all the education you can," Liza had cautioned them, "and never, ever rely on a man to take care of you." Yet it was still going to be awkward to plead Nelson's case with her mother.

As she weighed the tactics she would employ, Priscilla changed into the short-sleeved T-shirt, matching shorts and faded sneakers she wore to play tennis. She grabbed her racket from the front closet and headed down the stairwell for the courts.

Gymnasium-green paint overlaid the three tall fences that contained the quadrangular spaces of sunbaked clay. A wall for batting tennis balls buffered the adjacent townhouses from the rear of the courts and rendered the appearance of privacy, which suited Priscilla. No one else was on the courts, since the other townhouse residents were at work. The sun shone directly overhead.

Priscilla focused on the spot on the batting wall and swung her racket. Each time the ball met its mark, she fretted, *Why me, Lord, why me?*

She struck the next ball harder. *Whack!* Her Daddy wanted her to patch things up with her mother. *Whack!* And he wanted her to move closer to home. *Whack!* Priscilla was amazed at her strength. She had never been able to hit the ball so far.

Perspiration poured from her scalp. Uprooting herself from her teaching post and her life in Florida was his more consequential request. Instead—or was it because of that—mostly she worried about calling her mother. Should she get it over with and call her tonight? Or wait until tomorrow?

Priscilla was drenched in sweat when she made her decision. She would book the first flight she could and go to California to make her request in person.

She consoled herself, as she threw down her racket and wiped her face with a towel, that at least she was getting a good workout from all of this.

CHAPTER 4

Gone on Long Enough

Two days later, Priscilla looked out the window of her Delta Airlines flight at the clouds. She guessed she must be halfway to San Francisco. She had changed flights in Atlanta, and since then the flight attendants had served lunch.

But Priscilla was in no hurry to get to San Francisco and start another fraught chapter in her relationship with her mother.

The white clouds were, in their way, so calming. Priscilla told herself she could use something to quell her anxiety. Remembering some of the more troubling aspects of her history with Liza, Priscilla reflected how, by comparison, the love she shared with Nelson was pure and simple. Maybe there were just too many ambiguous layers of relationship between a mother and a daughter. Or were a mother and a daughter simply too much alike?

Moodily Priscilla reached up, pushed the call light and then ordered a glass of Chablis. Thus fortified, she let herself remember one of the most unsettling chapters in her relationship with her mother. And, she had to admit, what had happened was doubtless one of the low points of her life.

She sipped her wine and, as she leaned back in her seat, she shut her eyes and remembered that dream. That nightmare that had triggered all that came after … That terrible dream in the summer of 1976 that had made everything come to a head …

It had begun during a trip home to Prendergast during a break from graduate school.

The visit had started out just fine. Since her other siblings had long since vacated the nest, it had been wonderful to visit with neighbors and old friends from high school and to catch up with the changes in their lives and confide in them about her life in Buckeye country.

But then, not long after her arrival, she had experienced an eerie, graphic dream. She had seen herself flat on her back in a damp, dark and dreary place that seemed familiar, although she could not quite place it. She had thought, *If only I could command myself to move, then maybe just maybe …*

But in the dream, she had not been able to move.

The tips of her ears had ached because her blood felt like it had rushed up to her head. She had felt hot flashes. Beads of sweat had rolled over her face, underneath her breasts and under her armpits.

Where am I? What's happening to me?

In the dream, she had closed her eyes, opened them as she caught her breath, and then helplessly closed them again. *Now, why the hell did I do that?* Every time she closed her eyes, she had seen ghastly minnows. No, *eels!* The slimy creatures had reminded her of snakes. All she had to do was close her eyes, and from out of nowhere, the snake-like creatures had appeared and then surrounded her. They had intently stared at her, turned away and swam upstream—somewhere away from her.

What does it mean? What do they want?

Half asleep, half awake, she had tried to cry out for someone for help. But no sound had come from her mouth.

Why are you doing this to me?

Again, her cry had remained silent. And no one had responded.

When she had opened her eyes again and dared to gaze at her surroundings, finally she realized she was back in her bedroom at her parents' home.

She had assured herself all this had been a nightmare. Yet lying in her bed, she had been frightened because she worried her dream pointed to something religious, something maybe even profound and foreboding.

And, worst of all, something recurring.

The next time she had the nightmare, she had awakened and called out for her mother as she ran into the kitchen. The two had settled down at the table, but Liza had interrupted as Priscilla was describing her dream.

"Oh, child! Don't you *know* what all that means?"

Wide-eyed, Priscilla had shrunk away. Her mother had always had a gift for interpreting dreams. Neighbors and women from church would ask her what their dreams really meant.

But this time Priscilla had been afraid to hear whatever her mother was about to say. "No, Momma, I *don't* know." She stood up to go, but the keening tone of her mother's voice kept her from leaving.

"Child, I *knew* something was wrong. As soon as you walked in the door, I knew something was wrong. *But this?* I never would have guessed it was *this* ... " Liza had begun to weep. Finally she wiped her eyes and blurted out what she had to say. "You're pregnant."

Priscilla had stared at her mother in disbelief. "No ... I can't be —" She had not been able to even say the word, "pregnant." Yet part of her mind was racing. When was her last period? And when had ... *that other thing* ... happened?

"I told your father that something wasn't right with you. You've been acting strange. You just looked so sickly when you first came home." Liza had reached to the far end of the table for a tissue and wiped her eyes. "You had lost so much weight your father and I thought you'd become anorexic. And you were so temperamental! Hormones, it was hormones!" Her eyes had trailed to her daughter's figure. "And now, just in the past few days, you seemed to have gained back your weight. Now it all makes sense now. You're pregnant." She had leaped to the only conclusion that was even conceivable to her. "Have you told Sedge?"

Priscilla's mind had kept racing. Of course her mother would think her boyfriend at graduate school had to be the father. *Well,* she had thought, *this is neither the time nor the place to disabuse her of that naïve little motherly supposition.* Priscilla's mind began to skitter. Sedge? Dennis? The senator?

And then, with a sickening certainty, Priscilla had known whose child she carried. Maybe she would feel differently if she thought Sedge was the father. Or maybe not. Years ago she had decided she would never have children. And so it had not been her practice to have unprotected sex. *Except that once!* Priscilla had felt herself hardening with determination. Without further reflection, she had told her mother what she knew had to happen. "Momma, I'm getting an abortion."

Absolutely stunned, Liza at first had wordlessly stared at her daughter, and then she had covered her face with her hands. Finally she had straightened and said, "Now wait a minute, young lady! We are good Christian people. And your father and I raised you to be that, too. We don't believe in abortions. Anything but that."

Priscilla had closed her lips, her mind and her heart. She was not about to share how all this had happened. It had been bad enough to go through it. She was not going to let anyone else inside her secret. She would deal with this in her own way. She was a strong, educated, modern black woman. She was strong enough to do what had to be done.

Priscilla's voice had been resolute. "Oh, Momma, come on, already! I'm almost finished with graduate school and preparing for my career. I don't have any room in my life for a child. Or for marriage, if that's your next question."

As she had watched her mother's face crumple, Priscilla continued. "This is twentieth-century America, Momma! And abortions *are* legal. As for your religious point, in the Old Testament even the priests performed abortions. So please, let's not go *there*."

Priscilla had passed her mother another tissue and watched her blowing her nose. "Besides, Momma, this is my decision. Not yours or Daddy's. And it is not my belief that a fetus is a human being. It is up to me what I do with my own body."

Priscilla had been feeling stronger from her recitation of the rhetoric. "And know this, Momma. I am not getting married just to give my baby a man's surname. So do you really want me to be like those welfare moms walking around with all those ducks trailing behind them, unemployed and unwanted because I already have children? Well, that is not the life for me."

Liza had finally found her voice, although it sounded more like a wail than a mother counseling her child in crisis. "Oh, Priscilla! Where did Nelson and I go so wrong with you? How is it that you're so different from our other girls? *So different!* And in your heart surely you must know that abortion is murder, and that it's a sin to take a life … Abortion is wrong, Priscilla."

Priscilla got to her feet. *Enough. And more than enough.* "Momma, please don't try to make me feel guilty about this. This is just the way I am, and after all, it is *my* choice." Yet her voice rose with urgency. "And please don't go telling Daddy about all of this. I will never, *ever* forgive you if you tell him."

Liza had watched her daughter march back to bed without so much as a backward glance. Priscilla seemed as unruffled as if she had just closed a deal to buy a car or a house.

But back in her own bedroom that night, Liza had fallen to her knees and prayed for her daughter. Her tears had awakened her husband.

Yet when he had rolled over and asked what was wrong, Liza had just shaken her head. "Not now, Nelson, not tonight. I'll tell you later."

Nelson had sighed and sat up, as he held out his hands and raised his wife to sit beside him. "It's Priscilla, isn't it?" Again he had sighed, this time more deeply. He had shaken his head. "I don't need a baby doctor to tell me what's going on with my girl."

"Oh, Nelson." Liza had continued to cry. "She really doesn't want you to know. About it … and her decision not to have it."

"So that's it, then." Again Nelson shook his head. "I prayed I would not have to drink that cup." He took his wife's hands in his. "Don't let her know that I know. That will just kill her. She may not let on, but this must just be killing her. My baby's in a lot of pain."

Wordlessly Liza had searched her husband's face, wishing, if for only a day, that he would love her as much as he loved Priscilla. He had always spoiled this daughter so much that sometimes people outside their circle assumed she was an only child. Yet surely this Methodist

41

minister she had married was not going to countenance his beloved daughter having an abortion?

"You see, Liza, we both know that Priscilla is not like the other children. She has her own mind. Whipping her never helped, and so chastising her at this stage in her life won't work either. No matter the situation, Priscilla has never wanted children ..."

"But Nelson, what are you trying to say?"

"I'm saying that times have changed and that Priscilla—whether or not we think this is right—is changing with the times." He had hesitated and then resurrected the ghost of a previous family scandal that had not worked out as they had hoped. "Besides, you know what happened when we forced Ellen to give up her child for adoption."

Stung, Liza had withdrawn her hands from his. Ellen was one of her daughters from her previous marriage. Nelson was only her stepfather. But he, too, had agreed with the decision to talk Ellen out of keeping the baby after she had lost the father. But who, Liza asked herself, could have predicted the consequences?

Yet Nelson had continued as though he had not even noticed his wife's reaction. "We just can't go through all that again with Priscilla. But the difference this time is that Ellen wanted her child. Priscilla does not. No matter what else all this is about, having a child like this just goes against her very being." For the first time in this conversation, Nelson had nodded his head and retreated back to his side of the bed. "Anyway ... we need to find a way to help her to cope and move on."

Liza had never told her daughter about that midnight conversation with Nelson. And all three of them—Priscilla as well as her parents—never had another heart-to-heart about what happened in Prendergast over the next weeks.

After Priscilla had confirmed with her gynecologist that she was pregnant, she had almost immediately scheduled an abortion. She had refused her mother's offer to accompany her for the procedure and instead had called a taxi to take her, alone, to the hospital. Afterwards, there had been a lot of tip-toeing, as well as a general aura of sadness, in the Austin household. Priscilla had slept more than usual. Nelson had bustled here and there, and mostly had chosen not to be home much.

Liza had occupied herself making sure Priscilla was comfortable and shielding her from the occasional phone call from Sedge.

And so the time had passed until finally it was September. Priscilla had returned to graduate school in Columbus, thankful that she seemed to have survived the crisis—and without her father knowing.

Yet in the aftermath, Nelson as well as Liza prayed more often and with more anguish for Priscilla.

Priscilla awoke with a start as her flight to San Francisco encountered turbulence and the pilot was advising passengers to make sure their seatbelts were fastened.

She checked her belt and then reached out for her half-full glass of wine. It was warm, but she drank some anyway. She looked at her watch. She had napped for nearly an hour.

As she recalled what had been on her mind before she mercifully fell asleep, Priscilla wished she had not awakened. Having that abortion had been such a hard, sad experience. The whole thing had been awful. *But maybe it was a blessing that I didn't let myself even realize at the time how hard it was.*

She reflected that, in comparison, her life in Tallahassee had been a good time in her life. No trauma. Just good, solid work, and pride in doing that work. She would be sorry to leave it. For the first time Priscilla let herself realize that of course she would honor her father's request to relocate closer to home.

Priscilla drained her wineglass. She would deal with leaving Florida and relocating … But where? When? And do what? But first she had this trip to San Francisco and her own unfinished business with her mother.

Priscilla's mind trailed back to that abortion four years ago, and then the aftermath that had begun just last spring.

Oh, Momma! Why couldn't her mother have just let it all go? Why had she tried to resurrect it all with her old boyfriend from graduate school? But her mother had always been a meddler, and she had been true to form when she had done what she had done with Sedgewick.

43

Priscilla frowned as she remembered how unsuspecting she had been when the phone rang late one afternoon last spring. She had been relaxing in front of the television—laughing at the absurdity of a soap opera plot, when the phone had rung. Eyes still on the television, she had picked up the receiver. "Hello-o."

"Priscilla, I need to tell you something."

The unusual intensity of her mother's voice had rasped against Priscilla's ear. In a flash, she had no longer felt so cheerful. *Now what?* She had never been very patient with her mother.

Liza had continued, still in that raspy voice. "Sedgewick called." Liza had paused, meaningfully, at the mention of Priscilla's old flame from graduate school. "Did you know he's in Atlanta?"

"Nope. I certainly haven't heard from him." But she knew Sedgewick had kept in touch with her mom for years and years after their break-up. The two of them had always gotten along well together. "What did he want *this* time?"

"Priscilla, what I called to tell you was that '*this* time,' I gave Sedge your telephone number. He always asks for it, you know. But I did tell him to give me some time to contact you before he calls."

"Momma! Why, after all this time, did you decide to tell Sedge where I was? You know that I'm trying to get on with my life." A thought had struck her. "You didn't tell him *anything else,* did you, Momma? And don't pretend you don't know what I mean."

"No, young lady, I didn't, but I'm hoping you'll finally find the decency to level with him yourself. This has gone on long enough. Sedge deserves to know. I still say what you did was wrong. The man deserves to know the truth!"

Priscilla had sighed as she hung up the phone. The last thing she had needed was drama with the old boyfriend. And so when he had called not long after she talked to her mother, she had let the call go to the answering machine.

Priscilla had paced, sighed some more, and then dialed her mother's number. Before she rang Sedge back, she had needed to know exactly what her mother had told him.

"Oh, Priscilla, it's you." Liza's voice sounded excited. "Did Sedge call?"

Priscilla was reminded again how much her mother had liked Sedge. So much so that, after that first time she had brought him home to Prendergast, her mother—and her father, too—had kept asking her to bring him back. That particular summer the local NAACP had held a fundraiser at the Prendergast Country Club. It was a formal affair, so everyone dressed in their fine gowns and tuxedos. Priscilla did not own a gown, so Liza had made her a beautiful sleeveless silk tea-length dress. Priscilla had known she looked absolutely stunning in that dress and had received many compliments. But what she most remembered from that evening was how Sedge had spent most of the time dancing with the many unescorted women. *Oh, how handsome he looked. And all those women fawning over him!*

She reflected that Sedge had been exactly the kind of well-bred, serious, intelligent, middle-class fellow her parents had always wanted her to settle down with. In a way, Priscilla regretted that she had never been in love with him. She had latched onto Sedge because he had fitted the image of what her parents had wanted in a man for her. But for some reason, she had always suspected that Sedge had known she was not in love with him. So why, she wondered, had he continued to cling to her? Perhaps he had held a similar view of their "fit" as a couple, because he had also taken her home to meet his family in Akron. Priscilla remembered that as soon as they pulled into the driveway, his sisters and brothers and mother had all rushed out to meet her. His father had liked her, too, but he had not seemed as fussy as the rest of the family. So it was that, looking back on their relationship, Priscilla concluded that they perhaps had gone steady because they fitted some presumed perfect image of what their families had expected. *Oh well, such is life ...*

Priscilla had forced herself to concentrate on what she had to say to her mother. "Sedge left a message on my answering machine. Tomorrow. I'll call him back tomorrow. But first I wanted to talk to you some more."

"What's on your mind?"

"Well, Momma, I know that you and Daddy pray a lot. And I know that I hurt your feelings when I had the abortion. But now that it's all over and some time has passed, I need to know … where you stand."

"Well, child, I still think that what you did was wrong and that it was sinful." Liza's voice rose with emotion. "But what I can't understand, for the life of me, is how you got to be so *cold*? And why didn't you want Sedge to know? He's a good man. He would have married you."

No surprises here, Priscilla had thought. Her predictable mother had always been an open book. "Oh, Momma, I thought you'd think that way. But I'm not so cold-hearted that I don't feel hurt from having had an abortion. *Sad,* Momma. Having an abortion is a sad thing for anyone to go through. But I just didn't think that having a child because I got pregnant was right for me at the time. That's all it was about for me. And I certainly didn't mean to hurt you."

"Well, Priscilla, I have prayed over the matter. Time and again, I have prayed. And now I only want what's best for you. So do the right thing and tell Sedge about it. All right?"

"All right, Momma," she had said. Her mother always meant well. And she reminded herself that even now, her mother did not know the whole story.

But at the time Priscilla had not been ready to confront the truth about her pregnancy, and she would not be ready for a long time. And so she had set her mind to telling more lies, or at least half-truths. She would mislead Sedge into thinking that the child that she had aborted had been his.

Again Priscilla flicked her wrist to check her watch. Another hour before landing! Would this flight never end?

More to the point, she thought: *Would this trip down memory lane ever be over?* She had not been proud of how it had gone with Sedge.

Priscilla tried to square her shoulders in the airplane seat and once again reminded herself how strong she was. She could face her past as well as her future.

She remembered how, as she had promised her mother, she had called her ex-boyfriend the next morning. They had chatted about his administrative post at Atlanta University and her faculty post at FAMU. But it had not taken long to get past the pleasantries and knuckle down to the hints Liza had left with Sedge when she had called him the day before.

"For goodness sake, Priscilla," he had said. "Your mother told me you wanted to talk to me. To tell me why it was that you left me hanging like that. I've been racking my brain for nearly four years, trying to figure out what happened." He had seemed intent on pouring out his heart to her. "And then, out of the blue, there was your momma on the phone. I begged her to tell me what had happened. And you know what your mom said? 'It's time you and Priscilla talked. This has gone on long enough.' Okay, now, Priscilla, exactly what has 'gone on long enough?' What happened? Was it me? Did I do something to hurt you?"

Priscilla had hemmed and hawed as the distraught man continued to beg for answers. He had even begged to visit her in Tallahassee.

Reluctantly she had agreed. She would have been a coward to do this over the phone. "This weekend is good for me. How 'bout you?"

"I can be there Saturday by noon."

"OK. I'll catch you up on everything then. Meanwhile, take care, and I'll see you soon."

Waiting for him at the airport late that Saturday morning, Priscilla had recalled dating Sedge for a year or so. She had liked him but not loved him. So after the abortion, she had let the relationship die what she had hoped would seem a natural death. Nearly four years had passed without any contact between the two of them. She had mistakenly thought that she could have the abortion and simply forget about Sedge and move on with her life. But thanks to her busy-body mother, it had seemed he was at least temporarily back in it.

Chastely they had hugged. What, Priscilla had wondered, was the protocol for greeting an old lover to whom she was about to tell an intentional and important … but ultimately misleading rendition of what had happened?

Yet she needlessly worried. Sedge had always been a kind, thoughtful man and since graduate school his confidence had increased. His hug was warm and reassuring.

On the way to her townhouse, they had caught up like the old friends they essentially were, until finally they settled at her kitchen table and she made him sweet tea.

She had smiled. Slightly over six feet in height and pale in complexion, Sedgewick had fine facial features, a thin nose and thin lips and hazel eyes. When they first met at an interdisciplinary seminar at Ohio State, he had been a graduate student in business administration. Her first impression had been, *This guy sure fits the image my folks look for in a man.*

And so she had tried to be as kind as he deserved as she prepared to share her sad – but slightly *adjusted*, story. "Sedge, it's so good to see you again and to see that you're looking so well." Some time ago, Priscilla had learned how to stall until she had the right words or the courage to make her point, so that was what she did. "Let me try and start by saying that sometimes stuff happens that we just wish we could forget about, and what I'm about to tell you just might make you wish that you never knew me."

"Oh, come *on* Priscilla. Whatever happened can't be all that bad."

"Oh, but it is. You see, Sedge, during the summer in question, I ... well, I learned that I was pregnant."

Sedge had just sat there, astonished.

"And, well ... I had had all those plans for my education and a career and ... Sedge, you have to understand how shocked I was to find out that I was pregnant. And so ... I had an abortion." *There,* she had told him what had happened. Although she had not told him the whole truth, she had shared all she wanted for him to know.

Sedge had looked away from her and taken a sip of iced tea. When he finally spoke, he had seemed incredulous. "You're telling me that we could've had a little boy or a little girl running around, *if* you hadn't had an *abortion?*" He had spoken the word as if it were profane, and then he had cried out, "I really can't believe I'm having this conversation with you, Priscilla. My God, we're talking about an *abortion.*"

Priscilla had simply nodded. She had said what she had intended to say.

"Hell, you didn't even tell me you were pregnant. Why did you think you couldn't tell me? You always knew that I loved you. So tell me, Priscilla, what happened? *What happened?*" Sedge's voice had been a wail. "What made *you* decide not to have *our* baby? What about me? Didn't *I* have *any* say-so in the matter? My God, Priscilla, what's happened to you, to *us?*"

"Sedge, I already knew how you felt about me. That you loved me. But Lord knows, I didn't want to force you into marriage, and so I kept the pregnancy from you. We were both still in school. We needed to get our degrees. I didn't want to mess up your chances for success any more than I wanted to mess up my own. That's why I kept the pregnancy and the eventual abortion from you."

Sedge's face had reddened. He had stared at this woman whom in a way, even after four years, he fancied he still loved. But even after hearing what she had said, still he had yearned for acceptable answers to his questions. He had shaken his head, and then his eyes had trailed back to this woman who seemed so different from the young student he thought he had known so well. For the first time, he had been able to see a callous streak in Priscilla. But did he still love her? Did he still want her? He had supposed even back in Ohio, if he had been honest with himself, he had known she was not a paragon. But who was? Yet her revelation left him cold. Even if the two of them were to decide to give whatever they might still have another chance, he had to admit to himself that their relationship would never have the promise it once had. Forgiving and forgetting would be hard, so hard.

Priscilla had remained silent as she watched the play of emotions on the open face of this good man. She had no intention of renewing their relationship. All she had wanted was to explain what had happened to cause their separation. Yet sitting here with Sedge, the truth of what she had done and how she had hurt him overwhelmed her. She had never meant any of this to be as it was. Sedge had deserved better. And maybe she had, too. Yet she took solace in having faced up to one of the worst chapters in her life.

And that had not been the last time Priscilla—or her mother, too—had heard from Sedge.

But the pilot was announcing they were circling and about to land.

Priscilla broke into a smile. Finally! Whatever awaited her in San Francisco had to be better than all she had remembered on the long flight west.

CHAPTER 5

Acquiescing to Her Father's Request

Priscilla's first surprise was not just her mother but her father, too, waiting at the airport in San Francisco to greet her.

"Daddy!" She threw herself in his arms, and then she embraced her mother.

But a moment later she had her hands on her hips as she regarded the two of them. She had flown cross-country to fulfill her father's request that she advocate with her mother for an end to their estrangement.

And he had beaten her to it.

But they looked so happy together that Priscilla could hardly reproach him.

And who could be angry about an unplanned vacation—her first-time ever visit to San Francisco, one of America's most fascinating cities?

At Ellen's, Priscilla hugged her sister and then, arm-in-arm they walked out to the kitchen for a chat. Ellen made coffee, produced a plate of pastries she said were from one of the city's finest bakeries and confirmed that Liza and Nelson had indeed settled their long-simmering differences. Liza would be returning to Prendergast with him.

Priscilla nodded in satisfaction. One of her father's requests done, and one left still to do. But just now she was more interested in her reunion with Ellen who had always been one of her favorite siblings.

As Priscilla bit into a chocolate éclair, she regarded Ellen with admiration. Four years older than Priscilla, Ellen looked just like Liza—petite with long, thick, wavy black hair. But her arrestingly high cheekbones were her best feature. Liza's own heritage was part Cherokee, and all her children—Priscilla included, had inherited that trait. But Priscilla had always thought that, of all Liza's daughters, Ellen had not only the highest cheekbones but the prettiest face. She was stylish, too, as well as very proper and refined.

Priscilla enjoyed listening to her sister catch her up about what had been happening in her life. She was glad to see that her sister had evidently finally recovered from the major trauma—and scandal—that had once rocked not only Ellen but also all the family. When she found herself pregnant during her first year in college, Nelson had insisted she give the baby up for adoption, and so it was that even Liza's advocating for her daughter to keep the baby had fallen on Nelson's deaf ears. The tragedy had seemed to break Ellen's heart. As soon as she graduated from college, she had moved to California, where her birth father lived. Priscilla had always believed that the situation had created a rift between Nelson and Liza. But she was thrilled when Ellen said that she had been able finally to get in touch with the family who had adopted her baby, who was now ten years old. Ellen showed her photographs of a pretty girl who, like all the rest of them, had high Cherokee cheekbones. Priscilla rejoiced that this happier ending had obviously not only eased Ellen's sore heart but also seemed to be contributing to whatever reconciliation had brought Nelson and Liza together again.

Then it had been Priscilla's turn to share her news.

But before she could begin, Ellen started with compliments. "Priscilla, girl, I'm so proud of my younger sister, the big-time professor! You've got to know you've done the family proud, working on a doctorate and now teaching at a big university and all." Ellen glowed in happiness for her younger sister.

Priscilla smiled. Ellen had always been such a kind and generous soul—eager to share her natural joy as well as whatever material possessions she had. But she held out her palm for her sister to stop praising her to the skies. "Ellen, please … You're the one who's done well for herself. Imagine, my big sister working as a big-time accountant for a big-league contractor! And, from what Daddy's told me, you bring in the big bucks, too."

A very animated Ellen retorted, "I might make more money than you, kiddo, but you've got all the prestige. Everybody knows, money ain't never bought anybody prestige. And, oh yeah, before I forget, you ought to have been here earlier when *your* daddy, yes, child, the good Reverend James Nelson Austin, bragged about his little Ms. Prissy. Can't tell the ole Reverend anything now. Nothing beats his 'Professor Prissy.'"

Priscilla spent the rest of her long weekend in the city by the Bay basking in the love of her family. This was the first time they had heard the gory details about that car accident which had totaled her Mustang. Priscilla was selective in which details she shared because she did not want to alarm them. So she left out the part about her car having twirled in the air. She also did not mention her "miraculous" survival because even she still found it hard to believe that she had walked away from the wreck fairly unscathed. Finally, she did not mention the chronic vertigo with which she was diagnosed after the accident. No one had to know about the exercises she sometimes did or the caution she tried to remember to take about moving her head too fast, in too many directions.

And Priscilla took note that she was not the only member of this family to indulge in a little selective sharing. She did not hear one word pass her father's lips about having asked her to move north from Tallahassee "closer to home." So she, too, never mentioned it to the others. She would simply figure out how to honor his request. And then she would tell all of them—her Daddy, too—where she would be moving to and when.

Priscilla was happy to spend most of her California time with Ellen, mostly sightseeing in the Bay area and shopping in nearby Sausalito.

On her flight back to Florida, Priscilla finished her gin and tonic and fastened her seatbelt when the huge Boeing 747 on which she was boarded encountered major turbulence. She was, as usual for her, in the window seat. She looked out at the trembling wings of the aircraft with more interest than anxiety. She had never been nervous in the air.

She did notice however that the man sitting next to her—who had previously introduced himself as an IBM sales executive—was sweating, profusely. His eyes were red. The more the plane shook, the more agitated he became.

Until then, the two of them had sporadically shared small talk, but suddenly the tenor of their conversation changed.

"I don't get you, lady" the sales executive said. "Why aren't you afraid? I'm scared to death!"

"Well, one thing's for sure," Priscilla said, "there isn't a gosh-darn thing we can do *way up here* in the sky. Point number two, I already said my prayers. And point number three," Priscilla continued as she reached across from the man and waved her hand in the air, "Hey, stewardess, I'll have another gin and tonic."

Then she turned her attention back to her companion. She regarded expressions of fear in men as weakness and often was dismissive of such frailty. "Might as well," she said, "go down enjoying myself."

As soon as she took her first sip of her fresh cocktail, the plane dipped sharply. The storm raged as the aircraft burst into the puffy, dark gray mass. Frightened from the smacking and crackling sounds, many of the passengers panicked and pulled down their window shades. Then all at once, the storm unleashed a deluge against the nose of the plane. Lashing rain slapped against the underbelly until it reached the rudders. The plane shook ferociously.

Priscilla swigged her drink. She was not afraid. Not her. Not of a little turbulence. As she saw the flight attendant collecting glasses and bottles while moving through the cabin, Priscilla took one final drink that finished her cocktail. With a flourish she gave the empty glass to the stewardess.

Fumes from nervous smokers in the rear of the aircraft over-whelmed the nonsmoking part of the cabin. Thunder and lightning broke against the plane. "Ah!" the storm seemed to exult: "Thought you'd closed us out?"

"I don't want to die like this," said the man sitting next to Priscilla.

Another passenger in the seat ahead pleaded. "Can't somebody do something? Oh, God, please, don't let us go down, not like this."

Against the captain's better judgment, he had taken a path too close to the cyclone's eye. "Oops!" The captain had not meant to speak out loud, but Priscilla and the other passenger's overheard him over the public address system.

After realizing their situation, he and his copilot fumbled with the gadgets on the control panel. But their corrections came too late for the passengers' comfort. The jetliner wobbled aimlessly in the pitch-black night. The plane continued to shudder. Seconds seemed like hours.

As frayed as the captain's nerves surely must have been, he managed to press the intercom button and spoke to the cabin: "Ladies and gentlemen, this is your captain speaking. This is some storm, but we've made it through the difficult part. Now, we've got just a little more turbulence to endure. Even better news, our landing is in sig—"

Hearing what they wanted to hear, the passengers applauded. Some even shouted out premature cheers of joy.

"As I was about to say," the captain continued, "we're in for a bumpy landing. So *please* extinguish all cigarettes and make sure you remain securely seated with your seatbelts fastened. And all stewardesses, please return to your stations. Sorry folks, but we'll have to circle the airport and wait our turn to land. Otherwise, everything's under control."

"Yeah, like hell it is," the sales executive muttered to Priscilla.

In those final moments of the flight, the pilots tried to navigate the plane upwards, only to realize their maneuver failed. Vainly they made more efforts to ready the plane for landing. But no maneuver seemed to work.

"Sorry to disturb you folks again," the captain said, "but this ole storm just won't let us alone. Yet everything *is* under control. Just remain seated and keep your seatbelts fastened."

Priscilla's stomach ached. She wished she had not downed that gin and tonic, which was agitating like her belly was a washing machine.

Beside her, the petrified salesman was holding on to the armrests for dear life.

Priscilla silently prayed: *Oh Lord, end this horror soon. I'm sick, real sick, and my friend here, well, he's through.*

The captain managed to maintain control of the aircraft and fought to steer the huge, wobbly bird twice around the Atlanta airport, where Priscilla had to catch her connecting flight to Tallahassee. Each circle seemed more awkward than the last. During the third and final turn, the voice over the intercom said, "Looks like we're in line to be next, folks. For those of you with connecting flights, you might have to wait a bit due to obvious delays. Others of you, I'm sorry to report, may already have missed your connecting flights."

Priscilla cradled her stomach. "Ah hell, Bubba, I'll crawl to Tallahassee from here. Just land this bugger."

She gave a prayer of thanksgiving when finally the flight safely landed. But she knew that the hidden blessing in the very bumpy flight was that she had not been able to worry about beginning the next stage of her life. She had decided what she wanted to do. But she was not altogether certain anyone else would be willing to make it happen.

CHAPTER 6

Consider It Done

The very next morning, Priscilla made an appointment to submit her resignation to Dean Newsome in person.

He told her how disappointed he was. "But you've only just gotten started," he said. "From what you've told me, you haven't even met anybody special. You can make a good life here." She had already told him that a family emergency made it imperative that she honor her father's request to move closer to home in upstate New York. "Are you sure," the dean asked, "that the good Reverend can't find someone else to help out?"

At the time, Priscilla did not even consider asking the dean to hold her job open until she returned. For in her heart she knew she would not be returning to FAMU and that in a way she would always regret leaving such a plum job. But her father's need had to come first.

At the time, Priscilla had been so enmeshed in reweaving the tapestry of her life that it never occurred to her that although the dean had expressed disappointment, he had not seemed so surprised. It was almost as if he had expected it. Finally, after what seemed like a lifetime later, her father had confided that "Lionel and I," (Dean Newsome's first name was Lionel) had known one another not only from their shared Mississippi hometown but also from civil rights' marches in the Sixties in the South. So, as it turned out, Nelson had helped his favorite child not only get the job at FAMU but also to ease out of it.

Priscilla spent the rest of the day extricating herself from all the other commitments of her life in Tallahassee. She paid a penalty to the leasing agent after informing him she would be breaking her lease. She called the movers and arranged to have her possessions put in storage before being delivered to her next apartment. She arranged for disconnection of her electricity and phone service. She even called up colleagues and, once she had told them she was leaving, helped them plan a going-away reception in the departmental office later that week.

It was however, not until the next morning that she screwed up her courage enough to make the most important call of all.

Ohio State Senator Daniel P. Callahan was not only her former boss but her former lover. She had never thought she would be calling him again for professional or personal reconnection.

Damn it, she thought. *I don't even want to talk to that man. I thought I was finished with him. I need a drink, a serious one at that.*

Since it was eight o'clock in the morning, she contented herself with a big mug of coffee. She understood that what she really was about to do was to eat a big slice of humble pie. She, Priscilla J. Austin! Humility was hardly in her vocabulary, let alone her character.

She groused to herself about making so many big changes to honor her father's request. She told herself she would feel much better about this if her father had been more forthcoming about his reasons for asking her to move closer to home. She did not even know the full story about *why* she was turning her life upside down.

She had met Senator Callahan while she was attending graduate school in spring 1975. Someone from the university—and, funny, she did not even remember who that was—had taken her to the senator's office at the state capitol. At the time of their meeting, she had decided that he was not only intimidating, pompous and unpretentious but also, at the same time, strikingly impressive.

Apparently the senator, too, had felt the electricity.

Not long after, when again she was visiting his office on some university errand or another, the senator offered her an internship on his staff. At the time she had refused, saying she knew little about real-world politics—or so she claimed—and virtually nothing about Ohio politics. She had insisted her political knowledge was "theoretical, textbook." But finally that fall, after six months of repeated offers, she had accepted his offer for a legislative internship. As part of their agreement, she had also volunteered to cover his district office in Cincinnati, where she campaigned in his failed bid for Congress.

She had been working for him for months before, quite to her surprise, Senator Callahan had called and asked her out to dinner.

She had expected a working meal, maybe a proposal to begin work on a new project. And so, after asking him about the appropriate attire for the restaurant where he wanted to meet, she had dressed casually. But she had been embarrassed to discover how elegant and upscale the establishment was. That was her first cue that fashion, as she had joked with him, was not one of Senator Callahan's "strong suits." She had laughed at the unintended pun.

As the evening advanced, the senator had ordered the best of every selection on the menu, with the obvious intention of impressing Priscilla. But she was not at all impressed. This was not her first experience with fine dining. And at the time she was surprised when he teased her by picking the oysters from her shells. But what she had been the most preoccupied with at the dinner was how other guests made familiar gestures toward the senator. A few men had even come to their table and tried to speak to him as he was trying to eat his meal. Priscilla had been accustomed, back in Prendergast, to her father attracting some attention in public places because of his status as a pastor. But this was her first-time encounter with how political prominence, here in the state capital, could intrude on a legislator's personal business. Even so, she had been struck by this proof that there was no positive correlation between the senator's political stature and his command of social graces and etiquette. She was aghast when he ordered red wine with their oysters.

"Senator, its white wine with seafood," she had said, "preferably a pale, dry wine when eating seafood." And she wondered why she, the graduate student, was the one instructing this man of such stature and years. *What's wrong with this picture? Isn't he the older, wiser person?* But she had dismissed her misgivings. *Ah, I get it; he must just be teasing and testing me.*

Yet Senator Callahan had been unperturbed by her correction because he had lifted his glass and drunk with apparent satisfaction.

Before long, Priscilla had understood that whatever they ate and drank and said had been a mere setup for what followed.

When the senator took her home to her place, he had wasted no time before making a direct hit, "Now, sweetie, you can send me away whenever you want. The last thing I want to do is take advantage of someone who feels she owes me a favor."

Silently Priscilla had regarded him and considered. *Yeah, sure, you want to do it and I've never done it with an old geezer, at least none as old as you.* The senator was the same age as her mother, twenty-three years older than Priscilla. But her father was nineteen years older than her mother. So for Priscilla, her age difference with the senator did not seem outlandish.

When she did not say "no," the senator had been all over her. His hands had been gentle, and his body had been smooth and receptive to her touch. Within minutes, Priscilla had found herself wanting to do things with Daniel P. Callahan that she had never considered with anyone else. But before she could do much else, the senator's lips had gripped hers tightly and snugly. Thoroughly relaxed, she had let go. Her limbs had trembled; one by one, each cataract of Victoria Falls had seemed to burst down into the body of water beneath it. Never before had she experienced such an amazing quickening. *No doubt about it, this is the good stuff. Damned good stuff...* She had screamed so loudly when she came that she had turned her head to muffle her voice in her pillow.

Afterwards, the senator had grinned. "The oysters were merely the appetizer. You're the main course." He had sat up and looked around her place. "Now all I need is a drink of cognac. Well, we'll have to get you some to stock."

Priscilla had taken those words to mean Senator Callahan did not intend to make this a one night stand. He clearly desired more of her company.

When she walked him to the door, he had made that official. "Priscilla, you know I'm married, and I know you have that nice boyfriend of yours. Sedgewick, I think?" When she nodded, he had continued, in exactly the tone she had heard him use when he was sealing a deal for votes at the legislature. "So here's the deal: We'll see each other when we can. There'll be no talk about marriage or divorce. You just let me know when you no longer wish to see me. And, another thing, sweetie, this relationship is just between you and me. You're not to tell that boyfriend or anybody else."

Priscilla had always been a quick study, so she had acquiesced with a simple nod. As it so happened, she was acutely aware that the senator was beyond asking her to be available to him for sex; he was closing a deal of a higher order. And, as often the case in politics, the unspoken had consummated their deal. At the time, neither the senator nor Priscilla had any idea when she would call upon his services. Yet they both knew, in due time, she would need him before he would need her. It had been at that juncture therefore, that Priscilla first entered into the game of politics, Ohio politics, as it were.

Priscilla sighed. She was going to have to put her secure, dreamlike existence here in Florida behind her. If the call she was about to make turned out as she thought it would, she would be returning to a sector that would force her to deal with certain realities much more complex than compiling lecture notes on the American presidency or discussion points for radio talk shows during election campaigns on patterns of black voting behavior.

Again she sighed. Enough memories of the best and worst of her past with Senator Callahan. *Might as well get on with it.*

She had not forgotten the number she finally dialed. But she was taken aback by the voice that answered.

"Senator Callahan's office. To whom am I speaking?"

"Oh." Priscilla had expected to talk to the same secretary who had answered the senator's phone during her legislative internship five years ago. "Did Barbara step out or something?"

"Barbara's no longer here. She moved out West," said the woman with undisguised glee. "I'm Charlene. How may *I* help you?"

Priscilla ignored Charlene and her ego and instead got straight to the point of her call. "I'm Priscilla J. Austin, a former legislative intern in your office. May I speak with the senator, please?" With her dismissal of Charlene, Priscilla returned to the legislative world and the first battle over rank.

Charlene held the telephone up in the air and yelled out loud for all to hear. "Hey, Senator, it's that girl who used to intern for you ... Priscilla."

There was momentary silence, and then a whirling sound as the senator quickly picked up his receiver.

"Hello, honey," he called out. "Do I take this call to mean you miss the old man?"

Priscilla could not help smiling. *Same old Senator Callahan!* Obviously, he still had not joined the ranks of the politically correct. And even though he still commanded excellent enunciation, he had not done anything about his very arrogant and high-pitched tone of voice. The senator was among those who assumed a certain amount of power because of his political station.

Priscilla had rehearsed exactly what to say, and so she said it in a straightforward manner. "Well, senator, I never thought I'd ask. But I need a favor." She paused, aware of the significance of this first real favor she had ever asked of him. Because of all of the interactions among the lobbyists who represented special interests, the state lawmakers possessed untold ability to supply favors, especially employment and government contracts. "I need a job. Not interning. A real job. And I need it right away." Tersely she continued. "Senator, I need to return to Ohio as soon as you can 'make it happen.'"

She had not forgotten how it was at the Ohio capitol. Asking certain politicians for a favor was tantamount to giving injections of adrenaline, estrogen, steroids or testosterone. Much of each waking moment, politicians contrived ways to curry favors. Indeed, many such lawmakers thrived on "making things happen." Often the knee-jerk response to a request like hers was a simple: "Now ask me something I can't do."

But Priscilla had been careful not to ask specifically for employment at the Statehouse, and there was neither intonation nor intimation of such a search in her request.

So she clarified her request. "It doesn't matter whether government or private sector."

Senator Callahan did not hesitate. "Consider it done. You can be my AA. You'll make an excellent staffer, my legislative aide," the senator said.

Priscilla's eyebrows lifted. 'AA' was short for "administrative assistant," which at the time in the Ohio Senate was synonymous with the title of legislative aide. "Your 'AA?'" Priscilla said under her breath. Her thoughts raced. *He's offering me a job in his office. I just want a job, one where I can get lost in some big corporation for a little while. That's all, a no-nothing job, and not necessarily one at the capitol. Damn it all, I'll be right under his nose!*

But Senator Callahan was assuming that of course she would be eager to snap up the offer. "Yeah, Sweetheart, your timing is perfect. Rick, my aide is leaving me. The job is yours, if you want it. Now, when were you thinking to start?" He did not wait for her answer. "I'll alert the folks in the clerk's off—"

Priscilla understood that implicit in what he was saying was an indirect command that she start right away. As if she had met his bluff in a game of poker—and she knew that the senator was an excellent player—Priscilla interrupted. "I can be there later this month. I need to take a few weeks to take care of some —"

The senator sounded indignant as he cut in. "Oh, no, Sweetheart, you said you needed a job, and I offered you one. Do you understand 'pronto'?"

Priscilla understood "pronto," but she did not give a darn about the senator's intimidation. She had read somewhere that the best way to be taken seriously on the phone was to project a serious, sharp, stern tone, by standing up straight and speaking downward into the receiver.

So positioned, she struck back with precision. "Senator, I'll get back with you once I know more about my situation. Tell everyone 'hello,' and I'll be in touch. And if I didn't say so before, thanks for your help."

Before the senator could comment further, Priscilla hung up the telephone.

She stared at the phone. She realized that Senator Callahan thought that she had called because she had missed him and the excitement of political life in Ohio. And, knowing how he was, she surmised that he probably also believed not only that she wanted to resume their affair but also that he was the only one who could bring her sexual pleasure. Priscilla needed time and space to think—and to think fast, for her decision to return to Ohio certainly carried more significant repercussions than having a simple fling with a politician.

To keep the senator off her back, she took care to turn off her answering machine and not answer her phone for the next few days.

CHAPTER 7

Sometimes Ya Gotta Do What Ya Gotta Do to Get What Ya Want

Priscilla spent the rest of the day packing, or rather, trying to pack.

She had already engaged a moving company but had decided to do as much of the packing as she could. The movers had sent over the packing boxes she would need. When she had discussed costs with the company, she had been so appalled at how much it would cost to move back to Ohio that doing the lioness' share of the packing herself had seemed like a strong, independent and financially wise idea. But now she was not so sure.

Priscilla paced from room to room. She packed up two cartons of books from the shelves in the living room but then decided to begin with her dishes. After laboring over one carton of china, she decided she would rather pack her shoes. Yet she tired of that even more quickly than the dishes.

She poured a sweet tea, lounged on the sofa and put up her feet on the coffee table. She was usually highly organized, and approaching a task like packing would normally call forth her latent skills as a captain if not a general. Yet today she supposed her heart was not in it.

Priscilla looked around the living room of this townhouse where she had felt so free and so in control of her destiny. Now here she was, uprooting herself for some unknown whim of her father's. She had absolutely no idea what this new turn in her life would be like. How could her father be so selfish? And had she lost her mind, stepping back in time to a place where Senator Callahan clearly thought she would once again be under his thumb?

But then, just after a long, cool drink of iced tea, Priscilla felt a groundswell of guilt sweep through her. Tears blurred her vision. She was the selfish one, not her Daddy. All her life, he had been so compassionate, so loving and so protective. She loved him more than anyone, and she owed him everything. Yet when he had asked for her help that one time on the phone, she had responded like the spoiled child she knew in her heart she could still sometimes be.

Enough of this packing nonsense, Priscilla said to herself. *If I don't get it done on time, the movers will do it. I'll pay through the nose, but so what? I need a little time for reflection, and I am going to take it.*

In her bedroom she donned her bathing suit and grabbed her other swimming stuff. Only a few minutes later, she was sitting on the side of the swimming pool that was one of her townhouse amenities. She slid into the water and let out a deep breath of relief. *Better, much better.* She pulled her plastic float from the side of the pool and climbed upon it.

Priscilla basked in the brilliant sun and let her mind wander over some of the ups and downs of her early life. If she had not had the strong foundation of such a happy childhood in such a loving family, she doubted if she would have agreed to pull up stakes and change life as she was doing, just because her father had asked her to.

As she floated in the turquoise pool, Priscilla reflected on how her father had shaped her into the woman she was.

She supposed growing up a preacher's daughter had taught her about authoritarian power, economic insecurity and inner strength triumphing over adversity.

Priscilla remembered how she and her siblings had learned to tighten their belts and get ready to pack their bags whenever Nelson ran afoul of the Methodist church bureaucracy.

She could never forget the times when Nelson had been, in his own words "left out of an annual conference." Usually a pastor was denied the renewal of a church appointment or an assignment to a new one when his bishop determined that he had failed to meet his financial obligations to the global operations of the larger church denomination. In Nelson's geographical conference, bishops wielded tremendous authority and they could—and did—assign blame for financial shortfalls.

Priscilla, along with the rest of the family, had always known when their father had lost out in one church controversy or another. An obvious indicator had been one of their extended summer vacations at Grandma Lilly's in Sills Creek, Illinois. Lilly was Liza's mother. If summer turned to fall, and the children found themselves enrolled at Sills Creek Elementary School, they had told one another, "Daddy was left out of his conference again." Sometimes the Austins would stay at Grandma Lilly's as late as Thanksgiving, awaiting news from Nelson about his search for a new church.

But the children had rarely been anxious about such turns of events. That was just the way things were with the church. Neither did any of the Austins—Nelson included—harbor ill feelings toward any of the bishops, not even the ones who had denied Nelson an appointment. Everyone in the Austin family had understood church politics.

Priscilla did not doubt, either, that they all had also understood how acrimonious things could get when a Christian community seemed to forget that essential love-one-another message of the Gospel.

And of all the churches that Nelson had been assigned over the years, none had been as full of acrimony as the congregation at

Conner's Chapel in western North Carolina, which was the only black Methodist church in the area.

The Austins had arrived in Connersville in 1962, at the dawn of court-ordered school desegregation. One of Nelson's first acts as pastor had been to help select a handful of black children to integrate the Connersville School System. Included in the group of schoolchildren he selected for the desegregation process were Priscilla's two younger sisters Helen and Camille. But Nelson had told Priscilla that—because she tended to be too unpredictable and outspoken—she would continue to ride the bus to Central High in neighboring China Grove along with her two older sisters Harriet and Ellen.

But there had been hard feelings about which children from their church would be part of the desegregation team.

One day, a contingent of dissident church members, led by Buford Brawley and Ethel Mayfield, had arrived at Nelson's doorstep and made their position clear about who was to decide which children would be on the desegregation team. "Reverend," Buford told him, "you go ahead and preach whatever you wish, but leave the business of managing the church and community affairs to us." Yet what this angry contingent did not know was that the community's own power elite had originally approached Nelson for his input on integrating the Connersville School system. Taking the lead role had not been Nelson's idea.

Still some of the church members had continued to stew over their children being left out of the historic school desegregation initiative.

So it was that matters had come to a head in Conner's Chapel when Nelson received federal funds to operate a day care center at the church. One day while Nelson was away, Buford and Ethel had led a group of the dissident members into the lower level of the church. They had thrown all of the day care center's furniture, toys, supplies and instructional materials outside on a vacant lot next to the church. The staff had been so frightened by the dissident members that they fled the church on foot. When Nelson returned, he had simply taken his time, and, one by one, returned each of the items back inside the church.

Priscilla shook her head as she remembered how the situation had worsened during the Austin family's third, and final, year at Conner's Chapel. This time the congregation had stopped paying Nelson's salary. Liza had helped make ends meet by taking a job at a furniture plant. But when Buford and Ethel heard about her employment, they had gone to the work site and told her supervisor, "The Austins are troublemakers, the kinds your lot don't care for." Liza had promptly lost her job.

It was not long before the Austin family had been penniless. Since the church had also ceased payment for the parsonage's utilities, it had not been uncommon for the Austins to experience electrical blackouts and the loss of telephone service and water.

In spite of everything, Nelson had taught them all to "make do."

Sometimes he had filled the bathtub with water, and the family members had used it for all their needs, until the day came when a mysterious someone from the church would pay the water bill. For light, the Austins had used candles. For heat, they had put more linen and coats on the beds.

Through it all, Priscilla and her sisters never nagged their parents or criticized their situation. As she remembered it, they even had fun with their new adventures.

Of all these memories about poverty and deprivation, for Priscilla the most memorable began one day with Nelson telling them, "Get in the car, children, and ride with me down the street."

They had driven to the only grocery store in town, gotten out of the car and gone inside.

Nelson had asked to see the manager, a white man named Jeff Richards.

He had stood before that grocer with his hat in his hand and said, "Mr. Richards, these here are my children. We've fallen into a rough patch, and we don't have any food in the house. Is there any way you can give us some food until I can pay you back?"

"I'm really sorry, Reverend Austin. Honest I am," Mr. Richards had said. "But there are rules and laws governing grocers. Not to mention I report to someone else and need to account for my inventory."

Intently the two men had stared at each other. Nelson and the grocer had been personally acquainted, and each had seemed to realize how devastating it must have been for the other man to share those words.

"Surely, there's something you can do," Nelson had persisted, in a not-so-subtle plea. "I've seen some managers toss out food products that don't look too good to sell."

"I, uh … " The grocer had hesitated. "Perhaps there is some fruit, bananas or something like lettuce or cabbage I can place in the bin out back. But you'll have to drive 'round and actually take it out of the dumpster. I'm so sorry things have come to this for you, Reverend. I declare I am."

Then Mr. Richards had carefully collected some food to put in the dumpster.

Priscilla still remembered that moment. And she had never forgotten that, at the time, everyone in town had known what was happening at Conner's Chapel. Everyone!

Nelson had driven the children to the back of the store by the dumpster. They had gotten out and walked over to the bin. Before he placed his hands on the food, Nelson had looked at his children and said, "I'm sorry, kids, but your mom and I don't have a dime to our names, and we've got to feed you." And then he had smiled. "Oh, look, these bananas don't look too bad, not at all." So they had picked through the food items in the garbage bin of Jeff Richards' Grocery Store.

On other occasions when Nelson was rock-bottom broke and desperate, he would ask for financial support from his own brothers and sisters. Most of them lived in Indianapolis.

When he was too proud to call them, he would urge Liza to call her folks in Sills Creek.

"Tell them, it's a loan, Liza," he would say, "and that we'll repay them when we get back on our feet."

Despite all that animosity and those schemes and chaos, the Austin children still experienced the normalcy of childhood peaks and honors. That year Ellen was chosen homecoming queen and graduated with honors. Harriet joined the color guard and proudly marched with the band in parades. Priscilla learned to play the French and English horns, and she and her younger siblings also studied the piano.

But none of those accomplishments, as Priscilla remembered her childhood, could begin to match the remarkable roles Helen and Camille played integrating the Connersville Elementary School.

On their first day of school, a teacher had greeted them as they walked up the sidewalk, and she had escorted them throughout the day. There had been no large, angry white mobs. No one had spat on the black youngsters. No mayor or governor had blocked their entry into the formerly all-white school. In fact, the small group of black children had experienced only mild rejection during their first couple of weeks at the new school.

By the third or fourth week, Camille had become the darling of every teacher and every other student.

Yet Helen, who was fair-complexioned with ginger-colored freckles, had a somewhat troubling experience. She had resented being around some of the white kids, who, like other whites, would constantly ask her, "Are you sure your daddy ain't white or something else?"

Still, although the Austins had very little money, Nelson and Liza had somehow managed to dress Helen and Camille in much nicer clothes than the other three girls. "That's because we've got to put on our best for this moment in time," Nelson had told his children concerning their participation in this historic moment.

One day, not long after the integration of the schools, Priscilla remembered asking her father, "Daddy, are we po'?"

Completely taken aback, Nelson said, "No, child. Where did all of that come from?"

"Some kids at school says we're po' 'cause I never wear new clothes and never have any money."

"Child, when did you start using *poor* English?" Nelson had asked indignantly.

Priscilla had never forgotten what he had said next: "Try to understand that being poor says more about how a person sees himself than it does about social station or who he is. Your mom and I are simply going through a rough patch. That's all. You girls are from strong stock that provides all your needs and your hearts' desires. And one day, God is going to show you just how blessed you are. Priscilla, you will never be poor."

After giving her father's words some thought, Priscilla had blurted out, "Then why are those church folks so mean to us? People are only mean to poor folks."

Priscilla recalled how tears had filled her father's eyes. "Oh, Priscilla, child," he had said. "I can always tell when there's something hurting deep down inside you. Someday, when you're a little older, you'll learn that some people don't like it when others do what's right. Doing good and right by others is hard to do in the midst of deceit and treachery. That day care center helps a lot of youngsters who don't have any food and clothing and don't even attend school. Did you know that Priscilla?"

"Nah, Daddy, I didn't know that. So we don't just feed ourselves. We feed other people, too?"

"Priscilla, child, you do understand. Now stop talking like you have not had a day of schooling." Nelson had proudly hugged his daughter. Then he had gone back to reading his paper.

Priscilla reflected, as she floated around the swimming pool in her Tallahassee townhouse complex, that she had learned two important lessons from that experience. The first was how to behave in ways that pleased her father. The second was that she herself had an undeniable aversion to poverty.

Then Priscilla smiled as she remembered how finally the hard times had ended for the Austin family. Nelson's next appointment had been a keeper. He and his family had mostly thrived in Prendergast, New York.

It must be getting late. Priscilla squinted at the clock on the clubhouse wall and then quickly climbed out of the pool. Yes, it was late, and she had been out in the sun for far too long. She did not want to be burned to a crisp and have a painful ride all the way to Ohio.

Yet as she toweled off and prepared to return to her townhouse and belatedly address that packing which still had to be done, Priscilla was suddenly overwhelmed by all that remembering of how important and steadfast her father had always been to her. No matter what she ever did—and that included giving up her university professorship and moving back to the political world in Ohio—nothing she ever did could repay her father for all that he had done for her.

The first thing she did when she returned to her townhouse was to call her father. She told him that she had "worked things out" and that she would "be relocating back to Ohio."

"Oh, child!" Nelson added, "I am pleasantly surprised that you worked things out so quickly."

Priscilla took a deep breath. She had fulfilled her father's request. And she was aware, and not for the first or last time in her life, how much she needed his approval. She had also managed to please Senator Callahan, whom she was prepared at least to tolerate. Indeed, the path she chose was of her own volition.

With a far lighter heart, Priscilla went back to her packing. Yet as she sorted and packed, she worried just a tad that the path she had chosen in the political realm was one frequented by people who were desirous of money, position and power. As an intern, she had experienced a little of that world, but what she would encounter now at the Ohio Statehouse as a Senate aide was octaves beyond anything she had experienced thus far in her relatively sheltered life.

And then she laughed out loud when she recalled pragmatic words of wisdom from no less than Senator Daniel P. Callahan.

"Playing the game," he had once told her, "is *not* for the fainthearted. But sometimes ya gotta do what ya gotta do to get what ya want."

CHAPTER 8

Of Her Own Volition

Priscilla took her time driving to Columbus. The knowledge of how this would annoy Senator Callahan made detours and stops to see old friends all the more irresistible.

One was Sedge in Atlanta. She had not been sure, the last time she had seen him when he visited in Tallahassee, whether they would ever contact each other again. But she had always liked Sedge, and she had decided when she started to drive north from Florida that she would try friendship on for size with him.

"Yes, Priscilla, you know I'm glad to see you," he said, after she arrived at his home. "But your decision to work for the senator in that rat hole at the Statehouse is a mystery to me. You're not secretly in love with him, are you?"

"Nah, Sedge, you know better than that," she said. "I just need to take care of a little business. When I'm done, I'll move on. This time I'll also keep in touch. Okay? And thanks again for allowing me to visit."

Priscilla held back tears and drove away with a lump in her throat.

As life turned out, she would communicate with Sedge a few times after she settled back in Columbus. But soon, even Sedge would come to terms with the reality of their relationship having run its course. Eventually, he returned to Columbus and met another woman—someone almost the complete opposite of Priscilla in every way. They would get married and have three children. Both Sedge and his wife worked at Ohio State for the duration of their respective careers. Priscilla was glad for Sedge that he and his wife seemed to enjoy a happy life together.

A day or so later, stuck in traffic on the covered, dimly lit, old, unstable bridge between Kentucky and Ohio, Priscilla was beset with claustrophobia. She had always been frightened by close and dimly lit places. The traffic moved at ten miles an hour, or so it seemed. She had already opened her windows for the slight breeze to soothe her, but it did not help much. In fact, she became even more overwrought. With no way to turn her car around and escape, she slipped off her left shoe, opened her door and dragged her bare left foot for a few hundred feet along the pavement of that old, unstable bridge.

Ah, that's all I needed, she sighed to herself, relieved by the touch of her skin on the bridge. Priscilla had intuited that the touch of the earth would bring calm to her. She also knew that although the bridge was thousands of feet above water, it was the next best thing to the earth.

But as she had been carefully dragging her foot on the pavement of the bridge, she had not noticed the driver of a large, slowly moving tractor-trailer looking down at her out of his open window. Then he yelled, "Feel better now, young lady?"

"Oh! I didn't realize that anyone saw me do that," she said, and then she laughed, her composure restored.

"You'd be surprised what we can see from way up here," the truck driver said. "But it's good to know you worked it out. Have a safe journey for the rest of your trip."

There, at the Ohio River where Interstates 75 and 71 converged, at the crossroads between Covington and Cincinnati, Priscilla came to terms with her decision.

Lord knows, she thought, *I couldn't have gone back to being a computer programmer, and so life in the political underworld will have to do. Besides, it's only till Daddy tells me what's going on. In due time, I'm sure he will reveal all. Oh well, my choice.*

She took Interstate 71 North for the remaining two-hour drive to Columbus.

Priscilla arrived at the capital city early on a sunny afternoon in late August. The monumental old capitol occupied the heart of downtown Columbus, and it covered a whole city block.

Priscilla made a sharp turn off South Third Street and entered the Statehouse parking lot between its dingy gray stone columns. But before she could stop her car, the Statehouse guardsman had stepped out of the little stone house. By the time he reached Priscilla's side of the car, she had already gotten out, stretched her aching limbs and was standing upright. Nelson had taught his daughters, especially when they traveled alone, always to assume an assertive posture. Priscilla, who looked remarkably younger than her twenty-seven years, had found that advice particularly useful.

She was heavily bronzed and wore her hair short, in a curly, sun-blazed Afro. Having adopted the casual style of a native Floridian, she was also clad in a short-sleeved, pale, moss-colored silk blouse and matching safari shorts. She looked as if she had been photographed on the cover of a fashion magazine.

Emotionless, the guardsman stood at ease. "Hello, there, young lady. How may I help you?"

"I have an appointment with Senator Daniel P. Callahan. He's expecting me, Priscilla J. Austin."

"Hold on a minute while I check," the guardsman said. He walked back to his station.

Left alone for a moment, Priscilla surveyed the enormity of this huge stone edifice that looked like it had seen better days. *Gosh, I never thought I'd see this place again.* "Lord, please be with me for I surely know not what I'm about to do," she said, not conscious that she was praying out loud.

The guardsman returned and instructed Priscilla to park her car to a designated space in the underground parking ramp, three levels down. She did as she had been told and then hiked up the dimly lit stairwell to the top level, which was still underground. There she stopped and gasped for air. But she urged herself to keep going.

Priscilla was relieved when she finally saw signs of life: the governor's secret service vehicles parked slightly north of Mary's Café, which had always been popular with legislative staffers. She staggered toward the elevator shared by the governor's and the Senate's offices.

Still oblivious to her own appearance, she pushed the button and ignored the stares and comments she seemed to be attracting. At the second floor, she did not hesitate. She had not been gone so long that she had forgotten where everything was. At that time Democrats like Senator Callahan were the majority political party; and although he was not in the Senate leadership, he possessed the rare privilege of premium office space.

Her composure restored, Priscilla turned left and walked down the corridor past the leadership offices and turned left again into the last suite of offices. She walked across the reception area to the secretary's station, where she saw a young woman seated there.

Presuming the woman to be the senator's secretary, Priscilla said, "Good afternoon. Are you Charlene? I'm Priscilla J. Austin, here to meet with Senator Callahan."

"I'm Charlene." She was a bleached-blonde with a raspy voice. She admonished Priscilla, "The senator expected you days ago. What happened?"

Priscilla gave her a frosty sort of smile. "I had some things to take care of. I told the senator to expect that. Did he forget?" She looked past Charlene's desk to the senator's office. "Is he in? I hope you're not going to tell me I have to wait. As you can see, I'm fresh off the road. I'm bushed."

Charlene pursed her lips in disapproval but briefly talked to the senator on his phone before she ushered Priscilla into his office.

"Priscilla!" The senator smiled as if he had just won a big prize. He waved Charlene out of his office, shut the door and embraced his new administrative aide. "So you thought you'd give me a run for my money and arrive in your own good time, didn't you?"

As the senator returned to his high-back black leather chair, Priscilla took a far less imposing seat across from his desk.

She noted that he had not appeared to change at all since she had last seen him. Senator Callahan was dark-skinned, tall and slender, with a full head of curly black hair and wire-rim glasses rather like those Peter Lorre used to wear in old movies. He was still wearing one of those cheap polyester suits he affected. Yes, it came back to her. Senator Callahan was a cheapskate. It was a quality that had stood him in good stead as a legislator. He was often called "the numbers man" for the Senate Democratic Caucus.

Priscilla's eyes trailed from the senator to his office. There was, she thought, no mistaking whose office this was. Numerous photos and artistic renderings of the senator cluttered all four walls. Some of the pictures were of presidents and other politicians. Others were of celebrities. And there were enough commendations, plaques and trophies to start a specialty shop, with no space for any other mementos. The parts of the off-white walls not hung with images of the senator were smudged and had scuff marks. Besides his big desk and bigger chair, there were two smaller, unmatched chairs and a plain black leather sofa. Amid the piles of papers on his desk, only a black push-button telephone was discernible. Three ashtrays, filled with cigarette butts and ashes, sat amid the clutter on his desk.

After she had taken it all in, Priscilla shook her head. "My, my, Senator, you should keep this place a secret." The two of them had often bantered back and forth. That dynamic helped Priscilla keep some emotional distance from him, as did her refusal to call him by his given name. She had never called him anything but "Senator."

Unruffled by her remarks, Senator Callahan said: "Now that you're here, perhaps you can redecorate my office. You know, use your woman's touch to rearrange my plaques. Fix it up good." He nodded, pleased how he already was planning to make good use of her. "But where are my manners? We need to get you onboard first. A quick trip to the clerk's office to sort all that out. Then, have I got a surprise for you!"

Annoyed, Priscilla said, "Just tell me what I need to do to start the job and where I'll be situated." She was no longer the naïve graduate student he had first met. She was a professional. She had become more confident and focused.

Senator Callahan, too, was also not someone who could be told what to do. He gave her a dismissive nod and referred his new aide to the Senate clerk's office to complete the necessary paperwork.

Priscilla was not pleased with the salary offered to her by the Senate clerk. The senator had forewarned her that she would have to be willing to make some concessions. But she reminded herself that she did not need to earn a bundle of money, just enough to support her modest lifestyle. And besides, for her this job was temporary, mostly just a way to get closer to home as her father had requested. She could leave anytime, depending on what was really going on with her father. She signed what she had to sign to begin her new job.

Back at the senator's office, Priscilla had expected only a quick visit before leaving to rent a room and get some rest. And she had been determined to do so alone. She was exhausted. She had come straight to his office from the interstate.

But, no. An exhausted Priscilla was repelled to learn that the senator had been making plans that her "welcome home" would be done his way.

So it was that Senator Callahan led Priscilla to his apartment.

Hours later, they finally got down to some serious talking.

It had been very obvious after they arrived that the senator had had no intention of either of them going to sleep. He had accordingly kept Priscilla thoroughly engaged for longer even than she expected.

He had ordered out for food and then after it was delivered they had fallen on the steaks, baked potatoes and salads as if neither of them had eaten for days.

Between bites, Senator Callahan tried to catch up on what had been happening since she had left his employ. "My goodness, Priscilla, it's been nearly four years since I saw you last, and only a couple of times have we even spoken by phone." He continued, "Were you trying to avoid me?" When she did not answer, he ran his hand along her arm. "And now, look at you. Were you trying to get as black as me?" Then he played with her hair and kept commenting about her tan. "And I like your new hairdo, girl."

As the senator raved about her appearance, Priscilla found it odd that he never once asked her *why* she had asked for his assistance finding employment. She told herself that the senator was simply the senator. It was best just to let his ego rule him.

"A suntan comes naturally with life in Florida," she said. "I tanned easily because I was new to the area and unaccustomed to the drastic effects of the sun." Besides, she preferred to keep the conversation limited to her suntan and to avoid telling him—should he ask—that the reason she had moved to Florida in the first place was to get away from the likes of him. Then, unbidden, she remembered the relative innocence of her recent trip to Trinidad and Tobago. *My, how my priorities have shifted,* she thought.

Thoroughly exhausted from her drive from Tallahassee and then those unexpected hours on the sheets with the senator, it was not long before Priscilla fell asleep on the senator's sofa.

For a half hour or so, as he sat in an armchair and read some files he had brought home from his office, he was amused by the sound of Priscilla's snoring. But then Priscilla began to toss and turn. She wiggled her arms beside her, and she spoke, aloud: "No, Dennis. No, this is not right. You know, this is—Let me up." She moaned and turned her head from side to side and back and forth.

The senator grabbed at her shoulders and shook her. "Wake up, Priscilla. Please, sweetheart, wake up. It's me, Daniel, 'the senator.' I'm not going to let anyone hurt you. Priscilla, wake up."

When Priscilla's eyes flew open, awareness of her nightmare was still with her. Had she revealed her secret, or even portions of it? She did not know for sure, so she told herself to be careful what she said to him. But she was still trembling, and she was drenched in perspiration. Yet she struggled to get out of his embrace. "All right," she said. "I'm good. I just need to get up and get a drink of water."

The senator let go of her, and she went into the bathroom. She stared at her image in the mirror. Her reddened eyes were puffy and encircled in dark shadows. Her mascara was running down her cheeks. Her haggard face look drooped. She tried to freshen up by taking a drink of water and then splashing more of it on her face.

When she returned, the senator was seated on the edge of the sofa. He wore an expression of hurt and sadness. "Come sit with me, Priscilla. Please, let's just sit here together. We need to talk."

Priscilla recoiled and then took a step away from him. "I had a bad dream. That's all. And what of it, anyway?"

"Priscilla, sweetheart, let's not pretend it was nothing," the senator said. "It took me a long time to bring you back around. And you were squirming and fighting someone named Dennis. Who is this guy and what has he done to you?"

"Just somebody I knew once. A nobody. He meant nothing to me."

The senator reached for Priscilla's hand and pulled her toward him. "So, sweetheart, if that's true, why were you fighting this Dennis fellow? I'm an old pro. I wasn't born yesterday. It seemed to me you were fighting off a man in your sleep. Come on now, Priscilla, who is this Dennis guy and what did he do to you?"

"Whatever happened, *happened* a long time ago, and I've forgotten about it. Leave me alone with that now, will you, senator?"

"No. I will not leave you alone. Talk to me, Priscilla. Tell me exactly what happened. Because then, and only then, can you begin to deal with whatever happened and move on."

Priscilla bit her lip and remained steadfast. Maybe she couldn't control her dreams but she could decide who—and when and if—to share her secret with. "Not now. Okay, senator?"

CHAPTER 9

Engaging in the Game of Politics

Priscilla plunged into her new life.

Settling into the high stress political environment was, for her, duck to water. Her new lifestyle and profession were inextricably linked. The essence of her life was now political, an essence for which she had already been unwittingly conditioned. Adjunct and unknown to almost all those who knew her, she thrived on the sheer rush of an occasional storm, which life and work in the Ohio capital provided in abundance.

She had heard more than one of her A.A. colleagues, as well as the legislators themselves, call her "that new girl in the Ohio Senate with that smashing suntan." But she shared little of her background with them. Many seemed to know she had most recently been teaching political science somewhere in Florida, but she never bothered to mention her work for a doctorate, much less the yearning she had experienced to chuck academic advancement and live a simpler life in Trinidad-Tobago. Her inner drives, she believed, were nobody's business, so she did not bother to talk with such intimacy to anyone.

Priscilla mostly held herself aloof from the entanglement of relationships. Aside from what she continued to have with Senator Callahan, she did not want to be tied down in a relationship. She kept to herself, except for beginning to make casual friends with Julia, a medical student who lived in her neighborhood. She had been raised to rely only on family and to keep her personal business to herself or within the family. As for Roshan, that East Indian she had the fling with in the Caribbean, Priscilla had talked to him only once after she returned to Ohio. When he called her one evening, she almost had not recognized his name. They had shared a desultory conversation. Priscilla did not know it at the time, but his own parents had already cautioned him not to get his hopes up about the black American tourist with whom he had crashed and burned during that summer romance. Priscilla hardly even noticed when Roshan failed to call her again.

Instead, Priscilla J. Austin was totally psyched up for her new role in Ohio politics.

She recalled a maxim that had been taught to her as a teenager and that had been reinforced while she attended Livingstone College: "You're here for a reason, not for the season." That maxim fueled the equanimity that was necessary to do what she had to do to get what she wanted.

And what she wanted first of all was not development of a new social life but, instead, a new home in Columbus. Searching through the classified ads, almost immediately she found what she told family and friends was "an absolutely fabulous old house." She leased the main floor of the historically preserved Victorian house from a young urban "yuppie " professional couple—known as "yuppies" in the late 1970s—and wrote more in her letters about the new house than she did about the new job.

In one letter, she called her new home "humongous", with expansive rooms, three fireplaces and hardwood floors but no carpeting. It was situated among rows of restored houses in an area called Victorian Village. The neighborhood attracted a growing young professional class and was situated near the university and hospital among antique shops, boutiques, pubs and restaurants. Priscilla wrote home: "This place is the best." Tellingly she added that her new home reminded her of houses back in Prendergast, "although statelier."

In the midst of so much change, Priscilla had settled for the familiar.

She was especially thrilled with one particular feature. She wrote home: "Wouldn't you know it, I also have three huge fireplaces, each one of them unique. One distinguishes the spacious dining room, and the two others connect the two bedrooms, each back-to-back against the bedroom walls."

She added with pride that her furniture from the Florida townhouse "barely fills all the space here." Two floral-patterned Queen Anne chairs and a coffee-colored sofa set the elegant tone for the formal living space. She wrote to Liza, "Mom, you would love that room." Adjoining that living room, she added, "I made the parlor my office and moved the piano into it. French doors separate the two rooms. Can you *believe* this place?"

Sometimes, when Priscilla sat down at her piano, the past and the present would blend together. Back home in Prendergast, everyone who had heard Priscilla play had enjoyed her music, whether classical, contemporary, modern jazz or old gospel hymns. As Liza cleaned the house, she would often call out: "Play that one again, Priscilla. I like that old gospel song. Only this time, slow down the pace a little."

Nelson also would ask her to play the piano for him. He would position himself in his La-Z-Boy recliner in the den and then request his special songs—usually, just like Liza, those old gospel hymns.

Priscilla liked to play the hymns, too, especially "Eternal Father Strong to Save" and "Nearer My God To Thee." But at home in New York, the summer before she left for Florida, her father had become mysteriously troubled when she played them. "Priscilla," he had said once, "those hymns are usually played at funerals. Play something else."

"But I *like* these hymns," she had replied. So she had learned to play them when her father was not around to hear them.

The least decorated room in Priscilla's new home was her bedroom, which she intentionally left what she thought of as "drab." *The last thing I want to do is to mislead the senator into thinking he's got a little love nest here*, she thought. *This is where I crash after a hard day's work, that's all. If he comes here and dislikes the room, let* him *decorate it.*

Off her bedroom was the only bathroom. The homeowners, a husband-wife architect and designer, had chosen to retain the original design of the house, which included the bathroom fixtures. But they did install a hand-held shower hose.

It had taken Priscilla close to a year to adapt to the hot and humid climate in Florida, but it took far less time and effort to readjust to the more temperate Ohio climate and her new lifestyle in Columbus. When she did not drive to work, she would walk the maple tree-lined street and catch a bus for the short ride downtown to the stop adjacent to the Ohio Statehouse.

She had studied and worked in Columbus previously, so from the beginning she was on familiar ground in her new job. Yet, thorough as always, Priscilla intentionally oriented herself to a deeper understanding of this place and its history. Constructed in 1857, the Ohio Statehouse was among the oldest working capitols in the nation. Like the Florida Statehouse, Ohio's also anchored the downtown. But Columbus was more urbane, more cosmopolitan and much more densely populated than Tallahassee.

One day during her first week on the job, Priscilla happened to overhear a tour guide from the Ohio Department of Development's Office of Travel and Tourism describing the capitol to a group of visitors as she strolled through the rotunda. She had not taken that tour during her legislative internship. Back then, she had spent most of her time working in the Callahan-for-Congress campaign office in Cincinnati.

Intrigued, she lingered on the fringes of the crowd and joined them staring up at the huge dome and listening to his summation. "The rotunda is one of the most remarkable spaces in the Statehouse," he said. "It extends some one hundred and twenty feet to the skylight—its crown jewel. At its center is a hand-painted seal of the state."

Then the tour guide pointed to the stone floor below the rotunda and the stone walls extending down from it. "The original artwork symbolizes several victorious battles, mostly from the Civil War: the Lincoln-Vicksburg Memorial, a bust of Abraham Lincoln produced in *bianco carrara*—a fine white marble from Italy—and a relief of the Confederate Army's surrender at Vicksburg."

But Priscilla was mostly impressed with the imposing statue of Christopher Columbus, for whom the city had received its name. The larger-than-life figure sat atop a massive base on the south lawn, at a remarkable point of entry.

Still, eager to learn all she could about her new milieu, Priscilla continued to listen to the tour guide. "Ohio, the 'Home of Presidents,'" he was saying, "has provided the nation with eight fine leaders: Ulysses S. Grant, William McKinley, Warren G. Harding, William Howard Taft, Benjamin Harrison, William Henry Harrison, Rutherford B. Hayes and James Garfield."

Finally, Priscilla thought, *something to interest me!* But there were more pressing contemporary realities to the political terrain in Ohio.

Priscilla stepped away from the group of visitors and headed up the steep spiral marble staircase, catching her breath near the bust of Abe Lincoln on the landing between the first and second floor. Then on the third floor, she walked into the office of Senator Theopholus Madison. Of the eleven black legislators in the Ohio General Assembly, only two – Senators Callahan and Madison – served in the senate.

She smiled at the middle-aged black woman sitting at the reception desk. "My name is Priscilla J. Austin. I'm the new aide to Senator Callahan." Priscilla did not know it, but she was looking at the only other black staff member of the Ohio Senate.

"Hello, to you, young lady," Andrea, the receptionist said. "How may I help you?"

"I'm here to pay my respects to Senator Madison, Senator Theopholus Madison. Is he available?" Her smile widened. Even back in her teenage years, she had heard of him and his accomplishments. "It will only take a minute."

The receptionist nodded, impressed by Priscilla's courteous attitude. She checked with the senator and then led Priscilla to his office. As Priscilla entered, she noticed the contrast with Senator Callahan's. This office was so neat and organized.

Senator Madison stood up to greet Priscilla. "Hello there, Ms. Austin, I understand you wanted to meet me. How charming of you. Please, come right on in and have a seat."

Priscilla did as he had suggested, pleased by the senator's dignity and comportment. He was, indeed, a far cry from her own boss.

Senator Madison looked to be about sixty years of age. But it seemed to Priscilla that he must be a notch shorter than Senator Callahan. He had close-cut hair, a thin mustache and dark complexion. He wore a starched white shirt, a bow tie and a tailored dark Brooks Brothers suit—perhaps gabardine—with expensive and fine-looking cuff links. This legislator appeared much more refined than Senator Callahan.

"Well, Sir," Priscilla began, "I wanted to match the face with the name and that prominent portrait that hangs in the vestibule of our church in Prendergast, New York." Priscilla knew that they shared that home town. "If you don't mind, Senator, I would just love to know more about your life in Prendergast. Were you there long? And why did you leave?" Eagerly she moved forward in her seat.

The senator hesitated as he decided how exactly to say what should be said. "Ms. Austin, I'm sorry to have to tell you this, but my family's life in Prendergast was not exactly rosy. You see, my mother had to move us to Cleveland to find a better life. I think, however, by the time your family might have moved there, circumstances were a little better for you than they had been for us."

Priscilla sank back in her chair. She had never imagined anyone, especially any distinguished black leader, *not* finding success in Prendergast. To her, the town had always seemed so enlightened. "I'm sorry to hear that, Senator. I honestly had no idea, Sir." As she thought about what he said, she focused on his success in the Ohio Senate. "But you seem to have done well for yourself, anyway."

They held each other's eyes for a moment. In that look, Priscilla read his unspoken plea that she would keep their Prendergast connection to herself. It was only later, much later, that Priscilla would come to realize that unwittingly she had exhumed a part of the senator's life that he thought he had long ago buried. She had already heard, here in the Statehouse, that most people assumed Senator Madison was a native Ohioan. It was only because of his portrait back in her church that Priscilla had known otherwise. But sitting in his office this first time, Priscilla had never guessed that someday she might have to choose between loyalty to their hometown and allegiance to this senator.

At the time, she simply connected to this senator who, in a way, was so like her father. Like Nelson, Senator Madison was old school. He had "worked hard," he told her, to get where he was, "especially for acceptance by my colleagues in the Ohio Senate." Although politically conservative, Senator Madison, like Senator Callahan, was a holdover from the civil rights era. As for his views on race relations, Senator Madison told her that he believed: "The best way to get things done is through compromise. You've got to work within the system." Most of all, he seemed to be trying to make Priscilla understand how he differed from Senator Callahan.

"May I take the liberty, young lady, to offer you some advice?"

By then Priscilla had already begun to tire of his pitch. But he did remind her of her father, and Nelson had taught her to be courteous. "Sure, Senator, that's why I'm here, to get acquainted with you."

Senator Madison rose as if he were about to deliver his most precious pearls of wisdom. "I'm sure your father has told you that, 'In order to get ahead, we must possess more education.' But it's not uncommon to see young people like yourself enter this arena expecting to garner fame, money and power. Well, I'd think long and hard about all that if I were you. Mostly, around here, *respect* is power. If you don't command respect, then you don't have anything."

Finally, Senator Madison spoke in a prophetic tone: "I didn't get in this position without the *respect* of my colleagues."

Priscilla kept a respectful look on her face, although she was thinking: *He's way out there, on another plane.* She had indeed always been told to be better prepared than "the competition," which of course was code for white people. But for Priscilla, that caution did not mean that she had to be content with always accepting less than she deserved and had earned. Senator Madison was president pro tempore in the Ohio Senate, and he was the first black person to achieve that leadership post. Priscilla honored him for that distinction.

But in her heart as well as her head, Priscilla wanted more out of life. She could not have said exactly what it was that she wanted, only that it was more than what she had seen in Senator Madison.

Or, she told herself, as she thoughtfully returned to her office, than she had seen in Senator Callahan.

A short time after Priscilla met Senator Madison, Senator Callahan called her to his office.

"Close the door behind you, Priscilla."

She sat attentively and waited for him—as usual—to vent and then issue a new directive. The first time she had met him, she had observed that pattern of behavior. But this time, he seemed more agitated than usual. He seemed angry as he pointed to a large pile of papers on his desk.

"Most all of this very important correspondence requires personal attention—phone calls and letters to constituents and to the Department of Public Welfare." He pointed his long, skinny index finger directly at Priscilla. "And other members of my staff tell me that you think constituent affairs are *not* your job. And that you especially don't handle the 'indigent and downtrodden.'"

Priscilla usually was quick on the uptake. But this time, as she was soon to regret, she did not fully comprehend the significance of the senator's outrage. "Surely you don't want to use me on issues that produce little or no votes and certainly no money for your campaign?" As if that were not enough, she continued before he could set her straight. "Senator, it would be a more efficient use of my time and of my skills if Charlene ran off the form letters and pursued the inquiries with those folks over in DPS. If she took care of this welfare stuff, that would free me to do the real business of the committees and cater to the interests of the *lobbyists*."

Senator Callahan raised his already loud voice a full octave. "For the record, *Ms.* Austin, I grew up on public assistance. Yes, *welfare!* My mother raised my brother and me the best she could, and I vowed I'd do my best to take care of her and anybody else who desired a better life. I know what it's like not to have enough food to eat, to be hungry. I know what it's like to work unsafe hard jobs as a youth. Everybody in my district and this whole damn state, for that matter, is familiar with my story. Hell, I'm the poster boy for, 'Poverty makes good.' Even if I wanted to—which I don't!—how the hell would I look disavowing poor people? How the hell do you think I got elected in the first place? Explain that one to me, *Ms*. Austin."

Priscilla bit her lip and considered her disdain for the poor. She remembered how she had felt as a child when her father had held his hat in hand and begged that grocer to let his family scavenge in his garbage. She recalled, too, that perhaps she owed her life to those welfare moms back in that Tallahassee slum who had pulled her out of her car after the accident. But she held fast to her belief that she was not a snob. She liked to think that her disdain for the poor lay mainly in her belief that most poor people allowed their poverty to define them. She remembered one of her father's sermons. "Poverty is a state of mind," Nelson had preached. "And it's one of helplessness and despair, and of allowing others to govern one's life." She realized that she, in fact, had assumed that Senator Callahan, along with some other public officials, advocated for the poor merely for political expediency. She had also incorrectly assumed that the senator had overcome the impoverished state of his youth.

For the remainder of that dressing-down by the senator, Priscilla proceeded to do what she could to salvage his esteem—and maybe, she thought later, her job itself—but the incident continued to shadow her work. There were, she discovered, many layers and implications to this issue of poverty and political expedience—and some of those layers were cynical. Priscilla came to believe that Senator Callahan was not above using the poverty of his youth for all the political gain he could extract out of it. He was good at that game. Senator Callahan, in fact, was good at playing many political games.

For the next few days and weeks, Priscilla atoned for what the senator obviously believed was a great sin. With growing impatience and an indiscreet tongue, mostly she immersed herself in what she still characterized to herself as "menial tasks."

Yet she still had not learned to keep her feelings to herself. To Charlene she groused one morning: "I'm sick and tired of writing all these stupid letters, chasing staff for people to get *welfare checks*, of all things," she said. "My God, this is, well, this is just not what I do."

The receptionist lost no time in reporting that comment to the senator. Nothing came of that particular new bit of tattling, for Charlene had not had a glimmering of the personal dimensions between the senator and his new legislative aide.

But even if she had known about the affair, Charlene still might have reported Priscilla. In fact, the receptionist still had not forgiven Priscilla for blowing her off during their first phone interaction. She had nicknamed her "Miss Prissy," and she had been the one to bring Priscilla's disparagement about welfare recipients to the senator in the first place. "What," she had complained to the senator, "makes Ms. Prissy think she can just pick and choose the constituent work she'll handle?" She had stopped short of questioning the senator as to why he had even hired such a supercilious aide. But she had said of Priscilla, "She doesn't relate to the people in your district at all. Not in the least."

The situation ratcheted up the office stress. As each day passed, Priscilla became more and more upset. She was definitely out of favor, as well as out of the loop. While she continued working her way through a mountain of paperwork about welfare and related issues for the poor in the senator's home district, she no longer understood what was truly happening when the phone rang, when visitors came into the office and when the senator asked for assistance from other members of the staff.

And during that fall of 1980, plenty was happening in the Ohio Senate.

At that time, Democrats were still the majority party in the thirty-three-member Ohio Senate. They held eighteen seats to the Republicans' fifteen. That meant the Senate Democratic caucus, of which Senator Callahan and Senator Madison were members, held the leadership posts and committee chairs. The Democratic caucus would not be holding the reins of power for long. But they were doing their best to wield that power while they still had it.

By the traffic of legislators and staffers in Senator Callahan's office, Priscilla sensed that he was at the center of the legislative storm. But she was vexed that she was not part of it. So she picked up what shreds of information she could from seemingly casual conversation with other legislative aides.

At issue—she discovered, was passage in the Ohio Senate of the Minority Business Enterprise (MBE) legislation, which provided for fifteen percent of all state construction contracts and seven-to-ten percent of all goods and services contracts to be bid on by minority contractors. In addition, this proposed legislation, which became known simply as the "Set-Aside Bill," required that financing be available for bonding minority contractors to perform construction contracts. More importantly, Senator Callahan had been charged by the leadership with moving the bill through the Senate.

Priscilla was frustrated in general by being left out of the loop on this bill and in particular by not being part of Senator Callahan's day-to-day machinations in securing its passage.

When finally the senator released her from what she regarded to herself as "this damn desk job," Priscilla had to work exceedingly hard and fast to catch up on the details of the Set-Aside Bill.

CHAPTER 10

Respect

Near the end of a very busy day at the Statehouse, Priscilla was preoccupied with final preparations for accompanying Senator Callahan to Cleveland for a presentation on the Set-Aside Bill. While most staff members busied themselves with closing their offices, she and the senator were packing papers and other materials for their trip.

Priscilla was looking forward to hearing him wax eloquently on the bill. Finally she was going to get the inside scoop on the controversial legislation.

When he had finished with his part of the packing, the senator headed for the door and said he would wait for her in the parking lot.

"Sure thing, Senator. But I need to double-check some of this stuff. Then I'll arrange to get all this to your car before catching up with you." She worked a few more minutes and then called for a page to come and cart several boxes to the parking lot.

As she waited for the page to come, her mind wandered from the political to the personal. As close as she kept in touch with her family in Prendergast, still her father had not told her anything more about why he had asked her to move closer to home. Mostly she had come to accept that he had something very personal to share with her, but that she would have to wait until he decided she was ready. Still, she hated to wait for anything and everything. She was even impatient for the page to arrive to cart the boxes to the senator's car.

Her personal reflection, however, ended quicker than she expected. The page arrived with a cart. As they rushed toward the elevator, Priscilla let go all thoughts of her father's secret. She concentrated all her energy into setting off with the senator to sell the Set-Aside Bill.

Senator Callahan drove a big, ugly maroon-colored Buick. Sometimes when he drove into the Statehouse parking lot, even the guard took a second look before buzzing him inside. But early on, Priscilla had realized that encouraging him to consider buying a different make and model of car was useless.

As she approached the senator standing beside the car, he asked, "Do you want to drive or shall I?"

"I wish you would," she said. Fresh from the limbo of public welfare minutiae, she still was only partially knowledgeable about the Set-Aside Bill. "I need to take more notes on some of this stuff."

They got into the car. But as he put his key into the ignition, the senator was startled by the sound of tapping on his window.

A grinning Senator Marcus Tektonidis—slightly overweight, with heavy facial features, thick and wavy black hair and a swarthy Mediterranean complexion—stood waiting for Senator Callahan to roll down his window. "Hey, Daniel, where you headed in such a hurry?" His smile widened. He was the aspiring leader of the Senate Democratic caucus and was best known for his strong and ingratiating personality. Of course, he already knew where Senator Callahan was rushing. In the small and incestuous world of the Ohio Senate, Senator Tektonidis made a practice of knowing most everything about everyone. He peered through the window at Priscilla. "I see you have your bodyguard with you." He doffed his hat to her. "Hello, Ms. Austin. Are you prepared to help Daniel round up the troops in Cleveland? They're a tough bunch."

But before she could respond, Senator Tektonidis had his head together with Senator Callahan and was whispering the real message that had brought him to the car.

"Yeah, yeah, I see," said Senator Callahan, patiently.

"Daniel," Senator Tektonidis was saying in a voice now loud enough for Priscilla to hear, "the Speaker has agreed to stay out of this one. Andrew told me we should fight this out among ourselves."

Priscilla frowned. Andrew Olmstead was the Speaker of the Ohio House of Representatives. What Senator Tektonidis was telling Senator Callahan might impact the bill's passage once it was referred back to the House of Representatives.

"And," Senator Tektonidis was continuing, "I declare, Daniel, if we lose anything, a pint of blood, one single member, anything at all ... " He hesitated to call attention to what he was about to say. "Then I'm telling you that this time we will be taking Walt and his cronies out altogether."

"Yeah, yeah, I hear you," said Senator Callahan.

Priscilla looked from one senator to the other. She knew of course that Walter O'Leary was the president of the Ohio Senate and the leader of the Senate Democratic caucus. What was Senator Tektonidis really saying?

"Daniel," he continued. "A word to the wise. Try not to be anywhere near Walt and that lot when the sledge hammer falls." Then Senator Tektonidis slapped the hood of the car and stepped aside.

In silence Senator Callahan and Priscilla drove through the stone columns, out onto South Third Street and headed north.

They were on the interstate when he put the car on cruise control and cleared his throat.

"Priscilla," he began. "I need to explain something to you. Marcus and his boys are preparing to take over control of the caucus." When he saw her eyes widen, he nodded. "The only deal I ever cut with leadership—or those seeking it—has been for committee assignments. I don't need leadership roles or titles. I need good committee assignments so that I can get some things done."

Priscilla's curiosity ripened. "Tell me, before you go any further. Why do people always call Senator Tektonidis 'the Greek?'?"

The senator laughed. "Because he *is* 'Greek.' Greek-American, actually. And he wants everybody to know it." He reverted to the stream of his conversation. "What I really want is to chair the Senate Finance Committee. That's where all the bodies are buried and where all the possibilities lie."

But a determined Priscilla had more to ask about "the Greek's" behavior. "So Senator Tektonidis wasn't threatening you?"

"Sweetheart, in this business, whenever somebody wants something, they go after it. Marcus already knows my position on the impending takeover. He was simply informing me that his team has officially waged war against Walt's. That's all."

Still confounded, Priscilla said, "He sounded awfully threatening to me."

Senator Callahan gave her a knowing look. His legislative aide appeared to be more politically naïve than he had thought. He set about schooling her in what she had to learn about the game of partisan politics. "Priscilla, come what may in the November elections, Marcus's team intends to take over the Senate Democratic caucus. And that's that. Now, surely you already know coups are nothing new. Ambitious, the lot of them are so ambitious! Those fellas are always up to something." Then the senator laughed, "And they do the same thing over on the House side."

Priscilla did not comment.

"Regardless," the senator went on, "the point to remember through all of this, is to remain strong in your convictions and earn respect. Then, and only then, will you survive."

Priscilla remembered how that same word had rolled off Senator Madison's tongue. *Ah! There's that word "respect" again.* Finally Priscilla understood precisely what that other senator had been trying to tell her. He had used the word "respect," but it seemed the word "power" and "money" had been what he intended to imply.

She recalled how her father had worried, and with reason, whether he had raised enough money to satisfy his bishop before every annual conference. At stake had been whether he would lose his church congregation. And in her childhood losing his church had been a common occurrence for the good reverend.

Speeding north toward Cleveland, Priscilla let Senator Callahan's ongoing chat roll over her as she pondered all these implications. She figured that although "character" was part of "respect," "money" weighed more heavily. Without raising money, a pastor could forget about a good church appointment; and without money, a pastor could not even dream about a leadership post. Ergo, she concluded, the same held true in the political realm. The bigger the war chest, the greater the influence.

Now that she had begun to comprehend the situation, Priscilla peered out into the dusk as they flashed by the rural heartland of Ohio.

"Okay, Senator, so, how much *money* do we need to raise for either Walt or Marcus to give you the Finance Committee?"

Senator Callahan grinned. "You had me fooled there awhile, kiddo. I didn't think you'd be such a quick study. For starters, I need to command a statewide constituency, raise an unusually large amount of money *and* spread some of it around."

The senator had finally gained his aide's full attention. "OK, so now let's hear your whole plan."

He laughed. "I'm hoping this trip to Cleveland will shore up my base. I'm good in Columbus and the rest of the south in the state. It's up north where my standing needs a boost. We've *got* to pass the Set-Aside Bill. Once that's a reality, then I can attract more widespread support for our caucus."

Priscilla nodded. Now she saw the connection between this trip to Cleveland and that all-important piece of legislation. What this Cleveland foray was about was rallying the black business community for passage of the Set-Aside Bill.

The senator then elaborated further, explaining how the Black Elected Democrats of Ohio (BEDO) in the Ohio General Assembly had pushed for a Set-Aside Bill since 1966. "Right now, we're as close to getting a bill through as ever." He also told her that a white colleague in the House of Representatives had already drafted the language to finance the program.

Priscilla wrinkled her forehead. "Senator, you're joshing me."

"No, I'm quite serious, for real. The guy in the House who has been working on that bill was the one who pointed out the difficulty of passing a Set-Aside Bill without first addressing finances and bonds, which are the root causes of the problem."

Priscilla nodded again. Now some of the bits and pieces of what she had heard were beginning to make sense. In September, the Democratic leadership in the House had already sent that bill with the new language to the Senate's Rules and Reference Committee.

Senator Callahan teased her. "Yeah, remember, sweetheart. All that was happening around the time you were doing 'desk duty.'"

He smiled as he continued to give her the background she needed to be able to help him with the bill. He had urged his caucus to assign the bill to Commerce and Labor, his committee. Yet the Set-Aside Bill was considered by the Democratic caucus to be a higher priority for the black legislators than for the party caucus at large. "Priscilla, this is, after all, politics. We had to cut all kinds of deals just to get us to this point."

She could feel her rising anger and impatience. "But why disguise or lose ourselves in obscure language like 'minority?' Call the bill what it is, 'black.'" She did not care how impossible it would have been, at that stage of the legislative process, to try and change the title of the bill.

But she need not have worried. The senator was so engrossed in his own analysis that he had hardly heard what she had said.

"Right now," he continued, "we're working on a strategy for what to do next. Merge the two bills? Move only on the one from the House? Pick up mine later? I'm pushing for a merger, that is, an amended substitute version of the two bills."

"And the role of the Minority Business Enterprises in Cleveland?" Priscilla asked.

Somewhat disparagingly, the senator said, "Sometimes when you can't win a battle in-house, you go after support wherever-the-hell you can get it."

The meeting of the predominantly black business group had already begun when they arrived at the Cleveland Ambassadors Club after their two-hour drive.

As Senator Callahan glad-handed it all the way through the conference room, Priscilla followed closely behind, all the time trying to assess the gathering. She had been told back in Columbus that the group's membership had expanded recently to include those of Hispanic origin along with a few Indians from East India and Southeast Asians, several Native Americans and even several white women.

Trailing the senator and his aide, a hotel doorman pushed a rack of their cartons. Then when a recess was called, Priscilla handed out sample correspondence, talking points and contact information for each of the thirty-three senators.

She felt immediately comfortable in the throng of mostly black businessmen. Like many other affluent and middle-class blacks in the 1970s, the Austins had been staunch supporters of the Republican Party. Indeed, at that time most well-to-do blacks had merely played homage to Democratic Party officials. By now, however, in 1980, the political leanings of many black lower- and middle-class voters had already shifted to the Democratic Party. Yet the so-called "black Democratic voting bloc" had not yet solidified.

Priscilla was aware, too—as she joked and small-talked with these prominent businessmen—that the black middle- and upper-middle classes in Cleveland thrived as a formidable constituency in both of the state's major political parties. They had recently helped to elect one of the Drummond brothers as mayor of Cleveland and had sent another of the brothers to Congress. One of the few black-owned banks in the nation and one of the oldest black-owned publishing companies, the *Sentinel*, were headquartered in Cleveland. In fact, several black millionaires, some of whom were in their second or third generation of affluence, resided on the peripheries of Ohio's major urban centers. During Priscilla's youth, Nelson would talk about one such family, the House of Wills. Morticians by trade, the Wills were so prominently established it was said that the men who married into that family had to adopt its name.

Still, when the meeting resumed, it was soon apparent that this predominantly black entrepreneurial assemblage at the Cleveland Ambassador's Club sought more vigorous representation in the Democratic-controlled Ohio General Assembly.

The group's president challenged Senator Callahan.

"So what you're saying, Senator, is that if we support you on this bill, 'from time to time' you'll call on us to provide financial support for your campaign initiatives as well as for others in the Senate Democratic caucus?" He waited for the Senator to say he would. When he had that affirmation, the president shook the senator's hand. "Well, folks, I'd say that's a small price to pay to get in the game."

Many in the assemblage responded, "Yeah, yeah."

Priscilla felt like cheering. Senator Callahan had gotten what he came for.

Elated, the two of them continued to talk political turkey on the drive back to Columbus.

"The polls show our man—President Jimmy Carter—having grave difficulty in his bid for reelection," Senator Callahan said. "In fact, I hear he's even turning down requests for campaign events. Our own polls show Ronald Reagan winning big time. Reagan has already proclaimed his loathing for big government, welfare chiselers and other stuff they have been able to pin on to Democrats. And if and when he gets in, I predict he will try to change everything. By the time he gets done in Washington, we'll wonder where we are."

"If you're right," Priscilla asked, "what will all that mean here in Ohio—particularly in our Senate?"

"I hate to break it to you, kiddo," Senator Callahan said emphatically. "But the Republicans are looking for a landslide victory, which always brings with it a strong coattail effect. If that prediction holds true, we could lose the Senate. *That's* what it means. And if we lose the majority in the Ohio Senate, all plans of my becoming Chairman of Finance are off." He snapped his fingers to emphasize his point. "Blip, zap, gone."

Priscilla reflected. Just when she had a taste of life on the top of this particular heap, everything could change. She wondered what it would be like to experience minority status as a staffer in the Ohio Senate.

As they approached the outer limits of the capital, the senator regretfully turned toward her. "I'm sorry, sweetheart, but I can't stay with you tonight. Gotta make a showing on the home front. Do you mind if I just drop you off? I can call on you Monday." He reached for her hand. "And thanks for making this a good and productive evening. I think we scored really big time with the Cleveland folks."

Priscilla tried to look regretful. At her home, she closed the door behind her and sighed in relief. She always enjoyed a peaceful sleep when she was alone, and she did not dream any bad dreams, either.

CHAPTER 11

Minority Party Status

On the way to work the morning after the 1980 November elections, Priscilla recalled Senator Callahan's predictions. Everything—Reagan's landslide and that coattail effect resulting in a Democratic loss of the Ohio Senate—had all come to pass.

But she had not been prepared for the long faces and despair of politicians and staff. And despite the senator's warnings, she was shocked at how they expected the election returns to affect almost every aspect of their political lives. Democrats in the Ohio Senate had lost their majority, not by the anticipated one seat, but by three. Their eighteen-to-fifteen majority was flipped into the exact opposite and placed them squarely into minority-party status.

The first words out of Senator Callahan's mouth when she entered his office were, "Well, there goes the Finance Committee and chairmanship of anything else around here."

She tried to cheer him up by reminding him that he had predicted the loss more than a month ago, and that he had warned the party elite to pump more money into the campaign of one state senator who had lost the day before as well. "You did your part to hold on to the majority. And surely this isn't a surprise. After all, you've reminded me to no end that 'Ohio is a *red* state.'"

"Cold comfort," said the senator. "Ice cold, Priscilla."

He seemed to revive only when, musing out loud, he remembered what had been obvious to Priscilla last night as the returns were coming in. The Democrats had more than two months before the Republicans took control of the Ohio Senate on Inauguration Day 1981. "Maybe it's not too late for the Set-Aside Bill after all." But then again he slumped in his chair. "Though it won't mean as much without that committee chairmanship."

Priscilla returned to her desk to take a call from her father. He had voted for Reagan and was elated at the results. She was glad no one in her office could hear Nelson exulting.

Later that afternoon Priscilla, along with the Democratic senators and staff, crowded into the office of Senate President O'Leary.

The atmosphere was tense and acrimonious. Supporters of Marcus Tektonidis wanted O'Leary to resign from his leadership position because of the caucus's humiliating loss at the polls. But O'Leary obtained enough votes to become the new minority leader. Next on the agenda were contentious decisions about which pending Democratic bills to send to the floor to try to push through passage before they lost their majority in January. With such a small window of opportunity, tempers flared— including Senator Callahan's.

Senator Callahan was intent on pushing through the Set-Aside Bill now, while it still had majority party control. In the past weeks, the galvanized black business community had besieged every member of the Ohio General Assembly to pass the bill. Without even most of the senators being aware of it, an amended substitute version of the bill had cleared the Commerce and Labor Committee. Now, poised for consideration on the Senate floor, the minority businessmen had begun lobbying with legislators finally to pass it. So far as Senator Callahan had been able to discern, the black business lobbyists had determined that their best bet to get the bill enacted lay with the current Democratic-controlled General Assembly.

Senator Callahan advised the Democratic caucus to give the minority community what it wanted. "Put the Set-Aside on the calendar for a floor vote! We've got to act on that bill now!" Then he focused his demand on Senator Madison, who, as chairman of the

Rules and Reference Committee, was responsible for scheduling the bills on the Senate calendar.

Senator Madison got to his feet. "I'm really sorry, Daniel. I got a little behind on some things. But it's been taken care of now. It was a close call, but you're on at the start of the week of Thanksgiving." Then Senator Madison perused the room. "As for the other bills, I've prepared an unofficial list for your approval prior to posting. It's the best I could do under the obvious circumstances of yesterday's election results."

Back in his office, Senator Callahan called in Priscilla to crow about his accomplishment getting a vote scheduled on his bill.

But she was shocked to learn from the senator that the Set-Aside Bill had been "way down on the totem pole" and might never have come to the floor if he had not advocated so strongly.

"In this game," he told her, "one must choose his battles carefully. I've also told you about the significance of respect. No matter what our partisan status, a lot of these guys *owe* me. Keep in mind also that I've been around awhile and I've done a lot of favors for many of these little monsters. Some of them owe me *big time*."

Then he talked strategy with her.

Already, he said, both Democratic caucus leaders—O'Leary, the actual outgoing Senate president, and Tektonidis, his rival who was intent on taking his job—had insisted that Senator Callahan shore up adequate votes ahead of the actual floor vote on the Set-Aside Bill.

"The Greek" had been the most forceful when he called Callahan that morning. "I have no intention anchoring rock bottom," he had insisted. "We're going to get it to the floor, but it's up to you, Daniel, to make sure you have the votes. We need something to hang our hats on to recoup our damn losses. You know the problem selling sour grapes. When we hand over the reins in January, the people in this state must see us as positive and forward-thinking, not griping and groveling."

Senator Callahan rocked and swiveled in his big leather chair as he considered what he had to do. Finally he nodded at Priscilla. "I need eighteen votes. No more and no less. Though more than eighteen would be dandy."

Again he rocked and swiveled. "Some of those guys won't support the bill for fear of backlash from their conservative constituents. And the only Republicans I can count on are those with substantial black and Democratic constituencies. But that's only a few, at most, only a few. Then again, I do have a few favors hanging in the fringes." He spoke those last words with a subdued smile. He needed firm commitments from a handful of strong Republicans to offset the possible fallout from his own caucus. "Never can tell with some of these guys. I need to round up maybe five. Yeah, I need to line up five strong Republicans to hedge my bets."

Priscilla had never realized her boss was such a dreamer. Passage of the bill was clearly unlikely. "Are we talking about a crapshoot, Senator?" Her disillusionment with what went on with the political process in the Ohio General Assembly was as clear as a pane of glass.

"I'm saying this is one of those instances where my vibes are out of sync with my tabulations. But I'll be damned if I'm not running this ball."

Priscilla nursed her doubts as the senator again silently tried to decide what next to do. Yet she was about to learn that the politician for whom she worked commanded tremendous respect. Her own purpose in the Ohio Senate may have been transient, but politics had always been Senator Callahan's life's passion. He already relished the rare privilege of prime real estate in his Statehouse office. He appreciated, too, the quality of his ongoing relationships with the statewide leadership as well as perks typically reserved for Senate leadership including insider information, special committee assignments and travel. He particularly enjoyed his assignment to the State Controlling Board, which required appointment by the president of the Senate, with whom Senator Callahan was always careful to maintain favorable relations. That board consisted of lawmakers from the House and Senate and a representative from the governor's office. Its membership voted on all financial contracts awarded by the State of Ohio. Even with the Senate leadership change following the election, Senator Callahan would once again retain his prized seat on that board. So if the Set-Aside Bill were to obtain Senate approval, like all other state contracts, *all* contracts awarded to minority businesses would also require the approval of the State Controlling Board. That approval was the plum the senator was after.

Senator Callahan leaned forward. He had reached a decision.

"OK," he told Priscilla. "Write me a floor speech. Cover the history and legislative intent of the bill."

Priscilla had never before heard him speak with such intense conviction.

"Then," he continued, "give me two or three significant points to highlight. I'll adlib the rest."

Priscilla raised her eyebrows. She was unfamiliar with his gift for oratory, and that for him a written speech served merely as a sort of "Peanut's blanket".

He smiled at her obvious doubts. "I've been eating, sleeping with, and nurturing this baby for years. And I'll be a monkey's uncle if I'm carrying it any longer. And I'm no monkey's uncle. It's time to birth this baby."

Priscilla returned to her desk, pulled together the appropriate documents and told herself to write the speech. But she immediately hit a snag. "Damn, damn, damn, where should I begin? What should be the first words out of his mouth? How should he appeal to his colleagues, and play to the media as well as to the gallery?"

Priscilla had been so engrossed in her assignment that she had been unaware she was speaking out loud.

She shared an office with another legislative aide named Sharon, who worked for Senator Jamison Chouinard. The two women were neither friends nor enemies and usually did not talk much to each another.

Yet Priscilla rattled on, still aloud. "This is going to be hard. My first floor speech! Everybody's going to be watching. I've got to get it right."

Sharon broke into her thoughts. "Priscilla, are you talking to yourself? You're writing his floor speech on the Set-Aside? You and the senator have a tough road ahead, don't you?" She continued to needle her. "Listen, Priscilla, you *do* have the votes lined up, don't you?" Sharon's boss was in line for second-in-command of what would be the minority-party caucus. He was a supporter of "the Greek".

Priscilla barely acknowledged Sharon. She was writing on a legal pad now. Yet the words came slowly, very slowly.

It was full speed ahead for Senator Callahan.

He wasted little time in reflection. Senator Daniel P. Callahan had not gotten where he was on the basis of silent meditation. He needed five Republican votes, and he set out at once to secure them.

His first stop was the office of the president-elect.

He started off by sweet-talking the receptionist. "Good morning, sweetie. Is he in?"

Gracie, the middle-aged woman indulgently smiled. "For you, Senator Callahan, of course, go right in."

"Raymon," Senator Callahan said to the president-elect of the Ohio Senate, "how the hell are you? Listen, I need to offer my congratulations to you again on your big victory."

Senator Raymon Ferrari greeted Senator Callahan warmly. "I'm fine, Daniel, and thanks for the 'congrats.' Now, what brings you across the aisle?"

"Raymon, I'm calling in a favor. I need your vote on the Set-Aside Bill. Will you come through for me on this one?"

Surprised at Senator Callahan's request, Senator Ferrari answered almost immediately. "I don't see why not, Daniel. My constituency doesn't even know about the bill, nor does it carry any negative offshoot for me. Anyway, if you need my vote, you've got it on this one. And by the way, thanks for asking. Anything else, Daniel?"

"Nah, man. Thank goodness we still have a little civility left."

The two men shook hands, and Senator Callahan walked out of the president-elect's office.

His next stop was to see outgoing Senate Minority Leader Allen Van Vorst, who was regarded as the most conservative—even right-wing—member in the Republican caucus. That a substantial segment of Van Vorst's Dayton constituency was black and that he tended to represent mostly the conservative white constituency did not necessarily mean he was a racist. But only Senator Callahan and a few other, more astute lawmakers knew that he was not. Regardless of the reason, Senator Van Vorst had been the only Republican to lose his reelection bid.

"Allen, my goodness, man, I'm sorry we're going to lose you." Senator Callahan said. "Are you going to be okay?"

"Yeah, Daniel, man. Damn glad you dropped by, though I know this has to be more than a courtesy call. What can I do for you, Daniel?"

"I'm calling in a favor. I need your support on the Set-Aside Bill. Can I count on your vote, Allen?"

"Hell, Daniel, if circumstances were different, I'd give you the roundabout. But for the hell of it, you've got my vote, especially if no other member of my caucus breaks ranks. What a way to go! Thanks, Daniel. I couldn't have written a better departing script than one that will have me supporting minority business enterprises."

The two men laughed and then embraced.

Senator Callahan returned to his office, where he made his last three appeals over the telephone. Then he decided to begin working on his floor speech.

The senator called Priscilla into his office and asked to see her draft. As the two of them bent over her script, the seasoned politician did not share with his aide the news of the Republican votes he had secured. He had no intention, either, of sharing those details with his caucus. He would assure them only that he had collected ample votes for the bill's passage.

After reading Priscilla's draft, the senator shook his head. "Sorry, but this is too academic. Rework it more in line with prime time. I won't have all day to change those guys' minds. I need this speech to be tight, concise. I want it terse and clear."

Surprised and a little bruised at his criticism, Priscilla went back to her office to rework the speech. She was an academician. She had researched and written the pertinent facts. She had given the senator all the fodder he needed.

But she started all over again. This was her first stab at political speech-writing. But she would learn by doing. She had grown up at Nelson's knee, and she was used to approval. Used to excellence.

"Terse but clear," the senator had said.

Priscilla set about writing exactly what he needed.

CHAPTER 12

Act Like a Winner

On the day of the Senate vote on the Set-Aside Bill, Priscilla was tense but optimistic as she took her designated seat on the black leather bench reserved for staff. From her catbird seat inside the banister in the Senate chamber, she would experience her first floor speech delivered by the senator.

Everyone who was anyone was there. Officials from the governor's office, other statewide offices, the House of Representatives and the state agencies packed the gallery and every other available space in the Senate chamber. It was standing room only for the black businessmen, the lobbyists as well as the media, who had squeezed in where they could.

Priscilla scanned the gallery and chamber for familiar faces. She was gratified to see so many black businesspeople here. Many she remembered from her trip to Cleveland with Senator Callahan had come to Columbus for the final vote. The black business community had lobbied all 132 members of the Ohio General Assembly with letters, personal visits and telephone calls. Those same minority entrepreneurs had even engineered news editorials, primarily in print media, in support of the Set-Aside Bill.

Priscilla craned her neck to overhear snatches of conversations around her in the chamber. It was always good for her, as a legislative aide, to keep track of what folks were thinking about what had momentum and what was about to die.

Maurice, a lobbyist with the Ohio Contractors Association was talking to George, the Statehouse news reporter for the *Columbus Chronicle*.

"Word is," Maurice said, "that Callahan doesn't have the full backing of his own caucus. So where do you suppose he'll get the votes to pass his baby?"

"I don't know, man" George answered, "but word I've heard is that this is either a New Orleans-style requiem or a last-ditch partisan hurrah for the Democrats. Either way, both make good news copy."

A few minutes earlier, in the hallway outside the Senate, Priscilla had overheard two other reporters who doubted the bill's chances of passage. "This might be a funeral today, but whose is it? Senator Callahan doesn't seem ready to deliver any eulogy. I wager he's holding a few cards none of us has even considered—maybe two or three moderate Republicans."

"Whatever the senator's holding," the other reporter had answered, "this is going to be a last-ditch effort to shore up his caucus's fledgling image. I'm sure you know the thinking is that his own party is going to kill this bill, because there are just too many conservative Democrats."

Priscilla had hid a smile. They obviously did not know even the half of it.

Prior to the vote on the Set-Aside Bill, interested parties were still milling around the corridors for last-minute lobbying. But when President O'Leary called for the third reading on the bill, there was a rush as everyone present in the chamber hastened to take seats or at least find a comfortable place to sit or stand.

Nearly everyone in the Senate chamber had preprinted tally sheets to record the votes alongside the names and political party affiliations of each of the thirty-three senators. The magic number for passage was seventeen, a simple majority of the thirty-three senators.

Maurice was leaning forward in anticipation. "It looks like Callahan is about to take to the floor. What we want to do, right off the bat, is follow his mood and tempo."

Priscilla's eyes drilled into the back of Senator Callahan's head. Earlier she had seen his final version of the speech she had written: penciled notes and additions filled the margins. But this time Priscilla had been less thin-skinned. She figured her job had been to galvanize his thoughts, and she was proud she had done exactly that.

Senator Callahan stood. "Mr. President?"

"The Chair recognizes the distinguished gentleman from Cincinnati," outgoing President O'Leary said.

Blessings, Priscilla prayed. Senator Callahan's moment was *now.*

He turned to acknowledge all others in the chamber. "Mr. President, distinguished colleagues, ladies and gentlemen, I rise to urge unanimous support for the long-awaited Minority Business Set-Aside Bill."

Senator Callahan had a magnificent speaking voice that even eighteenth- and nineteenth-century statesmen would have appreciated. In his speech, void of fluff or slang, he employed simple logic and, on occasion, inserted a phrase or two from classical Greek literature, which he had borrowed from the books of his friend and colleague, "the Greek". Moreover, Senator Callahan possessed an essential quality for public speaking—that rare, high command of the English language. What gave his oratory particular power was how he coupled his rhetorical gifts with his political skills. He had worked in the trenches for the NAACP in the 1950s and 1960s, where he had learned to *demand*, not just to *ask*, and if necessary, to *demonstrate* and to *protest* for social justice.

"Thanks to our esteemed attorney general," said Senator Callahan, "we know the details of our abysmal situation, namely, that less than one percent of all state contracts is awarded to MBEs annually and that most black business owners aren't even registered with the state. Hence the need for this legislation."

He appealed to his undecided colleagues, who he knew were silent not because they *wanted* to be, but because they *had* to be. Some even feared rocking the boat in their home districts.

One legislator from a rural district rose to speak and was temporarily given the floor and objected to what he characterized as the bill's "unconstitutional preferences and quotas" in the governmental bidding process.

A moment later, Senator Callahan again had the floor and dismissed that objection, citing court and state governmental rulings to the contrary.

Priscilla nodded. Legislators and staff understood the dissenting legislator's objection had been the Republican caucus' perfunctory way of registering formal opposition to the bill. Yet Priscilla was unable to resist whispering to Sharon, her fellow staffer, sitting next to her on the bench. "Those guys needn't be quiet because they've won." Priscilla continued to whisper. "They're in control in a matter of weeks."

"Yeah, yeah," Sharon answered. "I know what you mean."

Priscilla felt rebuffed. She wondered why legislators, and staff as well, were saying so little. *Maybe nobody's saying anything because they don't want to be seen as racists voting against another bill that benefits black people, like that anti-bussing bill that was pushed through last month.*

Yet as hard as she was trying to listen and learn, Priscilla continued to be baffled by the scene on the Senate floor that day. It was hard to read the runes and interpret the hidden meanings in every word.

What she did not consider was that her sense of isolation was fed by her being the only black female legislative aide for the Ohio Senate. Rick, her predecessor as A.A. to Senator Callahan, had been the first black person to serve as an aide to a senator. The only other black Senate staffer was Andrea, Senator Madison's secretary. In addition, by the time of this vote, Priscilla had been on the job for fewer than four months. Most legislators and staff, not only in the Senate but also the House, had never even met or seen her. In fact, many news correspondents and visitors seemed nearly as curious about the new black female aide to Senator Callahan as they were about the outcome of the vote on the Set-Aside Bill.

Priscilla heard a whisper from a staffer almost out of earshot at the end of the bench. "Who do you think wrote Callahan's speech? He sure didn't. This speech is more organized than his other stuff. A tad long, but at least it's organized. Do you suppose that new girl wrote it?"

"Maybe," someone answered in a low tone. "Somebody else sure did write this speech. Daniel P. Callahan does *not*, I repeat, does *not* talk like this. Not at all. But these are definitely his issues, and he's making his point. He certainly has done that, and he's doing it without race-bashing, too."

As Priscilla wavered between being flattered and annoyed, she overheard another snatch of conversation from a female journalist.

"This is good oratory," the reporter was saying. "He's speaking with tremendous vigor, as if his speech is an invitation to join him and the others who've already pledged their support. He sounds so confident. Do you think he has all the votes he needs locked up?"

Priscilla's spirits rose, but even as she listened to Senator Callahan's speech, out of the corner of her eye she noticed that the aide to Senator Tektonidis seemed to be heading her way.

She had experienced run-ins before with Brad, who was neither meek nor mild and certainly was self-conscious of his status as aide to the senator who had been so persistently bent on taking over the Senate leadership.

Brad was behind her, leaning over the staff bench, whispering in her ear. "You should have given us copies of the speech before Daniel started speaking. This is a major piece of legislation. The caucus doesn't need any surprises. Got that, Ms. Prissy?"

Without turning around to acknowledge him, Priscilla regally handed him a copy of the speech. "Don't be in such a huff. He's not reading it verbatim, anyway. He's doing his own thing."

Priscilla knew she had conducted herself properly. She had given copies of the speech to the Senate clerk, and a page had put a copy on the desk of each of the thirty-two other senators on the floor. Brad of course had to be aware that the staff was of secondary importance. He was simply relishing the opportunity to flaunt his authority as a senior staffer in the Senate Democratic caucus and the aide to the aspiring minority leader.

Some of the news reporters had eyed this interchange and now were beckoning Priscilla.

She rose calmly and courteously told them she did not have any extra copies. But she felt caught off guard as she returned to her seat on the staff bench.

Priscilla did not have a clue about how to interpret the talk she was hearing from the lobbyists, reporters and staffers. Nor did she know that the silence among the lawmakers did not necessarily mean their opposition to the Set-Aside Bill. But then she remembered that Senator Callahan had always said: "In this game there's a time to speak for purposes of public relations, a time to demonstrate conviction and a time to speak with your vote." Most of the lawmakers, Priscilla suddenly realized, were waiting in silence for the opportunity to voice their vote.

Senator Callahan's mighty voice was reaching a crescendo.

"I'm sure all assembled believe, as I do, that this is a great day in Ohio" he said. "It is a great day in this great state because of the emancipation of black businesses ... for their inclusion in the economic fiber of this great state. The reality is that black business contributes to the general revenue of this state, enhancing its overall economic status, just like other businesses do. And as a consequence, MBEs deserve equal access to *and* equal opportunity in the state contracting process just like the other businesses do."

Senator Callahan paused and then rhetorically asked, "How can any among us disagree with anything I've said thus far?"

The senator brought home his point: "Ergo, we're not asking anybody for anything. This is an economic issue, and we're *demanding* our seat at the table, our *right* to participate in the state contracting process." His words echoed thunderously throughout the otherwise sedate Senate chamber.

Priscilla had never experienced the senator at full throttle. *Why's he carrying on like that?* She had written what she thought was a short scholarly thesis, from which the senator had extracted his declaratory phrases and pungent political rhetoric. In this, his moment, Senator Callahan's belief manifested itself in his conviction and his delivery. The result was very real, even electrifying.

When Senator Callahan finished his remarks and then his responses to the few questions that had been put before him, he took his seat.

The tenor in the chamber had now risen to fever pitch.

A few of Senator Callahan's colleagues walked over and slapped him on his shoulder. "Good job, Daniel," Senator Chouinard said. "Good job!"

"Excellent presentation, Daniel," Senator Gallagher said.

Priscilla overheard comments from all around her.

"I particularly like his handling of the overall economic impact of the bill," she heard one respected reporter from the *Sentinel* say. Somehow he had obtained a copy of the speech, and as he talked he flipped through it. I liked it when he said, 'This is an economic issue, and we're *demanding* our seat at the table.' But I can't find that in his written speech."

"Damn, he's good," agreed another reporter. "The man is good at this game. He knew exactly where to place his markers."

President O'Leary was gaveling for order. "The clerk will call the roll."

Priscilla had spent a restless night before this day where she believed Senator Callahan would face a major defeat on the Senate floor. She had not foreseen what was to happen after the calling of the roll.

"Aye," "Aye," "Aye" reverberated throughout the chamber. An occasional "Nay" brought soft booing from some in the gallery.

"Twenty-five 'ayes' and seven 'nays,'" said President O'Leary. He hammered his desk with the gavel. "The bill has passed."

At that, many in the Senate chamber leapt to their feet.

"Twenty-five frigging votes!" shouted one Democratic legislator.

"Can you believe this?" yelled another.

The otherwise august Senate chamber had erupted, Senator Callahan's personal lobby had paid off, and the Democrats had gotten their last hurrah.

"Phenomenal, just phenomenal," Priscilla murmured to herself. Her boss had just won a major battle, and Priscilla had learned that one important lesson about playing the game was to act like a winner.

It was November 24, 1980, just before the holiday recess. *Happy Thanksgiving,* Priscilla thought.

CHAPTER 13

The Real Pillar

Priscilla rushed home from that extraordinary day of triumph. It was Thanksgiving eve, and her parents were arriving to pick her up for the drive to Indianapolis, where the plan was to spend Thanksgiving with the Austin clan.

She leaped at the phone when it rang soon after she came in the door. When she heard her mother's voice, Priscilla was excited. "Momma, I'm here. Are you and Daddy on your way over?"

"No." Liza's voice was flat, almost mechanical. "We've taken a room at a hotel nearby. And we want you to come over here. We're ready for dinner."

Still exuberant from the victory in the Senate chamber, Priscilla did as her mother asked. She had no premonition of what was to come. She still had no idea why Nelson had asked her to relocate closer to home. In fact, she had pretty much forgotten about the matter.

But when she entered her parents' hotel room, she noticed it was dimly lit and that only Liza was up and ready.

"Come on, you guys," Priscilla said. "It's time for dinner. Why isn't Daddy up? And why's it so dark in here? Shouldn't we turn on more—?"

But Liza stepped quickly over and pulled her daughter's hand from the light switch.

"Priscilla, girl, your father's resting. He's a little tired from the drive over. So he won't be joining us for dinner. He'll join us in the morning. Okay?"

Priscilla bit her lip. Something was out of kilter. She knew how much Nelson loved coming to Columbus. He had always enjoyed sightseeing the grand university campus and would have crawled to Indianapolis to see his eleven brothers and sisters there. Yet as she pondered what exactly might be going on, she felt obliged to obey her mother. Nelson had conditioned her to do what her parents had asked of her, without question.

Priscilla approached her father's bed. "Are you sure you're all right, Daddy? Can we bring you something back from the restaurant? And don't you want to check out the campus in the morning?"

"I'm fine, Priscilla. Just do as your mother asks." Nelson lay still underneath the covers in the darkened room. "I'll see you in the morning. The old man is just a little tired. That's all."

Priscilla later was to wonder why she went off with her mother for dinner without insisting on knowing more about her father needing bed rest. She concluded that at the time she must still have been so high from the legislative victory that she was not sufficiently in touch with her parents' evident gloom.

But the mood at dinner, too, was not auspicious. Liza did not like the restaurant. And she seemed annoyed by the people who kept dropping by their table to offer congratulations on Senator Callahan's success in the passage of the Set-Aside legislation. Still basking in that victory, Priscilla had hoped to impress her parents with the adulation of her colleagues.

Instead, she gradually became aware that something was seriously wrong. Liza was a staunch Democrat, and she loved to argue about politics—especially with Nelson, the eternal Republican. But on this occasion at the restaurant, she seemed disinterested in what had happened that day in the Ohio Senate.

Finally, Liza said, "Oh well, Priscilla, I can see your mind is immersed in your work, so what news I have to tell you can wait." In her heart she understood it would never be a good time to break her "news" to Priscilla. But still she postponed that conversation.

Priscilla frowned but again she shrugged off her misgivings.

Back at the hotel, Liza said good night in the lobby. "Don't forget that your father is counting on you to drive us to Indianapolis in the morning. You need to be up early. So get some rest, will you, Priscilla?"

The next morning, there was no sightseeing around Columbus. Again, Liza said Nelson was not up to it. Priscilla was startled at the sight of Nelson experiencing difficulty walking to his car. Yet, she did not make much of it except for her thinking, *He must really be tired.*

Driving for nearly three hours in holiday traffic on Thanksgiving Day, all Priscilla was to remember later was that Nelson had been bundled up and had talked very little. That, and her own growing anxiety which built as she drove along that particularly flat, dull stretch of Interstate 70 to Indianapolis. *How on earth did Daddy drive all the way from Prendergast if he was so sick? Maybe he's got the flu or something and is only making this trip because it's Thanksgiving.* She reflected, too, how much of an ordeal the drive from Prendergast must have been for him.

So it was that they finally arrived at the house of Maxwell Austin, Nelson's younger brother, where the whole family gathered in the family room.

Maxwell's home was a large three-story structure that sat on a one-acre lot. The neighborhood was upper-middle-class and had exquisite landscapes and two-to-three car garages out of plain view. Maxwell Austin played the role of a successful physician, and his wife, Miriam, played the role of a dutiful homemaker. Several other aunts and uncles were also present.

As usual, Maxwell was concealing his emotions by the overconsumption of alcohol. A born extrovert, he kept the conversation lively. The occasional jokes and tall tales from his other brothers complemented his efforts. The youngest brother Robert paced back and forth.

So far, Priscilla thought, this was a typical Austin family reunion. Yet she admitted to herself that she still had an uneasy feeling. *I sure hope those guys don't start all that talk about their time in the war,* Priscilla said to herself. By "war," she meant World War II.

Then Aunt Bessie, one of Nelson's older sisters and the owner of her own beauty shop, spoke in her usual jaded manner. "Now Priscilla, you and Liza must be strong and look after Nelson and the rest of the family. We knew this day was coming, but none of us expected it to happen to Nelson, at least not before it happened to one of us."

What the devil is Aunt Bessie going on about now? Priscilla never paid much mind to her aunt, who was known as a character in the family and even carried "a piece" for protection. She had not quite *heard* what her aunt had said, mostly because she had not been intently listening. But she certainly noticed that her aunt was staring directly at her as she spoke. Yet Priscilla had heard *something* that seemed to be about illness. *Is somebody having a difficult pregnancy, dying, losing his job? What does she mean inserting Daddy's name into such a bleak story?*

Priscilla took a deep breath and decided not to get upset or too inquisitive about what Aunt Bessie had been saying. Instead, she let herself simply submerge in the sea of her aunts and uncles.

Of the twelve living Austin siblings, Maxwell and Robert sat near the middle of the spacious family room. Ted, the thirteenth and youngest sibling, had died young in a knife fight. Whenever his brothers and sisters talked about him, they spoke his name with disdain: "Ted lived a fast life." By that, they meant that he had not epitomized the image that the Austins had desired to project.

As Priscilla eyed her family, seated around the room, she took the time to reflect on the women.

The aging Austin sisters were big, brawny women and resembled mostly Bessie in how they related within the family—at the same time both in control of and supportive of their brothers. But the sisters did not have a high regard for the women who had married the Austin brothers. Yet in some ways the sisters seemed to envy their brothers' wives, who were generally more refined and did not look like the typical Austin woman.

Yet Priscilla had always known that the primary role of all the women of her father's generation was to service and support the Austin men. Indeed, every family member knew the views of the Austin men toward their wives. They had intentionally "married the right kind of 'ladies'; the kind that attended the right schools, like Sherwood and Winterfägen University, and the kind that looked good in public, especially on the arms of their husbands."

A smile lingered on Priscilla's lips. Today, the women who had married her father and his brothers' would be called "trophy wives," or even "desperate housewives."

Years ago, Priscilla had asked her father why all the "black" women that his brothers married looked the same—light-skinned or pale-complexioned— and why they behaved like light-skinned women.

"Gee, Daddy, I can't help noticing the obvious."

"Oh? What's that, young lady?"

"Well, for one thing, your brothers seem to have married light-skinned women. What's wrong with dark-skinned women?"

"Well, Priscilla," Nelson had said, "since you asked … You're too young to know this, but there was a time when our people were more likely to be accepted by whites if we looked more like them. Therefore, some of our people bleached their skin and straightened their hair. And of course, the more educated, the better the opportunities."

"Wow! But did it work?"

"It did for my brothers, but not everybody was successful," Nelson had said. "Anyway, the point you need to get is this: your generation can be yourself. You don't have to try and fit anybody's mold. You're free to be yourself, Afro hairdos, dashikis and all."

Later, when Priscilla went away to college, Nelson's comments crystallized for her. There, she learned other language to account for the phenomenon she had noticed as a young adult—why it was that so many black people who possessed a college education came from similar backgrounds and looked a certain way. These factors more readily enabled their social mobility. Yet Negro women of Priscilla's parents' generation were mostly homemakers or teachers. For them, other options were limited.

But unlike most of the other Austin wives, Liza had inherited her mother's features: she was mostly Cherokee, short in stature and possessed a striking figure. She was an attractive woman. Also unlike most of the other Austin wives, Liza was not among the socially prominent, nor did she aspire to be.

Still, Priscilla reflected as again she looked around that family room, not all of the Austin men had adhered to the practice of seeking light-skinned, college-educated wives capable of social mobility. And Clarence and Nelson, the oldest brothers, had married women with little formal education and with darker complexions.

Then Priscilla belatedly noticed that it was only her father's generation who had gathered in the room. Her many cousins and their children were nowhere to be seen.

And what about Daddy? Where's my father?

Openly she asked. "Where'd Daddy go?"

At that moment, the room fell silent.

Uncle Maxwell took to the floor and cleared his throat. "Nelson," he began, "has known for some time that he wasn't well. In fact, Nelson has spent the past couple years putting his affairs in order."

Priscilla stared blankly at her uncle. Later she remembered thinking: *What a horrible phrase, "putting his affairs in order."*

Uncle Maxwell let that sink in and then continued: "Nelson even traveled across the country to visit all our family and friends, especially those at the old homestead in Canton." The Austins of Indianapolis and Prendergast hailed from Canton, Mississippi.

He then reminded Priscilla and the others about "Nelson's surprise announcement to retire from his ministry and the big celebration held at the church in his honor last spring." He directly addressed Priscilla: "You remember that, child, don't you?" Maxwell asked. "Shortly before you went off to the Caribbean for that teaching program?"

Priscilla opened her mouth but no words came out. *Yeah, yeah, now cut to the chase, you bloody bastard.*

Finally, Uncle Maxwell spoke of Nelson's intent to join the united family for Thanksgiving. "He wanted to give everyone the news at the same time." He nodded. "Well, everybody, this is that moment in time."

Suddenly her uncle was standing directly in front of her. He took her hand and gentled his voice. "Priscilla, your father has been in the hospital. Tests confirm that Nelson has inoperable cancer—colon cancer—and he has approximately six months to live."

Uncle Maxwell returned to where he had been sitting, took his half-empty glass of liquor, threw back his head and drank to the dregs. He had expended every ounce of his energy to make that speech to the Austin clan, especially to Priscilla. She, Maxwell knew, was the only one in the family wholly unaware of her father's illness. Why Liza had not forewarned her remained a mystery not only to Maxwell but also to the rest of the family.

Priscilla remained totally still. She was numb and speechless. She was among her aunts and uncles, people she had known all her life; people she trusted. Yet all she could think was that everybody in the room was waiting for her loss of composure and eventual collapse. But she was strong. She would not break. Instead, she slipped into her secret place: the one that had rescued her before and that would rescue her from future situations that were almost but not quite as unbearable.

As if reminded of something important, Uncle Maxwell leapt back to his feet and headed to the bar, where he fumbled over a variety of decanters. He poured himself another drink.

Then he turned again to Priscilla. "Can I get you something, Priscilla? Water? A drink? Yes, maybe you would prefer a drink?"

Her senses dulled, Priscilla hardly heard him. *Who are these crazy people? What're they trying to tell me? What's all this talk about my daddy dying? Daddy can't die. We're not through being together yet. I have so much to talk to him about. This is madness.*

Vaguely Priscilla was aware of time passing. But still she did not move, talk or weep.

Sometime later—Priscilla had no idea when—she was sitting at the dining room table with the others. She had no recollection of how she had gotten there. As the voices she knew so well and had loved all her life floated around her, Priscilla remained stolid and said nothing. She did, however, have a conscious thought as to where her cousins were, and that she would like to be near her favorite cousin Kenny, Uncle Maxwell's son, who was her age and her friend since early childhood. She might have talked to him, she thought, but he was not there.

Finally, later that evening, Nelson was suddenly sitting in the family room. He was bundled up in sweaters and a shawl and looked tired yet eager to have company. He seemed especially at home in the midst of his brothers and sisters, who all surrounded him.

By then Priscilla could talk and move. Just seeing the person she loved most in the world gave her the strength to walk over and spend a moment. She sat close by him. *Daddy!* Soon, she knew, the others would go to bed. She would have him to herself soon. *For now anyway.*

"Well, young lady," Nelson said, "I suppose Max has filled in all the blanks you've been wondering about up to this point."

"Let's not worry about any of that right now, Daddy. I'm just glad to see you again. Can I get anything for you?"

"I'm fine. Go join in the fun with the others. We'll be home soon where we can spend some time together. Go on. Besides, your mom could use your company."

Priscilla was aware of the others all watching them. People often speak of the bond between a father and a son. But every member of the Austin clan knew that Priscilla was the *daughter* that was her father's son—despite the fact that Nelson had a son, Nelson, Jr., who had been raised by his mother (Nelson's first wife) and her second husband in Indianapolis.

When Priscilla decided she had to get away from the gathering, she went upstairs to the library where her bed was. She stretched out. *What a waking nightmare.* And then: *That's it ... it's all just a nightmare.*

Immediately she fell into a deep sleep, in search of someone or something to reconcile her apparent waking nightmare.

Suddenly, she awakened to a strange foreboding. She trembled. Footsteps tiptoed from outside her door and headed toward it. Her muscles tensed. Nausea set in. *Oh damn, not him, no ... Have mercy.*

God Almighty must have indeed heard her plea, because the footsteps receded back down the hallway.

Then she said aloud, "Thank you, dear God," and fell back into a deep sleep.

Several hours later, voices reverberated throughout the house, and sunlight graced the pale walls of the library. Uncle Maxwell's house bustled.

Priscilla sat up in her bed. *Wow, it's tomorrow already.* She rose, freshened up and headed downstairs toward the boisterous sounds. Her cousins had at last arrived and were now scattered throughout the house. Each one greeted her and Liza with great enthusiasm and exceptional politeness.

Like a looped message on a tape recorder, Priscilla recited over and over, "Gee, you guys, I've missed you. Where were you all yesterday?"

For Priscilla's cousins, this would always be remembered as the Thanksgiving that they learned Uncle Nelson was dying. Instinctively shying away from that—and not wanting to hurt Priscilla—they all wanted to know about Priscilla's new job working for one of the two black legislators in the Ohio Senate.

In her answers Priscilla conveniently left out that her boss was a Democrat. The household in which she stood was unabashedly Republican—conservative Republican.

Finally Priscilla herself broached her father's terminal illness: "On this particular Thanksgiving," she said to herself, "one of the Austin clan is known to be dying, the one who is *the real pillar of the clan*, not a pillar in the sense of wealth and social station—like Uncle Maxwell— but *the real pillar* because of his character and the nature of his work. He's a minister, a Methodist preacher and, unlike some preachers, Daddy's committed to his ministry."

Priscilla sighed to herself, *There, I've said it.*

CHAPTER 14

Quail Hollow Inn

Driving home at the end of the long holiday weekend, Nelson sat up straight and burst into conversation on the long stretch on Interstate 70 before Columbus. Priscilla was driving, Nelson was beside her and Liza was stretched out, sleeping already, in the back.

Nelson fully appreciated Priscilla's willingness to drive him and Liza back home to Prendergast—in his car. She would return Nelson's car the following Friday and take the Greyhound Bus back to Columbus that Saturday. In that way, she would not miss any time away from her job in the Ohio Senate.

"Gee, Priscilla, it sure feels good to be on our way home." He smiled that big Nelson smile she had always loved. With his illness fully disclosed, Nelson finally seemed liberated to share everything that had been such a hard secret. "I thought those doctors would never stop poking and prodding me. They already knew my condition, but they kept poking here, and poking there. And all those crazy questions!"

Priscilla grinned. She had always loved everything about her Daddy, and never more than now, when his days were evidently numbered. She was going to treasure every precious minute of their eight-hour drive back to Prendergast.

Near Columbus, they cruised north toward Cleveland onto Interstate 71.

"Well, folks" she said, "we have five more hours on the big road home."

For a while along Interstate 71, Nelson openly admired everything—the brisk weather, the trees and all the sights along the way.

"You know," he said, "fall is my favorite time of the year. The foliage is attractive and the weather so brisk. There's something special about leaving one season and entering another. And fall prepares us for the winters in our lives."

Priscilla missed the point of her father's allegory. But she was glad to hear him talk so freely. She did not want to think of the coming days when she would never again be able to hear him talk at all.

Near Cleveland, Priscilla veered off Interstate 71 onto Interstate 90 and headed east.

Now that they were in the home stretch, Priscilla felt her heart lift; from Nelson's elevated mood, it seemed he was feeling the same.

In more familiar territory now, he spotted a favorite restaurant, the Quail Hollow Inn. Cheerfully, he ordered, "Stop over there, Priscilla. We've eaten there before. You remember. You and I stopped there once on our way from visiting Maxwell."

A warm feeling came over Priscilla as she recalled that trip with her dad. "Yes, I remember."

That particular journey had begun in the early summer of 1978. Nelson had come home and announced his plans to "drop in on my folks in Indianapolis for a spell." At the time, even Liza had been surprised at his sudden decision to visit his folks.

Nelson had asked only Priscilla to accompany him and, of course, to do most of the driving. It was on their way home that father and daughter had dined at the Quail Hollow Inn.

Priscilla was regaling her mother, as the three of them prepared to get out of the car, about what she called "the magnificent ambiance" of this restaurant that she and Nelson remembered with such fondness.

It took some doing, but Nelson managed to get out of the car and walk inside the restaurant. Once seated, he insisted, "Order your favorite dishes. Go on. Read the menu and get what you want."

But Liza fussed. "It's so dark in here. I like to see my food when I'm eating. Why don't they turn on more light? Besides, I still don't get what the two of you see in this place. Looks like an ordinary restaurant to me."

As if on cue, Nelson and Priscilla both smiled and shook their heads. Sometimes, Priscilla thought, it did not pay to make a case whenever Liza missed the point, especially when she disagreed with Priscilla and Nelson.

After Priscilla and Liza placed their orders, they looked at Nelson and waited for him to say what he wanted.

But he said: "I don't have much of an appetite. Maybe I'll have some soup and crackers. I'll be satisfied just watching you enjoy your meals."

That's interesting. How can Daddy get satisfaction out of watching *us eat?* Priscilla, for a moment, either had forgotten about his illness or had managed to put it out of her mind.

But then she remembered the summer—last year, the year before, or was it even before that?—when he had come home and talked about some tests "his doctor" had performed on him. He had given his family the impression that he had seen his regular family doctor. But Liza and Priscilla found out later that the physician he had seen had been an oncologist.

At the time, he had informed them that he could not eat much of anything solid in the short term. "I had a piece of my tongue removed to be examined," he had said matter-of-factly. "It'll take a while for my mouth to heal, but I'll be okay soon."

Yet this time at the Quail Hollow Inn, as she and her mother began to eat under Nelson's fond eyes, Priscilla remembered other, though similar events that she now understood were the beginning of the end.

133

Later that same summer when he first visited the oncologist, Nelson had begun to pour much more salt than usual on his food at the dinner table. He did not use the saltshaker; he used the whole box.

"I can't taste the seasoning or flavor in anything," he had said in disgust. Liza then had insisted that he return to the doctor for more tests. By that point in time however, Nelson had already known of his cancer diagnosis and had begun to struggle with its reality.

On another occasion, in one of his sermons, Nelson had intimated his condition in an anecdote about "a man who'd lost his ability to taste, but who'd found satisfaction in watching others eat."

There were so many signs, Priscilla thought, dining at the Quail Hollow Inn on Thanksgiving weekend. *How much more warning did everybody need? We'd all thought those were simply interesting anecdotes, the kind that preachers use as fillers or to make a point. Sometimes we see and hear only what we want to.*

Finally, as Priscilla brought her napkin to her lips at the end of this meal, she fully understood the obvious. Her father's rationale in having asked her to relocate closer to home at last was so devastatingly clear.

Back in the car, Priscilla was revived by the good food and her father's obvious delight in treating them to a fine dinner in a place that held such warm memories for him.

She looked over and was about to share other happy times when she saw that he had drifted off to sleep. She glanced in the mirror, and her mother had also dozed off.

So I'm really the chauffeur. Priscilla smiled to herself and decided to enjoy a solitary jaunt down memory lane.

She remembered that New York Highway 394 took them past the Chautauqua Lake, home of the well-known Chautauqua Institute.

Priscilla turned pensive, remembering how she had almost missed her Class of 1970 Prendergast High School graduation at the Chautauqua Institute Amphitheater. Before the event, she had decided that in support of the Black Power Movement and its opposition to the Establishment, she would neither order a cap and gown nor send out any invitations. But when—unknown to Priscilla—her parents discovered her scheme, they had aborted it.

The outdoor amphitheater featured a covered stage, with seating slanting downward from a knoll. The amphitheater comfortably seated a graduating class of at least six hundred and fifty students and their guests.

As the name of each graduate was called, the student had stepped across the stage to receive the diploma and then processed up the knoll.

Priscilla had almost reached the crest when she was taken aback. She had assumed Liza was seated near the front by the stage, but her mother had been waiting here for her.

Tears had filled Liza's eyes. "Child, you made it. You finished school." For some time it had been uncertain whether Priscilla would finish high school. But that evening Liza had been proud of her daughter. "Thank you, dear Lord," she had prayed aloud. "She made it."

So many years later, Pricilla still recalled how surprised she had been to see those tears in her mother's eyes at the graduation ceremony. At the time, she had not realized her behavior in high school had caused Liza such uncertainty and anguish. Nor, even now, did she have any idea what she could have done in high school that was so god-awful that she had not been expected to graduate. She had a vague memory of a counselor saying to her once in her parents' presence, "Children like you won't be going to college." But Nelson had quickly admonished the counselor for having taken such a presumptuous role with his daughter. There had been, too, the many scuffles Priscilla had been part of in the school hallways.

She considered that perhaps her memory was somewhat selective, because she could hardly recollect what a troublesome teenager she had been.

On the other hand, she would never forget being sent away to a college that she had not chosen. Of course, she had hated that decision having been made for her. Still, now, nearly a decade later, she still did not care to relive any of *that*.

But another, happier memory—the day when Nelson expressed his pride in her decision to accept the faculty post at FAMU—tugged at her.

That day had begun in Prendergast shortly after she had committed to FAMU. "Goodness, Daddy" Priscilla had said, "If the temperature here reaches seventy-five degrees, folks start screaming 'heat wave.' I guess I'm going to roast to death in Florida."

Reading between the lines, Nelson had attempted to project confidence in her. "I realize Florida's the farthest away you've ever gone, but, you'll see, it won't be that bad. Besides, you'll be around lots of other young folk of promise like yourself, all highly educated and from good stable backgrounds."

But he also spoke more to himself than to her: "My daughter, a college professor! I can't wait to tell Maxwell and the others."

Though Nelson would never have admitted it, the Austin clan were highly competitive. Her father's generation had worked to send one another to college and set up their respective businesses. And yet they competed with one another. Each generation was supposed to do better or achieve more than the previous generation. If any member of one generation failed in his quest, he looked to his children to achieve it. When Priscilla became a college professor, she scored *big time* for Nelson, even though he was already held in high regard by the family. Yet Priscilla's drive for success was always tied to her yearning for a close relationship with her father. She still thrived on her father's approval and happiness, for his happiness was hers.

"This is something, Priscilla, really something!" Nelson had dabbed at his eyes, wiping away tears of joy. "You're going to be a college professor at one of the nation's most prestigious universities!"

"Wow, Daddy, you'd think that I was a famous celebrity or something. You weren't this pleased when I graduated from college."

"Oh, Priscilla, please. Even you know there's no comparison between graduating from college and becoming a college professor—*and* the first one in our family, too! Yes, Sirree, Bob, this is a big deal."

Remembering that moment, Priscilla wished it could have been frozen forever in time. Years later, she understood that had been one of the happiest days of her life, a day that in a way was never to be equaled.

At the time, she had simply savored the moment. Yet what had happened next was that she suddenly had blurted out a totally unrelated question. "Daddy," she had asked, "why did you really leave that other church? I thought those people were friendly and treated us well, but I never understood why you left there."

Surprised at her question, Nelson had gone silent for a moment as he decided how to answer.

Priscilla had continued her line of inquiry: "And did Momma ever get over your decision? I know we all thought you'd done all that you could do here. So why did you *really* come back to this church?"

Nelson had taken his time to explain the situation: "There are some decisions we preachers make that might elude you *and* your mother. Sometimes our actions aren't intended to make sense, at least not at the time. More important, someday you'll learn that situations aren't always as they appear. It's not that I gave up something—rather, certain circumstances had changed for me. That's all. So you see, Priscilla, coming back here to Prendergast had nothing to do with how those church folks treated us. Someday soon, maybe you'll understand, but now isn't the time."

He had stood and smiled down at her, and said: "Right now, we need to get you ready for your new life in Florida. Let's stay with that."

So she let the subject die. Her father's demeanor had led her to acquiesce to him without asking more questions.

As Priscilla continued driving on New York Highway 394, she remembered the serenity of that moment and how her father had gone on to extoll the many relatives and acquaintances who had pursued the teaching profession.

He had referred to it as a "noble profession" and said, "Just about all of my brothers are married to women who have taught school, and several of my sisters were teachers, too. Man alive, aren't they going to be outdone with this news! You are aware, aren't you, Priscilla, that you can make a good and stable livelihood in the teaching profession? It also gives you good standing in the community." Image had always been important to Nelson, but so too had been his desire that Priscilla start taking control of her life.

From deference to her father, she had overlooked the apparently sexist connotation in his words. Nelson did, after all, consider teaching a noble profession—for a woman. And if his words were sexist, did that even matter to him?

What mattered to Priscilla, driving him home after just receiving the news of his terminal illness, was her realization that her decision to become a college professor may have been based on pleasing her father.

Those memories helped ease Priscilla during the long drive home. They also kept her from stewing in the reality of her father's illness.

CHAPTER 15

The Scenic Route

After that reflective moment, Priscilla had already decided to take the scenic alternate route along New York 17J. She veered off the interstate where vineyards in Mourné Placid—home to Mourné Wine—surrounded both sides of the narrow highway. To the north were the Sinclairville ski resorts and beyond them, the stables for training quarter horses.

Often, while driving to Prendergast from Columbus, she had enjoyed this long way home. Especially in the winters, she had loved scenes of the snowcapped country homes and shops and the few people who braved the out of doors on foot. "Oh, we must be looking at two-to-three feet, at least knee-deep," was, she remembered, a common description of the average snowfall for Chautauqua County.

Besides the scenery, she had preferred this circuitous route because it had the more impressive entry into Prendergast. The sight of the imposing Lake Charles Cemetery always reminded her of her teen-age years when she knew it not so much as the place where famous, prominent and wealthy people were buried, but rather as the preferred hangout for her and her teenaged friends at Halloween. They had been fascinated with the monuments, the mausoleums and the encased statues, such as the one of a young bride in her wedding gown. So far as Priscilla knew, only one black person—Catherine Harris, operator of the Underground Railroad—was buried there.

That was one reason, she recalled, that her family had been shocked when Nelson had announced one night at dinner long ago when Priscilla had still been in junior high school, that Lake Charles Cemetery would be his final resting place and that he had already purchased two burial plots there. Looking back, Priscilla supposed it should not have surprised any of them that he wanted to be buried in Prendergast, since they all had been keenly aware of Nelson's love for the town. Yet none of them would have predicted that he wanted his final rest to be as a definite minority in that particular cemetery.

As Priscilla continued driving, she remembered something Nelson had said to her about Prendergast during her teenage years: "There's a warm spirit here, much more inviting and encouraging than in the South. Down South, we could never have bought real estate in an all-white neighborhood."

She remembered exactly how and why Nelson had sought—and had been able to afford—property in Prendergast. Shortly after the family moved to the town, he and Liza had begun to search for a home other than the church parsonage in which they had just begun to reside. Their search came about because Nelson had grown distraught having to leave his family with his mother-in-law in Sills Creek as he awaited a new church appointment. But with his new assignment in Prendergast, he had decided to be proactive so that Liza and the girls would never again be uprooted because of his work with the church.

"Besides," he had said, "New York has the best educational system in the country. It's called Regents."

After learning of the couple's desire to purchase their own home, the neighbor next door to the parsonage had provided the Austin's with what turned out to be their best option. A second-generation landlord, she owned a huge Victorian house at 14 West Seventh Street. "All income-generating," she had said to Nelson. "And it doesn't hurt that I happen to like your family, too."

One day later, the owner of a statelier Victorian house, just down the street, had offered to sell that house to the Austin's, as well. The second house was owned originally by one of the founders of Prendergast.

Nelson and Liza had immediately decided to buy *both* homes. To come up with the funds to buy them, the couple sought employment outside of the church.

But they soon had discovered there remained some racial discrimination in the North that was significantly different from what they had experienced in the South. In the North, it was subtle but deeply entrenched. Neither Liza nor Nelson had been able to find professional jobs. Liza took a sewing job at a manufacturer of voting machines, while Nelson donned a night watchman's uniform. For the next ten years, the couple had pooled their financial earnings to pay off the mortgages on both properties.

Then, true to form, Nelson had been appointed to another church in the vicinity of Buffalo. So the couple had moved into the statelier Victorian house at 19 West Seventh Street in Prendergast.

Most people they knew in Prendergast had been bowled over at the news that "the Austin's have moved into their own home." The church members had asked one another, "Where did they get the money?" Nelson's Rotarian associates had wanted to know whether one of their members had arranged for the purchase. The Austin's of Indianapolis had found great amusement that Nelson had "finally arrived." But perhaps no one had been as happy about the purchase as Priscilla, who had long since tired of having to explain to her classmates and friends the definition of a "parsonage."

The neighborhood into which the Austin family had moved was home to a growing middle class, into which the Austin's fitted, primarily because of Nelson's occupation. Compared to the other homes on West Seventh Street, the Austin residence was more stylishly designed and the only one with a striking cylindrical tower. Older neighbors would tell the Austin family that the original owner was one of the early settlers in Prendergast and that the home had long been known for its grand staircase.

The main entrance was a small enclosed porch. For their first years in the house, the Nelsons lived on the first floor and rented out the second floor to an elderly couple. At the time, only Camille was still living with her parents, so they had no need for all that other space.

The main entrance led inside to the den, where most guests preferred to sit. Liza had decorated the room modestly with moss-green fabric wallpaper, a deep cushiony sofa, a La-Z-Boy recliner, a durable but comfortable high-back chair and a tall glass cabinet filled with collectibles from the family's travels and various other mementos. The mantle above the huge fireplace showcased an array of family portraits, including one of Nelson and Liza in formal attire at a Republican Party fund-raising event. Nelson cherished that photo, which featured Governor Nelson Rockefeller.

To the immediate right of the den was the substantially larger though seldom used living room. Liza had painted the room crème and hung pastel satin drapery to cover the immense windows, which were held open by ivory and golden strands of braided rope. An elegant, embroidered white sofa with green floral upholstery was the highlight of the room, and it was flanked by a pair of small marble-topped tables. A new Baldwin upright piano sat against one wall of the room. Although the three younger siblings had all studied piano, only Priscilla had stayed with it.

Continuing her drive and reminiscing about her family's early years in Prendergast, Priscilla laughed out loud as she recalled the day when Nelson came home, strolled into the living room, took off his shoes and carefully placed them on the tea table.

Nelson had always regarded his home as a place to enjoy, not to be put on display. Priscilla remembered the time her mother had finally asked him, "Why'd you do that Nelson? Why'd you put your shoes on my tea table? That's so unlike you. What came over you?"

In his defense, Nelson had replied, "I need to feel like someone lives in this part of the house. The only time anybody ever comes in here is when Priscilla plays the piano *or* when we dress up to take pictures."

Priscilla remembered how Nelson would tell that story over and over, and how listeners always rolled in laughter because they knew the story was true.

The couple's bedroom was across from the den and next to the only bathroom on that floor. To the left of the den was a formal dining area, where Liza had placed her silver tea service on the buffet, the base of which contained several large pieces of pottery and other tableware. A secretary sat against the wall between the dining room and the den.

Next to the dining room was the small but comfortable kitchen. Adjacent to the kitchen were the two bedrooms in the rear of the house. Nelson had remodeled one of those rooms into his study and designated the other as Camille's. "The only child here now, and soon, she too will leave," he had said.

Priscilla had discovered when she decorated her own townhouse in Tallahassee and her home in Columbus that her own taste was influenced by Nelson and Liza's "eye" for simple elegance.

But the house that Priscilla remembered from her teenage years was not this stately Victorian but the parsonage. Situated on the front lawn and visible to passersby was a marker installed in 1936 by the New York State Education Department: "Here stood a station on the Underground Railroad (R.R.) in which Catherine Harris did heroic service for fugitive slaves." Ms. Harris had also been one of the founding members of the church where Nelson served as pastor.

One block north of the Austin residence was the huge, block-long Prendergast Library.

As a child, Priscilla had been impressed when, just after the family's arrival in Prendergast, Nelson took his children to that library. She still remembered the kindness of the librarian, whose name she forgot but whose pleasant demeanor had been unforgettable. As she led Nelson and his girls on a tour, the librarian had said, "Please visit us regularly, Reverend Austin. Your children can work on special school projects and read as many books as they want, either here or at home." She had shown them the section on New York State history and talked about the role of Catherine Harris in the Underground Railroad.

Yet Priscilla remembered how taken aback she had been by the librarian's talking about Catherine Harris. She even recalled saying to Liza after Nelson and the girls had returned home that day, "A white woman talked to us about slavery. Can you believe that, Momma?"

Over the course of nearly sixteen years in Prendergast, one by one the Austin children had grown up and left home to pursue their own careers and interests. Occasionally, however, they returned home, sometimes with boyfriends, husbands and children of their own.

Overall, Priscilla reflected, life for the Austin's had been reasonably serene and prosperous in Prendergast.

Yet as she approached her home town, Priscilla was not prepared for what lay ahead. She had assumed the family's serenity and prosperity in Prendergast would last forever.

While on the drive, she had been able to put it out of her mind; but, once Priscilla arrived "home," the reality of her father's impending death was inescapable.

She parked in the driveway, and then she and Liza helped Nelson out of the car and into the sanctuary of their house.

Priscilla had to be back in Columbus on Monday, and for the remainder of the weekend she seemed to have as much difficulty coping with her own grief and pain as Nelson initially had in accepting the reality of his condition.

Getting into bed that night, Priscilla wiped her eyes and wondered: *Is this what it feels like to lose someone you love? I don't ever want to go through this again. I'm crying uncontrollably. My nose runs. Why won't it all stop? And I can't get rid of this damn lump in my throat. Why won't it swallow? Oh, it hurts so much. Does he hurt? Do I dare ask Daddy about his pain?*

The next morning began as beautiful and snowy as Priscilla had wanted it.

Nelson got up and prepared for his routine Saturday morning outing. He put on his hat, gloves, galoshes and overcoat, and then he stood in front of the fireplace in the den.

"Priscilla, it's time for my haircut." He reached for his car keys. "Time to go to the barbershop."

Exhausted from the long drive the day before, Priscilla was not prepared to help with errands and chores, at least not so early in the morning. But she managed to collect herself.

Although her better judgment was to question Nelson's assumption that he would be driving, her heart gave way. She allowed him to drive.

On the way to the barbershop, Priscilla noticed that Nelson seemed distressed at his diminished capacity to perform simple tasks such as driving his car. He was right, she thought. His driving was a disaster. But she knew without being told that he wanted his friends at the barbershop to see him *drive*, not *to be driven*.

But when the car was about to careen into a pole, Priscilla struggled from the passenger seat for control of the steering wheel.

"Girl, move over, I've got this. I'm just a little rusty, but I'm not incapable of driving my own car. I'll let you know when I need your help." Nelson's demeanor was overbearing, but even with both hands on the wheel, he lacked the strength to maneuver the vehicle.

Priscilla held onto the wheel. She did not want to crash.

Although she had to help her father get out of the car and walk inside the barbershop, by some miracle of will, he managed to walk on his own once inside and make it to one of the chairs for his haircut. The rest of his visit went without incident. Nelson needed only to sit and talk, not to move about the room.

After Nelson was settled in his seat, Priscilla sat in a chair against the wall and began to doze off. But she rallied enough to overhear a few snatches of the barbershop conversation.

At one point Nelson told his friends: "Mother Nature has summoned the old boy. I've contracted something that can't be repaired; and the doctors tell me that I've got only a few months to hang out with you fellas. From now on, then, I want to hear *good* news such as your latest big-fish story."

Arthur, his barber, said to Nelson: "Rev, we knew you've not been at yourself lately. But we sure didn't want to hear this kind of news." Arthur was speaking for every man present.

By the time Priscilla awakened from her catnap, the shop was still filled with cheerful and lively chatter.

Nelson drove back home. Priscilla prayed the whole way, certain that it was the grace of God that spared them any accident.

145

As Priscilla helped her father out of the car, he turned to her and said, "I suppose I won't be doing much more driving, eh?" Then he managed to smile.

Sunday was another beautiful, snowy day. This time, Priscilla was in the driver's seat. Liza had decided to stay home.

After parking in the church lot, Priscilla had more difficulty getting her father into the church than she had experienced the day before at the barbershop. Yet she managed to help him out of the car and up the steep steps to the church.

Nelson had to stop to catch his breath in the vestibule. Then he walked slowly to his office where, with even greater difficulty, he donned his clerical attire.

Painstakingly, he dragged his feet through the main entrance of the sanctuary and waited for his cue to walk in the procession.

After observing the Reverend and Priscilla struggling to maneuver, a couple of men approached to assist them. The sanctuary was unusually quiet. Church members had been saddened to learn about their pastor's illness—news that had raced through the community after his trip to the barbershop the day before.

After tremendous difficulty walking to the pulpit, the Reverend James Nelson Austin stood feebly in front of the congregation. His voice was barely audible, and his posture slumped. His upper body trembled as he attempted to brace himself against the pulpit. Because he was unable to deliver a complete sermon, his presence made the point without explanation. He was ill "unto death."

Joseph Washington, the preacher's steward, stepped up to the pulpit. Tears streamed down his cheeks. He mumbled a few words and cleared his throat. Then he said, "Ladies and gentlemen, the Reverend has spoken." He continued: "Let us pray. Dear Heavenly Father, we pray for Reverend Austin and his family. We ask you to prepare us to do our part to ease their burden. Please be with us as we carry on the work of this church. Be with us for what is yet to come."

There was a moment of silence.

Then Mr. Washington said, "Please remain prayerful until we escort the Reverend and Ms. Priscilla to their car." Even though Nelson had already formally retired, every church member knew that this time the Reverend James Nelson Austin would not be returning to the pulpit. He had served out his tenure as their pastor.

Priscilla silently drove her father back home. To her knowledge, that was the last church service he ever attended.

Later that morning, Priscilla telephoned Amber, still her best friend in Prendergast. "Hard to imagine now, but until Daddy's trip to the barbershop yesterday, most of those people hadn't a clue about the extent of his illness. I never knew he was that good an actor."

Liza had meantime told her that even she had not known his prognosis until a few weeks before Thanksgiving.

As Priscilla was packing for her return to Columbus, she consoled herself that she was returning home for Christmas.

Then she dressed in layers to protect herself from the frigid weather. She would be leaving soon to try to beat the traffic and get back to Columbus before dark.

Before she left, Nelson sat her down and told her he had something important to share.

What now? Priscilla braced herself for another dark surprise.

"You know, Priscilla, you've always acknowledged my birthday to be December 18."

Priscilla nodded and waited for whatever was to come.

"When I realized how sincere you were," Nelson said, "I didn't have the heart to tell you, well, you've always had the date wrong."

Priscilla was caught by surprise.

"Even so, I let it go, Priscilla." Nelson fought hard to keep a straight face. "But things being what they are, you need to know the correct date of my birth. I was born on December 17, 1909, not on the eighteenth."

Priscilla looked at her father in a way that only he could have appreciated. Then with all the earnestness she could muster, she said, "You mean to tell me that I've had your birthday wrong for over twenty-eight years or however long I've been on this earth?"

Father and daughter hugged and laughed from the belly up and out.

CHAPTER 16

Back at work after Thanksgiving recess, Priscilla felt as if she had taken a job in the belly of political treachery. Some lawmakers, she thought, would make characters in *The Godfather* look meek, for they would actually "step over their ailing mothers for political gain," as Senator Callahan had once told her. The senator had also shared a story with her about one of his colleagues who had used his own wife's virtue to get something he wanted. When the man for whom he had asked the favor expressed dissatisfaction with his wife, "he sent the man his daughter!"

Priscilla had known that politics could be rough and raw, but she had no idea about the extremes some politicians would go to get what they wanted. And although many politicians and their constituents found it loathsome for a woman to have an affair with a married man, Priscilla's take on her arrangement with Senator Callahan was, "Now ask me something I won't do." Still, she was grateful that their personal relationship had remained secret.

All that intrigue weighed on Priscilla mostly because of the atmosphere in the Ohio Senate. The Republicans had returned from the holiday with great zeal, emboldened by their recent electoral victory.

They had already signed on a key new member of their team. Bill Scott had made a name for himself at the Legislative Budget Office (LBO), which determined the impact of bills and amendments on the state's economy. He held a master's degree in Business Administration, earned from within the state's university system. Reportedly, he had graduated at the top of his class.

Before lunch on her first day back, Priscilla had already heard about the new Republican aide. She had also been told that he was exhibiting particular interest in her role as well as why she, an outsider not only to the legislative branch but also to the state political apparatus, had chosen to work within it.

Priscilla, the lone black legislative aide for the Ohio Senate, was accustomed to such curiosity. Bill Scott was not the first to wonder: *Why a minister's daughter from upstate New York had left a perfectly good faculty position at FAMU to work for Senator Callahan?*

Priscilla let them worry and wonder. She knew that if any of them knew her as well as her parents did, they would stop their silly conjectures and simply accept her as the "player" she had signed on to be. Nelson and Liza had long ago accepted her ambition and her independence, which Liza had been prone to call "Priscilla's outlandish behavior."

It was only a day or so later that she heard, through the overactive rumor mill, that Bill Scott had been heard to say to his Republican bosses that so far as he could tell, Priscilla was doing a good job and brought more to the table than had Senator Callahan's previous aide. She had already established a reputation for no-nonsense hard work. One of the Republicans even told Bill that, in a way, Priscilla was just like him.

With so much politicking and posturing, the passage of the Set-Aside Bill in the Ohio House of Representatives and the governor's signing it into law on December 18 attracted little attention. The sensation had been its unexpected passage in the upper legislative chamber.

The first legislative victory in which she had played a part, however, helped Priscilla to honor that date. The fact that this happened on the day after Nelson's seventy-first birthday had made it all the sweeter for her.

One evening shortly before Christmas, Priscilla and Senator Callahan dined out after a particularly grueling workday. The turnover of power from Democrats to Republicans in the Ohio Senate was stressful, and the always heavy workload had intensified.

After dinner, they drove over to her place. Wholly exhausted, Priscilla was in no mood for anybody's company or any sexual activity. She went into her bedroom, quickly undressed and jumped into her bed. Almost immediately, she began to snore.

The senator sat in a chair in her living room and read some files he had brought over from his office. Yet every now and then, he rose and went to her bedroom. A few times he had to shake Priscilla because the sound of her snoring had disrupted his concentration even from where he had been sitting in the living room. Yet after only a little while, she would resume her loud snoring.

Eventually she stopped snoring, and the senator assumed she had settled into a restful sleep.

But Priscilla was having the same "Dennis" nightmare she had experienced in the senator's apartment back in August. This time, however, when the senator woke her up, he forced the issue. He slapped her cheeks. He shook her. Then, when Priscilla opened her eyes, the senator said, "This time you're going tell it to me straight, young lady. Who the hell is Dennis, and what has he done to you?"

Circumstances finally were ripe for Priscilla to release her devastating secret. Still shaking from the nightmare, she coiled up her body and began to talk.

"As I'm sure you're already aware, Senator, Ohio State (referring to *The* Ohio State University) is an enormous complex, a community of some 50,000 people within itself. Well, one time when I went to hear a speaker on existentialism, I met two young men, neither of whom I thought much about. One was tall, dark-complexioned and easy on the eye. The other one was more appealing to me. They said that they were cousins and that even though they weren't students here, they lived in the city. From what I could tell, both seemed all right.

"Dennis, who was the tall, well-built guy, befriended me. He asked lots of questions about my major, my hobbies, where I was from and where I lived. I did find it a little strange, though, that it was Marcus who asked me out to dinner. I accepted. Our time together turned out to be uneventful—to be honest, downright boring. Afterwards, we returned to the graduate towers, which, as you know, are co-ed. Nothing happened between us. Marcus left and I thought nothing else about him.

"In the meantime, I was dumbfounded when Dennis called me. When I told him that I wasn't interested in him, he got upset, like a madman. He even came by my room once and tried to make a scene. Then, I didn't hear from him for a while.

"A short time later, I heard that Lena Horne, one of my favorite entertainers, was coming to the Ohio Theater. The day of the concert, Dennis called me, which I thought was really odd. 'Had he been stalking me?' I wondered. Anyway, I got dressed, went downtown to the concert and returned to campus afterwards.

"By the way," Priscilla added, turning away from her story for the first time, "Lena Horne was simply stunning in person. Absolutely stunning!"

She paused before returning to her story, as though she dreaded what she had to say next.

"Once in the residential tower, I heard the phone ringing from the hallway. I quickly unlocked the door, ran in and picked up the receiver. It was Dennis. He said he was in the lobby and was on his way up to my room.

"I told him no. But before long, there he was. He made a ruckus. Some of the guys who lived on the floor came around to see about the commotion.

"But I told them everything was okay. That I'd be all right.

"Then, after I let Dennis in the room, he closed the door behind him.

"He said that he'd been watching me for some time and that he knew I wanted him.

"I remember thinking he was either misguided or psychotic. But before I could collect any more of my thoughts, he picked me up and forced a kiss. Then he set me down. He behaved as if he could not

152

decide whether to kiss me or molest every part of my body. The more I tried to push him away, the more savage he became. I realized he intended to force himself upon me."

Priscilla stopped talking, took a deep breath and then continued.

"I made a tactical decision to yield to him and let him have his way.

"Dennis lifted me up again, threw me on my bed and quickly pulled the clothing off the bottom part of my body. He did it fast, as if he had rehearsed his actions well beforehand. With one of his hands, he held my hands together above my head while he pulled down his pants with the other hand.

"Then he slapped my thighs and told me, 'Spread your damn legs, bitch, you know the drill.' Abrasively, he shoved his penis inside me. My vagina was not moist. He didn't use a condom. The roughness of his ... forced entry was excruciating.

"I clinched my teeth together to muffle my misery. Besides, I was too ashamed to scream out for help. I just wanted the horrific episode to end.

"But then Dennis stopped. He was still inside, but he stopped and turned my head to face him. 'Tell me you're enjoying this! Tell me how much you've wanted me!'

"I remember detesting him more than I feared him. He had controlled the rape. But now, although by then I knew he was mentally unstable, I was determined to challenge him. I had to catch him off guard. I remember thinking: *If I could just get to the door ...*"

The senator was spellbound. He muttered, "I had no idea, no idea my precious Priscilla ever experienced such an ordeal."

Priscilla met his eyes for the first time since she had begun telling her story. She could see that he hurt from the news as much she did. This was the first time she had told anyone any of it.

"Senator, I tell you, I don't know where the inspiration came from. But I looked straight into that man's crazed eyes and said, 'Have your own way, Dennis. Do with me whatever you wish. But don't you dare tell me what to say, or how to feel. You're raping me. This is called rape, pure and simple. You're raping me, Dennis. Now, hurry up and come and get the hell out of here.'

"Maybe he was peeved by what he thought was foolish boldness on my part. But Dennis rolled off the top of me, and mercilessly, with the strength of an ox, he walloped my face. My cheek throbbed. I was in so much pain! But I fell off the bed. And, God gave me courage to leverage my fall. Then somehow I bounced back up and sprinted across the room, half-naked. I opened the door and saw my neighbors were just outside there.

"I remember one of them. Russell, that was his name. A med student who lived at the end of the hall. He kept begging me to let them call security.

"But I refused. I said I didn't want any record of this. And I told them I didn't think we would have to worry about this madman anymore. He wouldn't be coming back."

Priscilla paused, remembering. She and her neighbors in the resident tower comprised an intimate community. They passed one another in the corridors wearing their bathrobes on the way to the showers. They knew one another's habits, and many were familiar with their neighbors' significant others and their spouses. They shared meals and other occasions. So, although Priscilla had never ventured into the hallway half-naked like this, she was at that moment unashamed. She understood that Russ and the other men knew she had been sexually assaulted, and that they would do whatever she asked of them. Her hall mates were keenly aware of how an independent woman thought, and they respected her for that. Besides, their mere presence had aided her freedom.

Priscilla resumed telling her story to the senator.

"The boys and I looked in the room, where Dennis was still stretched out on my bed. He raised himself up and yelled, "What the hell is wrong with you, woman? Close that f—ing door."

Once again, Russ begged Priscilla to let him call security.

"But suddenly, Dennis leapt up from the bed, pulled up his pants and ran out into the midst of the men. They immediately surrounded Dennis, and then, one by one, each man said, 'We know your face, buddy. We know your face.' Yet the men heeded my plea and allowed Dennis to pass by them."

Priscilla took a deep breath and then was silent as she thought over what had happened. After Dennis bolted, she had thanked her hall mates for their help and then implored them to keep her dirty little secret. She did not desire that her name be associated with a rape. It had been difficult enough in the 1970s for a woman to maneuver the corridors of a Big Ten university in pursuit of a doctorate, especially in political science, an academic discipline that had been historically dominated by men. And back then, no ambitious feminist had wanted to be connected with a sexual assault, not to mention "the victim mentality" which a sexual assault suggested. *I was nobody's victim.*

She gave the senator a shy smile. "This is the first time I've ever talked about that incident. That is, the rape. And you know something else? I've always heard similar or worse stories about assaults only on *other* women. But I never imagined anything like that would ever happen to me."

"Oh, Priscilla, I had no idea. I had absolutely no idea you'd been violated, not like that. Do you want to report it? I realize it's been a while, but you can still report the crime."

"Oh, no, Senator, no, I'm not dredging up that crap, not to make it a matter of public record. I may have been blindsided back then, but I won't be anymore. Besides, at this point in my life, I have other matters to deal with."

Tonight, she thought, she had shared so much with the senator. But enough was enough. She would keep to herself the affirmation that she had to be strong for her father, and that nothing, absolutely nothing, was going to interfere with her mission.

She let the senator give her a hug and a kiss, and she even drank the drink he fixed for her. But when she told him she would prefer now to go back to sleep—by herself, he still refused to leave her alone after such a terrible nightmare and her subsequent revelation. Yet he kindly told her he would settle back in her living room and give her time to get to sleep. He would tiptoe in and out only if and when he could see she was indeed asleep.

Priscilla agreed. She stretched out and let the senator tuck her in.

But when he left her alone, she lay awake for some while, remembering even more.

She had been so intent on not telling anyone—anyone at all—about the rape, that she had allowed her mother and Sedge to believe that the baby she had aborted was Sedge's. Looking back, she considered that she had been wrong to do that. She admitted to herself that it had also been wrong to lie about the reason for her behavior: that she had been so heartless as to arrange the abortion because she feared that a child would interrupt her academic and career pursuits. But at the time, many feminists espoused a rationale like that. She had also feared being shunned by certain circles, particularly those in the black community, where the thinking was almost always, that a woman was somehow responsible for the sexual assault in the first place.

Lastly, she feared that the image of "damaged goods" would penetrate her very being. But since she was not one to let herself off easy when it came to her own wrongdoing or sin, Priscilla was fully aware that what happened to her was wrong, but her response was just as wrong. She was willing to shoulder that much responsibility, but for her that admission was the extent of her penitence.

The last thought she had before she drifted off to sleep was that Priscilla J. Austin was nobody's victim.

CHAPTER 17

Tonight's the Night for a Good Fight

The next day Priscilla arrived at the office early. She walked down the corridor toward the Senate chamber and gazed up at the huge marble staircase because she had felt someone staring at her. There, at the top of the stairs, stood the new Republican Senate staffer, Bill Scott. Bill wore a starched white cotton shirt, cuffs turned stylishly back. *From here, I can tell there's no polyester in that shirt,* Priscilla said to herself. *Now* he's *worth talking about.* She nodded to acknowledge him, and then she walked back to her office.

Later that same morning, she sat in a dull Senate staff meeting. As she leafed through a news magazine, she paid no mind when she felt someone sit next to her. But then a tanned, hairy arm reached over and took her magazine, and a sultry masculine voice spoke, "There's a fascinating article in there about FAMU. I understand that you taught there before coming to work for Senator Callahan."

Priscilla's zone of privacy had been breached by this guy who some-one had described to her as "Ohio's boy wonder in Reaganomics." She did not like demonstrations of familiarity. But she decided to give him a chance. "And how did you know that I worked in Florida?"

Bill continued to talk casually as he leafed through her magazine. As though he presumed they were old friends, he said he had heard she was the daughter of a lifelong Republican preacher from upstate New York and asked her why she was working for a Democratic state senator from Cincinnati, Ohio. "Are your families related? What's the connection?"

Priscilla did not answer. Her father and her politics were not his business. Yet she noted his radiant complexion was darkened by a deep tan. She resented white people whose skin was darker than her own. Besides, she had to take care not to be too friendly with a member of the opposition. Ohio politics were downright cold, dirty and divisive.

Beside her, Bill looked puzzled. This young black woman's nod of recognition that morning was one of the only gestures of kindness that any Democratic staffer had made toward him. He had been eager to develop a civil working relationship with her.

Shortly after that staff meeting, Priscilla set about finding out more about Bill Scott. She asked around and found out that he had a reputation for fairness and efficiency, and that, as a result, he had managed to retain his position at the LBO under both Republican and Democratic majorities in the Statehouse.

Not bad, Priscilla concluded. She would consider cultivating a professional relationship with this fellow. If that upset members of either party, then so be it. She was Priscilla J. Austin, and she would do as she pleased.

Priscilla reflected that night, as she sorted out the clothes in her closet, that she had developed a lifelong habit of doing as she pleased.

As a child and even as a young adult, she had enjoyed reading the cartoon *Dennis the Menace.* She had identified with the character's perpetual youth and exuberance, and occasionally the cartoon even reminded her not to take herself too seriously.

But at this point in her life, she had chosen, in her quest to become a player in the Ohio Senate, to downplay her carefree nature and feminine joie de vivre. Even her wardrobe reflected her new attitude:

black, navy blue and gray suits, and occasionally for special effects, bright colors and earth tones.

Her clothes reflected an inner change. Again, since childhood, her father had noticed what he called "your streak of stubbornness and cunning." Priscilla had never minded it and had actually rather taken to that word "cunning." Nelson and Liza, too, had often told her that they never knew when this "streak" would assert itself and shadow her behavior. Over the years they had also told her that they simply prayed every time they saw those traits emerging.

Priscilla sank down on the sofa and remembered her most notable time of "stubbornness and cunning" as a teenager. At the time, her parents had even called her "incorrigible." And Priscilla supposed they must have had to pray overtime for her then.

It had begun one summer evening between her eleventh and twelfth grades. She had arrived home from work and told herself matter-of-factly: *Tonight's the night for a good fight.*

She had changed into a sweatshirt and her only pair of jeans and, as her younger sister Helen had told her parents later—"Priscilla was just in one of her moods"—she headed to the YMCA, where the youth of Prendergast often hung out.

She had come, specifically, to pick a fight with Marcia, who was the girlfriend of a guy named Jerome, neither of whom meant much to Priscilla. Marcia came from a large family with a reputation for defending one another. People used to call them "that bunch from the Virginia hills," like the famous Hatfields and McCoys from the hills of West Virginia.

After Priscilla arrived at the Y, she immediately scoped the dance floor for Jerome, and then started flirting with him. His attraction that night for Priscilla was simply that he was Marcia's boyfriend and the father of her son. Priscilla was aware that Marcia had long accused Jerome of having a crush on her. Accordingly, she thought he should have known better than to respond to her overtures. But Jerome, like many men, enjoyed the attention of women.

Even then, as a teenager, Priscilla had been easily bored. After she finished flirting with Jerome, she had looked for Helen and her friend Amber, who was not only refined—she had studied ballet and ice-skating and excelled at sports—but also the daughter of one of Nelson's church officers, Joseph Washington. Added to that, her father was a member of the Prendergast City Council.

"Guys, let's get outta here," Priscilla had told Amber and Helen. "Nothing's happening anyway."

But Helen had already been upset at her sister teasing Jerome. "Priscilla, why do you always have to instigate? You know how those women feel about their men. That was wrong what you did, and you know it. You shouldn't have danced with Jerome, up in his face and all."

"Yeah, Priscilla," Amber had agreed. But her objection had been highly practical. "There're only three of us. There's a lot more of them in Marcia's clan."

Yet the three of them looked at one another, remembering how they had been spoiling for this fight. A few days earlier, Priscilla and Amber had even outlined their strategy for such a fight.

"Since they're such a big family we're probably gonna need a weapon, something like a big butcher's knife," Priscilla had said.

"Girl, please," Amber had been aghast. "Our folks would kill us if they even heard us talking like this." But she and Priscilla had been forever friends. To maintain that friendship often she had gone along with her friend's shenanigans. And so she had shrugged agreement. "Oh well, I'm game if you are."

Priscilla had smiled in triumph. "Just remember, Amber, we can't take all of them out. The point is to face them and inflict enough pain that they'll never come our way again *and* to embarrass 'em in front of a whole lot of folks."

But that night, as Priscilla, Helen and Amber had left the Y and headed home, when—after having walked only a couple blocks up North Main Street to the corner of Fifth—they encountered trouble. Someone at the Y had gone to Marcia's family and told them, "Priscilla's with Jerome." Marcia's clan had come ready for a mêlée.

The two delegations had converged at the top of the hill.

The two contenders had stretched their necks searching the other side for their respective prey.

Marcia had caught a glimpse of Priscilla and belted out a battle cry: "You big-headed, red-boned preacher's kid."

Priscilla had stepped away from her pack of three and faced up to her opponent, who stood at the head of a much larger group. Then she had run forward and lunged into Marcia's chest. Then she had punched Marcia's face. "Do you really think I want that sissy Jerome? You can have him!" Then she had gripped Marcia's hair and had seemed to be struggling to swing her around by her head.

Marcia had fought back valiantly and landed a walloping blow to Priscilla's face.

Completely stunned, Priscilla had stumbled. "You put your hand on *my* face!"

At that point Marcia had begun to cry. Even with a long history of animosity between the two of them, she still had been shocked that she and Priscilla were actually fighting. Between her tears, she had screamed back at Priscilla, "Jerome's no sissy. You bitch, you damn bitch!"

With that, the fight had escalated. Each girl had twisted to dodge the other's punches. Each had whirled her arms and swung her fists at the other like blades out of alignment on a windmill. Priscilla and Marcia had tossed, tugged and kicked each other. Suddenly the fray had widened, and many bodies had been tangled into a huge heap. Underneath the heap, Priscilla had grabbed at any body parts to inflict pain. Her opponents had been beating and stomping not only Priscilla but anyone else near her body. They had not even been aware that mostly they were punching their cousins and brothers and sisters.

Moments later, Priscilla had clawed free. "My goodness, is this fun or what?" Yet Priscilla had been gasping for air. She had managed to raise herself from the ground and rub her eyes for a moment before she caught sight of her sister Helen, weeping on the sidelines. She screamed, "Amber, where's Amber?"

Amber was more than taking care of herself. This onetime ballet student held a broken beer bottle that she swung back and forth as she dared two of Marcia's female relatives to move.

That was the situation when the police had arrived.

At first, none of them had said they knew anything.

Then one of the officer's had picked up a butcher's knife from the ground. "And *this*? Where did *this* come from?"

Priscilla had quickly answered for all of them. "I can't imagine, officer. I really can't imagine."

Then the same policeman had asked, "Who started this fight, anyway?"

Ignorance and silence have long been essential ethics of street fighters, and such was the case that night.

The second policeman had shaken his head. "Okay, folks, let's break it up. Everybody go home now. The fight's over."

Priscilla smiled at her recollection of the night she had been a street-fighting woman.

But then her smile died as she remembered the not-so-exciting confrontation at home. She had fervently thanked God that night that Nelson was out of town. But Liza had been there, and so too had been Amber's mother.

Mrs. Washington had been livid as she shrieked at Liza. "How god-awful an example your daughter Priscilla is! She's simply a horrible child. My Amber was almost killed tonight. Liza, do you hear me? My daughter never behaved like this until she met your bad girl, Priscilla."

Priscilla remembered sulking at the accusations thrown at her by Amber's mother. *You'd think I was evil,* she thought. And then, *Boys do this kind of stuff all the time, and nobody says anything.*

"You and Reverend," Amber's mother had continued, "should send Priscilla away. I don't want *your* daughter associating with Amber anymore."

But Amber had interceded with unreserved contempt: "Oh, stop it. Just stop it, Mother. First, I did no less than Priscilla would've done for me. There was no fairness in that fight. That entire family and some of their friends were out to get her, not to mention that fight had been brewing a long time. It simply came to a head tonight. Besides, you didn't see what I saw. All those people were piled up on her. I had to do something! End of story, Mother."

Yet Amber had gone on anyway, as she peered into her mother's sad eyes: "Did it ever occur to you this incident had nothing to do with acting ladylike or who influences whom? We're talking about doing what's *right* and *friendship*!"

Throughout all this commotion, Liza had kept on apologizing profusely. Then she had turned her head in Helen's direction and asked, "And where were you during this darned skirmish in the street?"

A tearful Helen had said, "Momma, Priscilla's always getting into trouble. You know how she is, Momma. And I wasn't going to fight just because Miss Prissy, here, was in another of her outrageous moods."

Lost in thought, Liza had said, "One daughter stood idly by while the other almost got killed." She shook her head in consternation. And she, like Priscilla, had been grateful to God that Nelson had not been here to witness what had happened tonight.

In Columbus, nearly a decade later, Priscilla reflected that the more things change, the more they stay the same. Yet here in this high-stakes game of Ohio politics, it would not be enough to be Dennis the Menace. *I need to know how these guys think*, she reasoned.

Then she leafed through her Sunday edition of the *Columbus Chronicle* to the editorial section and deeply concentrated on what she read.

CHAPTER 18

An Austin Family Christmas

Priscilla was on the road again. With a sigh of relief at leaving the Ohio Senate behind, she had locked her front door, slid her luggage into the trunk of her dear Mustang and took off for Prendergast again.

As she pulled onto the familiar interstate, on the car radio she heard "Home for the Holidays." She was eager to be going home, yet she knew that what would be most memorable about this Christmas was that it was likely to be the last Nelson ever enjoyed. It would be a real family reunion, and as joyful as the determined family could make it. So far as Priscilla knew, all the children and grandchildren, except for Ellen and Nelson, Jr., would be coming home.

All the way, the weather was predictably cold and snowy. As the Austins often pointed out, "Christmas in Prendergast without snow? What a ridiculous thought!"

It might have been treacherous driving for some, but Priscilla knew the roads and how to drive in everything from light snow to real blizzards.

On the five-hour drive, Priscilla sometimes let her mind drift like the snow.

She was looking forward to spending time with her favorite niece and nephew: Germane, Helen's son, and Kimberly, Harriet's daughter. Her other niece—Ellen's only child—had been adopted at birth. Although Priscilla knew that recently Ellen had managed to establish contact with her daughter, the rest of the family still had never met the child.

Aside from playing Auntie, Priscilla was aware that she would field the usual questions from her siblings. She had been accustomed to shrugging her shoulders whenever anyone among her family and friends asked her what she would do with her education after she completed her doctoral degree program. "Whatever I do, I'll be darn good at it," she usually responded. Now, as a political scientist, she not only enjoyed the enviable opportunity to practice her profession in the Ohio Senate but also had enjoyed teaching politics in the university classroom. She recalled how her students at FAMU had marveled at how caught up she would get in teaching the subject. She was unsure, however, how exactly her profession would wholly crystallize. But in the meantime she prepared herself for hearing, as usual, from all her family how knowingly she talked about everything from the recent presidential election to the oil embargo and the Iranian hostage crisis. Priscilla assured herself that the reason she had no answer to the question about what she would do "with all of her education" was that she had already been living her ambition. Yet the only thing she was sure of was that she would avoid any serious, and intimate, relationships.

Her thoughts trailed to Ellen. Priscilla was glad for the time that she had spent with her in California before she went back to Columbus to work for Senator Callahan.

Priscilla had always had a soft spot for Ellen. She reflected on how her eldest sister's life had turned out, even though her educational pursuit for her accounting degree at Southern Illinois University near Liza's family in Sills Creek had been interrupted by her pregnancy. Ellen had overcome that unpleasant episode in her life, married, and was now managing the accounting for a large architectural firm and enjoying a fairly successful life in San Francisco.

Priscilla remembered that as perhaps the most traumatic time of her adolescence. She herself had been in the eleventh grade, and the family had resided in the parsonage.

What had happened and its aftermath were vividly etched in Priscilla's mind.

She had first become fully aware of the crisis one night when a distraught Liza called her daughters together. Equally distraught was Ellen, who, covered up in her bedroom robe, leaned against a small table in the family room. Once all the girls had assembled, Liza said, "What I have to say involves Ellen. As you already know, she came home unexpectedly a short while ago. Then she started working at Sears. Well ... Ellen's pregnant."

Priscilla had never seen her mom look so somber, pallid-faced. Crow's-feet-clad red eyes. Her signature cheekbones sagged. Liza appeared to have grown older by twenty or more years. Her voice cracked. Distraught. Hopeless. Powerless.

Priscilla and Harriet and Helen and Camille clung onto one another as if they could somehow prevent the onslaught of what else Liza was about to tell them. They actually trembled. They already knew that something was the matter, but they never imagined one of them was pregnant. Tears filled their eyes as they turned their heads from Ellen to Liza and back again. It was, however, the punctuated cadence of Liza's words that set the stage for what each of the girls knew would not be to Ellen's advantage.

"Since your father is a minister—"

"Oh, no!" the girls cried out.

"We can't go 'round proudly displaying such a condition as this—"

"No, Momma, no!"

"... especially out of wedlock," Liza managed to complete her sentence. Then she added: "We have your father's reputation to consider. It's been decided, therefore, that Ellen ... well, she's giving up her child for adoption."

"No, Momma, no! We can't do that to Ellen's baby," the younger sisters chorused in near unison.

By the hurt and pain visible in Liza's face, it seemed that the decision to give up Ellen's child for adoption had gone against her grain, too.

Ellen spoke up, her eyes aflame in a strong rebuttal. "Let me be clear. *I'm* not choosing to give my child up for adoption. It's your mother and Reverend Austin who's doing all this, not me. Can you believe that they're making me give up *my* child to spare your *daddy's* image?"

As the snow pelted the windshield, Priscilla turned on the wipers and kept her eyes tight on the road. But her mind continued reliving that terrible scene.

It had been a frigid night, so cold and snowy—much like this one. Misery had permeated the atmosphere. That night, the sisters lay still in their beds and listened in silence as Liza cried out loud, wailing as if she were in excruciating pain. Priscilla relived Liza's anguish for her firstborn, Ellen—who herself would soon give birth to what would be her only child and whom she would be forced to give up for adoption. Unbearable, that whole episode had been unbearable. As it happened, though, Nelson had been away again, perhaps at one of his church conventions; he surely had not been anywhere on the scene that night. From that terrible night to the day the child was born, no one had ever mentioned Ellen's pregnancy again. It was as if some sacrilege had been committed.

During that time, the sisters had grown even closer, as they felt the need to be strong to help Ellen. Priscilla remembered seeing Ellen reading love stories in the magazine *True Confessions*, or going with her to the movies at the Winter Garden Theater. Back then, the Austin girls had not been allowed to go out alone in the evenings, and Priscilla had felt privileged to be asked by her big sister to accompany her on some of her outings. Sometimes Ellen had imparted to her tidbits of life skills, especially about self-reliance. Most memorable of all the movies were *Doctor Zhivago* and *The Valley of the Dolls*, neither of which Priscilla had fully understood. She had been confused when Doctor Zhivago set up house with another woman, and when the character played by Patty Duke had used the word "dolls" to mean "narcotics." Because

Priscilla and her sisters lived such a sheltered life, she had failed to grasp the meaning of certain lifestyles. In her innocence, she had not known much about sexuality, either. She had thought, for instance, that homosexual men were comedic cross-dressers, like the men in Flip Wilson television shows.

Looking back as she drove home for what she understood was probably her father's final Christmas, Priscilla realized that she and her siblings had grown up oblivious to behaviors that went against the teachings of their faith— including adultery, drug addiction and homosexuality.

And then there had been Liza's constant ranting: "You girls are getting beyond yourselves. Don't you bring home any more babies, and especially no white boys!" Priscilla had never quite understood—as an adolescent or even now, as an adult—where Liza's admonition against bringing home "white boys" had come from. There had been a strange irony in Liza's admonitions, since, given the statistical insignificance of the black population in Prendergast, interracial dating and mixed-race children were common.

After the drama of her pregnancy, Ellen had given birth to a baby girl who was given up for adoption. Shortly afterward, she had briefly relocated to Missouri and then to her final stop in California. Priscilla reflected how parental reactions to their children's mistakes can produce unimaginable consequences. Despite all that had happened, Priscilla still deeply appreciated Ellen's teachings on being a self-reliant woman. As far back as she could remember, she had always wanted to be like Ellen, with whom she had acquired a certain *je ne sais quoi*. Besides, Ellen was strong, and Priscilla had already developed an aversion to weakness.

Such a long ride, Priscilla thought. *Good thing I have so many sisters to think about. My brother Nelson, too.*

Camille was the baby of the family. In high school she was a cheer-leader and hung around with the cool crowd. She was pretty and preppy with medium brown skin. Unlike Priscilla's life experiences, which had included those in a predominantly black world and those in a predominantly white world, her youngest sister Camille's life experiences had included only the latter. Because she had spent most of her life in Prendergast, Camille's exposure to black America had been so limited that during high school she had asked Priscilla to write a paper for her on the life of the Reverend Dr. Martin Luther King, Jr. At the time, Priscilla had been at Livingstone College. Priscilla also remembered that Camille had been the only daughter for whom Nelson and Liza had ever bought a car, and a new one, at that. Although she was the youngest, Camille had originally owned the Mustang that had been "handed down to Priscilla" and that had been totaled in her Florida accident.

Camille was also the only one of the sisters who had visited Helen in Hawaii and who now lived with Ellen and her husband in San Francisco. Both moves had occurred during the 1970s in the name of helping Camille to "find herself." In San Francisco, Camille had pursued her interests in graphic art and design. Eventually she worked alongside Ellen at a renowned architectural firm.

It was Harriet, of all the Austin sisters, who had taken a completely different path.

She was the tallest of the sisters, ebony-complexioned but the least confident. She had especially high cheekbones, other Cherokee facial features and long, thick, black wavy hair. Immediately after high school, she had enrolled in a school of cosmetology in neighboring Olean, east of Prendergast. But when she completed her program of study, she had come home one day with documents for her parents to sign. To the surprise of everyone, Harriet had enlisted in the U.S. Air Force. Nelson had signed the papers, and then Harriet was off to what ended up being a twenty-five year career. In the interim, she had married and later divorced a man and bore Kimberly, whom, in her infancy, Harriet had brought home to Liza "to keep for a while." In the military, Harriet worked in dentistry and sometimes had to identify the bodies of soldiers by their dental work. But she was sent to various international postings and often hosted her mother as her guest. Liza later inscribed her name in a book whereby she acknowledged her travels to nations such as Great Britain, Holland, Japan, Morocco and the Philippines—travels all made possible by her daughter Harriet.

A couple of summers earlier, Harriet had come home on leave and accompanied Nelson on one of his last trips to the Austin homestead in Mississippi. From what both Nelson and Harriet had said afterwards, both had treasured that special time together.

As she continued driving toward her homecoming, Priscilla did not doubt that each of her sisters—Ellen included—shared a special fondness for their father. Still, she thought, Ellen had found it a bit more difficult to come around because of the forced adoption of her child. Besides, being the eldest, she never quite let go of her own birth father. But Priscilla was certain that Ellen did regret not being able to join the others for Christmas. And Nelson knew she loved him, for they had grown even closer during his visit to her home the previous summer. But on this particular Christmastime, Ellen was working feverishly to help her husband with his Bay area real estate business. She had also taken over management of his family's group home for high-achieving men with developmental disabilities. Ellen and her husband were both workaholics.

Priscilla was almost but not quite home. There was time, she thought, for some serious remembering of the sister so close to her in age and appearance that often, while growing up, people had assumed they must be twins. Priscilla frowned as she remembered how competitive she and Helen had often been as children and adolescents. Only a year younger than Priscilla, Helen was very pale, with ginger freckles, and had seemed to resent being compared to Priscilla. But what had always seemed to bother Helen the most was that Priscilla had obviously been their father's favorite. Helen had yearned to get out from under the shadow of Priscilla and desperately wanted to study fashion design. But when Nelson and Liza insisted that they could not afford to send her to the private school of her dreams, she had enlisted in the U.S. Navy—"anything to get away from home," she had said at the time. In the military, Helen's work had something to do, she said vaguely, "with naval intelligence." She used words like "communications" and "radioman." Early in her naval career, she had met a man named Robert and brought him home to Prendergast, where Nelson performed their marriage ceremony. Germane, their only child, was born shortly afterward. But the marriage had not gone well. Its abrupt and even puzzling ending had troubled Priscilla as much as the forced adoption of Ellen's baby.

The beginning of the end of Helen's marriage had occurred when she and her family were stationed in Hawaii. One summer day, Helen had called home to Prendergast, out of sorts, and told Liza, "Robert says he has amnesia. He can't remember Germane and me." When Liza pressed her for details, Helen had said, "Robert was on a secret submarine mission, and when he came back to shore, he was totally out of himself. He didn't even know who he was or anything or anybody, including me and Germane." Priscilla had been standing nearby and—overhearing Liza's side of the conversation—never got over the sound of helplessness in her mom's voice. For a long while now, Helen and Germane had been on their own. Priscilla still grieved over Helen's loss and prayed that she would be made whole again. She had, as a result, vowed to herself that she would never get too closely attached to any man. And she never did.

As she drove the final stretch to Prendergast, Priscilla wished Nelson, Jr., had been able to make it home for this special Christmas.

But his immediate priority was to be with his own growing family in Southfield, Michigan. In this, his third or fourth marriage—Priscilla had lost count, because Nelson, Jr., had married one of his wives twice—his current wife had captured his heart. He would be missed by the whole family. Nelson was proud of his son, who bore a striking likeness to him and a handsome chap, too. Already a regionally acclaimed artist, Nelson, Jr., was fully aware of his father's love and pride in his career.

Of all her siblings, Priscilla realized she behaved most like Nelson, Jr. Although they had not grown up together, over the years they had grown close.

She particularly recalled flying to a Democratic Party convention in Detroit during her stint in Florida. She had been with "a friend" who was a prominent politician, a tad older than she was and married.

But when Nelson, Jr., arrived to meet the couple at the airport, he had grown livid and insisted on dismantling their plans. So Priscilla had left her friend at the convention center and stayed with her brother and his family in neighboring Southfield.

"I don't care who he is," an outraged Nelson, Jr., had said in the car en route to his home. "He's unacceptable. Girl, have you lost your stupid little mind? Can you imagine what Daddy would do if he knew about this bizarre scheme of yours? End of discussion."

When pressed, Priscilla had admitted she had been living out one of her occasional bouts "just for the hell of it." For her, Nelson, Jr., had long since assumed the role of father, of big brother, of protector, of whatever role was necessary to deal with his little sister's foolishness. But whenever brother and sister argued about issues like this, Priscilla had always reminded her brother of the double standard: "You were hardly ever chastised for your transgressions. Truth be told, you might even have been encouraged. Remember when you served in 'Nam and Daddy sent you money with instructions to 'Buy some condoms, Son'?"

From Priscilla's perspective, her brother had not been discouraged from his indiscretions. Instead, he had been encouraged to be a red-blooded male. However, she and her sisters had been taught "to save yourself for marriage," whatever that meant. Such teachings had long been lost on Priscilla. Instead, she had always wanted to do her darned best to do whatever it was she thought that men did.

Priscilla—finally home!—luxuriated in her family. At first what delighted her most was playing "auntie" to Germane, Helen's five-year-old son.

For the Austins, who had once resided in rural areas, it was a common practice to take children outdoors for fresh air before bedtime. And since Priscilla assumed that all children liked to play in the snow, she had dressed the child in multiple layers of clothing and took him outside.

But she had overlooked the fact that Germane had spent most of his life in Hawaii and was unaccustomed to the cold and the snow. So once outside in the small front yard, Germane moved about awkwardly, knee-deep in the cold, powdery stuff. He felt his way a few steps at a time, and he wobbled because he was overdressed. It soon became clear that he was not in the least bit thrilled with the snow.

"Aunt Priscilla, I'm cold. Can we go back inside?" he asked, and he meant it.

But Priscilla persisted and tried to get the child to play. She made snowballs and threw them at him. She fell backwards on the ground and made a snow angel. But none of those games pleased the youngster.

Then Germane fell down. Some snow touched his flesh, and he cried out loudly, "I'm cold, Aunt Priscilla! Take me back inside!" At that point, Priscilla got the message. Germane had cried so loudly that everyone inside the Austin house, as well as the neighbors, had heard him.

Priscilla helped him up and onto the front porch. When she opened the door to the den, everyone but Priscilla laughed at the child's displeasure.

The doorbell rang. Priscilla turned around and noticed two familiar faces through the window. There stood Harriet and six-year-old Kimberly. Stationed in the Philippines, they had been hopping flights for two-and-a-half days. They looked excited and exhausted at the same time.

Harriet walked in first and tugged an oversized duffel bag, with Kim in tow. The two appeared to be more traveling companions than mother and daughter.

Kim, who stood close to three feet in height, beamed. She took off her wooden Japanese sandals and placed them on the floor next to the door. She meekly stepped aside and stood in her socks, awaiting the next cue from her mom. Everyone stared at Kim in utter amazement, and then she said something in Japanese—or was that Filipino?

Though exhausted, Harriet managed to say, "Kim spends most of her time with our housekeeper, who's Filipino and speaks very little English. Give her some time. She'll come around."

Kim had needed only an instant. "Grandma Liza!"

The little girl was a tad uncomfortable with the other family members who at that point were still strangers to her. But as the evening progressed, she and Germane bonded. It was easy to see that each child had been accustomed to receiving attention—*all* of the attention. But they eventually settled into an amicable state.

The Austin sisters, in other reunions at home, ordinarily would have gone out to house parties and nightclubs with their family and hometown friends such as Amber. That Christmas, however, they opted to stay together at home.

Even their Christmas shopping was concentrated on the children.

For the most part, the adults had already purchased the usual gifts for Nelson: bedroom slippers, pajamas and robes. And it was generally understood that the gift for Liza was "a piece of money."

Priscilla had attempted to find special gifts for the children. She had first become intrigued with "heritage dolls" when she visited a museum named after Stephen Foster during her time in Florida. Patterned after a middle-aged African slave woman, the doll that Priscilla had chosen for Kim wore a colorful bandanna wrapped around her head with an equally attractive kerchief wrapped around her shoulders. The doll also wore a ragged, ankle-length print skirt. It was not the typical pink- or pale-complexioned Barbie that many young girls had come to expect for a gift, nor was it a replica of a contemporary black doll.

But Kim and Germane were military brats who had lived most of their short lives abroad and were unfamiliar with contemporary mainland American notions of race. Priscilla mused that both children probably saw more blacks in their grandparents' home that evening than they had ever seen in any other setting. Besides, both children were multi-racial. Kim's father was from an interracial marriage: a black-American father and German mother. Harriet, like Liza, had strong Cherokee features, but Kim resembled her father in skin color.

When Kim realized the heritage doll was hers, she tossed it down on the floor, and the coins hidden underneath its skirt fell out to the floor.

As Priscilla knelt to gather the coins, she said, "These are Susan B. Anthony silver dollars, Kim, and they'll be worth something someday. Let me help you pick them up and put them away. Okay, Kim? And the doll, well, it's not something you just play with."

Then she looked up at Harriet, "When you get back home, maybe you can place it on your mantle. I only wanted Kim to know how special she is. I didn't mean to upset her." Priscilla felt out of sorts as she tried to explain her gift choice, but she could see that Kim looked disappointed in her gift from Aunt Priscilla.

There were issues, too, with Priscilla's gift for Germane—an elaborate electric train set, with tracks and all. Before she left Columbus, she had gone to a specialty shop and described her nephew to the proprietor, who in turn had shown her several different kinds of model trains. Priscilla had selected a particular set in its entirety, one that was actually intended for a much older person, one that *she* had liked.

Germane told her that he was "very pleased" with his gift. "Very pleased, Aunt Priscilla," he repeated. The whole family helped assemble the elaborate train set, and then they mounted it on the tracks in a grand, figure-eight style on the living room floor. Before long, however, the two children squabbled over the train and their many other toys.

As the adults watched the children fighting so soon after the train set had been fully assembled, Helen was heard to complain about Priscilla's having "purchased such an expensive gift for *my* son without first having consulted me."

One of Priscilla's Christmas lessons that year was that it is best to first discuss one's plans for gifts for children with their parents. Her sisters' gifts for the children, on the other hand, all hit the mark with the children. They had brought home contemporary dolls, stuffed animals, trucks and transformers. Those were the toys that Germane and Kim played with and endlessly fought over.

Through it all, Nelson and Liza watched the activity and appeared to be deeply moved. Nelson still looked in fair health, though frail and slow of movement.

Yet he was thrilled to see his children and grandchildren, one last Christmas.

CHAPTER 19

Family time, although Priscilla did not fully appreciate it, mattered deeply to the Austins. So no matter the circumstance, the spirit of Christmas had to be kept.

Liza traditionally signaled the start of the Christmas holidays by decorating a tall Fraser fir, which she usually did by herself when no other family members were around. She hung not only strings of lights but also a variety of ornaments, including strings of popcorn and beads. That Christmas, she topped the large tree with a striking black porcelain angel.

This year, after decorating the tree by herself, Liza prepared the Christmas dishes from scratch including cakes, cookies, pies and candy—along with taffy pulled around popcorn balls. When her visiting daughters came to the kitchen to help pull the taffy, they sampled the cakes frosted with shockingly-colored icing and a variety of nuts. Liza's special Christmas dishes all tasted as good as they looked.

The Austins looked forward to feasting on the usual large turkey and assorted fixings including the rich stuffing and cranberry side dishes. After all was ready, the family gathered around the beautifully decorated table and waited for Nelson to give the grace for the meal.

"Thank you, Lord," he prayed, "for bringing us all together one more time and for this magnificent meal."

Then, less reverently, he said, "Rise, Peter, slay and eat."

Liza waited until the rest of the family had eaten their main course before she joined them at the dinner table. Then she started down memory lane, telling the first of the evening's many stories. "Back when you children were very young and Nelson and I had little or no money, I used to make your gifts. Do any of you remember those handmade papier-mâché dolls and ornaments and other toys?" Much chatter and laughter followed.

Priscilla and her sisters mostly recalled that they had played in that sticky papier-mâché concoction that Liza would make. They would dip their hands into that sticky, pale paste. Yet instead of helping to create dolls and ornaments, they would chase one another around the house and splatter the goo on everyone and everything in sight.

When Priscilla recollected the time when the family's economic circumstances finally improved, she yelled out, "I remember getting one of my best gifts ever—."

But altogether, the rest of the Austins finished her sentence for her: "Rin Tin Tin!" They were laughing as they remembered how much she had loved that gray, stuffed animal. It had been one of the first toys her parents could afford to buy for her. When she had not been sucking her thumb, the replica had served as her Peanut's blanket.

The sisters then recalled how Liza would make their clothes, how she would teach each of them how to sew and how she would dress Priscilla and Helen to look like twins.

The sisters also talked about the times when the family traveled by train on the Illinois Central from Canton, Mississippi, by way of New Orleans, to Sills Creek, Illinois.

"Those ole porters used to play with us kids," Harriet said. "Priscilla, you and Helen were too young to know what was going on, but we all had to sit in the back compartments because everything was 'for coloreds only' and 'for whites only.'"

Harriet recalled how some of the folks in the "colored only" cars were, like the Austins, of mixed race. Others looked pale enough to pass for white but did not seem to dare to try it. Others had complexions that looked Mediterranean or, like Harriet, had glossy Nubian-looking complexions. The main point of Harriet's story was how well they had all gotten along despite their differences in color.

Liza proudly reminded everybody that the children had free or reduced fare because her father had worked for the railroad. She was, in her way, as proud of her father as the girls were of Nelson.

Nelson cut in and let loose a wild chuckle as he told one of his favorite stories about his Uncle Charlie.

"I don't think I've told this story in years, but one time Uncle Charlie's horses broke out of the corral, and he came over to our farmhouse to get me to help him round them up. When I opened the front door, there he sat, mounted bareback on one of his horses, and he held the reins of another one meant for me. 'Come on out, Nelson, I need your help in the roundup,' Uncle Charlie said. Then he walked the other horse over to the porch for me to mount it, and I did. But no sooner had we started down that ole dirt road than along came Priscilla, screaming like the nuisance of a brat that she was, 'Wait for me, Daddy. Wait for me.' You should've seen her—hair unkempt, tattered dress, barefoot—but she was such a happy child, not a care in the world back then. I kept telling her to turn around and go back home, but she kept screaming back at me, 'Pick me up, Daddy. I want to ride the horsey, too. Stop, Daddy, *stop,* and pick me up.'"

"Was that here in Prendergast, Granddad?" one of the grandchildren asked.

"No, child, that was at our folks' place in Mississippi. Now, before anybody asks me why this and why that, allow me to explain a few things. First, I was no horseman. That means I couldn't ride as well as Uncle Charlie or any other rancher. For another thing, there was a fifty-fifty chance I'd have fallen off that horse trying to lift up Priscilla, not to mention the dangers of bringing her along on a roundup. Then it happened! A band of great big crusty turtles started crossing the road right dab in the middle of Uncle Charlie and me. I'd gotten behind because I'd slowed down to deal with Priscilla. Making matters worse, your Aunt Priscilla started playing with the turtles, which really slowed us down because those rascals withdrew into their shells and just sat there and blocked the road."

"Ah, come on, Daddy," Priscilla said as she waited for her father to catch his breath. "How was I supposed to know that turtles wouldn't play with me? For sure, I didn't know they'd pull their heads and limbs inside their shells."

Kim and Germane pointed their fingers at Priscilla and teased her as she and Nelson sparred.

"Eventually," Nelson went on, "I told Uncle Charlie that I had to take Priscilla back home. How I got back onto that horse remains a mystery to me. But I did and I finally caught back up with Uncle Charlie and did my best to help in the roundup. I laugh about all that today. But, back then, I was furious with your Aunt Priscilla."

One of the sisters remembered the time that Ellen had decided to run away from the Austin homestead. She had not planned to take anybody with her, but she had made the mistake of telling her younger sisters about her plan. The younger girls had jumped into the family's big, black Ford sedan along with their big sister. Somehow Ellen had managed to release the brakes. The car had begun to roll down a slope. But at the bottom was a deep, uncovered well. Less than four feet tall, Ellen had barely maneuvered the steering wheel. Then, by the time Nelson had appeared from somewhere and realized what was happening, he had barely reached the car in time to apply the brakes. After the near accident had come one of those rare occasions when Priscilla's hide had been spared. That time, the big whipping had been reserved for Ellen.

Other stories were told that Christmas. There was the time the girls had gone to a little red brick, dilapidated elementary school called Cameron Street; the day they had looked up in the sky and wondered what those big flying machines were; and the time they had watched Liza curse out a white sheriff who had come looking for a gun in their little shack of a home.

But the big story of the evening was Liza's story about "the day that Nelson got put in jail."

"Oh, yeah, kids" she began, looking at Kim and Germane, "your granddad actually went to jail. Here's what happened. One time in Mississippi, when we were going to travel up North, we'd barely gotten out of Mississippi when a sheriff pulled us over, right there in the heart of some little hick town. He might've been a policeman, but in the South they were mostly sheriffs. That man was really rude to us.

"He stared at Helen and asked, 'what y'all coloreds doing with a white child?'" Liza said.

"Making matters worse, your Aunt Priscilla perked up and said, 'Mista, ain't no white child in *our* car.' Anyway, we had to be stopped for something—"

Kim interrupted her, "Grandma, did you leave out part of the story. Was Aunt Priscilla wrong about the kid in the car?"

Then Liza realized that her grandchildren were not familiar with the notion of "the color line." They had no idea of their heritage, none whatsoever.

But hoping she could help them understand, she said, "Sometimes white people don't treat black people nicely, just because of our skin color."

Then she looked disapprovingly first at Harriet and then at Helen. Her glance accused them of failing in their parenting because they had not taught their children about "the color line."

Liza went on that maybe the sheriff just wanted to stop the "colored" family for something, so why not for having a white child in their car, presumably without authorization from its family? Added to that, the officer had also said something about "a traffic violation," which had been equally confusing to the family at the time.

To everyone's delight, though, Nelson interrupted Liza and said, "That mean ole sheriff told me to 'Git out of the car, boy. I'm taking you to jail.' Yeah! I left Liza and the girls all piled up in that great big ole black Ford just sitting there in the middle of downtown. Then I got into the sheriff's car, and we rode over to the jailhouse where they booked me for some crazy traffic violation."

Everyone at the table laughed vigorously at Germane and Kim's chant, "Granddad's been to jail. Granddad's been to jail." The grandchildren had understood that part of the story, but the rest of it had eluded them. The puzzled expressions on their faces seemed to say that their grandfather was much too big to be called "boy."

So Nelson addressed their obvious confusion. "Even when I was a young man, white people used to mistreat people who looked like us. One way to humiliate us or to put us down was to call us without using our names or to call a grown man 'boy.' I'm sorry, kids, but that's just the way life used to be for us. But we've come a very long way. Yes, by golly, we have. Anyway, it didn't take those ole fools much time to realize that there sat this Negro family stranded in the middle of *their* little downtown. Can you picture a black car packed with children that look like your aunts parked on a main street in the middle of a Southern rural town in the late 1950s? So they let me go, 'with a warning,' because they didn't know what to do with Liza and the kids. The sheriff took me back to the car, and then he escorted us out of town. Now, have you ever heard of anything sillier than that?" Much chatter and laughter followed.

Later that evening, after Priscilla and her hometown friend Amber were on the phone, Amber joined the Austins. It was generally understood that Amber loved the reverend as much as every Austin family member and that she also wanted to spend some time with him, especially while the sisters were home.

On that Christmas night, Amber stood in the midst of the Austin household and expressed deep delight to see everyone.

They gazed fondly back at her. They all remembered, although no one wanted to tell that particular sad story, how Amber had lost her eyesight more than four years ago. Frantic for a cure, her parents had taken her to see specialists in New York City and Boston. But the answer was always that her condition was irreversible and that she was legally blind. Priscilla had stood by her friend and learned to write to her in large block letters that Amber could see with the help of a magnifying glass. So in spite of her blindness, she and Priscilla had remained friends, and she had remained as close as a sister to the Austin girls.

On the brink of tears, Amber stood in the center of the den with the fireplace ablaze behind her. "Reverend and Mrs. Austin, you have no idea how grateful I am to be here. You have always been good to me and my family. You gave my father a place to stay when he struggled with his drinking problem. You supported my mom's candidacy for county commissioner. And Priscilla, you allowed me to visit you at Livingstone back when I got put out of school in Tuscaloosa. Then, when I got in trouble again at Butler University—the Reverend's alma mater—you came over to Indianapolis from Columbus and got Nelson, Jr., to come with you and check up on me."

Amber shook her head and gave Nelson a particular smile. "And now this. I don't know many people who would allow someone to share Christmas with them at such a time as *this*. Mom and Dad told me not to come over this evening, but I wouldn't miss seeing all of you for anything in the world."

While Amber talked, Priscilla was aware that her longtime friend, like all the Austins, was acutely aware of Nelson's illness. She was taking this opportunity to express her gratitude while she still could.

But then Amber said, "Come with me to the back bedroom, Priscilla. There is something I need to tell you."

The others watched the two young women leave the room. Most were aware of what Priscilla was about to hear. They had kept the news from Priscilla because they had known how the news would compound her grief about Nelson's health.

In the back bedroom, Amber said, "What I have to tell you is bad, Priscilla. I mean, it's really bad. It's about Tyler."

Priscilla sank down on the bed and tried to prepare herself. Tyler— tall, handsome and combative—was her first love.

During her teenage years, Nelson had forbidden Priscilla to date Tyler because, as he would say, "That young man is unsuitable for you." Priscilla never understood Nelson's meaning of the word "unsuitable." When she had been younger, she had imagined that maybe it had something to do with how he reminded people of the singer Marvin Gaye.

In the back bedroom, Amber strained to find a starting point for how to break the bad news. She began by addressing what she knew were Priscilla's lingering questions about Tyler's "suitability" in Nelson's eyes.

"You know, Priscilla, part of the reason the Reverend kept you away from Tyler had to do with the marital status of his parents. Remember when your father told you he was enrolling you in Livingstone College rather than somewhere in New York?"

"How could I ever forget being unloaded at that desolate place called Livingstone? Did I feel abandoned or what?" Priscilla laughed out loud.

"Tyler's parents," Amber said, "were never married."

"Come on! What are you going on about?"

"Priscilla, please listen to me. It's hard enough, what I have to tell you."

"I'm listening. But this had better be good."

Amber nodded. "We found out recently that Gilda used to be the nursemaid for Rufus's wife in Kentucky. She and Rufus ran away together and moved here to Prendergast to start a new life, but—"

"Stop right there, Amber. You're beginning to sound like a sorry version of *Peyton Place*." Priscilla wrinkled her nose. "This is what you had to tell me?"

"It's some of it. As you already know, all of their children were born in Prendergast, including Tyler. Gilda was pregnant with him when they came here. And she and Rufus have never married. You see, Rufus never divorced his wife in Kentucky. What I wanted you to know was that Rufus, when he found out how interested you were in Tyler, eventually confided that whole story to the Reverend. That's why Nelson didn't want you two together. But the Reverend kept Rufus's confidence all these years."

Priscilla's eyes filled with tears. "After all this time, I just assumed that Tyler didn't care for me as much as I cared for him. But you're trying to tell me that it was all about his parents not being married? And Tyler knew that all along?"

"Yes, but that's only part of what I'm trying to tell you."

"And are you saying that there's still a chance for us? Is that it Amber? Did you think I didn't care about him anymore because so much time had passed?" Priscilla stood up as though poised to run and find Tyler, wherever he was.

"No, Priscilla! It's too late!"

"Too late? Too late for whom, for what?"

Amber grabbed hold of Priscilla. "Tyler's dead. Priscilla, Tyler's dead. He was shot and killed last month outside of Buffalo in Mount Pisgah."

TYLER

Priscilla stood so still it seemed as if she were not breathing. Then she seemed to fall to the bed. "No, Amber. You've got it all wrong. This can't be what you had to tell me." Priscilla took a deep breath and shook her head, disbelieving. "Maybe you don't know it, but Rufus already gave Tyler his name. But what's all this talk about death? Surely, you've got that part of your story wrong, too."

"Oh, Priscilla, I'm so sorry to have to tell you this sad news about Tyler. I really am. We all are. The whole Austin family."

Priscilla looked at her friend in mute disbelief. Her "whole family" already knew about not only what had happened to Tyler but also about how she had always felt for him? Somehow, Priscilla found the courage to ask, "And how was Tyler supposed to have, you know ... died?"

Amber said that Tyler had begun to turn his life around. He had married, and he had had two children. He had even moved his family to Buffalo, where he worked as a bouncer at an upscale nightclub over in neighboring Mount Pisgah.

She reached out and took Priscilla's hand and told her what had happened: "One night, helping to close the club, Tyler had been walking two young women to their cars when a Volkswagen Beetle pulled up and one of the passengers called out Tyler's name. When Tyler turned to see who it was, another man from the car's backseat shot at him. Tyler tried to run to safety, but no one would help him. Some people in nearby buildings even rushed to lock their doors. Tyler limped down the street, fell and died within minutes. Meanwhile, the perpetrators had gotten away."

"No, no, no!" Priscilla cried out. "Why would anybody want to kill Tyler? Why?" She cried like a child.

Priscilla still sat on the edge of her bed, clinging to her friend. She was stunned at the news of the death of her first love. She was shocked, too, that apparently her "whole family" had known about her feelings for Tyler.

But now, for Priscilla, the news about Tyler's horrible death simply added one more layer of callousness to her increasingly impervious heart.

Nelson had a beatific smile on his lips as he watched his daughters moving about the house, preparing to depart. On this, his last Christmas, Nelson took satisfaction that each of his beloved daughters had grown into womanhood whole and even mostly happy.

This is good, he said to himself. *Good daughters. A good life.*

One by one, each sister drove one another to the Chautauqua County-Prendergast Airport or to the Buffalo Niagara International Airport. Since Priscilla would be driving back to Columbus, she would be the last one to leave.

But before she did, Nelson took her aside.

"Priscilla, I'm not sure what to say to you about Tyler. We've always known that you carried deep affection for him and that I never thought him a suitable catch for you. But I sure hope you know I never wanted anything like that to happen to him. I'm so sorry, child, I really am."

As she listened to her father, Priscilla realized this was the first time since high school that he had even mentioned Tyler's name to her. Despite her father's attempt to comfort her, her hurt still ran too deep. There was nothing that could be done or said to appease her. She simply stared at Nelson with her most stolid expression and kept her pain to herself. And yet, given Nelson's declining health, she chose not to begrudge his attitude toward Tyler. There was, after all, nothing either one of them could do about Tyler's death.

With that uncomfortable moment behind him, Nelson broached another subject. "Priscilla, do you have any idea when you'll be coming back this way?"

His question caught Priscilla off guard. She felt strange—not eerie or foreboding, just strange. She understood it was not that Nelson did not want her to leave; rather, he wanted to know whether his health would have declined when she saw him again. And although neither of them could prepare for such a contingency, he had still been unable to resist asking the question.

Priscilla replied that she was not sure exactly when she would return. Then they hugged, she bid him farewell and walked out of the door for her drive back to Columbus.

CHAPTER 20

The Exchange of Power

As soon as she returned to work after New Year's Day, 1981, it was depressingly clear to Priscilla how much the Democratic loss of the state senate affected all aspects of her political life. It was Inauguration Day, and she saw the Senate Republicans and their supporters celebrating all over the city.

Over the holidays, to her surprise, Priscilla noticed that the Senate Republicans had already converted and remodeled the office of their new leader, Senator Raymon Ferrari. Exquisitely designed, the suite displayed all the amenities of privilege. Unlike the minority leader's suite, the opulence of the Senate president's suite reflected the unmistakable appearance of leadership.

On her first day back, the Republicans' victory celebration spilled over into the reception areas of Senator Callahan and Senator Chouinard. Lost for a while in the crowd, Priscilla wondered whether she should have gone back home. But eventually she made it to the small cubicle she shared with Sharon. Although she recognized many of the guests, she knew they were waiting for the chance to congratulate Senator Aaron Caldiera on his appointment to chair the Finance Committee. She thought: *Talk about a slap in the face!*

Priscilla knew that Senator Callahan represented the greater Cincinnati area, which tended to vote Democratic; and that Senator

Caldiera represented the periphery and the more conservative parts of Hamilton County, which tended to vote Republican. She also knew that Senator Callahan, who was black, and Senator Caldiera, who was a Jew, shared a remarkable sort of gentleman's agreement that whichever senator served in the majority-party caucus would also serve the interests of the other senator, and she knew that the two senators had carried out "the gentleman's agreement" so well that some political observers had even referred to their pact as "a dying breed of bipartisanship."

Sitting in her cubicle next to Sharon, Priscilla riffled through papers as though she were busy.

Instead she was remembering what had once happened after Nelson had been transferred from his church in Prendergast to another in the vicinity of Buffalo. At the time, her family had resided at the parsonage at 12 West Seventh Street. After she arrived home from college one summer, she had been completely taken aback when a young woman opened the door to what she assumed was still her home. "May I help you?"

After Priscilla introduced herself, the young woman explained that her own father was the new pastor and had settled his family in the parsonage. Priscilla's family had moved next door to the lower level of their apartment building at 14 West Seventh Street until their home, a few doors down the street, was made ready for them.

After that surprise, Priscilla had found her mother next door. Liza had apologized for not informing her about the move. "It all happened so fast," she said. In their church, departing families are customarily given at least thirty days for the transition from one home to another. "We had to move in less than a week," Liza had said.

Then Liza explained why the church had been in such a rush to prepare the parsonage for the new pastor and his daughter. He was an elderly widower, and his daughter was his principal caregiver. Their situation was so desperate they had required immediate housing.

At the time, Priscilla had been disturbed that the church had laid out the red carpet for the new pastor while simultaneously casting aside her family. For once, Priscilla and Liza had agreed. "It's amazing how treacherous church folks can be," Liza had said, "But at least now we have our own home."

Priscilla, still trying to look busy in her office cubicle, considered how some of the same people for whom she had worked so hard seemed so eager to push her aside for a chance to get in a word edgewise with Republicans like Mimi, Bill and—of course—Senator Caldiera. She smiled a very little smile. *To think that some folks say, "There's nothing like church politics."*

Priscilla could not help taking such drastic changes personally, as a kind of public debasement. And she was aware, with her father's health as it was, that these feelings about work could not have come at a worse time. She did not care if cynical old politicos thought she was naïve or that she needed seasoning to acquire the aptitude and resilience necessary to withstand the "downs" of the political game. *Enough is enough!*

Priscilla stood and grabbed her handbag. *Mary's, here I come.*

Mary's Café, the Statehouse hangout located in the upper level of the underground parking garage, was named after a real person. Short and stout, Mary was everyone's friend. She sold plates of food, replenished coffee, made change and called all her customers by name. She could also unerringly discern the mood and tempo at the Statehouse. Intently peering through her smudged, thick-lens glasses into the face of her customer who stood at the counter, she said, "The usual, Miss Priscilla?"

Priscilla smiled. "The usual, Mary."

"The usual" was a cup of "rotgut," as Mary's coffee was called. If customers preferred gourmet blends, they went elsewhere. Still standing at the counter, Priscilla killed the taste with large portions of cream and sugar, the real deal, not those pink and blue packets of fake powdery stuff. "Anything interesting happening with you these days, Mary?"

"Nah, but I'd be interested knowing what you think about that new young fella in Senator Caldiera's office. You know, sweetie, he's an awfully good-looking young man." Mary shared a conspiratorial smile. "You got a boyfriend, Priscilla?"

Startled, Priscilla almost spilled her coffee. Bill was a Republican, and white. But she soon regained her composure. "You know I'm married to my work."

"Funny thing," Mary answered, "but that's exactly what Bill told me when I asked him if he'd met *you*." Then Mary laughed. By now, everybody knew what fun it could be to tease an easy target like Priscilla. Mary had meant no harm. Everyone needed a good laugh.

Priscilla ignored Mary's laughter and took her seat at a nearby table. Seated alone, she drank her "rotgut," and smoked her long, brown, slender cigarette. She skimmed the *Chronicle*, whose editorials were unabashedly pro-Republican. The editors at the *Chronicle* had endorsed Reagan for president and virtually every Republican and conservative Democrat in the 1980 elections throughout Franklin County. Now they wholeheartedly welcomed the new Republican leadership in the Ohio Senate. The only reason Priscilla read today's editorials was to stay abreast of the thinking of the Senate's conservative members.

Then, suddenly, Bill Scott confidently joined her, as if they had agreed to rendezvous.

Well, I'll be damned, Priscilla said to herself. *Does Mary know something I don't? Nah, its sheer coincidence he's here at this time. It's Inauguration Day, work's light and he's bored with all the hoopla. That's all. Don't get needlessly paranoid. Then again, if he weren't so good-looking and smart, I could deal with him.* As she continued talking to herself, her cheeks flushed. *Okay, Priscilla, calm down.*

Bill pulled up a chair and sat down across from Priscilla with the assurance of a husband at the dinner table.

Yet she hoped that their superficial indifference toward each other would be obvious to observers. She assured herself that their conversations with each other were about as interesting as the weather forecast. Yet she knew very well that staff from opposing sides did not discuss business, and fraternization was strictly prohibited. Recently

two staffers—one apiece from each political party's caucus—had been
fired for dating. Priscilla tried to step back and analyze the truth of the
situation. Not just she and Bill but Mimi, too, had not been following
those proscriptions to the letter. All three were virtual workaholics,
reclusive and not the kind of extroverted social favorites who were
popular with the other staff. Gradually, they had developed informal
ties with one another. And there was something else. All three of them
were aides to Senator Callahan and Senator Caldiera, who represented
contiguous senatorial districts. It was only natural that shared constituent interests would bring them together. Still, she understood that this
casual encounter over coffee with Bill would reap more than its share of
speculation on the part of others. The word would go out, and perhaps
it would be unkindly chewed over by others who would be seeking
ulterior motives. Priscilla and Bill had been seen together in Mary's.

After they had their caffeine-and-nicotine fix, Priscilla and Bill rode
the elevator back up to the second floor with the rest of the crowd.
When they got off, they looked at each other and reached a mutual
decision, without speaking about it, not to return to their offices.
Instead, they walked down the corridor and through the massive chamber doors onto the Senate floor, as if they were two distinguished Senate
colleagues.

Upon entering the chamber, Bill turned and headed left, and
Priscilla turned and headed right, toward the section where the
Democratic staffers were seated. She sat down on the staff bench and
considered the extent of the Republican electoral victory: Reagan's
coattails had fanned far and wide. *Man alive, did we lose big time! And
now we've got to sit here and carry on as if all is well.*

As Priscilla pondered the paradox, Sharon interrupted her thoughts.
"You are aware, aren't you, Priscilla, of the caucus's strict rule against
fraternizing with the other side?"

Priscilla collected her thoughts before answering. What she would
have liked to say was that apparently her office mate did not have
enough real work on which to concentrate. But she swallowed that
angry response, and instead marveled that word of her innocent coffee
with Bill had apparently already made the rounds of the Senate staff.

193

Eventually she said, "If you're suggesting I should have *no* contact with the staff in the Republican leadership, allow me to say how ludicrous that is. What's wrong with having a cup of coffee and discussing the weather and headlines with the number one aide to the chairman of the Senate Finance Committee?"

Having silenced Sharon, Priscilla looked around the Senate floor and realized one reason she had apparently breached that "fraternization" code was her isolation. She reflected that there were now no women; and, Senator Callahan and Senator Madison were the only black men. One casualty of the last election had been Angelica Marioneaux, a Catholic Democratic attorney who had been the only female member of that body. To Priscilla's mind, the loss of her seat could have been avoided, but the Senate Democratic leadership had grossly miscalculated how much support she needed to win and had even blamed her later for not fighting hard enough for herself. She had first won her seat in the historic "Class of 1966," along with the first notable group of black-elected officials since Reconstruction. Traditionally in Ohio, whenever there were civil rights gains by blacks, there were even more white women elected such as Senator Marioneaux.

Priscilla let the reality sink in that now there was not a single woman in the Ohio Senate. Another classic liberal—Joel Markham, who was Jewish—had lost his seat from the greater Columbus metropolitan area to a young conservative Republican who had accused him of being too liberal for his district. Priscilla had heard that the victor's ultimate goal was to get elected to Congress, and she did not doubt that he had a good chance to do just that.

Priscilla reflected that a third sitting Democratic senator—a relatively nondescript one-term senator from Lima—had also lost his seat. But the irony was that although he had not been expected to win, the Democratic leadership had poured a disproportionate share of its limited resources into the senator's campaign.

Priscilla mused that it was one thing to lose a seat or two, but the Democrats lost three and did not gain any new ones. She did not think the current Democratic leadership had done themselves any favors, or even acted wisely during the campaign. She wondered if the outcome would have been different if Senator Marcus Tektonidis, or "Marcus the Greek," had been in charge of the Senate Democrats.

At the podium, the transfer of party control from the Democrats to the Republicans was happening.

"Raymon Ferrari," outgoing-Senate President Walt O'Leary said, "I'm pleased to present you with this presidential gavel, signifying leadership of this august body." He handed the gavel to Senator Ferrari, who hoisted the heavy gavel high in the air. It was January 1981, and the Republicans were officially in control of the Ohio Senate.

Priscilla watched the exchange of power in silence. O'Leary, she was sure, would receive his reckoning for the devastating defeat of the Democrats in the 1980 elections. She knew plans were already being formed for how to retake the Senate. Election Day 1982 was expected to yield unmistakable reprisals.

CHAPTER 21

Priscilla's Rite of Passage

Senator Tektonidis strutted through the reception area and filled the threshold to Senator Callahan's office. "Hey Daniel, we're headed over to Chelsie's for dinner," he said. "Aren't you coming? Remember, we've agreed to put forth our best face in public. Tonight, we're going to be as exuberant as the Republicans."

Since he already knew about the caucus's plans for dinner, Senator Callahan nodded and asked Priscilla to join him and the others. "Besides, you look like you could use some cheering up."

Priscilla nodded and grabbed her purse. He was right.

Chelsie's was an elegant upscale restaurant located directly across from the Statehouse on the second floor of the Galleria. The restaurant faced the capitol's east side.

Still revved up from the events of the day, the Republicans had started celebrating early. They sat around a huge table set for twenty people.

As Senator Callahan and Priscilla entered the dining area, guests unaffiliated with the Statehouse just stared at the couple, whereas the large table of boisterous Republicans greeted them loudly.

"Come right on in, Daniel, Priscilla. Join in the festivities," hollered Senator Caldiera, along with a few other Republican senators. Their goodwill sounded genuine.

On the other side of the dining area, the Democrats had their own big table setting. But Priscilla was not surprised that Senator O'Leary and Senator Madison were absent. Then she came to an abrupt halt and turned around. "Where're my manners? Congratulations to each and every one of you," she said to the Republican gathering.

Bill smiled and waved back at her. Senator Ferrari and Senator Caldiera also expressed appreciation for her courtesy.

But Senator Callahan grabbed his aide by her arm and ushered her away from the Republicans' table. "Let's not overdo it, young lady."

As Priscilla and the senator made their way across the room, more greetings followed from several lobbyists, who all seemed to be in upbeat moods.

"Evening, Senator," said one lobbyist after the other.

"Senator, Priscilla," another lobbyist said as the couple brushed against his table.

"Evening, folks," Priscilla answered. She was in her element and she delighted in it. "Gee, Senator," she whispered to her boss, "I thought the point of the evening was to show 'camaraderie.'"

As the two of them took their seats at the Democratic table, Senator Tektonidis said, "Believe it or not, Daniel, we're actually enjoying ourselves."

"That's good to hear," Senator Callahan said.

Then Chelsie himself, the restaurant's proprietor, appeared with all the charm and grace of a head servant in the Queen's court. There was a professional rhythm in the way he bent down, assisted Priscilla with her seat and placed a napkin across her lap. Then he stood upright again, officially welcomed the couple and shared a few comments with the senator. For his finale, Chelsie turned his attention back to Priscilla: "*Bon appetite, Mademoiselle.*" Then he walked away to greet his other guests.

Before Priscilla could fully appreciate Chelsie's attention, a mannequin-like figure materialized to the left of Senator Callahan. The waiter made an abbreviated bow, and as his eyes met those of the senator, he asked, "Your drink order, Senator?"

"I'll have a Remy Martin up and a cup of hot tea with honey," Senator Callahan said. "Priscilla, what'll *you* have?"

Ignoring the senator's intrusion into his role, the waiter peered directly into Priscilla's eyes and asked, "And what may I bring Mademoiselle?"

"A glass of pale dry white wine," a nonchalant Priscilla said, as she looked around the table and pulled her chair up more closely.

Senator Tektonidis persisted: "You can do better than that, Priscilla. Order a real drink. Take a few moments off from being serious and join in on the fun with the rest of the team. We don't get many occasions like this one. If you could have your favorite drink, what would it be?"

This was not the kind of attention Priscilla wanted. Yet she tried to be gracious. "Thank you for asking me, Senator. I prefer gin and tonic."

A few of the others muttered, "Now that's more like it."

"Now she's a real team player," someone else said.

Senator Tektonidis echoed the sentiments of his colleagues: "She certainly is." Then he raised his glass and made a toast. "This evening we relax and let down our hair a bit."

"Hear, hear!" yelled the others.

Senator Tektonidis instructed the waiter: "Bring our lady friend a gin and tonic. Any particular brand, Priscilla?"

Instinctively, Priscilla suspected she had been set up, although she was not sure for what. *Now,* she thought, *when is the other damn shoe going to drop off of my frigging foot?* But she played along. "I prefer Tanqueray and tonic, with a twist of lime." Then, as she casually scanned the room, she noticed several lobbyists gesturing toward the Democrats' table.

Brad, Senator Tektonidis' aide, got involved. He nodded toward the lobbyists. "Those guys are offering to pick up our tab. Ignore them, Priscilla. Our tab's already taken care of."

Priscilla was familiar with the practice of lobbyists paying for meals and drinks for lawmakers, but she also knew that Senator Callahan did not generally go in for that.

That evening, however, was an exception. For once, Callahan *did* allow a lobbyist to "pick up the tab." And it turned out that Senator Tektonidis had been right about the occasion. At no point did anyone at the table discuss caucus business. The senators talked mostly about their personal situations, sports and other incidentals. The Senate Democratic caucus members had needed relaxation and release, and they got it.

When they headed back to the Statehouse, Senator Tektonidis, Senator Chouinard, Senator Callahan and several other senators ventured into a vacant room for a private discussion.

Priscilla, suddenly alone with Brad, walked with him through the upper level of the underground. They paused near Mary's Café, which was closed and dark.

"You know, Priscilla," Brad said, "the rules of the game for legislative staff are different from other state government workers."

Until then, Priscilla had not been paying much attention to Brad. But now, looking around the dim underground, she raised her eyebrows. "And you're going *where* with this conversation?"

Brad gloried in the moment. He had not intended to be graceful, and he was not. "Some of us think you need a different attitude, Priscilla."

But she was Priscilla J. Austin, and she would not be intimidated. "What's brought on this little tête-à-tête?" She resisted her impulse to move slightly away from him. She was her father's daughter. She would stand her ground.

"There you go again." Brad's scolding tone was contemptuous. "'Tête-à-tête?' Who the hell talks like that? You need to speak the language of the Democratic caucus—the downtrodden, folks who struggle." His eyes were narrow slits. "You don't even come off like a black person, and I'm not talking stereotype either."

"Man alive!" Priscilla said. "This really is the joke of the day. *You* have the nerve to talk to *me* about *my* so-called attitude?"

Priscilla was acutely aware how alone they were, and how eerie it seemed, after dark in the deserted parking lot. She felt short of breath and sensed the walls and ceiling closing in on her.

But her opponent continued his verbal assault: "You just don't get it, do you Priscilla? You're so aloof, even bourgeois. You have no ties to ordinary folks—blacks, or anybody else. With that kind of attitude, Daniel is always having to clean up after you back in his home district."

"Senator Callahan has never had any difficulty talking to me before," she answered. "So why have *you* been sent on this particular mission?" When Brad did not respond, she continued. "I think this is more a case of your ignorance about the political pedigree of certain black folks. I'm guessing that you're the one who doesn't know what to do with your own black constituents." Remembering the elephant in the room—the Democrats' recent loss to the Republicans, she said: "Small wonder you guys lost so many black voters to the Reagan camp. You Senate Democrats lumped all us black folks together. But you, my friend, will never hold onto your base with that kind of strategy. Come to think of it, I can't believe Senator Callahan plays with such a dim-witted lot."

Brad did not respond, although a small smile did play at the corner of his lips. Maybe he had, as she said, blown the part about race. But he took great pleasure in having provoked her. He had been told by several other Senate and House staffers, who wanted to discover what made Priscilla tick, to "get her reaction to being black." He had done as he had been told. But now he took another tack. "You know, you really blew us away with that floor speech on the Set-Aside Bill. *Everybody* knew that you wrote the damn thing." Then he leapfrogged to his main point: "Our caucus has come up with a strategy to retake the Senate in two years. But we'll need *you* to do *your* part."

Priscilla tensed. *What's he going on about? None of this foolishness makes any sense.* Surreptitiously she kept looking for the others to join them. To steady her resolve, she clenched her moist fists.

Brad began to steamroll her. "We need you to work with us in Cincinnati, Cleveland, Toledo and Youngstown. And I'm not talking about upscale supper clubs and art galleries. Do you hear me, Ms. Prissy?"

Under her heavy wool coat, Priscilla felt drenched with sweat. "Are *you* hearing *me*?" Her voice raised several decibels. "The future of the Democratic Party is not solely in shoring up the working class, which is already in the Reagan camp. You suckers have got to cultivate the *new* wing of the middle class. When are you going to get it in your thick skulls that the new wing, including us blacks and, oh yeah, baby boomers, too, are all looking to align with something more meaning-ful?" She nodded with brisk finality. "And listen to me, Brad. I don't much care hanging out in this dreary place." She took a step toward the elevator. "Unless we're done with this little chat, let's finish it upstairs."

But Brad had wanted to catch her off her guard and had inten-tionally chosen both the occasion and setting. "Sorry, Prissy, but we don't need to campaign for support of the black middle class." His voice hardened as he seized the opportunity to drive his words into her chest cavity. Like wooden splinters, his words drove through her rib cage as though in search of her very soul. Each merciless word he spoke drilled painful incisions. "Right now, we need to rally the troops among ordinary workers. And we want you to help us to do that."

Priscilla thought, *How can he chastise me and ask for my help at the same time?* Her voice was incredulous. "You try to beat me down, and then you tell me that I possess the wherewithal to get myself out of this fix, but only 'if *I* help you.'"

Brad went for the kill, declaring why he, and so many other staffers, disapproved of her.

"You know, Ms. Prissy, when you first arrived last summer, some of us had mild heart attacks. You came on the scene like you preferred to be anywhere but here. Like you were doing somebody a favor and the Ohio Senate was merely means to some personal endgame. When we asked Daniel why you were here, all he could say was something about you needing a job. But that didn't wash, because you already had a job teaching at that college in Florida."

Priscilla stood silent, mouth half-open. She felt thoroughly confounded.

Brad shrugged his shoulders and continued his assault. "And so, under the circumstances, *young lady*, we have no choice but to tell you how it is. You have to become one of us, or at least pretend to be. Bottom line: We need to know we can count on *you*, Priscilla. Can we count on your help to regain the Senate in the Eighty-two elections?"

"Whoa, Bubba, so *that's* the point of this little chat? First, you kill me off. Then you pretend to resuscitate my remains." Priscilla was nearly beside herself. "Why on earth would I help any of you bastards? Do you take me for a *complete* fool?"

Brad had dreamed of this moment. To prepare, he had rehearsed his lines and considered virtually all of her possible counterarguments. He returned to his main message: "I'll give you this, Priscilla. You've done a lot to make Daniel look better than he's ever looked. But right now we need your help on behalf of the *team*. Daniel and you are part of a *team*. You're not stand-alones."

Priscilla's head throbbed. She felt blood rushing to the top of her ears. Briefly, she felt dizzy—the "benign positional vertigo" that she was told she was destined to suffer after her traffic accident in Florida. Then she felt waves of anger reverberating throughout her body.

"And yeah, Pris-cil-la, you are the most *Up-pa-dee* ... My God, are you uppity." Brad let out an exasperated sigh.

Priscilla's eyes flashed with contempt. But she knew the political realities behind what had just happened with Brad. He was the top aide to Senator Tektonidis, who was a member of the minority leadership and the aspiring leader of the caucus. Since Priscilla's boss was not in the leadership, she was supposed to yield to Brad and not make a habit of operating on her own. Since she evidently had missed an important lesson of how things *were,* Brad, as a senior member of the Democratic caucus staff, had been given the honors of reeling her in.

Priscilla wiped her moist hands on her coat. "If you wanted my help, all you had to do was ask. But no, you had to try to degrade me first. You'll live to regret having played that hand with me. Yes Sirree Bob, prepare to pay handsomely for that!"

Brad gave her a brief, mocking smile before he made a stab at inflicting more personal injury on his prey. "I, too, have a warning for you, Prissy. Stay clear of your Republican friends. No more hanging out with that Mimi and even shopping together over in the Galleria. And no more sitting with Bill all cozy-like in Mary's, not to mention your little strut together onto the Senate floor today. Watch it, kiddo! Besides, what on earth can you possibly have to talk about with that chump?"

Priscilla was on the brink of tears but blinked them away. She was not going to cry. "What the devil brought on all *this*? What have I ever done to cause you to launch such a personal attack? Surely you don't think that *I* want *your* job?" But suddenly she remembered hearing that Brad had connections with some unsavory types. His boss represented Youngstown, an economically depressed district with rampant unemployment and where major industry had either shut down or relocated abroad. Organized crime thrived there. The congressman from the area was a notorious hustler and would later serve a prison sentence. Was the key to the ferocity of his attack simply that he was so insecure? Did he resent her confidence? Could it be that he had it in for her because she had never showed much interest in him? She was Priscilla J. Austin, and as usual she had behaved as if she could make it on her own.

Priscilla took a deep breath. "Brad, my man, thank you. Thank you so much, dear fella. Is there anything else? You've already killed me off. Now, go right ahead and toss the rest of your dirt. Or is the point to display my bleeding corpse for all to see?"

By then, even Brad knew that he had done more damage than he had set out to do. "Ah, come on, Missy, what I'm trying to get you to understand is that we need for you to work with the caucus now more than ever. All I'm saying is that you need to start doing what it takes for 'the team' to win."

Brad slapped Priscilla's shoulder and forced a smile. Then he headed toward the elevator and pushed the button. He had done what he had been commissioned to do, though he might have taken too much liberty in doing so. Callahan's uppity aide had been rattled, and her body still shook from their rendezvous in the dark underground garage.

Priscilla endured the elevator ride with her enemy. His little tête-à-tête had been equivalent to a rite of passage for her. Brad had been the clear winner of this round, but the fight was not over. Doubtless he would be rewarded with more respect from his peers and perhaps even a perk or two from the caucus for having taken Ms. Prissy down a peg or two. All the aides would be watching in the next day or so to see how or whether Priscilla would be able to ascend from the abyss.

That night, Priscilla went home alone and brooded.

The nerve of that scum-ball talking to me like that, she thought. *He even implied he had the senator's blessing. Well, I'll fix him. I'll fix the lot of 'em. Things must be really bad to bring that kind of pressure on a pawn like me. But just how damn bad is our situation anyway?*

She was determined to contrive ways to get back at them, "the whole damn lot of 'em."

That decision made, she fell asleep.

Vengeance did not come quickly or easily.

Instead, what came first for Priscilla and indeed for the rest of the staff and their legislators was hard work, perpetual jockeying for position and much ado, always, about money.

She had to live with the fact that her nemesis was far more powerful than she was. Brad had earned his newly appointed, and highly visible, post to assist Senator Callahan and the other Democratic senators on the Finance Committee. In that post, he wielded a huge influence on the Finance Committee—not only because he considered himself an expert in finance but also because he knew the interests of the individual caucus members.

Yet Priscilla took secret delight that Brad was always outranked and outshone by his Republican counterpart Bill Scott, whose mastery of finance was far above Brad's. She reflected, too, that Brad had been right about one thing that night he had verbally assaulted her in the parking lot: Brad had assessed Priscilla's presence in the Senate correctly. She did indeed have some "personal endgame," but she did not seek publicity or recognition for her work from anyone other than Senator Callahan. So Brad's new role meant very little to her.

As it turned out, Senator Callahan had given Priscilla the opportunity to demonstrate her own expertise, which was the power of persuasion. What she set about doing that winter was conducting a public relations campaign on the home front concerning the actions of the Senate Finance Committee. She issued press release after press release criticizing Republicans for their "lack of compassion for the least of us." One press release emphasized "the debilitating effects of the proposed excise taxes on poor people," particularly those levied on cigarettes and alcohol products. She scripted her press releases from actual statements used by the Democratic committee members, and she quoted them verbatim: "This is a travesty of justice," or, "This is an outrage," or, "This amendment to raise taxes disproportionately on the poor and the working class is unconscionable." Much as her father had once predicted, Priscilla's natural skills at persuasion surfaced.

One day in early April, Leland Stanton sent over a package from the LBO to Senator Caldiera, chair of the Senate Finance Committee. But the package was mistakenly delivered to Senator Callahan's office.

When Priscilla opened the package, she discovered a set of amendments typed on sheets of paper. She kept them on her desk until Senator Callahan returned, and then she showed him their unexpected gift.

As he leafed through the sheets, Priscilla said, "You know, Senator, we *could* have Leland draft a corresponding set of amendments for our side. What a jolt that would give them." Then she was inspired to make a record of her chance discovery and her proposed course of action, and she took note of the unexpected gift in her log.

Instead, Senator Callahan instructed Priscilla: "Take the damn package to Brad. He knows the drill."

So Priscilla—hiding a smile—did exactly as her senator had instructed. "All things," she said to herself, "come to those who wait." She knew Brad, and she was beginning to know the Ohio Senate, too. *Gotcha, Brad!*

CHAPTER 22

Going the Way of All the Earth

"And now I am about to go the way of all the earth."

— Joshua 23:14 NRSV

Around mid-April, Priscilla was once again happy to go home. During her previous visits, she had seen Nelson up and about. Maybe sometimes he had seemed a little weak, but at least he had looked like himself, especially when he was seated in his favorite recliner.

But this time, when she arrived at the Austin home in Prendergast, she was woefully unprepared for her father's deteriorated condition. Priscilla had little personal experience with terminal illnesses, and she was disturbed to see Nelson experiencing bouts of severe pain and that his weight was considerably reduced. But Nelson still possessed his mental faculties, and he was able to walk a little.

On her first day back home since a brief visit in February, Priscilla also observed that Nelson sat mostly in his big, moss-green upholstered recliner near the fireplace.

It was from there that he called her. "Come and sit with me a while, Priscilla."

She had been busy helping Liza with errands—mostly, busy for the sake of being busy. So she was relieved when she pulled over that old ottoman from across the fireplace and sat on it, pitifully knee-high to her father.

Moments later, she caught herself in a reverie, realizing that Nelson had been telling her how much he and Liza loved her and the other children. She fought back the mounting tears as she noticed the faded color in her father's face and the diminished depth in his voice. *He's not leaving me*, she assured herself. But she knew her father was dying. How she yearned for it not to be true!

Nelson's eyes glistened, and a wide grin spread across his face. "I've been fortunate to marry your mom and raise you girls and watch you all grow into fine young women. I've been fortunate to travel to places I never imagined possible." Nelson recited a litany of other blessings.

Then he said, "You know, Priscilla, we want what's best for each of you. You do know that, don't you, child?"

As Nelson paused to catch his breath, Priscilla reacted in her usual brisk way. "All right, now, where're we going with all this?"

Knowing his daughter as only he could know her, Nelson continued, "But there's one concern we both have with you, Priscilla."

"Priscilla, Priscilla, Priscilla," was all that she had been able to hear. "Please, stop calling my name! I just hate that. Just say whatever it is you have to say." Then, before she could restrain herself, her voice became a wail. "What on earth have I gone and done this time?" It was always easy for her to behave like an adolescent in her father's presence.

Nelson dismissed her annoyance and painstakingly corrected her. "It's not what you've done, child, but what your mother and I believe you haven't done. We believe you've spent the greater part of your life living for us, trying to satisfy and please us, not you."

After a long silence, Nelson leaned forward, close to tears, and peered down at her. "What would please the both of us would be for Priscilla to start living her life to please Priscilla, not us. And for heaven's sake, be happy, child. Do you think you can handle that?"

His tears pooled in his eyes. "You know something else, Priscilla? One of my most sincere wishes is for you to find someone you really care for and love. Yet for some reason I feel I should tell you that not everybody is meant to marry. So please don't take a husband just because you think that's what your mom and I want for you. That part of your life belongs to you and only you. Try to be happy for *you*, Priscilla."

He let out a long sigh as he released his long-held burden. He had been planning to say this for a long time. Those words were the most intimate he had ever said to his beloved Priscilla, and those words were about as far as even he knew he could have gone. He had known he had to say what he had said gently, and at the right time. He was satisfied that he had been gentle, and that this had been the right time.

A bewildered Priscilla stared straight into her father's eyes. "I'm not sure I understand. All these years, I thought I was supposed to do what you and Momma wanted."

Nelson did not respond. For all her intelligence, his daughter was incredibly immature and had not yet taken complete charge of her life.

Now, Priscilla asked herself, *what will I do?* She had always managed to do almost everything her parents had ever asked of her. But this request of her father was so different from all his previous requests. This time Nelson wanted Priscilla to make her own decisions.

"And for heaven's sake," Nelson was repeating, "be happy, child. It would please the both of us for you to start living to please yourself."

If Nelson said anything else, Priscilla did not hear him. There she sat, twenty-eight years of age, released by her father from some presumed state of obligation, one that was all she had ever known.

One question kept running through her mind: *Now what'll I do?*

Nelson's voice changed, as he sharply caught her attention. "All right, now, Priscilla. Is there anything you want to know about me, anything at all? Ask me, please. *Now!*"

Priscilla said, hastily, "I can't think of a single thing that I want to know about you, Daddy. Not a single —"

Nelson cut in. "I know there's something. I can see it on your face. What is it, Priscilla? What's on your mind?"

She nodded. She never could hide a thing from her Daddy. "Well, this might seem a little strange, but I've often wondered why it's so hard for me to settle on a boyfriend. You know, I mean, why can't I get all excited and even passionate like other women get over their men? It's as if I'm missing some genes or something."

Nelson was not surprised at her forthrightness. "Surely you know people who've never married? And there's nothing the matter with them either. Your cousin in Canton. Mr. Sonyer, who lives across from the Washingtons. And there are others."

"Yeah, yeah, I know."

"What I'm saying is this: if you marry against your will or out of forced circumstance like a pregnancy, it's highly unlikely the relationship will work. Or, if you consider marriage because the menacing women in the church, relatives or girlfriends push you, shrug them off. This is your life, Priscilla. Do with it as *you* please, not *others*. Now, if you can see yourself with someone long-term, fine, go for it. But only if that's what *you* want."

But Priscilla had already taken to heart the unfortunate marriages of her sisters and Nelson, Jr., not to mention that both Nelson and Liza had themselves suffered unsuccessful first marriages. Besides, she had also already determined there was no such thing as a perfect or good marriage. So the last thing she had ever really wanted was a serious relationship. Still, she had sometimes wondered why Liza had never discussed the subject with her. Priscilla hid a sigh. Regardless, she knew her Daddy. Nelson had said as much as he ever intended to say on the matter.

"Now, Priscilla, there's one more thing I need for you to do."

"Gee-whiz, Daddy, I thought special requests came in ones and threes. Then again, since you ask such big favors, I suppose you're allowed to package yours in twos."

Her father smiled, mostly because he had been relieved to change the troubling subject of marriage. "Look after your mom, Priscilla. Until I married her, Liza hadn't been anywhere nor had she done much of anything. That first marriage of hers hadn't amounted to much. I rescued Liza from Grandma Lilly's front porch. She was a virtual innocent. As you know, I handled everything, even writing the checks and paying the bills." Though what he said was true, Liza always resented hearing it. But Liza was not in their conversation; Nelson spoke directly to Priscilla, reminding her how he and Liza had "raised you girls different from the way she was raised."

At that point, he spoke with immense pride. "But I'm not worried about you taking care of yourself, Priscilla. You've always known how to get up and go after what you want. But your mom is different. Liza doesn't possess those capabilities. Look after your mom, Priscilla." That was Nelson's final request of Priscilla.

It would take some time for Priscilla to fully comprehend that Nelson had not only been asking her to "look after Liza" in the literal sense. Rather, she would come to understand that what he had been alluding to was for her to develop the same admiration and respect for her mother that she had always held for him. Just as it was common knowledge among the Austins and their friends and neighbors that the good Reverend had favored Priscilla over the other children, everyone had also known that Priscilla had favored her father substantially more than her mom.

It was, actually, two months earlier, during a brief visit back to Prendergast, that Priscilla had begun to form a better and deeper relationship with her mother. The occasion was a speech Priscilla had made for the Missionary Society's annual tea entitled, "My Mom, My Sweet Inspiration."

After her speech, the church folks were pleasantly surprised: in fact, her friend Amber's mother told Priscilla afterwards how deeply moved she had been by the speech. She had even bestowed a compliment: "How far you've come, child. I only wish Amber spoke as highly of me as you do of Liza."

But Liza herself was the most surprised of all the church folks. Until her speech, Priscilla had never told her mother that she loved her. Yet she had stood there in front of the Missionary Society and the other guests in the church and credited her mom with pretty much all that she had achieved.

But she did not say that it was Nelson who had asked her to make the speech in the first place. Though he had not told her *what* to say, he did say, "It's high time that you displayed some public sentiment for your mom."

Nelson was standing on the threshold between the kitchen and the dining room, watching Priscilla get her things together for the ride back to Columbus. He uttered dreadful, foreboding words: "You know, Priscilla, I'm probably not going to be here when you come back." Plainly at peace with himself, James Nelson Austin also wanted his daughter to know how much he loved Liza. "But I do hope to be around long enough to see Liza's next birthday." Liza's birthday was May 15th.

Then he casually added, "I can't promise you anything but I certainly hope to be here."

On the morning after Chautauqua County had been almost buried under another heavy snowfall, Priscilla drove out of Prendergast, traveling along New York Highway 394. As she drove along the narrow meandering road, her throat tightened every time her father's words came into her mind. She pushed away those words of love and finality. She willed herself to think about the road, the beautiful snow—anything but those ominous words of farewell.

She wondered: *Is it crazy to hope for a miracle, that all this has simply been a nightmare? There's no way on earth for me to go on without Daddy. I'll just stop thinking about him.*

Suddenly, she found herself and her car stuck in a ditch. Had she momentarily dozed off or lost control of the car? She could not allow herself even to think the obvious, that she had been frozen by thoughts of her father dying. She realized that she had forgotten to put the chains on the tires. But she assured herself that since there were no visible signs of other traffic, there was also no reason to panic.

She looked out the car window at the ditch. It was deep and filled with snow. *How the devil am I going to get out of this?* Calmly Priscilla prayed, "Oh, God, get me out of this ditch," and she did not mean just the ditch in which she sat in her car. The next thing she knew, she stopped fumbling with the steering wheel, took her foot off the brake pedal and then the car rolled back up onto the highway.

She patted the dashboard and said aloud, "Well, now, Lord, this will be another of our little secrets." She drove off as if nothing out of the ordinary had happened.

Once on Interstate 90 headed west, she noticed that the bulk of the snow had been cleared. Her thoughts brightened with the ever-present glow of the sun overhead. *Looks like smooth sailing from here.*

But soon she witnessed the strangest scene. The car of a female motorist in one of the oncoming lanes on the other side of the interstate began to weave back and forth. The woman pulled her car onto the right shoulder and then slumped over the steering wheel and, from what Priscilla could see, seemed to be weeping uncontrollably.

Priscilla steered her car into the far left lane and found a break in the median labeled, "For Emergency Vehicles Only." She steered into it and when there was no traffic, she crossed over and parked behind the weeping woman's car. She ran to the driver's side and beckoned for the woman to roll down her window.

The woman blurted out: "I don't have the slightest idea what's come over me. I was just thinking about all the lives I've disrupted and the mess I've made. What I did was wrong. I know that, but I've moved on, alone. I'm not with him anymore!"

Priscilla welcomed the opportunity to console the woman. *What the heck, nobody can help me. But I can be pretty good at this sort of thing.* She later forgot the words she spoke to the woman, but she did not forget how the woman's face lifted at her words.

The woman said, "I'm so relieved after what I did that anybody even cares about me. I only needed to know that somebody cares about me. That's all." She wiped away her tears.

Priscilla asked, "Are you sure you're well enough to drive? Do you want me to stay with you awhile?"

But the woman insisted she was all right. "I needed only to know that somebody cares."

How interesting, Priscilla thought. She watched the woman drive away and then returned to her own car. *Now I know what I'll do. I'll be nice to others and just pretend my own situation will resolve itself, just disappear.* Priscilla understood that the operative term in her vow was "nice." She was well aware that her personality was not "nice." She wondered if this vow might lead to a major transformation in her life. Or would it just give her another wall to hide behind and avoid her feelings? *Nice,* Priscilla thought. *Could I, would I, ever be nice?*

CHAPTER 23

The Republican's What-if-Package

Back at work in Columbus, Priscilla threw herself into the business of the Senate Finance Committee. For once, she enjoyed this submersion in numbers and money. Anything to divert her from her inability to cope with her father's impending death, or from her inability to cope with the recent news about the death of her high school sweetheart Tyler. *Can things get any worse?*

Although she said nothing to anyone at work—not even Senator Callahan—about Nelson's condition or about Tyler's death, she did confide in her friend Julia, a medical student who had befriended her shortly after she had resettled in Columbus and with whom she had grown comfortable and shared at least some details about her private life. Priscilla was careful, however, not to tell Julia everything, such as the times during the next month when her mother would telephone with dire updates on Nelson's continuing decline.

In days, if not hours, after she returned to work, Priscilla forgot her interstate vow to be nice. It took all her energy to keep going, work harder and stifle her feelings that her world was crumbling because her father was dying and because Tyler had been murdered. Until now, Priscilla had not personally known anyone who had been murdered. Most of the people whom she knew of who had died, had had heart attacks, had died from alcoholism or of old age. And she knew of only one relative who had died from a tumor, an elderly distant cousin in Canton. In fact, as far as Priscilla could recall, the word "cancer" or "terminal illness" was relatively new to her. So her father's illness was her first experience of someone dying from a terminal illness. Was her near perfect, serene and sheltered life coming apart? Or was it that reality was finally settling in? Perhaps Liza and her siblings were onto something after all, because they had always criticized Priscilla for viewing life through rose-colored lenses.

Further compounding her seemingly unbearable situation, her first day back she noticed that tensions between the Democrats and the Republicans in the Ohio Senate had escalated to a war footing. And sometimes Democrats fought other Democrats and Republicans fought other Republicans more fiercely than the two political parties fought each other. Even so, there she was in the trenches with the rest of them. *Not here, too*, she said to herself. *Is there anything good happening anywhere?* Plainly Priscilla was unaccustomed to conflict, hardship and seemingly unbearable circumstances, but not for long.

During one Finance Committee hearing, Priscilla watched as Senator Callahan became such an unhappy camper—and a furious one at that—that he snarled, "Why is it that every time I submit an amendment, the other side votes it down *without* discussion, and then offers another one with just the opposite effect as mine?"

In response to Senator Callahan's fury, Committee Chairman Caldiera looked straight out into the huge committee room and said, smiling, "Well, you see, Daniel, that's why we pay our aide the big bucks." His smile widened as he nodded at Bill Scott. "He's ready for you. He even has amendments to anticipate any what-if moves."

Senator Callahan beckoned Priscilla to come closer. Underneath his breath, he asked her, "Where's that package of amendments that Leland sent over?"

First she simply stared at the senator. Then she faintly smiled, thinking he wanted to make the Republican committee members think his side had something significant to offer. In a tactful whisper, she reminded him that he had told her to give the package to Brad and that Brad was supposed to take it to the other Democrats in the caucus. "Senator," she said, "surely you remember saying, 'Brad knows the drill.' I did as you instructed."

Priscilla sat back in her seat and tried to appear nonchalant. She knew that Brad had in fact ignored the message from Senator Callahan, just as she had suspected he would, and so, except for her senator, not a single other member of the Democratic caucus had been privy to those amendments in the Republicans' "what-if package." *Bummer*, she thought, unable to keep the corners of her mouth from turning up in the slightest of smiles.

Senator Callahan blinked as his mind flashed back to that day in early April when Priscilla had shared her unexpected find with him. Then he hissed in her direction. "Wipe that damn smirk off your face. We are dying in here."

Priscilla beamed back brilliantly: *That may be, Bubba, but you and Marcus's boy laid that egg.* Her sentiments shone like a chorus of dawns.

On that day the previous month—the day that Priscilla had opened the package meant for the Republicans—Bill Scott had come by her office and asked, "Did you *inadvertently* receive a package from the LBO that was intended for delivery to our office?"

In a very matter-of-fact way, she had said, "Oh, yeah, Bill, and it was full of a lot of budget amendments. I gave that package to Brad."

Then, after feigning indifference, she had also said, "Is something the matter?"

Priscilla knew what she had done, and Bill knew that she knew, but that was all part of the game that they both knew well.

The day that Senator Callahan had said that his party was dying in the Senate Finance Committee seemed endless. It was now almost two-thirty on the next morning in the committee room, and the committee members were still doggedly trying to complete as much of the public-welfare section of the bill as possible. Amid all the drama, Priscilla and Bill drank coffee, smoked cigarettes and collegially chatted. The Republicans might be making phenomenal progress in achieving their agenda, but Brad and the others on Priscilla's "team," were at the end of their tether.

"Good grief, Priscilla," Bill said with a chuckle. "And to think everybody wondered how you'd fare with Brad getting all the attention on the Finance Committee. You never cease to amaze me!"

"Now, Bill, what on earth are you going on about?" Priscilla hid a satisfied smile.

"Ah, come on! You must have known exactly what you were doing when you gave that package to Brad, since ordinarily you would've copied its contents and used it against us yourself. But no, this time you did exactly as you were told. You knew Brad was too busy with his own little agenda to give any attention to our amendments. But we both know it's going to cost him. And to think you were only 'doing your job.'"

Priscilla lowered her voice another register. "My dear Bill, you'll never know how badly that scumbag has pissed me off." Then she looked up at the clock on the wall. "And to think all I had to do was practice a little patience."

That marathon Senate Finance Committee hearing did not adjourn until dawn. So when Priscilla finally arrived home, she was so exhausted by the long deliberations that she collapsed on her bed and fell at once into a deep sleep.

When she awoke at nearly noon, she saw sunlight pouring through the bedroom windows. Since she already knew that the Finance Committee hearing would not be in session over the weekend, she spent the rest of Saturday mulling over what she feared was happening back in Prendergast.

She heard from her mother several times a week, and clearly her father's health was continuing to decline. Bravely, Liza kept telling her she did not expect Priscilla to put her life on hold and her job at risk by returning home. "Not yet," Liza said. "Not yet, child."

But Priscilla considered that maybe her mother was trying to carry too much on her shoulders. She was the only child near her parents' home. Her father had taken care of that, when he had so mysteriously asked her to "relocate closer to home" from Florida. Yet Nelson had not been thinking of the intricacies of the Ohio Senate's Finance Committee when he had made his heartfelt request of her. And so here she was, a long but manageable drive away from Prendergast.

Priscilla felt the warmth of the sunshine as she lay in bed. Yes, she admitted to herself. Her parents needed her at home. But then she looked deeper inside and came to grips with the reality that she did not want to go home. How would she handle the situation? What would she say and do? She had never dealt with the end of the life of someone she intensely loved. And it never occurred to her that it might be enough for her father simply to see her beloved face. Or that Liza may simply have been comforted by her sitting in a chair next to her at Nelson's bedside.

Priscilla looked at her phone. Should she call the senator and finally break her silence about her father dying? She shrank from that intimacy. Her personal life was her business, not Senator Callahan's. Then her thoughts veered from her father's dying to the senator's incessant demands that she spend so much time working on his behalf in the Ohio Senate. Her admiration for Daniel P. Callahan began to diminish by the bucketsful. It never occurred to her that maybe she was confusing one father figure with another.

She turned over and went back to sleep, but this time it was a troubled sleep.

Two mornings later, Priscilla was awakened by the phone ringing on the small table beside her bed. Groggily, she looked at the clock: seven a.m. She had overslept. Her eyes shot open as she picked up the receiver.

Before she could even speak her usual "hello-o," she heard Liza: "Your Dad is going down fast, Priscilla. He's comatose. He goes in and out a lot, and I really don't know how much longer he's going to last."

Before Priscilla could answer, Liza hung up. Sitting wide awake on the edge of her bed, Priscilla regretted not responding sooner to what she realized now were Liza's emergency calls over the past month.

As Priscilla showered and dressed, she remembered what her friend Julia had said to her yesterday. "Go home, Priscilla, first thing in the morning, not later. You can always find another job and another lover, for that matter. But you only get one father in this life."

Priscilla packed a bag but went to work. As soon as she entered the office, she told the senator she had to go home at once because her father was imminently dying. Almost as an afterthought, she told him Nelson had been terminally ill with colon cancer and declining for at least the last six months.

Often Senator Callahan was kind, but not this time. He responded abruptly, as if he were cruelly brushing the matter aside. "Well, apparently you knew your father was dying. The issue is whether you want to be there *before* or *after* he dies?"

Priscilla understood he was angry for her not confiding in him before. Still, she expected more sensitivity from this boss who was also her lover.

But she told herself, as without another word she left the Statehouse behind, that she had a bigger life crisis than Senator Callahan's ego to deal with now.

CHAPTER 24

An Endless Ordeal

When Priscilla drove into the driveway, somehow she was not surprised to see her mom waiting on the front porch.

But she was shocked that Liza spoke no greeting and talked as though they were already in the midst of a conversation: "Do you want to see your daddy before the ambulance gets here?"

Was he already dead? Priscilla gingerly stepped onto the porch. "Tell me, Momma. Why do we need an ambulance?" Two thoughts struck Priscilla: an awareness that she had yet to accept the reality of Nelson's condition, and that she never imagined that today might be the last time she would see her father.

"Priscilla, your daddy's beyond comatose." Liza seemed surprised that, as many times as she had talked to Priscilla in the last terrible weeks, her daughter was apparently unaware of Nelson's decline. "I think he's catatonic."

"Catatonic? My goodness, Momma, what's that mean?" To Priscilla, that term might mean someone out of one's mind, or uncontrollable.

When her mother did not answer, without another word, Priscilla followed her inside the house and to her parents' bedroom. Priscilla realized she was walking on tiptoe and that she had no idea what she would see in their bed.

An instant later she stood at the foot of the bed, shocked beyond words at the horrid caricature lying there. The image before her was not her daddy. It was a relic, the remains of the father that used to be. Gone was the shimmer in Nelson's eyes; instead, what looked like dirty marbles were loosely held in place in his eye sockets, seemingly focused upward. The once distinctive high cheeks and full jaws had sunk into what she could clearly see was the structure of his skull. The mouth, slightly opened, revealed an upper dental partial plate disconnected from its bridge. Gone was the striking bronze complexion; now what looked like cracked, dried-out leather covered a structure of bone. A huge mound replaced the once-sleek stomach and abdomen. But, oddly, that full head of hair still crowned him. Oh, how Nelson had admired his hair! Otherwise, there was not much semblance of the man she so loved.

"This can't be!" Priscilla cried out. "What happened to Daddy? He looks so.... This can't be Daddy. No!" A terrible thought struck her. "Is he dead?" Her voice was a croak.

"Not yet, child." Liza put her arm around her daughter. "But soon."

Time seemed to have stopped.

Then the paramedics arrived and were in the bedroom. One told Priscilla to step aside because they needed to put her father on the gurney.

Priscilla stood spellbound, oblivious to all that surrounded her. Then she said, "Momma? What's that you say? I didn't quite understand what you said, Momma."

Another paramedic then spoke to Liza with familiarity, as though this were not the first time they had come to the house in response to an emergency call. "Ma'am? Mrs. Austin? The Reverend's condition has deteriorated critically. This time, you need to be prepared to leave him at the hospital. You do understand, don't you?"

Liza nodded her head. She understood that, and more.

Then the paramedic said, "Mrs. Austin? Do you want to ride with us in the ambulance, or do you want to drive over on your own?"

"My daughter and I will drive over in our own car. Thank you."

Then she turned to Priscilla. "Do you want me to drive? Are you up to this?"

The two Austin women followed the gurney out the door and locked up the house. Priscilla sat in the driver's seat of her Mustang and stared into space, once more oblivious to all that surrounded her. But then she came to. She was about to drive her mom to the hospital to go through the formalities of having the doctor declare her father's death.

When Liza and Priscilla arrived at the hospital, they were invited into a sterile, empty room that reeked of a strong cleanser like bleach or ammonia. Priscilla was aware of a conscious thought, that she detested the smell of hospitals.

Two people in white coats —a doctor named Jeremy Spangler and a nurse called Ms. Lundstrom—came into the room. It was such a solemn moment that the doctor insisted they all sit down for what he called "a short discussion."

"Dr. Spangler, you must've gone through this scene many times before," Priscilla said, as though there were a formal etiquette for this interaction. Dr. Spangler smiled, briefly fixed his attention on Priscilla and then began to brief the two of them.

"Ladies," Dr. Spangler said peering from the one to the other, "I've known Nelson a long time, and unlike some of my other patients, Nelson prepared for this moment. Your husband's wishes are well-known to me and very clear." After a momentary pause, Dr. Spangler continued. "Nelson was most emphatic that—once it was clear that he was dying—he not be attached to a respirator or other life-sustaining devices. Well, it's clear that he is dying. His previous decisions will save you considerable pain and agony."

Dr. Spangler then led Liza and Priscilla into a spacious room with dull white walls. They all stood beside the stainless steel bed on which Nelson's body lay. The bed had no side rails and was elevated to chest-height of those standing around it. A utility table was positioned to the left of the bed. No hospital machines or appliances were in the room.

Already Priscilla noticed how different Nelson looked here compared to at home. He seemed to be at rest, and the huge mound on his midriff had been substantially reduced. The nurse said his eyes had seemed dried out and so for his comfort were now covered with pads.

Neither tubes nor machines were attached to his body. The nurse told them they could give him oxygen if the family wanted it.

Liza shook her head. "I don't think we should alter Nelson's wishes."

Dr. Spangler and Nurse Lundstrom both knew the Austins were not demonstrative with their emotions; and, unlike most families, the Austins talked about death and dying. So—with the obvious exception of Priscilla—the Austins had long since accepted Nelson's impending death.

Priscilla's mind drifted back to the time when Nelson had called her sisters and her together several years earlier. "The day is going to come when your mom and I will not be here." Well, it was not so much what he said that had bothered Priscilla, rather how definitive he had been. "Now, if Liza passes before me, I will probably remarry," he had said to Priscilla's surprise. Then he had added: "But if I pass before Liza, I am leaving everything to her. Young ladies," he had stared into their eyes, "you will be on your own."

Immature in her early twenties, Priscilla had not fully grasped the implications of what her father told her sisters and her. Shortly thereafter she had gone to him and asked: "Daddy, if you die first, what do you suppose Momma will do?"

Nelson had realized that Priscilla was ready to hear the details, so he spoke in the Austin's customary matter-of-fact way: "Oh, Priscilla, I hate to tell you, but your mom has already said she will sell the property and move on with her life. She doesn't like Prendergast as much as you do."

"Wow!"

Nelson had always known that Priscilla loved Prendergast as much as he did, but Priscilla was his daughter not his wife. So he had tried to prepare her for what he knew would be a painful yet inevitable situation.

224

As Priscilla's mind returned to the present, she realized that painful yet inevitable situation was upon her.

"Mrs. Austin, why don't you and your daughter go to the waiting room? Or perhaps you prefer to go home? One of us will call you. It shouldn't be long now."

On their drive back home, there was virtually no traffic. It seemed as if time stood still to allow for their safe, unimpeded passage.

At home, they moved about slowly and found themselves at the kitchen table, reviewing the events of the day. They wondered about "the difference between 'receiving some oxygen' and 'being put on a respirator.'"

Then Liza offered to fix breakfast, recalling that Priscilla had just arrived from her long drive from Columbus before the ambulance had arrived.

Priscilla said breakfast sounded good. But as soon as her mother fixed it, she felt nauseated and dizzy.

The telephone rang. Their eyes met, and then Liza picked up the receiver from the wall unit. She nodded once, said something about "Powers," thanked the caller and replaced the receiver.

Then she turned to Priscilla. "That was Dr. Spangler. Your daddy has died. The doctor said he passed a couple of minutes before six o'clock this evening.' I confirmed that Powers was the funeral home. They'll take things from here."

Liza sank back down in her seat at the kitchen table. "Well, it's all over now, Priscilla. Your daddy's at peace. It wasn't too bad a struggle for him until this last month. But he was strong. My goodness, was he a strong man!"

Priscilla remained silent. Then she forced a slight smile and listened. Her mother seemed anxious to talk about her experiences during Nelson's final days.

"You know," Liza said, "your daddy did something peculiar the other night. Saturday evening, Nelson said, 'Get me a mirror, will you?' He wanted to know if he still had his hair. I had no idea how much Nelson cared about his appearance. Well, he still has his hair, and all the way to the end it still looked good on his head. And I thank God

225

for that! When Nelson saw himself in the mirror, he smiled, and then he told me to go in the back room and get some sleep. Apparently, then he was contented enough to let go. He slipped into a coma and never recovered. When I looked in on him again, he was the way you saw him when you came into the bedroom."

Since Liza and Priscilla had never been physically affectionate with each other, at this most precious moment they shared no warm embrace, clasping of hands or even simple words of consolation. As Liza poured out her heart, she fidgeted with her hands and merely glanced across the table at her daughter.

Yet Priscilla did take a kind of comfort from Liza's account of her last moments with Nelson before he sank into his final coma.

"I'm glad Nelson expressed satisfaction in our last conversation," Liza said. "Your father was blessed. You know, Priscilla, not everybody's ready when they die. But Nelson was ready."

Priscilla began to weep at the realization that she herself had not been ready. When her mother suggested she go to bed and try to rest, Priscilla found her way to the back bedroom.

She sat on the edge of the bed and cried with tremendous vigor, letting out wild, raging sobs. She felt guilt beyond description. "Why didn't I come home the minute Momma called?" she moaned out loud. "Why did I even bother talking to the senator about my Daddy dying? Why couldn't Daddy have held on long enough for me to get the courage, the nerve, to tell him I loved him? Why? Why!" She cried out to God. "Why'd you take my daddy? Why did he have to die? Out of nowhere, God, you just took him from me." Priscilla was shaken by despair, but this time she did not cry out loud. *What will I do now? Who can I turn to when I need help? Daddy's always been here for me, always. Now what is it I'm supposed to do? Oh God, why'd you do this to me? Why'd you take away my daddy?* Suddenly she realized how she had always seen her father as omnipotent and all-powerful, traits usually attributed to the Supreme Being. In anguish she wondered if now her god, too, was dead.

She threw herself down on her bed, moaning: "This can't be. This can't be happening to me ... " For all her life, for nearly twenty-nine years, she had thought she was a Christian. But Nelson had been her god. She had little spiritual connection to the deity known as God, at least none to her awareness. She had never known the God of her father. That realization made her feel so, so alone.

Exhausted, Priscilla continued to cry. But before long, a short, deep sleep overtook her, and during that time a new spiritual realm opened up to her. Something eased into her very being, while something else escaped.

When she awoke, she felt limp. She whispered, "My goodness, I can't move. Am I asleep?" Her body trembled, and then a sense of calm came over her. That calm exceeded all other experiences she had ever known, and it was good. She now knew with a wonderful certainty that there was *Someone*, or *Something*, that would sustain her, especially at times when she felt most in need of sustenance. And although she did not understand what it all meant or how it came about, she felt its calming grace. Her heart still ached miserably, but the anger over the loss of her daddy had subsided.

She fell asleep again, only this time more soundly.

Later, when she awakened, she walked into the dining room where she saw Liza sitting at her desk there and asked, "What're you doing, Momma?"

Liza was startled. "Oh, Priscilla, you're up already? Did you get enough rest?" She had heard her daughter wailing in the back room. But once she had quieted down and Liza had begun calling the other children to tell them it was over, she had almost forgotten that Priscilla was even in the house. Yet Liza, too, was still in the first flush of grief. She turned from her daughter back to the papers she had been perusing. "You know, child, your daddy sure knew how to take care of business. He took care of everything. Obviously he tried to make things as easy as he could for me."

Priscilla frowned and nodded. Unfortunately for her, even the spiritual comfort she had just experienced had not been enough to overcome her lifelong habit of refusing to acknowledge her deepest feelings. Already she had reverted to denial about her father's death.

Liza handed her one of Nelson's papers. "Your daddy wrote his own obituary. The only thing missing is the date of his death."

Robot-like, Priscilla sat down and looked at her father's notes. "I'd forgotten about Daddy's work in the civil rights movement. I should be ashamed because he and so many other preachers put their lives on the line back then."

Liza did not comment. She was old enough that she would never forget what life in the South had once meant. Then she said, "You know, Priscilla, Nelson's insurance policy will cover the funeral *and* provide us a little stipend, too. He also left each of you kids a whole life policy. Your daddy was so thoughtful. He's taken real good care of us." Her voice softened. "You know, we go to hear the reading of the will *after* his funeral." Then Liza said, "If you're up to it, you can go with me to the funeral home in the morning. Mr. Powers called a short while ago to inform me that they have Nelson's body."

As her mother was mentioning other details of what now had to be done, Priscilla was remembering her father asking her to "look after" Liza. She wondered what that would entail. Liza already knew, better than she did, what steps had to be taken now.

"I'll understand if you don't go with me to the funeral home, Priscilla," Liza was saying. "I realize how painful all this is for you. You know something else, Priscilla? Nelson knew how much you loved him. He even said to me once that he thought it was 'a wee bit unhealthy,' but that he was so proud of you. You do know he favored you over the others."

Priscilla muted listening to her mother, nodded when she thought she should and wondered if this terrible day would ever end.

In a way, for Priscilla, the next day was no better.

During their visit at the funeral home, Liza could not decide between a wood-grain and a metallic coffin.

It was then that Priscilla made what turned out to be a ghastly suggestion: "Why not cremate him, Momma?" she said in that matter-of-fact way of hers. "Since he's gone and everything turns back to dirt, save your money. Have Daddy's remains cremated. Besides, what are we looking at in terms of cost for a casket and all that other stuff?"

Priscilla reflected later that one would have thought the devil itself had entered the room.

Liza shouted, "Shut up, you evil child! How can you be so cruel and thoughtless at a time like this? Your father would never have allowed such foolishness."

Suddenly Priscilla remembered the exchange between Senator Callahan and Senator Caldiera during a Finance Committee debate on providing "adequate burial" for the indigent in the state budget. She had not thought much of their debate then, and she did not understand her mother's point now. "If you didn't want my opinion, why'd you invite me along?" Priscilla asked. "I don't want to be here anyway."

Mr. Powers interceded. He had witnessed many similar, and even more dramatic, exchanges from other grief-stricken families. "Young Ms. Austin," he said to Priscilla, "I understand your sentiment. Believe me, I do. But I also knew your father."

The funeral director paused until he was sure he had Priscilla's attention. "Nelson was a minister and a fine one at that. He also was my good friend, someone I could rely on in all sorts of situations. This isn't an easy service for me to arrange, either. You see, if we cremate Nelson's remains, especially ahead of any services, then people won't have any opportunity to pay their respects the way most are accustomed."

Mr. Powers then turned his attention back to Liza. "Mrs. Austin, Nelson asked specifically that his funeral service be managed by you and, of course, by someone from the annual conference of his church. But I'll do as you wish." With that, the funeral director completed his business and then prepared to leave the mother and daughter alone.

"Boy," Priscilla muttered before she could stop herself, "you guys sure know how to turn a dollar from death." She had forgotten about the role of the church, not to mention the numerous organizations in which Nelson had held membership.

Priscilla could never remember whether it was later that terrible day, or the next day, which was also awful, that she and her mother first saw Nelson's remains at the private viewing.

Mr. Powers said, with great pride and reassurance as he ushered them toward the open casket, "Well, Mrs. Austin, I think we did pretty well. We dressed Nelson in one of those nice black suits he was so fond of, and, as I'm sure you're aware, everybody knew him for those thick, black horn-rimmed glasses, his signature trademark."

Priscilla stared into the casket. Indeed, she thought, one would never have known the Reverend James Nelson Austin had succumbed to colon cancer. She had wanted her father's remains cremated because she had been unfamiliar with the techniques, cosmetics and other means used by morticians to generate an attractive and lifelike appearance on corpses.

But for Priscilla, it was an ordeal. All of it was an ordeal. An endless ordeal.

CHAPTER 25

His Name was Howard Thurman

On Wednesday evening, the chapel at Powers Funeral Home played host to one of the wakes for the late Reverend James Nelson Austin. At the start of the wake, the Austin sisters and Nelson, Jr., first embraced Liza at the front of the chapel, and then they all sat in the front row. Members of a variety of organizations stood up before those gathered in the chapel and spoke about Nelson.

"How," Priscilla whispered to her siblings, "can Momma stand this exhibition?" But none of them answered her.

After a while, Helen whispered, "Don't you find all this a little strange? Here we sit at Daddy's wake, when, in the past, he was the one who would conduct these services for other families. I keep expecting to see him walk up to us and say something."

Her sisters and brother nodded. And as Priscilla looked around the chapel, it seemed to her that Helen's words were the sentiments of all the others.

At the viewing of Nelson in his open coffin, Priscilla stared and almost laughed as she saw several black men march into the chapel and said to herself, *And they ain't bad looking, either.* They wore dark suits and cream-colored canvas satchels wrapped around their waists, from which hung hammers and other tools. As the men sang a hymn that Priscilla did not recognize, it occurred to her, *They're Masons! I get it now: "fraternity, service and faith."*

She recognized some of the men from her teenage escapades at the Elks Club, a favorite black-owned nightclub in Prendergast. "Now," she whispered to her sisters," I see why one of them never acknowledged my advances. He was one of Daddy's 'brothers.'"

"Lord, have mercy, listen to Priscilla," Camille said to Helen. "She's up to something—even at a service like this. What're we gonna do with Miss Prissy? Is she something else or what?"

After hearing some of the other speeches about Nelson, Priscilla stopped listening. With some bitterness, she mused to herself: *Now I know why Daddy had so little time for us. He was too busy taking care of all these people and their problems.*

On Thursday, there were more rituals centered on Nelson's passing.

That morning, Amber phoned Priscilla and said, "I've always been told ... " And then the two friends completed the old maxim together: " ... When a woman feels a little down, she should go shopping for a hat." And later that morning, they did.

That evening the Austins of Prendergast played host to a wake for a multitude of family and friends, which included several clergy from the New York Conference of the AME Zion denomination, in which Nelson had served. After the wake, Nelson, Jr., recommended that the Austin siblings and their cousins and friends all go to the bar at the Holiday Inn Downtown Prendergast.

"Lord knows, we need some air," he said. "I certainly could use a drink."

Convenient, Priscilla thought. After they arrived at the bar, Priscilla remembered, from a phone call with Charlene earlier in the day, that Senator Callahan, who apparently had read Nelson's obituary in a Columbus newspaper, had driven to the Holiday Inn and taken up lodging there. She managed to slip away from her family and friends to join the senator in his suite.

First, she briefed him on the facts: the date of Nelson's death, the wakes and his funeral service to be held the next day. Then she went berserk: "Why on earth would you dare come here, and expect me to be with you as we behave in Columbus?" As she paced about the room, she ranted, "My God, man, you really do think more highly of yourself than you ought."

"But, sweetheart, I've missed you," the senator said. "And now that I'm here I'm wondering why you haven't bothered to introduce me to your family."

"Are you out of your mind? We're burying my daddy, and you want *me* to introduce *you* to my family? You want them to see us together? You're a married man! Don't you know they'll be able to see there's something between us? I don't think so, Senator. Oh no. I will *not* introduce you to my family."

"Oh, Priscilla, you can't be serious. I'm not only your boss. I'm here as your friend."

"You can define our relationship as you wish, but you can't make me bring you into my family. That is simply not going to happen. Please go back to Ohio and to your own wife and children. And another thing. I haven't decided whether I'll even return to that stupid rat hole."

"Oh, Priscilla," the senator said as he pleaded with her, "I realize now how much your father meant to you. But, for the life of me, I can't fathom your shutting me out like this."

"Senator!"

"It's Daniel. When are you going to call me by my name? *It's Daniel, Priscilla.* Call me Daniel."

"*Never.* Don't you remember that it was you who set the ground rules for this sordid relationship? It was you who said no mention of marriage or divorce. It was you who said no mention of 'us' to my girlfriends or anybody else. Therefore, as far as I'm concerned, you do not exist outside of the workplace. There is no respected friendship between us, at least none that I will share with my family. You and I as friends of any sort are wholly off limits to my family."

"Oh, Priscilla. You can't mean what you're saying. You're grieving. That's all."

"Whatever. Go home. Please, Senator. Go home and leave me alone." Then Priscilla stalked out of the senator's suite.

When she reconnected with the Austin gathering at the bar, she was nonchalant, as though she had perhaps only spent an unusual amount of time in the powder room. But before the night ended, she drank enough gin and tonics to intoxicate a large animal. She hardly noticed how her behavior embarrassed the rest of the gathering, but she could not ignore her bad hangover the next morning.

Friday morning, the day of Nelson's funeral, began as a typically mild spring day. Yet it soon grew dark with cloud cover.

By then, Uncle Maxwell and the Indianapolis delegation had already arrived and parked in front of 19 West Seventh Street. They had driven the whole way in a blue-and-black limousine borrowed from one of Maxwell's doctor friends. There, they assembled with Liza and her children in the limousines provided by Powers Funeral Home.

For Priscilla, some details of the funeral were etched in her mind but others were a blur. She later told her friend Julia, back in Columbus, that she distinctly remembered arriving at the church. "I must have floated up those steep steps, because I certainly don't remember moving my legs and feet."

When the family entered the small sanctuary, Priscilla noticed that everybody began whispering and that the congregation seemed to be trying to identify the individual family members in the procession.

"And then there was more darkness," Priscilla later recalled to Julia. "Girl, you should've seen all those black men in those dreary black robes all crowded together. The bishop sat in the tallest high-back chair in the middle, flanked by two presiding elders. Frankly, Julia, the only person missing was Count Dracula. I mean, please, it was a disgustingly morbid scene."

Because the seating area was limited in the small sanctuary, the over-flow of clergy and dignitaries had to sit on the side pews off to the right.

"I realize Daddy was a preacher and active in the community and all, but Julia, that scene at the church was, well, it was just disgusting,"

Priscilla recalled. "But tell me something, girl, why on earth would anybody leave a casket open, especially after all those darn wakes?"

Julia told Priscilla that "lots of people" leave the casket open. She also said, "It's rare for black people to have a closed-casket funeral." Since Priscilla did not consider the Austins "lots of people," she disregarded Julia's explanation.

"And another thing, Julia," Priscilla continued, "when the church clerk started reading the obituary, she said, 'Nelson *was*.' Past tense! Well, that about did it for me."

Priscilla related to Julia how she could no longer contain herself. She had been livid as she erupted, "What does she mean, 'Nelson *was*?'" Later she wondered if her outburst was those gin and tonics talking. But at the time, Priscilla remembered, "that about did it for Momma, too, who was at her wit's end with me, anyway."

Liza had snappishly said, without even turning around in her seat: "Somebody, take her out of here, *now*!"

Then Ellen had volunteered to escort Priscilla out of the sanctuary.

"The next thing I remember," Priscilla told Julia, "was Ellen and I sitting on the sofa in the ladies' room downstairs."

As she tried and failed to calm her sister, Ellen finally told her some of what she had said upstairs.

"I said *what*?" Priscilla remembered asking.

Ellen had shaken her head. "Yeah, girl," Ellen had said, "you said 'damn open casket' and 'what the hell does she mean, *was*?' You let her rip." Ellen had then given Priscilla the option of returning to the service or waiting it out in the ladies' room.

"I wouldn't miss Daddy's funeral for the world," Priscilla had said as she wiped away the copious tears she had shed from her laughter and sadness. So together she and Ellen had returned to the service.

"So what happened next, Priscilla?" Julia was intent on getting Priscilla to recount how her father had been eulogized. She knew on some levels that Priscilla still refused to acknowledge Nelson's death.

"All right, Julia … We went back upstairs and walked all the way back up front, where we rejoined the rest of the Austin clan. And the damn casket was still open!"

Throughout the service, occasional weeping had come from some of the guests, but no outbursts. The Reverend James Nelson Austin had been a formal and proper man, and most people in attendance had been familiar with his strict adherence to liturgy. So his funeral service had been conducted with the highest order of dignity. It was only Priscilla who had fallen out of line.

Toward the end of the well-synchronized service, the pallbearers stood up and surrounded the casket.

"Girl, they could've carried me out of there on a stretcher," Priscilla later confided to Julia, as she remembered keenly, "the sound of those levers turning and turning, followed by that slow, screeching, sucking sound of the casket being sealed."

For Priscilla, that sound and that moment had been terrible. She screamed out to Julia: "That's why I *hated* the casket open during the service. I thought, 'Well, if he wasn't dead, he's dead now.' I hated that sound. I just hated it. Why couldn't they have just closed the damn casket before the service? That was awful, just awful."

But Priscilla did not mention in her report to Julia that she had also behaved badly during the recession. Some pain cuts too deep to share.

As the limos lined up behind the hearse, Priscilla had asked her sisters in bewilderment, "Where're we going?" Then she had said, "I've never been to the black cemetery. Where exactly is it?" During the sixteen years that the Austins had resided in Prendergast, Priscilla had never once attended a funeral there.

Ellen reminded her that they were burying Nelson in Lake Charles Cemetery.

Priscilla was stunned speechless as she sat back in the limousine.

But then Liza stunned her even more when she said: "Nelson loved this place so much that he bought two plots here, not in Canton or Indianapolis, but here in Prendergast. 'I want to be buried in Prendergast at Lake Charles,' your father said shortly after we'd moved here. As for myself, well, I've not made up my mind. I'm just not sure yet."

Priscilla remained still and silent. Whenever she was confronted with devastating news, her hands would moisten. She clung to the hem of the jacket of her linen suit as if she were being taken away from the black cemetery against her will. Helen and Camille sobbed because they, too, were devastated at Nelson's choice of his final resting place. Priscilla felt baffled. How would she explain to her hometown friends that the good Reverend had not been buried in the black cemetery?

Liza, overwhelmed with her own grief, took this moment to explain more profound facts to Priscilla about her father. "My goodness, Priscilla, where the devil have you been all these years? First, you've got all those rosy pictures about life in the South. And now we find out that you don't have a clue about your daddy. Well, let me tell you something, Priscilla: towards the end of your daddy's life, he got philosophical, or is that theological? Nelson talked about humanity and spirituality, which created rifts in the black community here. He talked a lot about how 'we're all the same in the kingdom of God' and about 'common ground.' He talked less and less about race and gender. And I'm sure you know his man was Howard Thurman. It got so bad until he quoted Thurman as much, if not more, than biblical text. Racial integration! Multi-cultural churches! Everybody around here knew of your daddy's admiration for that man. If Howard Thurman said it, it was all but gospel. Better you know all that now than get embarrassed at some point later. That was your real daddy, Miss Prissy."

Then, attempting to comfort her younger sister, Ellen said, "I'm sorry, Priscilla, but I really thought you already knew all this. Really I did."

Priscilla shivered in her seat. Her mind raced. During the funeral service, she had missed similar commentary on Nelson's life because she had been downstairs at the time.

Soon, the remains of James Nelson Austin lay in lot number ten, section twenty-six, location fourteen, grave number twenty. His marker read, "James Nelson Austin, December 17, 1909 – May 18, 1981."

Afterwards, back at the Austin residence, everyone behaved as if all had gone well. No one dared tell Priscilla how outrageous her behavior had been at the church or at the gravesite. Then again, they were all so enveloped in their own grief that no one much cared. At least, Priscilla had dealt with her feelings instead of keeping them latched up. She had felt entitled to let go for her daddy, and that was exactly what she had done.

So it was, too, that even later, back in Columbus, Julia had no luck getting Priscilla to acknowledge her father's death. Nor did Priscilla tell her friend much about the site of the burial.

It took little time for Ellen and her husband, Nathaniel, a licensed realtor, to make arrangements to sell the Austin property. Liza was anxious to leave Prendergast, although Priscilla never understood why. Having to lament the loss of her father was hard enough, let alone the loss of her connection to him and life in Prendergast. *No more homestead. What is it about my family that brings about so much joy yet so much sorrow?*

And there was also the realization that, for the first time in her life: *I'm on my own now for sure.*

Priscilla returned to work in the Ohio Senate, where she tried to put the events of the past week behind her and where, one by one, colleagues and personal acquaintances dropped by her office to offer their condolences.

Even Charlene expressed sympathy. On the morning of her return, Senator Callahan's receptionist followed her into her small cubicle. "All right, Prissy" she said, "I know you and I have our differences, but I do feel badly for you. I know how it feels to lose a parent. I'm sorry for your loss." Then a tearful Charlene went back to her desk.

Priscilla had never before experienced condolences like that. The next person to greet her was her officemate. "Welcome back," Sharon began. "I was saddened to learn about the death of your father. You know something, though, you never once let on that you were going through anything like that. You've been here almost a year, and you never once said a single word about your father's illness. Why was that? I would've understood. I told you that my father died of a heart attack at age fifty, and afterwards, my mother and I had to deal with all that, plus start over again."

"Oh, Sharon, I'm sorry," Priscilla said. "I don't know why I didn't say anything to you before. I mean, we were told there was nothing anybody could do. So I decided it best not to dwell on it, that's all. I never meant to hurt your feelings."

At that point, Priscilla sensed her officemate's sincerity. The two women hugged.

Priscilla continued to trust no one absolutely.

In the few weeks that remained before completion of the state's budget, Priscilla resumed attendance in the Senate Finance Committee meetings with Senator Callahan. With them now, too, was an LBO intern who had covered the committee with the senator almost single-handedly during Priscilla's absence. Brad's status had diminished a notch or two.

Priscilla took much of her frustration out on the new intern, but to no avail. The Republicans had a lock on the budget in the Senate. The Senate Democrats had to take whatever the Republicans doled out, essentially kicking them down the totem pole.

On the day of the Senate floor vote on the budget bill, the usual crowds turned up. Since staff and several lobbyists had heard about the death of Priscilla's father, many paused for kind words and condolences to show their respect.

Priscilla was wading through the mob when she was unexpectedly embraced by Bill Scott. "Sweetheart," he said in his deep, seductive voice, "I wanted to come see you earlier, but I thought I'd let all the others speak to you first. *Now*, I'll bet I know why you came back here to Columbus to work in the Senate. Maybe only your love for your father would've brought you back here, and this wretched place is closer to your home than Tallahassee. Am I right?" Bill spoke with confidence. "You do know I'm here for you, no matter what else goes on."

Touched, Priscilla smiled at her Republican friend.

Bill added: "When Senator Callahan returned from Prendergast, he told us all about the situation. He even admitted that you hadn't said *anything* to him until that final week or so. And one thing's for certain, my fine lady friend—you're made of iron and steel, so God bless the poor sucker who gets in your way. I sure hope I'm on your good side!"

Priscilla cracked a smile, and his own smile widened. He was happy to see Priscilla smile again.

"Ah, heck, Miss Prissy, I just want you to feel better. I know it'll take a while, but I'm here to help you get through it, *if* you'll let me. That's all. Otherwise, I won't bother you. Do we have a deal?" Bill held Priscilla close and then he walked away.

Priscilla felt enough of her old self to enjoy that here, especially in plain sight for all to witness, once again she and Bill had flaunted their unlikely friendship.

CHAPTER 26

Intervention at King's Island

For the rest of the year, Priscilla suffered tremendous anguish, but kept it to herself. She refused to allow anybody into her private space. Habitually, she would pick up the telephone to call home, only to realize there was no one to call. Or sometimes she would grab her shoulder bag to "take a drive up the road," only to catch herself and ask, "What am I doing?" Liza had sold the Austin property there and was making plans to relocate elsewhere. Priscilla had not even thought about what her mom would do once she had sold the property. Apart from Amber, she had no more family and friends in Prendergast.

Most disturbingly, she sat alone in that huge Victorian house and sobbed, "Who the hell cares?"

No one knew that Priscilla was spending so much time distressed—not her friend Julia, not Senator Callahan, not even her family members.

She had also honed her ability to hide her feelings as she moved through crowds and passed people with ease. She had used her self-discipline to act whatever part she wanted to play. Since she mostly rode the bus to work, she had learned to carry a newspaper or magazine to read and so lessen the possibility of any personal interaction. Whenever and wherever she walked at work, she had consciously looked nonchalant or stark and cold—perfect expressions to lessen interaction with that Statehouse crowd. But the minute she left the public stage, often she had nearly come apart. She had learned how much energy it took to be an actor on the stage.

She had one respite early that spring, during Holy Week, when an old friend came to Columbus to visit. Cathy—a former classmate and close friend from her undergraduate days at Livingstone College, now lived in Cheyenne, Wyoming with her husband, Sleeter, and their son.

At the time of her visit, Priscilla's grief over the loss of her father was almost unbearable. Going to church was especially problematic because Priscilla had to watch a minister other than Nelson conduct the act of worship. Sporadically she tried to heal from her deep loss, but it seemed resolution was premature.

Cathy did her best to help Priscilla resolve her grief and get on with her life. Soon after she arrived, she noticed that her friend was almost wholly unfamiliar with her neighborhood. So she said one morning, "Priscilla, except for the time you spent in Tallahassee, Columbus has pretty much become your home. Yet you still don't know the communities here, not even the black communities." Cathy waited for that observation to sink in. "And you know something else I notice about you? When you want to, Priscilla, you can be so outgoing and vigilant, but you're still very aloof."

Priscilla chose to ignore the intent of her old friend's message. "At least I know where our church is, plus I know the pastor." In fact, at the time of Cathy's visit, Priscilla could not remember the last time she had even gone to church. As for her aloofness, Priscilla ignored that comment altogether. But she also proudly pointed out a couple of nightclubs where, in happier times, she had occasionally hung out with Julia.

During that visit, Cathy had only one special request: "Take me to Kings Island, Priscilla. I hear it's the largest amusement and waterpark in the Midwest."

"Isn't that for kids?" Priscilla frowned.

But off to Kings Island they drove, approximately two hours south of Columbus, near Cincinnati. When they got there, Priscilla said, "Just looks like a great big amusement park to me."

"Wow, Priscilla, you really do need to get out more," Cathy said, "which brings me to something I've been meaning to talk to you about. I see you're still keeping pretty much to yourself. But I'm mostly troubled by your playing second fiddle … to that man."

"Playing second fiddle?"

Cathy nodded. "Well, girlfriend, let me begin with what's on my mind. First, I understand why you left Florida to come back here. But you've upheld that commitment to your father. So there's no further need to tie yourself down with the senator. You can do better than him anyway—and better than that job, too."

Before Priscilla could interrupt, Cathy moved on hastily to her next point. "The Priscilla I remember from Livingstone was someone who the instructors all lifted up as an example. Remember what Professor (Abna Aggrey) Lancaster told you in class that one day? Remember how she put you on notice: 'I see great potential in you, young Miss Austin—your gift for oratory and your unusual style of writing.' I know you remember that, Priscilla. You still have what it takes to succeed. Please don't throw all your talents away fooling around with that user, that Callahan. He's not worth it."

Cathy had more to say, but she allowed Priscilla time to react.

"I hear you, Cathy, but what exactly is it I'm doing that makes you think I don't have control of my life?"

"My goodness, Priscilla, have you forgotten everything all those other instructors encouraged you to do? Professor (Albert Clayton) Boothby, your favorite of them all, bragged about you in his Diplomatic History class. 'Why, Miss Austin, *why* do you hide your talents?' And all those books from his personal collection! I can see you now, running down the corridor in Goler Residence, hollering: 'Cathy, look at all these books Dr. Boothby gave me! He gave *me* these books!' You were so proud and cheerful back then. What's happened to you?"

Priscilla simply smiled and said, "Girl, you sure have an excellent memory. I'd forgotten much of that stuff."

"And Karen Rawling, the only female professor in the History and Political Science Department, remember how she helped you to get into Ohio State and Yale? I mean, Yale! Come on, now, Priscilla; you seem to have forgotten that you were Yale material. And why did you turn Yale down? Because, once again, 'Daddy wanted me closer to home.' Well, now, I'd say it's high time 'Priscilla started living for Priscilla's sake.'"

Cathy's repetition of Nelson's parting words smacked Priscilla hard.

"And I know," Cathy continued, "that you don't want to hear this either, Priscilla. But the senator's not stupid. He recognizes your gifts and talents just like those professors did at Livingstone. Only the difference is that he's bleeding you for everything he can get. Promise me you'll hurry up and do whatever else it is you need to do and move on. It would be a tragedy to lose yourself in the senator's shadow."

Cathy nodded in finality. She had said what she thought needed to be said, with little regard for Priscilla's feelings. She knew her old friend would not have respected her advice any other way.

After a moment of charged silence, Priscilla said, "Are you sure you and Julia haven't been talking behind my back?"

Then they laughed like the old friends they were and continued to walk and talk on the grounds of that great big amusement park. That afternoon Cathy rode on just about every ride that she could, while Priscilla sat and thought about what Cathy had said to her. Priscilla had not realized how far off track she had gone.

Priscilla had another visit shortly thereafter from her mother, with Helen's young son Germane in tow.

Shortly after Nelson's funeral, Helen had arranged for Germane to stay with Liza, to keep her company and perhaps stave off her grief. But not long after that, Liza had decided to stay with Harriet's family in Spokane.

Priscilla's place in Columbus had been one stopover on their way to Washington State. As Liza and Germane waited for Helen to arrive and drive them to Spokane, a trip to the Ohio State Fair, which featured Gladys Knight and the Pips, became a major family excursion. When Gladys' brother Bubba sang a solo, Priscilla was one of many in the audience who jumped out of her seat; and Germane said, "Gee, Aunt Priscilla, I've never seen you get so excited before."

Then Priscilla took Germane and Liza to an equestrian show. Germane was amazed by the imposing size of the Clydesdales and awestruck when the owners allowed him to stroke them. But what impressed him most was seeing young people feed and walk their horses and then competing in the various contests. Overwhelmed, at one point, he called out, "Oh, Aunt Priscilla, this is so much fun! Wait 'til I tell my friends about this!"

Once Priscilla realized she had her nephew's attention, she decided to share a story about how the city of Prendergast had used big horses like the Clydesdales.

"When we lived in Prendergast," she began, "sometimes the snow fell so deep it would cover up everything—trees, landscapes, cars, ah heck, *everything*. Anyway, instead of snow removal trucks, the city used Clydesdales to pull steel wedges to clear the snow."

"Aunt Priscilla. I'm too old for fairy tales," Germane said, in utter disbelief.

"No, Germane, this is true. You know those fancy horses we see in the Anheuser Budweiser Busch Beer commercials and all those holiday parades? You know the kind of horses I'm talking about."

But Germane just laughed out loud. He thought his aunt was trying to amuse him.

Then Liza spoke up. "No, Germane. Her story's true. The streets were made of brick, cobblestone or something like that. They weren't paved like these streets here in Columbus. And since we got so much snow, the best way to clear it was with those big horse-driven plows."

"Wow, Grandma, that's incredible!"

Lisa nodded and smiled. "Well, young man, you can't imagine how shocked we were when we first moved there. The first time we experienced a serious snowfall, your granddad woke up the kids to see it. And those girls jumped up and down and ran all over the place screaming. They'd never seen that much snow! You only saw a mild case of it last Christmas. But it usually falls just as deep as your Aunt Priscilla told you."

Germane's eyes were as round as saucers.

Of course, no trip to the state fair would have been complete without a ride on a Ferris wheel. One ride was enough for Priscilla. But she put Germane on as many rides as he could endure—either alone or in a seat next to another child who was eagerly awaiting a partner.

As successful as their State Fair excursion was, the most memorable day of their visit occurred when Priscilla took Germane to her Statehouse office—and although he loved it, she regretted it almost immediately. From the point when they caught the bus, Priscilla was unable to control her nephew.

Once they arrived at the capitol, Germane acted as though the Statehouse lawn was a huge playground. He took out his secret weapon—a squirt gun—and sprayed everything and everybody in sight.

To Priscilla's relief, Bill came to her office. "Let me keep him a while," he offered. "After all, he's only a child."

At home that evening, Germane reported to Liza that he had the time of his life.

Perhaps the most important happening for Priscilla came a year after Nelson's death, when Liza reached a major decision. After a nice long visit with Harriet, Liza announced, "I'm ready now to move on with my life."

She had decided to return to her family's home in Sills Creek. Her plan was to fix up her mother's old house and bring her mother to live there with her. At that time, her mother was living with Madelyn, Liza's eldest sister. But Liza did not want to fly or take any other mode of public transportation. Instead, she wanted to be driven by one of her dear daughters, and this time she called on Priscilla to do the driving.

So it was that Priscilla's anguish over living a life without her father was suddenly compounded by Liza calling in a favor. She asked Priscilla to come to Spokane—where she had been staying with Harriet and her family for the past year—and then drive her and Germane to Sills Creek, Illinois.

The request took Priscilla by surprise. She still harbored ill feelings toward her mom for having sold the Austin property in Prendergast. And she never expected that Liza would decide to return to her Midwest hometown. To Priscilla, Sills Creek was just "that little flea-ridden hamlet where the biggest thing there is the mosquitoes."

And the timing of Liza's request coincided with the onset of primary election campaign season in Ohio. Senator Callahan was expecting her to work by his side. The governor's office and one-third of the Senate seats were in play. Although he did not face any serious challenge to his seat, Senator Callahan, too, was up for reelection.

Yet family was family, and she had promised her daddy to take care of her mother. So Priscilla put in the request for time off.

Senator Callahan, as she expected, was incredulous. "My God, Priscilla, all those people in your family, and your mother chose *you* for this mundane task? Didn't you explain the significance of your work to her? What I do affects people's lives."

At his resistance, Priscilla's resolve hardened. "I'll inform the clerk's office to take me off the darn payroll for my time away." She enjoyed seeing the stunned look on Senator Callahan's face. "I'll do my best to make up the time when I return. But I don't have much choice about this. You see, Senator, I'm one of those crazy people who doesn't put anything—certainly not my work—between my family and me. So don't you ever try forcing my hand like that again!" Priscilla noticed, with some surprise, how her level of self-assurance seemed to have increased immensely. Or, she wondered, had it always been there?

Senator Callahan's eyebrows rose, it seemed, nearly to his hairline. "Sweetheart, I *know* you're not threatening me." His voice had a dangerous purr. "I brought you in here and I can take you out."

Priscilla's eyes narrowed. The senator had always acted like he held something over her, probably this stupid job. But she sensed that now even he must recognize that something—whether he wanted to call it confidence, assurance or simply renewed strength—had changed in her. Much annoyed, Priscilla let loose: "Senator, get a grip! This isn't one of your committee hearings; I'm your only audience this time. I'm thinking part of your problem with *me* is your refusal to accept the fact that I have a life apart from yours and this wretched Statehouse scene. And yes, it *was* imprudent of you to force me to decide between you and my mom. That was wrong, and you know it." Then she walked out of the senator's office.

But at home that evening, Priscilla had second thoughts. Should she disappoint her mom or put her job at risk? She called her three closest girlfriends: Julia in Columbus, Amber in Prendergast and then Cathy in Wyoming. Julia and Amber, to Priscilla's surprise, weighed in on her mother's side. *But surely Cathy would give different advice?* Priscilla dialed the Wyoming number. "Cathy, girl, how the devil are you? Now sit down and get a load of this." After Priscilla explained her dilemma, she asked, "Can you imagine Momma asking something like that?"

But Cathy responded differently than Priscilla had expected. "No matter what you might think you feel right now, Priscilla, your mother is all you've got. You lost your father, but your mother lost her husband—her second husband, at that. You'll *never* know your mother's pain and grief."

Priscilla felt as if the wind had been knocked out of her.

But Cathy was not finished. "Priscilla," she continued, "your mother is not one of those stupid politicians that you decide to make or break on a whim. She's your mother!"

A stupefied Priscilla held a steady grip on her receiver but kept listening.

"Now," Cathy briskly continued, "you make a flight reservation to Denver. I'll drive over and pick you up. It's only a little over an hour's drive from Cheyenne. You can spend a couple of days with Sleeter and me, and then go on to Spokane and pick up your mom and Germane."

Priscilla hung up the phone, still surprised that none of her friends had a problem admonishing Miss Prissy when they thought she needed it.

Feeling that she was acting solely out of stunned instinct, Priscilla nonetheless booked her ticket to Denver. She then placed the call that she knew Liza was waiting for. Part of her still was fuming at having to make this trip in the first place. But remembering again what she had promised her father, she did it.

Cathy was alone when she met Priscilla at the Denver airport. Her husband Sleeter was still at work. On their drive to Cheyenne, Cathy tried to build her interest in shopping for Western clothes and silver jewelry.

But Priscilla made no attempt to be a gracious guest. Instead, she dismissed life in the entire Western region of the country. "What do you guys do out here? Are there any museums or theaters? And what about shopping centers? How on earth do you survive, girl?"

Cathy did not take offence, even though Priscilla's attitude was insulting. She knew her friend was still grieving her father and that she simply was not herself. Before they arrived at Cathy's home, Priscilla said to Cathy that she expected "a log cabin of sorts," and she seemed surprised that Cathy's spacious home was a split-level ranch constructed of brick and wood. As Priscilla walked throughout the house, she said, "Your home may be a bit sterile and orderly for me, but it's delightful all the same." And she had to admit, "Girl, you did all right for yourself."

Since Cathy did not permit smoking indoors, Priscilla found herself perching outside on the deck for a cigarette break. It was nearly summer, but she shivered; she realized she had misjudged the weather and had forgotten to pack sweaters and a coat.

Cathy seemed to sense her chill and brought her a shawl. "Girl," she said, "this is the West, the Great West, at that. No matter the temperature in the daytime, at night it gets cold. It still snows this time of year, too. Even in May!"

That evening, the two friends went shopping at a mall. Priscilla had always loved Western wear—boots, jeans, silver belt buckles and yes, the cowboy hat. But on this shopping expedition, for reasons she did not even try to understand, she chose to buy an earth-tone pair of rayon print culottes, "the perfect outfit for an event I plan to attend back in Columbus." The outfit was well chosen. The earthen colors brilliantly brought out Priscilla's facial features, gave her a very visible waistline and even accentuated her shapely legs. "This will do. I'll take it," Priscilla said, much to the surprise of the saleswoman.

Cathy laughed and then whispered, "Priscilla, these salespeople aren't used to people like us buying such nice things. In fact, most of us don't even shop here. But something told me to bring you here. Are you satisfied?"

"Cathy, girl, how'd you know what kinds of clothes I like? It's not as if we're still in college."

"Priscilla, please, stop acting like I don't know you." Cathy gave her a hug of total acceptance. Priscilla had her ways, but they would always be friends.

Later that night, Priscilla poured out her secrets—some secrets more than others. Indeed, the dynamic seemed like a much-needed therapy session. Priscilla still could not talk much about her father in the past tense, but she had no problem rambling on about her work in the Ohio Senate, including her relationship with Senator Callahan. But through all their conversations, Cathy never flinched. She took in all of Priscilla's revelations with ease. And she did say, "Girl, your life is so interesting, you ought to write a book." The two friends laughed.

"Yeah, sure, Cathy. But who the hell cares?"

CHAPTER 27

Cherokee on Mamma's Side

After Priscilla arrived in Spokane, she became overwhelmed with what felt like too much family.

Priscilla loathed Harriet's second husband, Judson, almost at first sight. He was just the sort of man she despised, most particularly for how brazen he was in his self-regard—most often at Harriet's expense. He often used expressions such as: "What I do for my wife," and "How, because of me, Harriet's very existence matters." Priscilla was disgusted by him.

Harriet did not make it any better when she insisted to Priscilla, "Judson's a good man because he provides for me and the children." When she heard her sister's words, Priscilla imagined herself in the Middle Ages.

Priscilla would have liked to hit the road to Sills Creek the same day she arrived, but instead—although Liza, too, was eager to leave—they all spent a whole day together in Spokane. Instead of sightseeing, Priscilla decided to go shopping at the Air Force Base Exchange. After she, Harriet and Liza entered the huge military shopping facility, Harriet cautioned Priscilla: "You can find just about anything in here, but I have to buy it for you. So don't go prancing up to the counter without me, Miss Prissy."

After strolling about the massive facility, Priscilla soon held up a pair of military-issued green pants and said, "Finally found myself a nice pair of straight-leg fatigues. Boy, this stuff's good quality, double-stitched and natural fabric." She used the same language that Liza had taught her about well-sewn and tailored clothing. She also picked out a navy blue sweater with reinforced arm pads. "It gets a little chilly in Columbus," she said, to convince herself to buy the item. But the catch of the day was a gorgeous piece of jewelry she had not anticipated finding there. "Will you look here?" Her eyes were locked on a huge topaz cocktail ring.

Taken aback by Priscilla's purchase, Harriet complained: "I could never buy anything like that now. I have a family to provide for. Wait till you have children. Just you wait! Besides, if you keep buying all those things for yourself, what'll you leave for the man in your life?"

Liza was only mildly interested in Priscilla's purchases, but she also offered up commentary: "You'd better listen to Harriet, Priscilla. She knows what she's talking about."

"But Momma, it was you who taught me how to shop. Have you changed or something?"

"And your daddy was alive back then," Liza said. "I don't have him to back up my buying habits now. You should learn a thing or two from that."

As Priscilla moved away from the other two and continued to shop, she recalled one particular day when Liza had taken her shopping back home in Prendergast. It must have been, she thought, sometime when she was in college. They had gone to The Village Corner, a favorite boutique of Liza's. There, Liza used a layaway plan, which meant that she paid only in cash for her purchases.

"And who is this charming young lady with you today, Ms. Liza?" the sales clerk said as they entered the small shop.

"This is Priscilla, my middle daughter. The one in college," Liza's maternal pride seemed much in evidence.

"Young Ms. Priscilla, you should know how proud your mom is of you," the saleswoman said. "Virtually every word out of her mouth is about something you're doing." Then she asked Liza if she was looking for anything special.

"Today, I'm actually here to teach Priscilla how to shop." With that, the sales attendant left them alone.

As Liza and Priscilla moved about the boutique, Priscilla noticed the many designer labels she had seen advertised in magazines. She would never have dreamed that her mother could afford clothes like this, yet here they were, in the shop that her mom had most frequented. Liza picked up a few items and described the color, fabric, fit, texture and stitching. She even turned some of the garments inside out to point out the buttons, the lining and the zippers. Priscilla was unusually attentive to her mother and asked questions of her.

When they came to a rack with an assortment of summer suits, Liza pulled out a couple of outfits and held them up against Priscilla's face and neck and said, "Ah, yes, just as I thought. These are your colors, Priscilla—coral, peach, pastel and earthen tones. Otherwise, stick to basic black-and-white, gray and navy blue for business occasions."

Their next stop was another of Liza's favorites, The Prendergast Fur Company. Here, too, the furrier, Joseph Jordan, was obviously acquainted with Liza. He informed Priscilla that he knew Nelson from the Prendergast Rotary, and that he was fully aware that Priscilla was the reverend's favorite child.

Then Joseph inquired about Helen, Priscilla's sister. He told the Austins, "Whenever I talk about Nelson and Liza to my son Bart, he always asks me what I've heard about Helen."

"Oh, Helen's fine," Priscilla said, her eyes still on the fabulous, fluffy furs. "She's been in the Navy since leaving that insurance job here. She likes it, too."

"And where's she stationed?" The furrier did not seem to want to drop his line of questioning.

"The last I heard she was in the Philippines," she said. "Or was it Hawaii? Anyway, Momma has her address." Then Priscilla changed the subject. She remembered the furrier's son from high school. "Hey, listen. Does Bart still have a crush on Helen? I always thought that was so-o funny for a cool guy like Bart."

Joseph ignored Priscilla's impertinent question and said, "Bart didn't want to work in the family business. He said, 'there's no future in it.' We disagreed a lot during his last year in college, and then he went off to law school. The next thing I knew, he was working in some big law firm in Manhattan."

"Wow," Priscilla said, "that's good news, isn't it? He's done well for himself." Priscilla was puzzled by Joseph's evident disillusionment in his son's career.

Nearly a decade later, shopping in the Air Force complex in Spokane, Priscilla wondered why that long ago shopping tutorial of her mother's had come back to her in such detail. Funny, too, she thought, that what the furrier had said about Bartholomew Jordan had stayed with her.

But then her mind went back to gnawing over why her mother had said what she said about strained finances. She knew for a fact that Liza was far from destitution.

Up early the next day, Priscilla readied Liza's small gray Nissan station wagon for the long journey halfway across the country to Illinois. Liza had bought the car to make a new start in Spokane, and here, not so long afterwards, she was making another new start in Sills Creek. Priscilla folded down the back seat to create space for Germane to stretch out. She also packed Liza's and Germane's personal belongings and her suitcase into the vehicle.

"All aboard," Priscilla called out, jokingly.

To his credit, Judson fulfilled his "manly role" and got in his car to lead the three travelers to the road that connected to Interstate 90, the main highway.

The weather was cloudy, damp and cold. *What a dreadful morning*, Priscilla thought, as she shivered.

Spokane was situated one-third of the way down the eastern border of Washington State. Soon they crossed the border into Idaho. In the uppermost part of the Bitterroot Range, they rounded a sharp curve and saw beautiful, sun-lit mountains where, without warning, heavy snow sloshed on the windshield.

Priscilla pumped the brake pedal and asked, "Where'd that stuff come from?"

"Welcome to the Rocky Mountains," Liza said.

"Folks, looks like this is going to be one heck of a trip," Priscilla said. "Brace yourselves. But maybe it's not going to be too bad. Germane, do you know what Idaho is known for?"

The disinterested boy said, "No, Aunt Priscilla. What's Idaho known for?"

"Potatoes, my boy, potatoes," Priscilla said, and laughed. Then she mumbled, "I wonder how it feels to be from a state known for potatoes."

They spotted a sign for what appeared to be a general store just beyond the next exit. Priscilla drove off the interstate and parked in the store's lot. She went inside alone because no one else wanted to join her. She bought chips, chocolate candy, peanuts and soft drinks; then she spotted some beef jerky. She asked the salesman what it was, and he tried to explain it to her, but without success. Priscilla bought some anyway.

Back on the road, they crossed the Montana state line. The drive through Big Sky Country seemed to take a lifetime. Everywhere they turned, they passed through another national forest.

Germane's constant chant, "Why do they call them 'national forests?'" began to annoy Priscilla immensely. After she had said, "I don't know," many times, she said, "Maybe it's because the government wants to preserve the trees and some of the wildlife."

When Germane continued his chant about the national forest, Priscilla resorted to scare tactics: "Germane, we'd better hope this little wagon doesn't break down 'cause there're lots of big bears in these forests, lots of 'em."

Her strategy did not last long. Soon Germane fixated on other questions. "Do you think they're black bears or brown? Is one color meaner than the other is? I don't think bears eat people, but they'll squeeze you to death!" Germane laughed.

Eventually, Priscilla gave up answering his questions. "More jerky, Germane?"

Then, still without seeing a single major metropolitan area, they were in Bozeman. *Montana's so flat*, she thought.

They spent the night at a locally owned motel. Liza's credit card receipt documented the exact place, "Billings. We're no longer in the Rocky Mountains," Liza said.

"That's for sure," Priscilla said.

The next morning they passed through the vast Crow Indian Reservation. None of them had ever seen an Indian reservation. In plain view off the interstate were numerous cream-colored, cone-shaped tents that looked as if they were constructed of animal skins. "I wonder if the Indians actually live in those tepees or is that done to attract tourists?" Priscilla asked, but there was no response.

"You do know we're Cherokee on Mamma's side, and Choctaw on your Daddy's," Liza finally said. She talked as if someone had asked a question. "I thought we told you kids all this back when you were young."

"Can't say that I remember that exactly," Priscilla said. "But I do recall someone talking about Indian blood on both sides of the family, and for years I've been telling people we're part Cherokee. But I'm only vaguely aware of the Choctaw connection."

"You know, my grandmother—that's Mamma's mother—was full-blooded Cherokee," Liza went on. "She told us that her dad was an African, but she never knew which tribe, and that he and his parents were slaves. That's all Mamma can remember about her parents." There was no comment on Liza's story because neither Priscilla nor Germane knew what to say.

Priscilla drove along in silence. But she had not failed to notice that Liza had not mentioned Grandpa Nelson's roots. Like her father, the good Reverend, her grandfather (Liza's father) was also named Nelson.

Nelson Meeks was the son of a mulatto father, Owen Meeks, and an Irish mother, Elnora, and they had owned a farm in Henning, Tennessee. That was the farm where Grandma Lilly, Liza's mother, and others like her used to sharecrop. Although she never had a birth certificate, it was known that Grandma Lilly was born in the late 1880s in Brownsville, Kentucky, in the southwestern corner of the state. Priscilla was also aware that mixed-race marriages like that of her grandparents and great-grandparents, for that matter, were illegal in most Southern states until the *Loving v. Virginia Case* overturned such statutes in 1967.

Yet Priscilla remembered the story told to her and her sisters that went something like this: Grandpa Nelson often used a horse and buggy to run errands for his father's farm. One day, he decided to take the sharecropper known as Lilly (and who became known to subsequent generations of Meeks as Grandma Lilly) along to assist him, which he had thought was a clever ploy because no one questioned white men, or even men who could pass for white, who were accompanied by their sharecroppers. But later on that day, Grandpa Nelson (who was not really white but of mixed race since his father was a mulatto) and Grandma Lilly eloped to Sills Creek, Illinois. And they never went back to Henning, Tennessee.

Priscilla delighted in that story because she could picture her grandparents in that old horse-driven buggy as they raced along the dirt roads through the mountains and valleys along the Mississippi River. Herself a romantic, Priscilla was pleased to know that her ancestors had known adventure and romance.

She also remembered that whenever Liza and her siblings talked about Grandpa Nelson's side of the family, they would say, "Well now, we don't see all the fuss in claiming the white side. That's just messed us all up anyhow." But the memory that stayed with her most was Liza and her siblings saying: "T'aint no shame being black, but where's the pride in being white?"

Priscilla reflected that Liza and her siblings well knew about the challenges and ordeals of their racially mixed family, some of whom had even passed for white. One of Grandpa Nelson's sisters had committed suicide because she could not cope with her mixed-race dilemma. Even Priscilla did not dare to force discussion of the issue with Liza.

After the travelers continued their journey for a few miles along the interstate, Germane piped up again. "You know, Grandma, all these signs about Custer remind me of what I learned in school. Custer was a famous general, and he did a lot to help the North win the Civil War. Did *you* know that, Aunt Priscilla?"

Priscilla already knew that whatever else her nephew was about to say would only corroborate the prevalent historical record of the fall of the heroic general during one of the most devastating losses in the history of the U.S. military on American soil—a loss to the Sioux Indians after General George Armstrong Custer and his cavalry descended on an Indian encampment on the Little Big Horn River in the summer of 1876. During the battle that followed, the Sioux had defended themselves so successfully that the loss was later called "Custer's Last Stand."

Priscilla wondered: *But instead of studying about Custer, what about the thousands of Indians who'd been rounded up and forced onto reservations? Where was the empathy for them?*

Then Germane paraphrased one of the popular textbook versions of the battle: "After the Civil War, Custer came out here to help the country grow. But he got stuck with a bunch of unprofessional soldiers who didn't know how to fight the Indians. Anyway, the Sioux wiped out General Custer and his men. I think they were Sioux." Then he pointed to something else that had captured his attention. "And *there's* a sign to Little Big Horn. Wow!"

"Want to stop, Germane?" Priscilla asked frantically. "Momma? Say something before we pass the exit." There was no response.

Germane continued with what he had learned in school. "General Custer was also very young when he died. That's all I remember. But he was really, really famous because he'd won all of his battles up to the last one when he got killed."

"Gee whiz, Germane, that's incredible." Priscilla was honestly impressed. "How do you know all that stuff?"

"'Cause I like history, that's why, sort of the way you like politics, Aunt Priscilla."

"Well, blow me over, will you, Germane. Just blow me over." *And he's so young*, Priscilla added to herself.

"Well, Aunt Priscilla, do you remember anything from when you were in school?" Already the competitive spirit of the Austin clan had apparently taken root. Only this time, Priscilla chose not to comment.

Still on Interstate 90, the family headed southeast into Sheridan, Wyoming. "I flew near here on my way to Spokane," Priscilla was proud to report. "My friend Cathy lives in Cheyenne."

"That's nothing," Liza said. "One time your dad and I *drove* all the way from Prendergast to San Francisco."

Something told Priscilla just to nod in encouragement.

"But on our way back home, Nelson got sick. We were in Cheyenne when it happened. The doctors at the hospital diagnosed him with phlebitis. Obviously, he couldn't continue the trip. It was your sister Camille, Priscilla, who flew out here from Prendergast and drove us back home." Then she paused and said, "So you see, Priscilla, you're not the only one that I've asked to do me a favor."

Liza's words provided Priscilla with an effective answer to her frequent fretting, "Why me?"

A little later, Priscilla announced: "Okay, folks. We're headed into another state. South Dakota!" Bored with the monotonous flat terrain, Priscilla looked out her window at not only more national forests but also the Buffalo Gap Grassland and Fort Pierre and then more grassland.

"I'll spare you, Aunt Priscilla," Germane said. "I know you don't know what grassland is."

"Right, Germane."

"Finally, Sioux Falls." Priscilla never imagined she would be so happy to see Iowa. "This is where we change over to Interstate 29 and start our descent into Iowa. If we can just make it there today, then we can get some sleep and the rest of the trip will be a piece of cake."

The family took shelter in Sioux City. As they settled into the small motel room, Priscilla felt groggy, numb, limp and virtually lifeless. But she told herself to hold on just one more day. *Just one more day,* she thought, and then she fell asleep.

CHAPTER 28

Your Backup's Gone Now

Bright and early the next morning they ate breakfast, refueled the small vehicle and continued on the last leg of their journey.

"Look at all those tall leafy blades, fanning all over the place," Priscilla said out loud. "Where's the traffic? I don't even see any farm equipment, nothing." She had thought that yesterday's drive was monotonous, but this was much worse. "Please let it all end soon, please."

They all grew dizzy from the drive through what Priscilla thought were crops of corn, wheat and barley.

"The really tall stalks are corn," Priscilla said. "That much I know. Anyway, daydream, that's what I'll do. Just pretend you're somewhere else, folks. Lord knows, this is nowhere."

Suddenly, she said, "At last! A sign for Missouri, the end of our Iowa nightmare."

Into the next state sped the little gray station wagon. Everybody came alive. But they saw no notable signs between Council Bluffs, Iowa, and Saint Joseph, Missouri, so they became concerned at a posting for Iowa Sac and the Fox Indian Reservation.

"Oh, no! Are we still in Iowa?" Priscilla asked. But a moment later she said, "Ah, I see. We're at the junction where Iowa, Kansas and Nebraska all converge."

At that point, they exited Interstate 29 South and merged into Interstate 70 East.

"Boy was that refreshing," Priscilla said, with relief. As her second and third winds kicked into gear, she drove the breadth of Missouri ten miles an hour over the speed limit, all the while looking out warily for Missouri state troopers.

The family was *finally* homeward bound.

As they neared Saint Louis, Liza said, "Germane, you know Papa used to bring me here to baseball games."

"Really, Grandma!" Germane said, much intrigued. "You've been to Major League Baseball games?"

In her heart Liza hoped to bond again with her home, her mother and her sisters and brothers. Germane sensed Liza's feelings, and he connected easily to his grandmother's expectations. But Priscilla had made no effort to understand her mother's changing motivations and needs. Her own sentiments remained in Prendergast.

Liza let that conversation die and then started a whole new tack as she turned her attention to her daughter. "You know, Priscilla, you haven't said a word about your job. I find that strange, especially since you were so high-strung when you first started there. Has something happened?"

Completely taken aback, Priscilla tried hard to give an acceptable response: "Well, Momma, I'm not sure where to begin or what to say."

"Try the truth."

"Did you ever wonder why I came back to Ohio in the first place? I'm not sure whether you know this, but Daddy *asked* me to move 'closer to home.' Otherwise, I had *absolutely* no plans to leave my job at FAMU. But lately, I *have* been reconsidering my options." Priscilla paused. Was now the time to share her hopes and dreams with her mother? *No*, she thought, *not now, not yet*. She hoped that her vague explanation would suffice.

But no. Liza chose to dredge up the past. It was a long ride, and Liza seemed to think she had plenty of time to pursue her inquiry. "Now wait a minute, *young lady*. Your daddy's gone, and he's not coming back. You don't have the backup you once had. You can't just leave this job like you left the one in Prendergast." Liza had completely overlooked Priscilla's faculty post at FAMU. She launched into the ancient history of Priscilla leaving a desk job in Prendergast. Then she wanted to know why Priscilla had just hinted she was planning to leave what she thought was "a perfectly darned good job."

"Oh, Momma!" Priscilla sorely regretted agreeing to be shut up in this car for so long, with no escape from her mother's relentless harping. She tried to distract her with another line of conversation. "But surely you know this is a new day for women."

"Really? Tell me, what makes things so different for women today than before?"

"Well, for one thing, women no longer cling to men to take care of us, at least, not all of us. For another, my work in the Ohio Senate is political. And yes, it's gosh-darn confining. I'm feeling really boxed in."

After Liza kept interrupting her many more times, Priscilla decided it was best to relent so Liza would get off her back. "Okay, stop worrying, Momma. I'll hang in there a little longer."

A thought struck her. Even though her relationship with Senator Callahan had never been mentioned, Priscilla had always assumed that Liza knew there was something inappropriate between the two of them. Yet at this moment, she felt that Liza was encouraging her to cling to the senator for security. *What's wrong with this picture?* She wondered.

As Priscilla pondered the absurdity of the conversation, Liza fretted, "I certainly hope you don't go and do something rash. Good jobs are hard to come by these days." She repeated what she had earlier said. "You just remember that your daddy's gone now, child. Your backup's gone now."

Liza looked out the window and sighed under her breath. When Priscilla had gotten the job offer from FAMU, Liza and Nelson had allowed their daughter to think that she had done so on her own. But she had been hired there because Nelson had a personal connection with Dean Newsome. Liza had also known that even back in Prendergast her daughter had been hired as a computer programmer because Nelson had a personal connection with the company's CEO. Finally, Liza had always intuited that Priscilla had been hired as an

Ohio Senate aide because she had a personal connection with Senator Callahan. So Liza's view of Priscilla's employment history was wholly out of sync with the thinking of contemporary feminists. But mostly, Liza's return to Sills Creek—where most of her relatives had even less enlightened worldviews—would further thwart her ability ever to comprehend Priscilla's way of thinking.

So how did Priscilla reconcile herself to her apparent dilemma? She did as she had learned. As usual, she relented for the moment.

"Oh, Momma, please stop fretting. I *told* you! I'm not going to go and do anything 'rash,' not anytime soon. Okay?"

Liza sighed again. She had wanted her daughters "to get as much education as possible and to get out into the world," but she had great difficulty letting them go, especially Priscilla. Yet after Nelson's death, Liza had reverted to even more archaic ways of thinking which were even more at odds with contemporary feminists. Yet she also knew that Priscilla, unlike her other daughters, had already lived dangerously on the edge. With Nelson gone, she had no idea how she alone could help her daughter hang on. And Liza was no fool. Even she understood that her daughter was saying whatever she had to say to appease her and to end the conversation.

A long silence ensued in the car.

Both Priscilla and Liza were greatly relieved to see the Gateway Arch, which, for them, was like seeing The Pearly Gates.

"Gateway to the West—or is it the East?" Priscilla said. "But I thought this would be a much bigger bridge and a wider portion of the Mississippi."

Yet Liza was happy. Her face was alight with joy. "Germane, we've reached Saint Louis! We're home now! Child, we can almost walk to Sills Creek from here! Are you excited to meet your great-grandma?"

The three travelers were soon cruising into Sills Creek. But when they arrived in the semi-rural town, none of them knew how to get to Aunt Madelyn's home. She had moved since Liza's last visit.

"Now where the devil is East McCord Street?" Priscilla asked.

They had driven across the country for three days without any problems, only to arrive at the one-horse town of Sills Creek and get lost.

Priscilla recalibrated her bearings and weaved through the maze of small streets.

"There it is, East McCord," she said. "I sure hope someone's home."

She drove into the driveway and had barely stopped the car before Liza and Germane jumped out.

For a moment, Priscilla could not move her travel-tormented body. She sat still until she collected herself. Then she joined the others inside Aunt Madelyn's house.

Aunt Madelyn was ecstatic to see her younger sister Liza and "the kids."

"I mean," she said, "I'm so happy to see you all."

Uncle Joshua—her husband—was equally pleased to see his in-laws. But he expressed disapproval that they had "made such an extensive trip without the company of a man."

Uncle Joshua looked like Paul Robeson: tall, dark-complexioned and stately. Aunt Madelyn was the exact opposite in appearance: well under five feet and white like her mulatto father. But Priscilla could not help noticing that Liza and Madelyn shared similar characteristics: accentuated cheekbones and fine, wavy hair, small-framed bodies and an ostensibly regal comportment like the many Indian women she had seen during their cross-country trek.

Priscilla said to herself, *Wow! Granted Uncle Joshua is up in age, but is this near the end of the twentieth century, or what?* Aloud she said, "But we did it, Uncle Joshua, we did it. And we did it on our own. Besides, my sister drove them all the way from Columbus to Spokane last year, and I don't recall any criticism about that trip. So why is it a problem for me to drive them all the way back?"

"I'm glad you remembered that tidbit about your sister, Miss Priscilla," Liza said, continuing to checkmate her daughter. "As I said before, you're not the only one who's done your mom a favor."

However, both Madelyn and Joshua were focused on the younger member of the family. They reached out to touch him, saying, "Let me look at you, Germane." But the boy was not pleased to be put on display.

Then, seemingly from out of nowhere, shot a high-spirited, small-framed elderly woman in a wheelchair. "Liza? Is that my Liza's voice?" Grandma Lilly screamed out in cheer.

"Yes, Mamma, this is Liza," said the tearful daughter.

"Ah knew you'd come and git me," Grandma Lilly said. "Ah told all these crazy folks, 'My Liza will come and git me.' And Ah told 'em 'you'd take me back home, back to *my* house.' Liza's here now!" Her prayers had been answered.

They all yielded to her small, yet magnificent presence. She stood no more than four-and-a-half feet in height, if that much, and she weighed less than one hundred pounds. Her hair was fine, shoulder length, wavy and worn in a small bun. Her eyes sparkled. Beyond any doubt, Grandma Lilly bore the Cherokee blood of her mother.

"Grandma, you sure are something else. You most certainly are that," Priscilla said, to join in the conversation. She leaned over to hug her grandmother, who grabbed her head and slapped a huge kiss on her cheek. Then Grandma Lilly smiled and wiped away streams of tears.

Poor Germane was next. Since he was small enough to manage, Grandma Lilly hugged him up until he begged for release. She wore the same expression of happiness as Liza had on the drive when finally they arrived at Sills Creek.

A few years earlier, Grandma Lilly had contracted a serious infection in the big toe on her right foot because she would pick and clip away at an ingrown toenail. Of course, she did not believe in medical doctors. Then, on a routine visit one day, Uncle George—one of Liza's older brothers who lived a couple of blocks away—noticed some discoloration and swelling in his mother's right foot. Immediately, he picked up her small frame, put her in his car and drove her to the local hospital.

There, after Grandma Lilly was examined, she was diagnosed with a major case of gangrene. At first, the doctors advised against amputation, primarily because Grandma Lilly was nearly eighty-five years old. Then the doctors changed their opinion and decided to remove her foot. Eventually, they determined that it was best to amputate her leg up to her knee. Throughout the surgery, the doctors were concerned that she might die from the trauma of such a drastic operation.

But Grandma Lilly had proved more resilient than anyone imagined. Soon, the family was concerned about keeping out of her way. She maneuvered her wheelchair like Mario Andretti on the speedway.

"Priscilla, chile, look at ya, looking like your Daddy," Grandma Lilly said. Then she teased, "She axes like him, too."

Priscilla did not understand what she had done to "axe like him, too," but she understood Grandma Lilly's words were not a compliment. While Priscilla looked puzzled, the others snickered. Maybe Priscilla did not "get it", but she was as aloof as her father had been. Everybody recognized that trait in her and took it for granted, yet Priscilla gazed in bewilderment from face to face.

That night, she lay in bed, gazed up toward the ceiling and said aloud, "Well, now, Daddy, do you suppose I've done my part by Momma? May I please get on with my own life?" Then she went to sleep.

The next morning, one of her cousins drove her downtown to catch the bus to Columbus. What would have taken her six hours to travel by car took close to a full day on the local Greyhound coach.

But Priscilla did not mind. She was in no hurry to resume her work in the Ohio Senate.

CHAPTER 29

The 1982 Elections

As soon as Priscilla entered the reception area of Senator Callahan's office suite, she encountered tension in the air. To be sure, she knew that the Senate Democrats were still fuming from their mortifying electoral defeat in November 1980 as well as from their more recent humiliation during the budget deliberations. *But enough of the pity party,* she thought.

Without waiting to be announced by Charlene, Priscilla made her way to Senator Callahan's office, where the wrath of her boss awaited her.

"Well, *young lady,*" he began. "I'm glad you remembered where your place is. But how long does it take to drive someone across the country? I started wondering whether you'd even come back."

Priscilla stood before the senator's desk in grand, stoic fashion and tolerated his angry outburst of the obvious. She only half-listened to his litany and hid a yawn as she waited for him, as usual, to blow off steam. Clearly he had not known her itinerary and apparently assumed she was driving all the way across the country, not just from Washington State to Illinois. But for the first time ever, she observed a strikingly unfavorable similarity between the senator's attitude and that of her mom: hectoring, disparaging and definitely disapproving. As Priscilla's eyes locked onto the senator's, she was clearly dismissive. *Whoa, Bubba, do you think I owe you something?*

PRISCILLA

But she knew, and the senator knew, that he needed her to help with the 1982 primary election campaign season which had begun while she was off chauffeuring her mother. The big prize, the governor's office, was up for grabs, and during this election cycle the Senate Democrats were finally showing the sheer will to win.

The senator's voice finally calmed. Then without waiting for any response from Priscilla he began summarizing the primary campaign. "As you know, we've got three excellent contenders on the loose for the governor's office, and the attorney general is heavily favored to win that race. And since I don't have any serious opposition, I'm exerting my energy and resources to help the caucus regain control of the Senate and, of course, to help the successful Democratic candidate win the governor's office. So, sweetheart, I need you to work closely with me on a major fund-raising project."

Priscilla knew that, except for her father, people in positions of power were often unable to express need. Because they could not or would not say what they *wanted* from other people, they resorted to other tactics. First—just as Brad had done in that tête à tête in the parking garage—they might degrade, demean and even intimidate their intended targets, and then maybe hope their targets would opt to work their way out of their unfavorable situations. For example, preachers in Nelson's conference were known to resort to bribery— carrying black leather cases filled with cash in the hopes of winning their bishop's favor. And closer to home here in the Ohio Senate was ongoing rivalry with Brad. She doubted that he had even considered a statewide event in support of Senator Tektonidis's quest for leadership of the Senate. She would be one-upping Brad by working on *her* senator's fund-raising project. "All right," she said. "How 'major' should this event be?"

"I was thinking fifty or sixty thousand dollars or so should cover everything to make my case," the senator said. "Provide a reception, a meal and an outstanding speaker. The way things seem to be going with campaign costs, someday soon we might consider that peanuts. But I've got a safe seat. The money isn't for *my* reelection campaign, but to spread around to help in other campaigns. We're not out to break

270

anyone's bank. I simply want my new donors to get accustomed to the image of me as the new chairman of the Senate Finance Committee."

Priscilla nodded.

The Finance Committee Chairman was the bagman for his caucus. Priscilla had heard some time ago that Senator Caldiera had raised one hundred and twenty thousand dollars. She wondered about her boss's goal. *Why so little? Why not more? Hum.* But what the senator wanted to do was test the waters for his capacity to generate funds, and expeditiously at that.

As it turned out, Liza had won Priscilla's grudging promise not "to do anything rash" about her job and that she would "hang in there a little longer." Priscilla reflected that now she had a more personal understanding of how women throughout the ages had to endure similar, or worse, circumstances contrary to their will. Yet she figured there were worse assignments. Born with a God-given talent to envision and execute, Priscilla possessed a natural propensity for planning events and marketing them.

Nelson and Liza had marveled at Priscilla's ability to accomplish her goals during her teenage years. If there was something she wanted, she would set out to raise the capital, and she seemed to do it effortlessly. She would sell products such as flower and vegetable seeds door-to-door. She would even pick grapes by the crate at Mourné Vineyards.

But her biggest accomplishment had been a fund-raiser that she had conducted in the name of her father's church. One summer, the young people in the church needed funds to attend a quadrennial church convention out of state. To acquire the funds, Priscilla devised a plan to sponsor a trip to Crystal Beach in Ontario, Canada. She easily filled two tourist busses with excited participants of all ages. She even had the temerity to "call a truce" with her archnemesis, Marcia, and the Virginia clan. In fact, on the evening that she called Marcia, Nelson had stood flabbergasted in the family room and listened as she made her pitch over the telephone.

"Okay, now, Marcia. This is a friendly call. I know you've heard about our trip to Crystal Beach. Do you think this is something you guys want to do? If so, then we've got to put our differences on hold."

A decade later, a more mature Priscilla was equally capable of managing a major fund-raiser for a state senator. Pumped up for her new project, she called her friend Julia: "Girl, the senator asked me to conduct a major *statewide* fund-raiser for him. The ultimate aim is to secure him the chairmanship of the Senate Finance Committee. This is going to be big. We'll start with personalized teasers to a select group from the donors' list. How do you suppose those guys on Madison Avenue produce their ad campaigns?" Priscilla paused for breath but cut Julia off as she tried to interject something. "We'll create a little flurry before sending out the actual invitations. Also, no preprinted labels. Everything must be hand-addressed. And the senator won't like this, but he'll have to handwrite a bunch of personal notes."

Julia managed to cut in. "Priscilla, slow down! You haven't even talked about your trip with your mother yet." The friendship of the two women had deepened in the past months after Priscilla used her political connections to help Julia win an important fight she was having with her professors in the medical school at the state university. Julia's advisor had recommended she switch her major from general practice to psychiatry, but she had refused. At Julia's request, Priscilla had taken the issue to the state senator from Julia's hometown of Toledo. But when that senator had lost her re-election bid, Priscilla had championed her friend's cause herself. As Julia waited for a favorable outcome, the two women had formed a habit of talking over their personal as well as professional concerns. Although she had often admonished Priscilla about her relationship with the senator, Julia had come to understand that it was only a matter of time before Priscilla ended it—and on *her* terms. Otherwise, Julia's primary criticism of Priscilla was her tendency to be openly picayune and obdurate and—at the worst times, for which she had often urged her to "Let it go, Priscilla. Just let it go."

Priscilla, habitually, did not seem to hear her friend. She was now focused on the biggest fund-raising campaign she had ever managed: "Doing it this way, people will feel like they're being personally invited, and they'll talk about it, too. Word of mouth! That's the kind of impact we want. And Julia, don't let me forget the gavel. I'm placing a great, big gavel on the cover of the invitation to depict authority and power. And the union label, can't forget that, either. Tell me I'm good at this game. Never mind. I *am* good and I *know* it. Never forget: 'Act like a winner.'"

Julia's voice was a wail. "How do you *know* the Senator will get the chairmanship of the Finance Committee? And why all the complicated mailing? What exactly are you up to?"

"I want each recipient to feel personally connected to the work of the senator."

"Stop it, already," Julia snapped, tired of Priscilla's lofty attitude and dismissal of her concerns.

"Julia, just let me finish my game plan, and then we can talk about the personal stuff. Okay?"

But Julia's concerns lingered. "Just tell me one thing. How do you *know* the Democrats are going to win back the Senate? What happens if you lose?"

"My dear Julia, the verb 'lose' is nowhere in a winner's vocabulary or mind-set. Winners view defeats as mere setbacks, something to learn from, launching pads for future campaigns, which, of course, will be victories."

Julia caved in. "Okay, Missy."

Priscilla had a big smile on her face as she informed Senator Callahan whom she had invited to speak at the event.

"What!" He became unglued. "You spoke with *whose* office?"

"Senator, I wrote a letter, enclosed your résumé and asked the senator if he'd like to come to Ohio and 'make a showing for such a man' as you. The next thing I knew his staff were on the line asking me for more details."

"This time, Priscilla, you've gone over the top. I'm not running for statewide or national office. I'm seeking reelection to the Ohio Senate. And besides, those gubernatorial candidates will be absolutely peeved with me if I bring in a United States senator. Call Senator Fitzgerald's staff back and tell them there's been a misunderstanding or something."

But Senator Callahan should never have used the word "major" to describe the type of event he had wanted because Priscilla had taken him literally. She had successfully solicited the support of Massachusetts Senator Teddy Fitzgerald.

After he had compelled Priscilla to withdraw the invitation, she became convinced that Senator Callahan would remain small-fry and never rise to higher office. So she sought the participation of one of the state's most prominent and eloquent black Baptist ministers, which was more suitable for the senator, anyway.

Former Lieutenant Governor Antonio J. Scalise handily won the Democratic Party primary over his two main opponents. The attorney general had been heavily favored to win, but both he and the former secretary of state lost out after significant political missteps. Over the summer and fall, Scalise had campaigned as if his life depended on it. A Rhodes Scholar and seasoned politician, Scalise presented himself as a centrist, and many political pundits were certain he was bringing refreshing substance to the 1982 gubernatorial race in Ohio. News media carried stories headlined, "Scalise Running For and Against Himself" and "Republican Candidate Poses No Contest to Scalise."

As the campaign heated up, Senator Callahan once again called Priscilla into his office. She had indeed delivered him a successful fund-raiser with that Baptist minister, and now he proposed that she conduct one more major event in support of Scalise's campaign for the governorship.

Priscilla silently considered what was at stake. Whenever a politician wants something from another politician of much higher rank, he must bring plenty of financial capital instead of alms. The senator had just told her the setting for the event was the governor's mansion, and the invitation list was to include the Who's Who of the state. She plainly understood Senator Callahan believed he needed Scalise's support to clinch the chairmanship of the Senate Finance Committee.

"Well, at the least, his support wouldn't hurt," he told Priscilla.

Again Priscilla was silent for a long minute as she considered the political realities.

Considered a slow-growth state, Ohio had been losing population for so many years that by 1982, the state's number of electoral votes had been reduced to twenty-three. With the state's dwindling population also had come a sharp reduction in federal funds, which was worsened by the departure and shutdown of heavy industries such as steel and rubber. Ohio had suffered not only high unemployment but also huge debt, and, ultimately, the despicable image of "the Rust Bowl."

Finally—and thoughtfully—Priscilla nodded. The successful Democratic contender had much to change for the better, and she was about to be part of that.

One of her first challenges was to assemble Statehouse liaisons for the fund-raiser from the gubernatorial campaign team. That way, she would ensure that the proper protocols would be followed in both the preparation and the execution of the event. The elaborate protocols included such details as who would stand where in the reception line and the proper titles for introductions and toasts, as well as the honorable mentions on the invitations and any statements to the press.

Also, she mentioned to Senator Callahan, the ticket price was a little steep.

"But we're talking about the next governor," he blandly told Priscilla.

For food, she hired one of the best-known caterers in the area, who had previously served at the governor's mansion; for entertainment, she booked a well-recognized black jazz ensemble.

Since the honoree had already served as lieutenant governor, Priscilla, with the senator's backing, decided to take the editorial liberty of showing only the word "governor" near his name on the invitation and in press statements. Priscilla and the senator were also hopeful that readers of the invitation would be further influenced by the name "Scalise" associated with "Governor's Mansion."

So the elegant but simply designed invitations read:

*You are cordially invited
to a reception honoring*

Antonio J. Scalise

The next Governor of the State of Ohio

*At the Governor's Mansion
Columbus, OH*

Thursday, Aug. 25, 1982 ~ 7:30 p.m.

After five attire – Open Bar

Senator Callahan's name appeared in fine print on the invitations as "the sponsor" of the event.

As Priscilla expected, rumors and speculation began as soon as the invitations were received—and leaked to the press.

"No, Senator Callahan is not looking for some special appointment," Priscilla felt obligated to say when the queries began. "We're simply showing our support for the successful Democratic contender for governor. That's all there is to the event. Period." Sometimes she would add that the senator's sponsorship was not about his own recognition but his deference for the candidate for governor, who was the head of the Democratic ticket. She did not feel obligated to confide that the senator had already made certain the event was in accordance with the campaign finance laws, and that of course he had cleared it with the Scalise campaign team.

The evening of the reception brought out virtually all the Democratic members of the House and the Senate and many local Democratic officials from across the state. Also in attendance were numerous staff and lobbyists and the many Republican supporters for the Scalise candidacy.

But most notable amid the gathering was a small and tight-knit group of young gentlemen who held power positions in Ohio banking, unions and construction, and who were commonly called, by those in the know, "the big wigs." They had come not only because the event was significant and that it was therefore "the place to be" but also because they wanted to size up the young woman known as P. J. Austin, who had pulled together yet another spectacular political event.

Indeed, although she did not know it, Priscilla was playing in high cotton.

On Election Night, they all sat in front of the imposing computer screens in the overcrowded, smoke-filled rooms of the Hamilton County Board of Elections. Republicans and Democrats alike squirmed, bit their fingernails and cursed at the early returns. Screams of adulation clashed with those of anger—and sometimes one's ears could not distinguish the difference. For some races, early returns signaled defeat; for others, such as Senator Callahan's, early returns were familiar indicators of favorable turnout and a likely win. Late returns arrived from the periphery of the senator's district.

After the "over-the-50-percent" mark was reached, Senator Callahan turned his attention to calling the secretary of state.

"How's it looking for our boy? What's that? Oh shit, that's not good." The senator asked about a few others and then, after beckoning to Priscilla, curtly spoke into the phone: "I'm on my way up. See you shortly."

Priscilla had already learned that not much of what the senator said in such conversations ought ever to be taken literally. He was, after all, a politician.

On their way out of the Board of Elections building, Priscilla and the senator ran into Senator Caldiera, who seemed disturbed about something. He and Senator Callahan spoke sparingly, and out of earshot. Callahan was upbeat, but Caldiera remained somber.

In the car, leave it to Priscilla to ask the obvious: "Why's Senator Caldiera so down? I didn't know this was his year, too."

"It wasn't his own reelection but the defeat of Republican control of the Senate," Senator Callahan said with much exhilaration. "We're back in the saddle, and you're looking at the new chairman of the Senate Finance Committee. Cheer up, sweetie. That means you rise, too."

As they drove up Interstate 71 to Columbus, the senator talked nonstop. Priscilla had never seen him so enthusiastic. "Remember when I asked you to plan that statewide fund-raiser for Scalise?"

"Of course. But why bring that up now?"

"No matter how well-known and respected a politician may become, if he doesn't command a significant war chest, he can't play in this game. It takes *big* money to play this game."

In Priscilla's life, there was very little she had cherished or sought with great desire. Yet now she was in an arena where people's existence centered on winning elections and appointments to public office. In this arena, people raised and spent untold sums of money—all used to hedge major commitments. For the time being, however, Priscilla was experiencing the belly of politics; the bile would come later.

She and the senator arrived at the capitol in the wee hours of Wednesday morning, after Election Day, Tuesday, November 2, 1982. Together, they pushed their way through the massive crowd as they, like many others, headed up the steep spiral marble staircase to the third floor office of Marcus the Greek, the heir apparent to the presidency of the Ohio Senate.

CHAPTER 30

A Defection in the Ranks

Later that morning, Priscilla, and all the other Ohio Democrat politicos, learned to their chagrin that all was not what it had first appeared to be. Yes, they had won the election; but no, they did not automatically resume control of the Ohio Senate.

The reason was that Senator Theopholus Madison—a man of immense political stature and seniority, and one of the two blacks in the Ohio Senate—was defecting from the Democratic Party ranks.

Priscilla and many other up-to-then jubilant Democrats read the news in various newspapers and wire services. Their hard-fought electoral victory had been transitory. The newspaper headlines ran the gamut: "Shake up in the Ohio Political Landscape;" "Overnight, Senate Democratic Coup Restores Majority Control to the Republicans;" and "Political Farce in the Ohio Senate." Although the Democrats had captured all of the state-wide offices and even regained control of the Senate in the polling, they would not be able to exercise majority power in the Senate because of a defection from within the Democratic ranks. The Republicans would retain control (leadership) of the Ohio Senate.

Priscilla was shocked to read that the defector was Senator Theopholus Madison, who for nearly twenty years had represented the largely black and Democratic district that comprised most of

Cleveland. He had served as president pro tempore—second only to then-Senate President Walt O'Leary. And before the Democrats' 1980 electoral defeat, for several years he had also chaired the powerful Rules and Reference Committee.

Reverberating throughout the corridors of the Statehouse and in the newsrooms of every media outlet in Ohio and beyond was the question: why did Madison break ranks and join forces with the Republicans?

No one could recall such a maneuver before. Most Democratic lawmakers shook their heads and told one another that Madison's defection made no sense.

Among those who shared that assessment was Priscilla J. Austin, who felt as though she had awakened to a nightmare akin to a Greek tragedy.

That evening, Priscilla returned home early. Senator Callahan had sent his staff home, saying there was no reason to hang around. Priscilla had nodded, aware that the Democratic caucus had ordered the shutdown to avoid leaks to the press.

She brewed a pot of coffee and settled down in front of the television in her bedroom. The news of Senator Madison's defection and the resulting Democratic loss of control of the state senate was sensational. As Priscilla flipped from one channel to the next, she caught sight of Cheryl Tupper, political news correspondent for CBS affiliate WBTV.

Cheryl was standing in front of the massive doors leading to the senate chamber where she poignantly stated, "The political adage of 'one-man one-vote' couldn't be more apropos than here and now. Here, it takes *one vote* from *one man* to determine the outcome of the leadership in this august body."

Priscilla thought: *How ironic. There aren't any more women in the Senate, either.*

She continued watching as Cheryl moved about the floor of the chamber, seemingly measuring her steps and waxing poetically:

"It is here that thirty-three state senators work to pass laws ranging from abortion, education, highway construction and minority-business Set-Aside Bills to birth, death, marriage and divorce, public welfare, redistricting and taxes. And it is here that Cleveland Senator Theopholus Madison holds the decisive vote to determine which party's agenda will control such legislation."

Cheryl paused and a photo of Senator Madison appeared on the television screen. Priscilla almost knocked her cup of coffee off the nightstand. She now realized that, for the first time, most television viewers were able to see that the subject of the news story was a distinguished, middle-aged black man.

"Oh no! Is she going to show Senator Callahan, too?" Priscilla said aloud.

Then, she steadied herself as, gradually the camera focused on an elevated podium, flanked by decorative flags and ornately framed portraits of historical figures.

Cheryl stood behind the huge rostrum, and once again the camera zoomed in on her.

"It is within this very chamber that the prestigious Club of Thirty-Three, as it is unofficially known, conducts the affairs of this state. Ladies and gentlemen, welcome to the Ohio Senate."

Near the end of Cheryl's report, she picked up the big heavy gavel and clutched it. It was then that Priscilla came to another realization, this time, about her boss: "That's it!" Senator Callahan was a lineman, not a leader. Priscilla even remembered how once he had said so himself when he told her, "I don't need leadership positions. It is in committees where the bodies are buried and where I can get things done."

Priscilla finally realized that the man for whom she worked, Senator Daniel P. Callahan, would never clutch that presidential gavel nor would he hold any other leadership post in the Ohio Senate. *Oh crap. No future for me here.*

Plainly Priscilla's enthusiasm about working for Senator Callahan had dissipated. So she came to the decision that, while still here, she would make the best of her own situation—and then move on.

As it turned out, the recent election results would have given the Senate Democrats a seventeen-to-sixteen majority. But Madison's defection would keep Republicans in power and forfeit the powerful committee chairmanships from the Democrats. Senator Madison had apparently stated only that he believed he would be "more effective with this new arrangement" and then refused any further comment.

Priscilla kept flipping to more channels, but there was no additional news, other than that there was apparently precedent for a change in party identification after an election. The consensus, at least among the television political news correspondents, was that there could be no court challenge or other legal reversal to Madison's defection.

Priscilla's anger intensified, and her voice rose as she berated the television in lieu of Senator Madison. "Does that man realize the ramifications of his actions? Does he even care?"

And there matters stood. Republicans kept the committee chairmanships. Reporters tried and failed to get anyone to go on camera and denounce Senator Madison. Senator Callahan was a particular media target, as though, being the other black legislator in the state senate, he would have unique racial perspective to share about Senator Madison's surprising defection.

While Senator Callahan and his Democratic colleagues deliberated strategies about what to do, Priscilla became tired of their seemingly prolonged inaction. That night she awakened from a series of bad dreams. She was soaked with sweat, but now, suddenly, she had a plan.

Priscilla jumped out of bed, went into her study, and commenced writing down her thoughts in the form of a letter:

Dear Senator Madison:

As a product of Prendergast, we've always celebrated your accomplishments; there, as you know, we display your portrait in the vestibule of our church.

Priscilla paused. Inadvertently, she had revealed not only that Senator Madison had come from Prendergast, New York, of all places, but also that she had lived there, too. But she continued to write:

It was from there in your teenage years that your mom moved your family to Cleveland, 'where there were better opportunities.'

Senator, as I'm sure you are aware, you were *among a few prominent citizens that Prendergast laid claim to, including Industrialist B. F. Blackwell and Actress Marilyn DeSantos—that is, until your recent defection.*

Although Priscilla's conversational style of appealing personally to Senator Madison remained constant, her tone suddenly shifted dramatically:

Some of us find your recent action unfathomable, and others, unacceptable, regardless of the reason why. Accordingly, dear Senator, people remember more that Faust sold his soul *than the reason why he sold it.*

As her pen chased her thoughts, even Priscilla felt the penetration of her words.

Does it matter that Senator Callahan, your friend and colleague and the only other black member in the senate, is being denied his well-earned historic chairmanship? What of the implications of a Democratic majority in the Ohio General Assembly for the black constituents in this state? Can you honestly say that you've given serious consideration to the ramifications of your actions?

Priscilla was mercilessly unrelenting as she continued to write of Senator Madison's *deplorable demeanor, selfishness, and your outright jealousy towards Senator Callahan.*

In an era of rapidly changing telecommunications, Priscilla's ability to portray an apt image of what she believed was a reprehensible act by Senator Madison was essential.

But even though she herself had been naïve, although thorough, forthright and scathing, little did she know the ramifications of *her* actions. She had acted alone, and she had stood out, alone, in the tempest. She had put her fortitude at stake.

A day or so after she edited the final version of her letter, she called Julia and asked her to come over to help "with a special mailing." Meanwhile, she thought about her next move and realized that she did not know of Senator Madison's whereabouts. So how could she deliver her letter? Priscilla shrugged. *Let him read about it in the newspapers,*

much like the way we learned about his defection. At that point, she also decided to make hers an open letter.

When Julia arrived and read Priscilla's letter, she suggested they simply hand-deliver it to his office at the Statehouse. "Surely," she said, "the senator's staff knows how to route it to him."

Priscilla shook her head, sure now she knew exactly what she would do. "I want this letter to hit him hard, not sit on some staff member's desk and collect dust." It took little coercing on her part to get Julia's cooperation, just as she had done many times before, back in Prendergast, with her friend Amber.

Priscilla and Julia took the three-page letter and Senator Callahan's campaign stationery to the university's main copy center and printed over one hundred copies under Senator Callahan's letterhead. When they returned to Priscilla's home, they spread out all the copies and envelopes on her dining room table and commenced to sign, fold and stuff each letter into an envelope. Next, they hand-addressed each envelope to a news organization, affixed first class postage and loaded up the mailing in Julia's car. Then they drove around the city and deposited their mail at different postal stations.

The next day, every major news organization in the state published parts of Priscilla's letter, particularly the reference to the soul-seller Faust. Her open letter to Senator Madison had effectively illuminated the dark nooks and crevices connected to this political farce.

From one newspaper article: "Senate legislative aide Priscilla J. Austin signed the letter." And from another: "But who really wrote the letter, and why, so boldly, did Ms. Austin, aide to Senator Daniel P. Callahan of Cincinnati, allow the use of her name?" Suddenly, local talk show hosts had ample fodder for their top-ten segments; and political pundits clamored to explain the significance of the latest event.

As for P. J. Austin, well, she stewed.

As Priscilla later learned much earlier that same morning, Senator Callahan was awakened at his Cincinnati home by the telephone. He grumbled and yanked the covers over his head. "That's got to be a wrong number. I was just getting to sleep." Then he slid his arm from underneath his bed linen and grabbed hold of the telephone. "Yeah, who's this at this ungodly ho—?"

Jokingly, the Greek said, "Wake up, Daniel, it's me, Marcus. Yeah, man, Tektonidis, your new leader."

Senator Callahan raised himself up in his bed. "For heaven's sake, Marcus, what's up for you to call me at this hour?" He swung his legs over the edge of his bed, reached for his eyeglasses and squinted at the clock radio on the nightstand. "Hell, man, is that five-thirty? Damn it, Marcus, this'd better be good."

Senator Tektonidis waited while Senator Callahan pulled himself together, and then he said, "Wait till you get a load of the editorial section in the morning newspapers. Apparently, someone *very* close to us has taken it upon herself to contact Theo Madison via an open letter."

Senator Callahan gripped his bed covers. "Oh yeah, man, who's that?"

Senator Tektonidis had difficulty maintaining control. "Ever heard the name Pris-cil-la J, that's middle initial 'J,' Aus-tin?"

Senator Callahan abruptly sat up and said, "Ah, come on, Marcus! You poured too much ouzo in your coffee or something?"

"Daniel, it's all here. Besides, I'm drinking my coffee black, thank you."

Senator Tektonidis read one of the editorials out loud. After he finished reading it, there was a prolonged silence.

"Now how the hell am I to deal with this shit?" Senator Callahan said. "Why didn't she come to me? I knew she was upset, but not like this." He swore silently to himself as he considered the possible implications to his achieving chairmanship of the Senate Finance Committee. "Ah shit, man, am I screwed or what?"

"Sorry to break it to you like this, ole friend, but I thought it best you knew the latest episode in this little farce *before* stepping out of your front door, 'cause they'll be waiting for you. But we can thrash this out once you get to the office. And take it easy coming up the road. I want you around when the dust settles."

Senator Tektonidis hung up the telephone and turned to his aide, who so thoughtfully had brought him the newspapers after being tipped off by a reporter friend. "Well, Brad," he said, "that takes care of that. You heard for yourself. I woke up Daniel in his bed at home, and he was genuinely shocked at the news. He said he didn't have anything to do with it. That girl is something else. She put herself right smack in front of the eight ball, all by herself."

Senator Tektonidis took another swallow of his coffee, and then continued: "But it's a good thing, 'cause the hunt is well underway. Once our guys catch up with Theo, and Walt, too, for that matter, it'll be all over." He paused. "Oh, I know, 'It really ain't over 'til it's over.'" A raw edge was in Senator Tektonidis' voice. "Still, I don't much care what you or anybody else thinks. I'm damn glad for this little diversion. It'll give everybody else something to focus on while we sniff out the bastards."

"Yeah, Marcus, you're right on that, but—," Brad began.

"I knew a 'but' was coming. 'But' *what*?" Senator Tektonidis said.

"I was about to say, but what're we gonna do about the speculation that the caucus put her up to it?"

"Snap out of it, Brad! At this point, I'm willing to let everybody believe Santa Claus wrote the damn letter. But if it'll make you feel any better, contact a couple of the fellas and put them on Daniel's tail. Tell them to probe him about the letter. Still, haven't you noticed that girl's behavior hasn't changed one bit? From day one, all she's ever done was to look out for Daniel. Nor has she slipped away from the scene like our little émigré Theo. Nah, Brad, Ms. Prissy will be in the office today: money on it." Then Senator Tektonidis winked at Brad.

Well before the legislative offices opened that morning, lawmakers, lobbyists and reporters descended on the Statehouse and crowded into Mary's Café.

Questions and declarations flew:

"What happened?"

"Why'd they publish an open letter under the name of a staffer?"

"Now we *know* she didn't write the letter, but what we don't know is why our mystery writer chose to release it under *her* signature?" Curiosity ripened.

Priscilla sat alone and pensive at her desk. *What the hell have I gone and done this time? How did I even get myself into this darn mess?*

She found herself far from her once-staid life, caught up in the bile of the political abyss. It seemed that few people believed she had written the letter—at least not by herself. Yet they understood why she had written her signature at the end of the letter: she had been keen on saying to everyone who would listen, "My boss deserves that chairmanship. The results of that election were valid."

But more unsettling for Priscilla was that many political observers did not think she had written the letter—mainly because "it contained several political implications, the kinds someone much shrewder than she could have conceived." *Oh well,* she thought, *so much for being recognized for my cognitive skills.*

Already media attention had shifted from Senator Madison to Priscilla J. Austin. The investigative report in the *Chronicle* stated: "Financial papers filed with the Secretary of State's office reveal Ms. Austin as having been compensated for her work on several political campaigns, though her compensation was legal because she had been off the state payroll at the time. She performs her political campaign work through her consulting firm, P. J. Austin and Associates, Incorporated, which she operates from her West Third Street home-office in Columbus." The slant of the news story was what upset Priscilla. The slant and the implications.

CHAPTER 31

The Ramifications of her Actions

Across from the Statehouse, Leland and Bill shared a coffee confab—seated across from each other in a booth—in the first-floor diner of the Galleria.

"Well, I tell you something else, Bill," said Leland, who was executive director of the LBO. "I compared her letter to the editor of the *Chronicle* with the one she wrote as a graduate student to the editor of the university newspaper. And in my opinion, this is authentic P. J. Austin, all right. It'd take more than a copycat to have written that letter. Priscilla's style is unmistakably straightforward. She sucks you in, then she spits your heart out like a pit from a peach. She leaves nothing to chance. Once she attacks, she completes the job."

"I know, but I still don't get it," Bill said angrily. "I just *do not* understand her having done this, especially because of her connection to Theo Madison, who none of us even knew was from Prendergast." Bill was perplexed because it had long been established that Priscilla's presence in the Ohio Senate was related to her father's illness. However, since Nelson's death, the question had become, "Why's she still here, and with Senator Callahan, of all people?"

Both men tensely stared at each other. Leland broke the silence and said exactly what was on both of their minds. "You don't suppose she was recruited for such an occasion as this, do you?" Bill shrugged.

As Senator Callahan entered the reception area of his office suite, he instructed Charlene to send for Priscilla.

He looked unkempt, his hair poorly combed and sheet lines in his face. When Priscilla arrived, he waved his skinny, intimidating index finger back and forth in front of her. "Can't you see how your actions have essentially put my fanny in the fire? I'll bet you never gave a second thought to the 'ramifications of your *own* actions.'"

Priscilla did not answer because she naively had assumed the caucus had wanted someone to bring the debacle to a head in order to obliterate it—like the command of Captain Jean-Luc Picard aboard the star ship *Enterprise*, "Just make it so." Yet even Priscilla wondered where she had acquired the propensity to behave so boldly.

The senator continued. "I've got my hands full just trying to convince those guys what I haven't done, not to mention the swarms of media and lobbyists nagging me." Then he tried to make Priscilla name what he described as her "collaborators." But she just shook her head.

Characteristically, he screamed at her, "Are you the least concerned how your actions have impacted *my* chairmanship? *Who* put you up to this? *Who* was it?"

"How many times do I have to tell you, Senator? There was no one else. Besides, what's with you? Why can't you believe that I wrote the darn letter *all by myself?*"

"Oh, I believe you *wrote*, as in *typed*, 'the darn letter' all by yourself. But I hardly believe that you alone wrote the contents. So *who* helped you?"

Priscilla stood still in absolute astonishment and said nothing more.

Outraged, the senator told her, "Just go back to your desk and stay there for the remainder of the day. And if you must eat, order delivery."

As soon as Priscilla returned to her desk in the small corner office that she and Sharon shared, Sharon and Brad showed up and settled in chairs near her.

"My goodness, Priscilla, couldn't you've found another way to air your opinion?" Sharon asked. "But an open letter?"

"Well, I know one thing for sure," Brad said. "You can hang it up if you ever have considered running for public office in *this* state. That's for damn sure." Brad made no secret about his ongoing animosity toward Priscilla, but he was disappointed with the Democratic caucus's appreciation for the "unexpected diversion created by Priscilla's open letter."

Priscilla did not respond.

"Are you *sure* you can't tell us who put you up to this?" Brad asked. "We already know that somebody must have made you a lucrative offer to go after Theo. Regardless, you're the one left standing." After he had exhausted all of his other ways of forcing Priscilla to talk, he said to Sharon, "I've done all I can; now it's *your* turn."

"You mean there's *more*?" Priscilla asked sarcastically.

"I'm sorry to have to ask, Priscilla," Sharon said, "but did Senator Callahan ask you to be prepared ... well, to be prepared to resign, that is, should the question arise? You must have known that to be a distinct possibility."

"Guys, please, give me a little breathing room *and* credit," Priscilla said. "I wrote the letter all by my lonesome self, grammatical errors and all. And, as I told the senator, I had no idea how influential an open letter would be. Otherwise, I might've taken a different course. Perhaps I'd have had it professionally edited?" She did not even try to hide her signature smirk. Then she prayed to herself that the two intruders would go away.

But no such luck.

"Come on, Priscilla, we don't want to see you lose your job over all this," Sharon added. "You're too valuable a team player to be forced to resign because of this mess."

Again Priscilla's smirk. "Try another angle, okay, office mate?"

"All right, then, if it helps, forget the letter. We all know it's not your fault," Sharon said with an air of finality. "Everybody's really mad at Theo, which makes it much easier to jump on you. Now that's what bothers me—you being made a scapegoat." Then she got up and stalked away.

"Damn it all, Sharon," Brad murmured, "why did you have to go and let on about the 'scapegoat' angle?" He realized some of the pressure had been taken off Priscilla, and he preferred she stew.

As the morning lingered—and for Priscilla, it lingered into eternity—she fielded several phone calls from reporters for follow-up comments on her letter. But eventually Charlene told the senator about the calls, and he instructed her to "screen all of Priscilla's calls and tell those blood-crazed reporters, 'Ms. Austin has no further comment.'"

Once again, Charlene was pleased to see Priscilla in the lion's den. She gossiped with others, "This is *it* for Miss Prissy. I'm sure of it. She won't last through the holidays."

But it was not long before Charlene buzzed Priscilla and suggested that since the senator had stepped out of the office, she might want to take this particular call. "It's from Washington," she added.

After she picked up the receiver and identified herself, Priscilla heard, "Yes, *young lady*, Mallory here. I'm senior aide to Congressman Louis Drummond, calling from his office in Washington. Let me get straight to the point: Why you haven't been *released* is the issue with us, *Ms.* Austin! The congressman wants you to know that he is 'outraged and appalled at your indiscretion.'" With that, the black community from Cleveland, by way of Washington, D.C., had spoken.

But Priscilla retorted, "Mallory, you deal with matters in Congress and leave the Ohio Senate to me. Besides, can you find fault with anything that I wrote? No, I submit to you that you cannot, nor can anybody else. The issue is not '*what* I wrote' but, 'it was *I* who wrote it.' That's all. Now, lose this telephone number." With that, Priscilla hung up the phone.

Yet she reflected, so alone at her desk, that she plainly had not taken into account the reaction from the black community—just herself, and herself alone. This was not the first time in her life that thinking for herself caused reproach from other blacks. But she did not care only about a person's race. So long as that person did something that she found disagreeable and she felt like criticizing that behavior, then she would do so, regardless of that person's position, race or gender.

Nevertheless, at home that evening, Priscilla winced as she read through more daily news editorials. The one that really rattled her was published in the *Sentinel*. The editors took Priscilla to task: "A black female senate staffer ruthlessly lambasted a respected black elected official." They concluded their editorial with the sentence, "Ms. Austin's removal from office is imminent." Priscilla took the newspaper's attitude to heart because the editorial board and the publisher were black—and staunch, old-line conservative Republicans, at that. *Oh well. At least Nelson wasn't alive to witness any of this*, she thought.

She called Julia to discuss the fallout from their little scheme.

"Folks in this game know the drill. Staff goes off the state payroll and signs onto that of the political campaign," Priscilla said. "This is politics, not philanthropy. Surely, no one expects me to perform my services gratis? Where the devil are they going with this crap anyway?"

"Priscilla, think character. Girl, they're playing the character card with you," Julia said.

Priscilla crumbled the *Chronicle* ferociously. "*'Character'?*"

"Those guys know you did everything legal, ethical and aboveboard. They even know your name is on all those financial reports filed with the secretary of state. So they're coming after you where it hurts—your image. You're not dirty, but neither are you squeaky clean."

"I tell you what hurts, Julia. No one gives me any credit for my little gray cells. Everybody—Senator Callahan, Sharon and Brad, the lot of 'em—thinks there's someone lurking in the background pulling this puppet's strings 'cause Ms. Prissy isn't resourceful enough to have scribed that stupid letter 'all by herself.'"

"Priscilla, part of your problem lies with that very fact. Remember, it was *you* who insisted we insert the letters in those manila envelopes and postmark them outside of your neighborhood. Well, girlfriend, in your attempt to create 'a little mystique,' you caused the recipients to think that someone else actually wrote the letter and copied it onto the senator's campaign stationery. That tactic didn't work too well. Nor did you consider other ways that people might consider your signature. To use your own words, 'plainly put,' the net effect of this little scheme has crashed before your very eyes. Yes, Priscilla, 'sometimes we outsmart ourselves.'"

Priscilla hated to hear her own words thrown back at her.

"Keep in mind also," Julia continued, "that we have no idea who could have copied your writing style. Everybody knows you attended Ohio State. Everybody! A few even know you wrote a letter to the editor of the university newspaper, and *everybody* knows the writing you do for the senator. Girl, those are only a few reasons why your critics are having difficulty believing that you wrote that letter 'all by yourself.'"

"Oh, Julia, do we have to keep reliving all that?"

"Yes, we do, because you still don't get it. Almost everybody in that Statehouse circle, including the lobbyists and reporters, have described this little fiasco as 'a farce,' and then you go and inject your reference to Faust 'for more literary intrigue.' For sure, 'one of them put you up to it.' In other words, Priscilla, there's as much evidence supporting your claim to sole authorship as there is to the contrary. Now that's the real irony in all this. I suggest you let it go and let them scurry, every single one of them. Especially your boss."

At her wits end, Priscilla still found a way to inject humor—or was that sarcasm?—into the ever-escalating political farce. "Yeah, well, as things stand, even Faust might be offended."

Bill visited her the next morning. She looked up and saw him standing on the threshold of her office, his starched, white cotton shirtsleeves rolled back.

"Surprise, Missy! Yeah. 'Tis *moi*. Bet you didn't expect to see me just now, did you?"

"Can't say that I did." Priscilla fought an impulse to jump up and hug him, but under the circumstances, she did not want to risk being castigated for *that* indiscretion, either.

"I don't know why I'm always offering words of encouragement to you," Bill went on, "but right now I feel that you need to hear somebody tell you that they're thinking of you. Also, I don't know much about this cesspool you've fallen into, but I do know that I don't like seeing you all caught up in it."

"Well, ole buddy, ole pal, I tell you, I had no idea the ruckus I'd cause. Then again, are you sure you want to be seen in the company of one held in such widespread contempt? Why, even damaged goods and road kill fare bet—"

Bill's complexion darkened. "Stop it, Priscilla. From what I can see you're maintaining your own just fine. Anyway, it'll all be over soon, and you'll emerge the better for having withstood it."

Then his effervescence and natural skin tone returned. "Just hang in there, which reminds me, the mere fact that you've kept face and carried on business as usual has been the best move you could've made. I only wish I had your genes or whatever's in your DNA. You're something else. Something else, indeed."

Priscilla was close to tears, but she quickly collected herself and said, "Honest to goodness, Bill, even crazy people like me sometimes need to hear a word of encouragement. You're a good man, Charlie Brown." Priscilla smiled again and said, "You most certainly are that."

"Thanks, but what I'll never understand is why you allow yourself to be used by the senator. And this time, he's using you big time. This is major. Even though something tells me you're going to be all right, I just hate seeing you used like this. But, as usual, let me know if you need anything."

"If I need anything? Damn it, Bill, don't you know you're pretty much *it* for me in this wretched hellhole? I don't need to see you to feel your support. From the start, I've always sensed a precious spirit in you. It's all these other blokes I tire of. I repeat, thanks for being you!" Again Priscilla fought back her tears.

Bill winked as he walked out of Priscilla's office.

Priscilla dropped her head in her hands. *Yes, I know I'll be all right, but right now I feel so all alone.* But not entirely. She prayed: *Well, Lord, I'm in another ditch. Only this time, I dug it myself, all by myself.*

Yet even at this low point, a tiny, brave, resilient part of herself pondered her next move.

That evening Priscilla dialed a number that she had not dialed in a long time. Then: "Yeah, Momma, it's me, Priscilla. How's it going?"

"My goodness, Priscilla, what on earth moved you to make this call? Are you in trouble or something?"

"I'm fine, Momma. Just thought I'd call to see how you were." She tried to sound nonchalant. "Say listen, have you heard any news about the goings on in Ohio politics?"

"Nothing that I can think of. But wait a minute," Liza paused as if she remembered something. "Strange you should ask but your cousin Roland was home from Springfield over the weekend, and he said something about some crazy man in Ohio having done something weird. I didn't fully understand what he was going on about, though."

"Okay, Momma, now, try and recall exactly what Roland said." Priscilla, after all, was as transparent as a pane of glass.

"'Okay,' my foot, Priscilla. What's it you're trying to tell me? You haven't gone and gotten mixed up in something else, have you? Not again! Dear Lord, Priscilla, you know how you are, girl."

"Oh, Momma, it's nothing. By the way, has anyone out of the ordinary called, like some opinion pollsters or newspaper reporters?"

"Well, if they have, I haven't been home to take their calls." Liza did not raise her voice, but it did sound more intense. "Now Priscilla, I know you've gone and done something outrageous. What's it this time? Otherwise, you wouldn't be calling me."

"Momma, please, I've not done anything, at least nothing bad."

"Dear me, Lord, here we go again. Priscilla, when are you going to learn that there are serious consequences for some of your actions?"

CHAPTER 32

The Collective Force

While Priscilla reflected and stewed and held herself together, others in the inner circle of the Ohio Democratic Party summoned its resources "to make it so"—or, "plainly put," to bring Senator Madison back into the fold. In the world of organized crime, such "resources" are best labeled as "lieutenants." In unsavory corporate circles, they are called "operations' managers" and "troubleshooters." In the Ohio Democratic Party of the early 1980s, those resources were surreptitiously known as "the collective force." Like sleepers, this three-man team prepared for special assignments and were proficient in producing magnum opuses. When called upon, they would perform their roles with the utmost skill and effectiveness.

The men of "the collective force" gathered at the Cheltenham Arms penthouse apartment of Tommy Wozniah in Cleveland. No party operatives or elected politicians had been invited, least of all Priscilla J. Austin. Yet she, like every other politico in the Ohio Democratic team, was aware of their power, and not just from their listing among the state's registered lobbyists. Whenever these men surfaced at the capitol or at Democratic Party events, Priscilla, like many other legislative staffers, behaved like a groupie. Otherwise, she had yet to make any personal connection—or so she had thought.

The grandson of Polish immigrants, Tommy Wozniah had risen to become chief operating officer of Chesterfield Bank of Cleveland.

Frequent tutoring had eliminated his coarse dialect, and expensive Italian-tailored clothing had provided him with the look necessary to fit into high-powered financial circles. Tommy had gotten involved in politics shortly after graduating from business school; but rather than run for public office, his role had been backing contenders in Democratic Party politics. He had also delivered the ethnic European vote to a select group of Democratic Party candidates. Tommy Wozniah played high stakes political poker.

Grandson of a successful highway construction contractor, Angelo Delgato, also third-generation American-born, was Italian. He had expanded the company's portfolio with untold non-bid and sole-source contracts from the City of Cleveland, Cuyahoga County and eventually the state of Ohio. Meanwhile, Grandson Angelo had earned the nickname "Angel" because of his uncanny ability to achieve positive results for presumably unsolvable problems. Unlike Tommy, however, Angel used his heavy southern Italian dialect liberally—for special effect.

Completing the triumvirate was Bartholomew Jordan, a New York-born Jew, who had relocated to Ohio as legal counsel for the AFL-CIO. As such, Jordy, as he had become known, represented the big city union bosses from Akron, Cleveland, Columbus, Dayton, Toledo and Youngstown. Like his associates, Jordy appreciated the finer things in life. He wore classic Armani blazers, cashmere turtleneck sweaters and loafers; the rest of his wardrobe was tailor-made in New York. His circle of acquaintances often marveled at his deceptive demeanor, for "Jordy," it was touted, "could walk unnoticed among the Wall Street tycoons"—mostly because he had been one of them.

Angel managed to be both effusive in words and detached in emotion as he walked into his friend's Cleveland penthouse for their get-together. "Tommy, Tommy, always a pleasure to visit you at home. I 'specially like the view from your window overlooking the wharf and Lake Erie. Is simply a gorgeous setting to do business."

"You said, it Angel," Jordy agreed. "This is the finest getaway in the whole of the city. Now, what's our game plan for reeling in the fish? Can you guys imagine that little twerp Madison thinking he could just snatch up everything and run? I'd give anything to see his face when we catch him."

As Tommy waved them to the table that looked out on the Cleveland skyline, the operatives sat down and began to eat as they chewed over their action plan.

"What *exactly*," Jordy asked, "do the boys in Columbus want us to do? After we locate the bastards behind this, how far do they want us to take this little charade?"

"Hold on awhile, fellas," Angel said. Rapid-fire, he named several politicians in Columbus and Washington, D.C. "And what about that little lassie who wrote the letter? Doesn't she have a part to play?"

"Hell," Jordy agreed, "I'd like to know those answers myself, Tommy."

"Well, for starters, the boys in Columbus *and* Washington, too, for that matter, want low-spotlight-to-none, which eliminates some of the U.S. congressmen, who, incidentally, wanted too much for their parts," Tommy said. "And Daniel P. Callahan, well, he gets no recognition because he didn't do anything. By the way, fellas, Leland really came through for us this time. I still don't know how he does it, but some of his data from the LBO turned out to be the best possible lead. It saved us lots of legwork, too. As far as Ms. Austin goes, the consensus is that, she acted of her own volition. Therefore, she's to be taken care of, but later."

Jordy nodded.

Just after Priscilla's open letter had been published, Jordy had divulged to Tommy that he had a "personal stake" in the matter and did not want Priscilla tarred and feathered.

Even in those early days, Tommy had concurred. "Luckily for you, the big wigs don't want her canned. It seems they want her compensated, even elevated."

With that understanding between them, the two of them behaved as if their conversation had never even taken place.

"So?" Tommy asked his two pals. Angel and Jordy nodded to acknowledge complicity.

Then Tommy elaborated: "The deal is to deliver … delicately," he paused, "the 'bill of goods' back into the fold *unscathed*." He met the eyes of the others, searching for accord that they had understood his meaning that Senator Theopholus Madison was not to be harmed in any way as they conducted their mission. Then Tommy went on to allude that nobody else, including outgoing Senate bigwig Walt O'Leary, was to suffer retribution, at least before the leadership vote in January. "Got that?"

Jordy was dismissive but agreeable. "That's all?"

"You bet," Angel agreed.

Tommy cleared his throat, took another drink and called over his manservant to bring over the telephone that had the secure line.

Back in the capital city, another powerful trio also shared a meal—this time in the backroom at Chelsie's. Their mood, however, was not as convivial.

As the phone he had waiting on the table rang, Senator Marcus Tektonidis yelled into the transmitter, "Tommy, is that you?"

"Yes, Mr. President, and I've got Angel and Jordy here. We're all eager for further instructions and a few more details."

With tremendous restraint, Senator Tektonidis divulged his information. "'The bill of goods' is in Fort Lauderdale." Tersely, without actually naming names, he related the address and the information that this was the home of the sister of Marcus' longtime rival. They were now certain that Walt O'Leary was behind it all.

The others at his table—the Governor-elect and the House Speaker—nodded.

"No one is to be hurt," added the Governor-elect.

"Psychological intimidation only," concurred the House Speaker.

On the other end of the line in Cleveland, Jordy asked for clari-
fication. "Intimidate him psychologically? What exactly do you want
me to say or convey to him?"

The Speaker told it like it was. "Tell the bastard to have a seat and
explain in plain language how his actions have pissed off a whole lot
of folks. Remind him why his momma moved to Cleveland in the
first place. You get my drift, Jordy? Make the error of his ways plain to
him, psychologically speaking. That's what we mean." He left enough
of a long pause so that the diners at both tables had time to remember the money and power involved. Once Madison returned to the
Democratic Party, all of the statewide officeholders, including the legislative leadership, would be controlled by the Democrats. Every major
decision—including all contracts—that pertained to the state of Ohio
for the next two years would be made by the Democrats. "You-know-
who must be made aware of the ramifications of his errors. Got that?"

Jordy nodded. "Okay, Mr. Speaker, I will use plain, unadulterated
language."

"Right. You're the point man." Senator Tektonidis regained his
composure. "Tommy and Angel, we want you as reminders of the *mag-
nitude* of the 'ramifications of his errors.' Be unambiguous. Remind
the scumbag how capable you are at delivering the goods and services
of your clients. Apply plain old-fashioned psychology. Our deadline
is New Year's Eve."

As the Greek was elaborating, the Governor-elect and the Speaker
chuckled.

"Okay, everybody on board?" Tommy asked.

Echoes of agreement bounced back and forth across the telephone
line.

"One more thing, fellas," Governor-elect Scalise said. From a
prominent political family, Antonio J. Scalise had been primed to run
for president of the United States, but first, he needed a successful
uninterrupted two terms as governor. As a matter of political expedience, the Madison defection had to restore Democratic power in Ohio.
"We need advance notice the deal is done *before* 'the goods' resurfaces.
Why not call Marcus directly when your mission is accomplished?

He needs reassurance more than we do, though we all need this crap cleaned up before too much more time passes … And, if the scumbag asks about the open letter, disavow any knowledge of it."

There were grunts of assent from both sides of the conversation.

The Governor-elect asked for a final confirmation. "We good?"

"We the best," Tommy amended before pressing a button to disconnect the call.

Priscilla was in the window seat as the sleek airliner circled a final time and began its descent towards the boot-shaped palatial sea island of pristine beaches and luxury resorts nestled along the South Carolina coast. It was close to Thanksgiving and it was as if she were there again onboard the flight to Savannah, Georgia.

Beside her was Senator Callahan, who had not stopped talking since they took off from Columbus on their junket to Hilton Head Island for a joint meeting of the National Black Caucus of State Lawmakers and the Congressional Black Caucus.

Priscilla looked down at the terrain that reminded her of her hopes and dreams when she had flown to Tallahassee to begin her life as a FAMU professor. Not so long ago she never would have believed she would be enmeshed in an Ohio political scandal. She had felt so beaten down by the aftermath of the Madison defection, that without much fuss she had agreed to Senator Callahan's request that she accompany him on this trip.

Just now, he was lecturing his aide on what he called the "ramifications of her actions." A half hour or so ago, he had almost shared with her what he knew about the search for Senator Madison, but instead he had been uncharacteristically discreet. He wanted to be sure he retained the confidence of Marcus the Greek—not, he assured himself, that he was in danger of losing Tektonidis' trust. But Priscilla, he believed, needed to be more in touch with political realities. "Marcus and the boys, you know, air-dried my derriere over that entire little episode. But it didn't take much effort for them to realize there was nothing here. Still, they're hard-pressed about why you acted *outside* of the team." He pressed her hand against his chest. "We act as a team, Priscilla. Mavericks and loose cannons are unwelcome in politics."

Priscilla stared back at him. "I understand. But *somebody* had to do *something*."

"I surely do agree. Only next time you decide to be that 'somebody,' run your plan past me first. Are we clear on that?"

Priscilla nodded. She knew full well that she was not only "clear" but also finished with this whole game. She no longer desired to be a team player, certainly not in Ohio politics.

"And, sweetheart, you should also know this. Your resignation has never even been an issue. I hope you know that."

Priscilla did not respond. There was no need to do so.

The senator continued. "Some of us are in fact in public office today because we, too, expressed dissatisfaction over something someone else may or may not have done. But your dissatisfaction should *not* have been transmitted in an open letter. You can't imagine the people who think I wrote that letter and got you to sign it, or that I know who did write it." Finally he segued to his main point: "Some people are still having a hard time believing you wrote that letter 'all by yourself.' Are you absolutely sure no one else worked with you on it?"

In an instant, she pulled away from the senator's grip. Anger competed with hilarity, and before Priscilla could stop herself, she laughed in his face: "Oh goodness, Senator, that's a good one!" She leaned over and whispered, "I can write a frigging floor speech and bullshit newsletters and press releases. Yet I lack the acumen to write a letter full of crap as that one?" She shook her head in disbelief.

Senator Callahan stared back at the woman he had underestimated. He had assumed she had done what she had done out of loyalty to him. But now he understood what Nelson and Liza had always known. Priscilla was capable of just about anything. She had her own agenda and would do whatever she had to do to accomplish it. He asked himself: *Now, who was the pawn?*

303

On Hilton Head Island, just across a tall bridge from Savannah, tall palm trees adorned the main passageways to gated residences that sporadically appeared amid the stately hotels. Tucked away from plain view were the resort bungalows, where, one by one, the drivers unloaded their passengers.

At their private bungalow, Priscilla luxuriated in the beautifully appointed accommodations. For once, she did not care whether a lobbyist or the Ohio Senate had paid for their trip. All that mattered was that her stay at Hilton Head was one of those perks that came from her association with the senator.

The senator still had more to say about the scandal that Priscilla was intent on forgetting.

"Did it ever occur to you, Priscilla, that Theo is in more than a little hot water—that there are some folks out there who are more disturbed about this than you, or any of us, for that matter? Guys who don't handle matters in committee meetings and letter-writing campaigns."

Priscilla was not listening closely enough to hear the warning behind his words. She was weary of being lectured as well as angry that even the senator did not believe she had written the letter alone.

At a stalemate, the senator agreed when she suggested they "breathe apart from each other."

However, when they entered the convention site, they immediately encountered crowds of adrenalin-enriched lawmakers, staff and lobbyists who hugged, slapped shoulders and told tall tales to upstage one another. But no tale surpassed the one about "the fiasco in the Ohio Senate."

Harold, a prominent congressman from Tennessee, threw his arm around Senator Callahan. "Here's the man of the hour," he joked. "Say, Daniel, can't you folks in Ohio hold your own together? Listen, man, I'm feeling Theo Madison's pain. Was he even thinking when he pulled that stunt? Is he going senile or something? By the way, how're you holding up?"

"I, too, pain for Theo and pray he's going to come through in one piece." Senator Callahan sounded very sincere. "As for what he was thinking … beats the hell out of me."

Harold laughed and then nodded toward Priscilla. "But it's good to see you here with your little bodyguard." His loud voice dropped to a near-whisper. "Damn, she sure pulled off a fast one. Want to trade her in?" The congressman then walked off as if Priscilla had not been present and listening.

Senator Callahan nodded at his aide and lowered his voice. "Suppose you never thought how far news about our little debacle would spread? Kiddo, it's all over the whole damn country. And look, whatever else you do, steer clear of some of our volatile congressmen. But I brought you along to relax. Try to make a few friends. Go swimming or something. I am."

She watched as Senator Callahan disappeared into the crowd of the other, mostly black politicians. Yet Priscilla maintained a certain amount of respect and even fondness for the senator. He had not cut bait and run from the controversy. Nor had he been an ostrich.

But since she had no desire to make friends in this crowd, she headed back to their bungalow.

CHAPTER 33

Groomed to Be a Player

The walk back to the bungalow, in the escalating heat and humidity, was miserable. Priscilla could not imagine why anybody would plan a conference here at this time of year. It was nearly Thanksgiving and this junket came on the heels of one they had taken in Chicago to learn about President Reagan's new welfare reform. Why was the senator so intent on getting her out of the capital?

Before she reached her bungalow, she was accosted by an intoxicated man.

"Hey, baby, you lost or something? Why don't ya come home with me?"

Priscilla barely looked at the man. Probably, she assumed, he was one of the conference guests. Her stomach churned, but she kept pace in a steady stride on the pathway to her bungalow.

"So," he called out, "you're too good to speak, eh, bitch!"

"Whatever," Priscilla said. Except for the two of them, the pathway was deserted. Where was her bungalow?

"Hey, hussy, I called you a bitch. Ain't you got nuthin' to say?"

Priscilla kept up her stride, but she did say, "Be a sweet little boy, bubba, and go on back home to your momma."

"What's that? You little bitch, you damn bitch." The drunken man was livid.

But at last, Priscilla spied the bungalow. In a moment she was inside. She leaned against the door and took a deep breath before she felt safe. She let the cool air-conditioned temperature surround her and then changed into an oversized T-shirt.

She paced the cold tile floor in her bare feet. What had she missed about that scandal back in Columbus? Priscilla often applied basic logic, and sometimes math, to solve perplexing problems. *My letter did more than provide a smokescreen. But was that all it did? And if it was a smokescreen, for what purpose? Or for whom?*

Then her feminist and counter-racist instincts kicked into gear. If she had been a man or white, what would have been peoples' reactions? Her mind raced. She gained more confidence.

That's it. I'm a woman, a young woman, a young black *woman in a predominantly man's world—a white man's world, at that.* Voila! *Someone else was supposed to have done what I did.*

With that revelation, Priscilla poured a drink and looked out onto the beautiful blue sea.

All right, now, she thought, *the senator also said something about 'some folks out there being more disturbed, only they don't handle ... ' Ah yes, now I've definitely got it.* She finally accepted the fact that her letter *had* created "a welcome diversion" for some other "folks" to advance their own course of action.

It was time for that old black-and-white movie reel to play out its grand finale.

"Yes, I remember now," Priscilla said to the woman who faced her in the bathroom mirror. "Homeroom. Homeroom was our sanctuary."

It was the place where her high school classmates and she had confided family secrets. But there, Priscilla's classmates told *their* versions of the crime stories about their parents—versions that tended to differ somewhat from the news reports of professional executions, arson, corruption, embezzlement, extortion and more. And what did

Priscilla do during those stories? She prayed that no one would openly implicate her father as an associate of her classmates' parents.

As she stood before the bathroom mirror, the super-stratum of her impervious heart cracked, secreting her deeply repressed memories. One by one, each episode played itself out.

Priscilla saw herself as a youngster, perhaps in first or second grade of the Cameron Street Elementary School in Canton, Mississippi.

It had rained that day, and the sparse lawn of the campus was filled with potholes of muddy water. Priscilla was with one group of youngsters as they walked along the rugged pathway. Another group of children approached. Some of Priscilla's classmates stepped aside to make way for the approaching group, but Priscilla rushed toward them and pushed some of them down onto the muddy ground.

When she was asked why she had behaved so badly, she said, "I just felt like it. Besides, they're retarded." At the time, in the late 1950s or so, there were few, if any, separate schools for the developmentally disabled or challenged. So in young Priscilla's realm of reasoning, there was no place for them in her world. Now, years later, her regret was nearly overwhelming.

In her memory, she watched as another scene unfolded. The Austins had gone out for a Sunday drive when, out of nowhere, a car rushed them from behind. Nelson had kept repeating, "What's the matter? Why are they rushing us?" She had trembled as her father's face and hands beaded up with sweat. He had fought to keep his car from swerving off the highway.

When the car pulled up beside them, Priscilla had noticed it was filled with white teenagers. They had hollered out, "Where'd you coloreds get the money to buy that car? Get off the road." The game of chicken had seemed unending as Priscilla watched her daddy tremble and then bemoan that his family had to experience a situation in which he seemed so helpless. She had hated those white boys for humiliating her daddy.

Next, in her memory, she saw her father loading his lawn mower into the trunk of his car. Then he had driven to a neighborhood of some well-to-do white residents. He had parked his car on the street in a shaded area and then pushed his lawn mower door-to-door and asked, "Do you need for me to mow your lawn? I need cash to support my family."

Those little Southern impoverished parishes had not been able to compensate him financially. Besides mowing lawns, Nelson had sold women's apparel. Since black people were not allowed to shop in the stores anyway, and certainly not to try on clothes, they often purchased their clothing from catalogs.

Oh, what Daddy wouldn't do to provide for his family.

Then, again in her memory, she witnessed that awful day when Nelson came into the den at their home in Prendergast and asked her to come with him to the garage. He had something "magnificent" to show her.

"See here, Priscilla," he had said. "President Ford has commended me on my invention, a gasless engine."

But Priscilla's reaction had been downright cruel as she said, "You can't be serious, Daddy. Have you lost your mind?"

Why could she not have allowed him a moment of joy? Why had she been so heartless? Back in the present, she sobbed at her mean spirit.

The next scene, she again remembered, took her back to Connersville, North Carolina. That evening menfolk from two families—Priscilla even remembered their names, the Brawleys and the Mayfields—had called the parsonage and cursed and threatened Liza and the children. Then they had stormed out of a church meeting that had become a shouting match. They had returned to their cars and trucks and taken out their pistols and rifles, gone back inside the church and demanded that the Austins leave.

On that same night, an incident had occurred to rival anything the Ku Klux Klan had ever done to the family. The Brawleys and the Mayfields had surrounded the parsonage and shouted out all sorts of obscenities. But then another contingent—Priscilla remembered those names, too—Walter Smith and his sons, had shown up. They, too, had been armed to the hilt, so the perpetrators had disbanded. For the next several days, the Smiths had kept watch over the Austins.

This incident was one more, among many, which Priscilla had never divulged to anyone she knew.

Then, she remembered Wilber Blankenship, the drunkard who sang in the church choir. One night, Wilber had broken into the Prendergast home where Helen was babysitting. He had carried a knife and threatened Helen and the children. The next day, a Sunday, the Reverend had stood erect in the chancel and called out Wilber Blankenship. Then he had said, "My work as your pastor is one thing, but my obligation to my wife and children is another." Then he had raised his rifle and taken aim at Wilber Blankenship, who hastily walked out of the choir loft.

Priscilla had never spoken of that incident, either.

Looking back, Priscilla reflected that it was one thing for an adult to experience shame, hurt and humiliation. It was another thing for a child to witness a parent experiencing those emotions. Whoever coined the phrase, "Sticks and stones may break my bones, but words will never hurt me," had probably never felt the tinge of certain words.

Once again in memory, Priscilla replayed the scene as her parents prepared their home for a visit from one of Nelson's Rotary friends, a white man by the name of James Peterson. James had also been the principal of Prendergast High School. To prepare for his visit, Liza had polished her silver tea server and even baked some tea cakes. On the day of the visit, James had arrived at 19 West Seventh Street, pressed the doorbell but returned to the sidewalk. So when Nelson opened the front door, he had seen no one on the porch. But as soon as he stepped outside on the porch, he had spotted James standing on the sidewalk with his back to the Austins' home.

At a total loss for the reason for James's behavior, Nelson had called out, "Come on inside, James. It's good to see you, my friend."

But with reserve, James had answered, "Ah, come on, Nelson, you know I can't be seen entering your house. Folks round here'll never let me live that down."

This had been, Priscilla recalled, in the late spring of 1976 in Prendergast, New York. At that time and place, someone who Nelson honestly had believed was his friend had refused to enter his home. Hurt beyond measure, Nelson, who had until then been an affable man, had immediately grown distant, particularly with his Rotarian "associates" for whom he would no longer apply the term "friend." The most tormenting effect, however, had been his difficulty explaining the incident to his family, particularly Priscilla, as well as Liza and Camille, who had also been home at the time.

But Priscilla recalled how her daddy had handled that.

Nelson had decided to follow his own advice: "Talk about what ails you." But instead of a parable to explain the incident, he had shared a story with his family.

When the Austins lived in Mississippi, Nelson once had a hound dog named Spot, who actually had spots. The dog used to follow Nelson around the farm as he performed his chores. Nelson had also enjoyed Spot's company when he hunted or when he walked the long dirt road to the highway to get the mail.

One day, as Nelson was doing his chores, Spot, out of habit, chased after a car that was traveling down the highway. But soon the sound of Spot's barking ceased, along with the sound of the passing car. By the time Nelson had realized that something was the matter, he saw a white man walking across the front yard; he was carrying Spot in his arms. Tears streamed down the man's face as he said, "Mister, I didn't mean to hit your dog. I declare I didn't mean to do this."

The man handed Spot's limp body to Nelson. Nelson held the dead dog close to his chest, thanked the man for his care and then walked away and cried.

At the end of his story, Nelson had said, "That man, who'd *accidentally* killed my dog Spot, befriended me. A friend is someone who does what's right by you in spite of social mores and norms."

Even at the time he told it, Priscilla had easily grasped the moral in her father's story. Meanwhile, Nelson had shared that story with his friends at the barbershop, the members of his church, his neighbors and his Rotarian "associates"—all of whom were white men. In fact, the story about "the visit that wasn't" went full circle, and eventually, it boomeranged back to James Peterson. When James tried to reconcile the matter with Nelson, Nelson viewed his gesture as purely fabricated, which, despite James's best intentions, it most probably was.

But Priscilla also remembered that some Rotarians, unlike James Peterson, never had any problem stopping by the Austins' residence,

312

where they often sat in the living room and expressed no reservations about asking Liza for something to eat or drink.

Later, as Priscilla and her siblings had grown older and become more curious, Nelson had moved those meetings elsewhere, mostly to the diner at the Y.

But the phone calls had continued: "Yes, young lady, just tell the good Reverend that Bob from the Rotary called. Yes, sweetheart, tell him I've got some more jobs for him."

Priscilla had serious difficulty, however, grasping the full dimensions of Nelson's relationship with his Rotarian associates—perhaps because Nelson would dole out his Rotarian colleagues' jobs on behalf of the black people of Prendergast. But most of those jobs were the mundane, grubby jobs in a factory or in highway construction. Yet eventually, Nelson had complained and demanded better.

Priscilla remembered once overhearing her father on the telephone in the kitchen.

"Now come on fellas," he had said. "We've got some young people who can do office work. Surely, you can find some more appealing work for our women, too—especially the young, educated ones."

Priscilla remembered, too, how, once the deals had been cut, Nelson had taken his pickings to the barbershop, where he had held court and doled out the jobs.

She had never discussed that part of her father's life with anyone—not Amber, not Cathy, not Julia, not her boyfriends, not Senator Callahan. Yet her former high school classmates had been intimately aware of the jobs because it had been their parents with whom Nelson had associated.

Priscilla crouched on the floor of the bathroom and sobbed. *Oh, Lord, will it ever stop? Must you throw all that up in my face?*

The final episode on that old movie reel featured a story that ran on the front page of the *Prendergast Post Journal.* The headline read, "Priscilla J. Austin Returns Home: Local Girl Makes Good."

Shortly after the incident with James Peterson, Nelson had secured a job for Priscilla as a systems analyst at Marlin-Rockwell, Division of TRW, which was the largest manufacturer in the city. This was one of the most prestigious professional jobs ever obtained by a black person in Prendergast.

But such an achievement had made Amber and her other friends curious about how Priscilla had managed to get such a position, when no other black person had gotten such a job before. They also wanted to know how she had landed a good-news, front-page story in the local newspaper, when, as Amber had said, "The only time black folks ever appear on the cover of that rag is in crime stories."

Priscilla remembered answering, "Amber, please, the white folks in this town just need to do something noble for our kind. That's all there is to the story. I just happen to fit the bill for their agenda."

But since Priscilla lacked computer programming skills, her supervisor had arranged for on-the-job training. The stakes were high for the company and for Priscilla to succeed.

Yet after being on the job for less than one year, Priscilla had realized that computer programming and software development were not for her. She had developed severe pain in her lower back and consulted a doctor when she was off work for a week. The physician had told her, however, that her problem was psychological, not physical.

"What do you mean 'psychological'?" Priscilla had asked.

"Well, young lady, is there something going on in your life that's bothering you? Are you happy with your work? What about your personal life?"

At that point, Priscilla had realized how much she hated what she thought of as "that darned desk job." She had been stressed because she was looking for a way out of it without hurting her father.

A short time later, she confronted Nelson about the matter, and almost immediately, her back pain had eased. After she resigned her post at Marlin-Rockwell, she also learned of Nelson's ulterior motive for getting her the job in the first place: "Since you didn't know what you wanted to do, I figured it wouldn't hurt if you made a few dollars and beefed up your résumé in the meantime."

Nelson had been quite disappointed that his favorite had turned her back on the plum job that virtually every young, educated person— and many older individuals—had openly coveted. But he had been absolutely thrilled that Priscilla had confronted him about her dissatisfaction with the job, for what he had most yearned for was that she would find her own way.

So it was, Priscilla remembered, that over the years her father had groomed her to play the role he wanted her to play. She had hated that role, but she had learned to act as if she were enjoying it.

And so, little by little, Priscilla had become the darling of the Prendergast community's social and political elite. She had attended house parties and all the right social events, played tennis, went boating on Chautauqua Lake, skied on the slopes near the Mourné Vineyards and had been recommended for positions on several community boards. Overall, she had enjoyed a pretty good life in Prendergast, even though she hated that computer job.

After she resigned from her job at Marlin-Rockwell, Priscilla had learned of, and readily accepted, the faculty post at Florida A&M University.

Priscilla looked in the mirror and admitted that she had moved to Florida to escape the influence of her father and that relentless spotlight shining on her life in Prendergast.

With that spectacular epiphany, the movie reel ended.

I'm good with myself now, Priscilla said to herself, as she felt the pain and tension recede from her head.

Still in her bare feet, she padded out to the sitting room and sank down on the sofa.

But politics, she thought. *How did I get in over my head in politics? Ohio politics at that.*

Again, her father came to mind. On the whole, although Priscilla had never dared to acknowledge this, it was small-town politics that had garnered Nelson power, prestige and social status. At work for Senator Callahan, the most she would say about her father's involvement in politics was, "My ole man's a Republican, poor fellow." To use Liza's words, "Priscilla sees most of her life, and that of her father's, too, through rose-colored glasses." But mostly, Priscilla had always disavowed that Nelson had been a player and that he had even enjoyed playing the game.

So when Nelson had said, "I'm not worried about you, Priscilla, you've always known how to get up and go after what you want," that was precisely what he had meant. For Nelson had groomed his daughter well.

So, she wondered, *what happens now to Senator Madison?*

Beyond a doubt, she understood he would be dealt with expeditiously and professionally. *Did he really think those guys were going to roll over and say, 'Sure Theo, you've got our blessings to take all of the bounty with you?*

Suddenly, Priscilla was afraid for her homeboy.

CHAPTER 34

Reeling in the Catch of the Day

Tommy and Angel sat and talked in the luxurious cabin of the custom-built Boeing jet. As the chief operating officer for the Chesterfield Bank of Cleveland, Tommy had access to such amenities as the private jetliner. They were awaiting landing in Fort Lauderdale.

Angel was already, or was it *still,* fuming about the Ohio scandal. "I still can't believe the gall of that man. After all that money we poured into those elections, he can't possibly believe he's getting away with this."

"We're about to find out for ourselves," Tommy said. "And remember, this one's Jordy's lead."

Meantime, Jordy was in the lavatory soaking his warm face in crushed ice. *Ah, that feels good. I need to be fresh and calm when I talk to the little twerp.* He grabbed a fluffy towel from the rack, wiped his face and smiled at his handsome image in the mirror before joining his associates in the lounge just in time to hear the overhead announcement to prepare for landing.

"Okay, fellas, I'm good," he said. "Let's do this job."

A chauffeur in a sleek, metallic-gray limousine with crimson, leather interior—Buckeye colors—awaited the three men outside the arrivals gate. They drove a little over thirty minutes to the Miranda Parkway address.

At their destination, they walked up the sidewalk to the house's front door. Jordy rang the bell.

An elegant, platinum-haired white woman in her late seventies opened the door.

"Oh, my, company! And it's only ten o'clock in the morning." Susan was the sister of Senator Walt O'Leary, the erstwhile Democratic president of the august upper chamber of the Ohio General Assembly. Graciously, she smiled. "May I help you, gentlemen? Who may I say is calling?"

Jordy was on best behavior as he gravely introduced his associates and himself. Then: "We're friends from Ohio visiting your brother Walt and Senator Madison. They're not expecting us because we'd hoped to surprise them." He gently pushed the door wider. "If you don't mind, please don't announce our presence."

Susan stepped aside. "They are going to be so surprised to see you young men." She lowered her voice. "Senator Madison has seemed a little down since he arrived. He's going to be so pleased to know you cared enough to come all the way from Ohio to visit with him." She gestured toward the rear of the house. "He's in the living room or maybe out on the patio. But Walt's off running an errand. He'll be back shortly. Meantime, I'll go and make you some tea."

In another moment they saw Senator Madison standing at the patio window, his back to the three visitors. He was wholly unaware of their presence.

"Good morning, Senator," Jordy said as he alone walked closer.

Theo Madison turned around. As he recognized the three men, his posture slumped. He even stumbled as he walked toward the uninvited guests.

"Oh, Senator, you needn't move away from the patio window," Jordy said. "Lovely day. The weather here is marvelous. Back home in Ohio, it's so dreary and frigid. Hope we don't catch our death of a cold when we get home from this visit." Jordy reached for the senator's hand and gazed directly into his eyes. "You know, Senator, we thought we'd best surprise you. We knew if we called ahead, you might not be willing to see us. Please, won't you allow me to state our case? And then we'll leave you to your serenity."

A terrified Senator Madison looked from Jordy to the other two men. He was keenly aware of the constituencies they represented: finance, banking, building and trade unions and construction contractors, among other interests. "Why are you fellas here? What do you want from me? And who told you where I was?" His voice faltered. "Was it Walt? Is that why he said he had 'a sudden errand to run' this morning?"

"Shall we sit, Senator?" Jordy asked. "I find it so much easier to discuss business while seated. Don't you agree?"

He and Senator Madison sat down and faced each other. Jordy was calm and in control. Senator Madison had already begun to perspire profusely.

"As I was saying, Senator," Jordy continued, "we're here to discuss some important business. And then we'll leave."

But Jordy's reassurance only served to disturb the senator even more. Tommy and Angel sat across the room on a huge sofa, their presence only compounding the effectiveness of their surprise visit.

Susan glided into the room with her formal silver tea server and a plate of crumpets. Soon all the men were fidgeting with their teacups and napkins.

"This is awfully kind of you, Madame," Tommy said.

"Yeah, no need to make a fuss, Ma'am. I'm good," Angel added.

"Thank you, Susan," Senator Madison said, as he prayed she would not go too far away.

She smiled a bright hostess smile and then left the men to their talk.

"Now, Senator," Jordy said, to refocus the frightened man's attention, "allow me to explain our presence. Mutual acquaintances of what I will simply term 'concerned investors' in the recent elections called upon us to meet with you. We mean you no harm, Senator. We're here merely to deliver their message. You see, Senator, there's concern over your defection from the Democratic Party, which, granted, is entirely your busi—"

"But young man, I need to—" Senator Madison stopped mid-sentence because he observed Jordy's look of surprise at being interrupted.

"As I was saying, Senator, our mutual acquaintances are concerned with the adverse effects of your defection on their business," Jordy said. "In a nutshell, Senator, several are in limbo over important decisions they have already made based on the results of the November elections *and* the impending votes for leadership in the Ohio Senate. Those 'concerned investors' are anxious to know whether they must now cover their losses or proceed as originally validated by Secretary of State Taglione. Do you understand so far, Senator?"

On the facing sofa, Angel held a clinched fist to his mouth as he tried desperately not to laugh, while Tommy occasionally kicked him on his ankle. Jordy glanced their way and then pointedly ignored them so he would not lose his own composure.

Senator Madison ran his tongue over his dry lips. "I meant no harm, Jordy, but I—"

"I am sure you 'meant no harm,' Senator," Jordy assured him. "Allow me also to impress upon you that my associates: Angel Delgato is with Delgato Construction and Tommy Wozniah with Chesterfield Bank." As they nodded, Jordy smoothly continued. "Senator, can you understand the dilemma we all face? We need to know your sentiments."

"Well, now, young man, as I tried to say earlier, I never intended to hurt anybody," Senator Madison said. "This all began because I wanted Marcus and his cronies to back Walt for leader of the caucus. When that … did not materialize, we … no, *I,* asked the Republicans to reinstate Walt as president of the Senate. To assure that outcome, it will fall to me to cast the deciding vote to achieve the magic number 'seventeen.' That's all we were trying to do. But we—or at least *I*— never expected this kind of reaction to what was supposed to be a simple plan."

The three visitors let that sink in. This was the first confirmation of what their Democratic bosses had suspected. Walt O'Leary—former leader of the Democratic caucus as well as former president of the Ohio Senate—was the mastermind of the grand scheme, after all.

Then Jordy smiled slightly. "Yes, I see. Now we see. But I wonder, Senator, if you calculated the fullness of the unexpected fallout from such a plan? For example, your son manages one of our banks. I believe another of your children as well as your wife are also experiencing unfavorable reactions on their jobs as a result of your actions.

"I realize that some people back in Ohio want to know the reasons *why* you defected. But my clients merely wish to invite you *back* into the fold. That's all we want from you, Senator."

While Senator Madison fidgeted, Jordy contemplated his next move. Then he leaned forward and asked, "May I call my people and inform them that you're returning to the fold, Senator Madison? What shall I tell my people?"

Tommy and Angel were disappointed that the discussion seemed over so quickly.

Tensely, Angel and Tommy leaned forward. There was a brief lull as Jordy stared at his prey. Senator Madison visibly wrestled with himself.

"All right, Senator, my associates and I need your answer before we fly home. May I tell my people that you're returning, say, between Christmas and New Year's Eve *and* that you'll confirm all this in a telephone call to Senator Tektonidis *prior* to your return? That's all we need from you, Senator, nothing more." Jordy sat back in his chair and clasped his hands together. He had presented his case, or was it his ultimatum? The next move belonged to the senator.

Very circumspect, Senator Madison said, with much hesitation, "But I need to talk to Walt first. There's a lot on the table, Jordy, unless, of course, Walt already knows about this little visit of yours."

"Sorry, Senator," Jordy said. "My instructions were to meet with *you* and to report back *your* decision. Have we reached a decision, Senator? Shall Tommy send the company jet to pick you up, say, the morning of New Year's Eve? You'll receive a call from the pilot to confirm the time of your departure."

The sound of silence has served many politicians well. Senator Theopholus Madison made the politically expedient decision. He took a deep breath and simply nodded.

Tommy and Angel stood up and walked across the room to participate in the consummation of the deal.

Tommy extended his hand to greet the senator for the first time. "I will inform my people of your decision to return on New Year's Eve. We will see you again upon your return to Buckeye country."

Angel was next. He, too, shook Senator Madison's hand. "Senator, you've sure made a lot of folks *very* happy with this little decision of yours. I mean a whole lot of folks. Enjoy the remainder of your stay here, and try to bring back some of this lovely weather."

"Well now, everybody, looks like our business here is finished," Jordy said. "Senator, thank Ms. Susan for her fine hospitality. Like I said, we'll be leaving you now."

The three associates headed toward the door. But Jordy turned back around. "See you New Year's Eve, Senator."

In the limousine, Angel and Tommy agreed that all had gone smoothly and maybe faster than expected.

Jordy had already dialed Senator Tektonidis on the car phone. Then: "Brad? Jordy here. The senator, please." He flashed his friends a smile as he waited for Marcus to come to the phone. "Mr. President? Yes, 'The bill of goods' is back in the fold. As we speak, we are headed for the airport." He paused. "No. No sign of the other one. His sister said something about him having to run an errand."

Senator Tektonidis made a sound that could have been a chuckle. "He's on an errand all right. He left his little lackey high and dry."

"You want," Jordy asked, "that we should do something about that loose end?"

"Down, boy." Marcus paused, then he asked, "But what else did our little émigré have to say?"

"Like you all wanted, he'll be home early New Year's Eve," Jordy said. "Our pilot will contact him about the schedule. It was quick and easy, really. Didn't even take any arm twisting. I was as straight as an arrow and, like you all said, used elementary psychology. I tell you something else, though. He was scared out of his wits. No trust there for you-know-who. He kept asking whether he'd been set up. Something strange is going on between those two."

But Marcus was intent on nailing down the details, not Jordy's speculation. "So I *will* receive a telephone call *directly* from 'the bill of goods' himself?" When Jordy confirmed that, Marcus hung up without so much as a word of praise.

Meanwhile, Senator O'Leary was breaking the speed limit along Florida Highway 27, en route not for a "short errand," as he had led Senator Madison to believe, but instead to a meeting with the Senate Republican leadership in Coral Gables.

Unfortunately for Senator O'Leary, he did not realize that he was being tailed by three men in a black sedan not far behind him—or that the driver was on his car phone with the other triumvirate who had just visited Senator Madison.

Charlie, the driver, barked into the phone. "Yes, boss, he's past Miami and definitely pushing his peddle toward Coral Gables."

In the back seat, Charlie's companions named Eduardo and Onslow—posed as thugs, fixed their gaze on Senator O'Leary.

"*Si,* that is him," confirmed Eduardo as he looked at a faxed photograph he held in his hand.

"Right plates, just like the DMV said," added Onslow. "And he thought he'd fool us taking the back road. Old man, crazy old fool."

With that verification, Charlie easily overtook Senator O'Leary's car and then deftly forced him off the road. Eduardo and Onslow jumped out and rushed over to the senator's car.

Senator O'Leary, his mind still focused on his meeting with the Senate Republicans in Coral Gables, rolled down his window. He had no clue what had just happened or what was about to happen.

Onslow stood in full view. "Think you're going somewhere, Senator?"

Eduardo reached through the open window and unlocked the door. Effortlessly, he snatched the senator from his seat.

"Who are you men?" Senator O'Leary blustered. "What do you want with me? It's broad daylight. The highway patrol's all over the place!"

But it did not take long for the senator to realize that these men meant business—and to understand exactly what sort of business they meant.

"Charlie," said Onslow, "call in and tell them we've nailed our quarry fleeing the scene." Then he gripped the senator by the waist, pulled him to the black sedan and handed him Charlie's car phone.

"Walt," said the voice on the other end of the telephone, "you're out. When you return, you will vote 'yes' to Marcus' presidency. After that, you'll enjoy an early and quiet retirement from the Ohio Senate. And I'm afraid, my friend, this isn't open for discussion. Sorry, Walt." The line went dead.

Angel and Jordy sat astounded in the lounge of the luxurious aircraft.

"Whoa, Tommy!" Jordy exclaimed.

Tommy flashed his associates a victorious smile and then placed a call to Senator Tektonidis. "Well, Mr. President, we've reeled in the 'excess baggage,' too."

At that, Angel and Jordy gave a high-five to each other, and then to Tommy. Of course they had always understood that Tommy was the real "point man" on the force.

"Excellent." The Greek hung up the telephone.

Angel signaled to the stewardess for a celebratory round of drinks. "Ah, Tommy, we knew there had to be more to this than the Fort Lauderdale piece."

"You bet." Jordy grinned. "I'm smelling a really *big* Christmas bonus for this catch." His smile widened. "Hey Tommy, man, when I grow up I want to be as smooth as you are."

They clinked glasses and drank to the dregs before the jet took off back to Ohio.

CHAPTER 35

The Ultimate Force

Late that next Saturday night, (which he told Priscilla about later) Senator Callahan was among the fourteen Democratic senators who met in the smoke-filled meeting room just off the Senate chamber. The two other senators, Walt O'Leary and Theopholus Madison, had not yet returned from Florida.

"Just when you think you know everything, you find out something new, like our Republican boys holding a retreat in Coral Gables," said Senator Tektonidis. Each of the Senate caucuses held an annual retreat. The Senate Republicans often held theirs at a posh Florida resort, while the Senate Democrats opted for more austere accommodations.

Senator Tektonidis gave a brief and edited summary of the clandestine happenings in Florida, and then said: "Okay, fellas, looks like we're going to enjoy Christmas *and* New Year's after all. But save your jubilation until New Year's Day. We damn sure don't want anybody knowing we've restored our situation before then."

Yet several senators still did not get it and demanded more answers.

The Greek sighed but complied. "It goes like this: Walt O'Leary just wanted to be reinstated king of the hi—"

He was interrupted with a surge of laughter and sighs of disbelief.

Senator Tektonidis held up his palm. "No lie. That *was* the game plan. But Walt got Theo to play the front man, and then he took the deal to the Republicans, who he hoped would promise to vote 'yes' for his leadership. And then Theo was to seal the deal and cast the decisive seventeenth vote."

The Democratic senators exploded.

"That's crazy, man!"

"The goddamn Republicans surely weren't falling for that foolishness?"

"What a farce!"

Without the aid of a gavel, the Greek silenced them again. "Anyway, Walt actually seemed to have believed that he would come out smelling like a rose and on top again."

"But the Republicans would never have voted for a Democrat at the helm," one senator said.

"Walt sounds as desperate as Theo," said another.

"And exactly what was in this" asked another, "for Theo?"

Senator Callahan spoke up as if he were waiting for that moment: "A goddamn title and some perks, like more trips. Theo really did sell his soul for a 'bill of goods.' He wanted to retire on top, and in the end he's getting *nada*."

"That was insane, Daniel," Senator Chouinard said. "Just plain foolishness."

The other senators nodded in agreement, and then resumed talking among themselves until the Greek again commanded their attention.

"There remains one loose end. Or, shall I say, loose cannon." His eyes locked on Senator Callahan. "This concerns your little Miss Prissy, Daniel. We need to finally discover the extent of her involvement and whether she had any ulterior motives. Supposing she's one of the angels, which of course is *our side*, and that we need to close out this deal publicly, she will be the one served up to issue an apology to Theo. Not you, Daniel, or me, or anybody else from the caucus. Only Ms. Prissy." He cracked the tiniest of smiles. "And Lord knows, I've got a funny feeling she can handle that, too!"

There was a groundswell of relieved laughter before the Greek brought the meeting to a close.

Perfectly according to script, Senator Madison and Senator O'Leary returned to their offices at the Ohio Statehouse. Not a single news story about the reappearance of either senator was printed or aired.

Finally even Priscilla understood why no one but she had acted, at least not publicly.

The same day of the senators' return, Senator Callahan called her into his office and let her know how and why it had happened that Senator Madison was back in the Democratic fold and that Senator Tektonidis was going to become Senate president.

Then he cleared his throat, hoping what he had to tackle next was not going to be as difficult as he feared. "Priscilla, you're going to have to *apologize* to Theo. I know it's going to be tough for you, but it's the right thing to do. Theo deserves a professional courtesy, and we also have to have some acknowledgement for the public record. Besides, it's only appropriate." He hid a smile. "And for goodness sake, lose that smug demeanor!"

Priscilla made the appointment with Senator Madison and carefully rehearsed her lines. But no matter how she phrased it, she could not bring herself to include the word "sorry."

The time of her meeting arrived. Priscilla walked quickly from her office, through the reception area and out into the huge corridor. With each step, she felt as if everyone knew her mission. Most of the senators and their staff were aware that an apology was in the works, but they had no idea that Priscilla was on her way to apologize at that moment.

She climbed the huge marble staircase to the third floor, where she avoided glancing into Bill's corner office. Then she hurried into Senator Madison's reception area. As she waited for the receptionist to call back to the senator, she fervently prayed that she would leave Senator Madison with his dignity restored. *Surely he deserves that much.*

Priscilla had barely taken her seat in his office, when the senator began his reproaches. "I was saddened," he said, "to read the complete text of your open letter to me. My God, Priscilla, you quartered me in the public square. But it also disturbed me that you circulated your letter throughout all those media outlets. My goodness, young lady, we were swamped with telephone calls and walk-in traffic because of your letter."

Priscilla merely said, "I considered sending the letter to you. But I didn't know where you were, Senator. No one did, or so it was said." Even to her own ears, her response sounded weak.

"But you could have delivered your letter directly to my office," the senator said. "Staff would have routed it to me. Couldn't you've done it that way, Priscilla?"

"I could have," Priscilla conceded. *Is now when I should say I'm sorry?* But she could not quite frame the words.

Senator Madison's voice rose. "And all that stuff about Faust and the devil!" The senator felt hurt by that analogy, and Priscilla could not suitably explain it.

Ah, she thought. *That's what hurt him the most.* She felt his pain. "Senator Madison, I truly apologize for the anguish I've caused you."

But the senator did not let her off easy. "Then why are you having so much difficulty merely apologizing for your actions? Can you at least express regret for having written the letter in the first place?"

Priscilla's head ached, and she flushed. Yet anger replaced remorse. *Why should I apologize for something I did in reaction to something he'd initiated?* "Senator Madison, I can honestly say that I truly wish that the entire incident had never happened and that I had found another way to express my views. However, I kind of think—Don't you agree, Senator?—that a piece is missing in your equation."

She paused, aware that she was asking the senator to offer his own apology for having created the mess in the first place. As the silence grew, she looked into the sadness of his eyes. What had happened to change this man who had radiated such admirable aplomb and impeccable style? His eyes had become dark and swollen. His shoulders had slumped. He had aged. She was appalled at how broken he had become.

Her voice fell to a whisper. "What did they do to you?"

Senator Madison did not respond, nor did he explain the reasons for his defection. After all, he was a state senator, and Priscilla was a mere staffer.

The two had reached an impasse.

In the silence that followed, Priscilla continued to pray that he would not press the issue. And she asked herself if she would handle this differently if a similar incident were to occur again. The only answer that occurred to her was that she was finished with all of this. She was through playing the game.

"It appears as if we have reached a little stalemate." Senator Madison's sadness seemed to deepen. "I would never have taken you, Priscilla, for someone who would have difficulty apologizing. I'm sorry that you don't see the error of your ways." He stood in dismissal.

They shook hands, and then she departed quickly.

Oblivious to all who spoke to her, Priscilla dashed around the corridor and down the stairs. By the time she reached her office suite, she had to stop to catch her breath. Then she almost tripped into her boss's office, where she gasped for more air.

"Senator Madison," she said, "looked broken." She wiped away tears from her eyes. She had felt the aging senator's pain. But she was also conscious of her own principles. She had grown accustomed to political wins and losses, yet something she had witnessed in Senator Madison's eyes had caught her wholly off guard. She finally realized another repercussion of playing, and then losing, in that political game: *respect is irreplaceable*. For Senator Madison and Senator O'Leary, too, the entire horrific episode had indeed been a farce.

"What did they do to him?" Priscilla asked Senator Callahan.

Senator Callahan did not answer and instead allowed Priscilla to endure her moment of anxiety. Then he said, "Now, Priscilla, I do hope you've learned an important lesson or two from all this. Never, unless it's *absolutely* necessary, show your hand. Because if you lose, the costs to you may very well be prohibitive. Yet, in this particular case, 'the force was with you.' Even more remarkably, most of us didn't even know that for certain until it was almost over."

Senator Callahan did not expound on his remarks. That would have been futile anyway, for the Ultimate Force had apparently been with Priscilla J. Austin, never mind "the collective force" of three who had flown to Florida.

The inauguration of the new Senate leadership team occurred with much celebration. Like all the other statewide officeholders, Governor Scalise and House Speaker Olmstead exuded satisfaction and pledged their support for the new Senate leadership team. But it was mostly Senate President Marcus Tektonidis who welcomed the restoration of the Democratic-controlled Senate. In January 1983, Democrats had finally regained complete governance of the state of Ohio—but not for long.

CHAPTER 36

The Delgato Offer

Early one spring day, three handsome men appeared at the Statehouse. For the heck of it, they stopped by Mary's Café for coffee because, like so many in the game, they wanted to enjoy a moment of celebrity.

After much glad-handing and bear hugs, the notorious trio rode the elevator to the second floor and walked to the reception area of Senator Callahan's office.

"We are here for our appointment with Senator Callahan," Tommy said pleasantly.

Charlene looked up and nearly gasped. Everyone knew these three men. Instead of using her telephone, she sprang up and ran into the senator's office. Overcome by the sheer presence of the men, she said, with her whole body trembling, "Senator, you're not going to believe this, but Tommy Wozniah, Bartholomew Jordan *and* Angel Delgato are in our reception. They claim to have an appointment with you, but I don't have them on your calendar."

Senator Callahan peered over the top of his wire-rimmed glasses and said, "Where are your manners, Charlene? Invite the gentlemen in, please."

After briefly glancing back at his mail, he looked back up at her. "And ask Priscilla to join us."

"Priscilla? But—"

"You heard me, Charlene," he repeated, without even looking up.

By the time Priscilla arrived, the visitors were already seated and engaged in informal conversation. Of course she recognized them, although she could not guess why they were here. "Welcome," she said. "Such a pleasure to meet the faces behind those organizations that supported us so generously at our Scalise fund-raiser last year. I'm pleased to have this opportunity to thank you personally." She shook hands with each of them.

The threesome looked at one another and smiled.

Tommy spoke first: "Well, Ms. Austin, truth is, we asked Daniel to call you in so we could make your acquaintance. We've heard a lot about you, and we're quite impressed with your work here."

"*Really?* I mean, my goodness! You guys are a big deal statewide, nationwide and, for all I know, internationally. How could you possibly be interested in *my* work?" Already she had put the Madison defection and her role in it behind her.

"Well, Ms. Austin ... ," Jordy smiled. "Or may I call you Priscilla?"

For a brief moment, their eyes connected. Priscilla blinked. *What! No, can't be!* Again she blinked. Well over a decade ago Jordy had been voted "the coolest guy" in their senior year in high school. Since then, he had grown remarkably more handsome and more sophisticated. Though his associates thought he was from Westchester County, Bartholomew Jordan was none other than the son of the local furrier in Prendergast.

Senator Callahan and the two other men wondered why Priscilla looked so flummoxed.

Jordy's smile widened as he repeated his question: "'May I call you Priscilla?'"

"Sure, Jordy, I'm good with that."

"You see, Priscilla, we want to know whether you're interested in employment advancement elsewhere," Jordy said. "Say, legislative agent for Delgato Construction? You'd serve a similar capacity as you do for the senator, only you'd be working for Delgato's corporate offices out of Cleveland. Also, you'd have an office in the nation's capital, where, of course, you'd represent our operations with the federal government."

Until this very moment, Priscilla had assumed that her open letter had placed her on the "Do not touch list" and that she had been quietly slated for the nearest exit ramp. It had never crossed her mind that her actions would result in a ticket of her own choosing. In her mind, she could almost hear what Nelson would say: *Child, there's no comparison between being a computer programmer in Prendergast and a lobbyist for a major corporation headquartered in Cleveland.*

Jordy had just offered his former classmate a big juicy plum.

"Wow! Are you sure you've got the right person?" Priscilla asked. "And another thing, what about the senator? I just can't leave him stranded." Actually, she was sure that she could have, but she preferred being seen in her most considerate and professional demeanor.

"Don't worry about me," the senator said. "These men are offering you the opportunity of a lifetime, and we realize this is a little unexpected. So why not take some time to think it over?"

"That much I can do, Senator. But I sure wasn't expecting anything like this." She smiled. "I still say you guys have me confused with someone else, I really do."

Angel, too, was smiling. "Another thing, Priscilla. I understand you like scuba diving and other sun sports?"

Now it was Senator Callahan's turn to be surprised at something new about his aide, the woman that he had slept with and thought that he had controlled. He leaned back in the gulf of his seat to watch the rest of the show.

Priscilla nodded. "I'm almost certain that you know I prefer deepsea diving." *Just how much of my background did these bastards check out?*

Angel was entranced at what he perceived as Priscilla's two greatest assets: her seemingly innocent behavior and her youthful appearance. Gifts like that, he knew, would put any of their adversaries to a disadvantage. "How about this? Part of our package includes access to one of our properties in the Caymans. You'll also have an unlimited expense and travel account. And pardon me for talking money, but your salary, which will be more than adequate, is negotiable. Young lady, I assure you that my folks would *love* to have you on board."

"We all would," Tommy and Jordy chimed in agreement.

"Wow!" Priscilla exclaimed. "Thanks again for this impressive, though unexpected, career option. But as I said, I'll need a little time to think it over. Okay, fellas?" Then she excused herself.

On their return trip to Cleveland, the men talked of nothing but Priscilla.

"Well," Jordy said, "she's a good-looking young woman. She's certainly intelligent, and she knows the game. At least *now* she does."

"Yeah, man, we made her a darn good offer, too," Tommy said. "If she bites, we can groom her for the real deal later. Let her get her feet wet first, though."

"Do you fellas think she'll bite?" Jordy asked. "There's something about her that suggests her mind is elsewhere."

"Maybe," Tommy said. "But frankly, I don't know where her 'mind is,' but I've been instructed to let her know she's got a job, a good one at that, *if* she wants it. Those were my instructions to the letter."

For several days afterward, the Statehouse hive was abuzz. Rumors flew. There was speculation that the trio had been the ones behind the open letter. But mostly everyone tried to figure out why they had wanted to see Priscilla. Brad and Sharon could not leave it alone. They did not stop harassing Priscilla for answers. Senators from both sides of the aisle even asked Senator Callahan about his impressive visitors.

But both Senator Callahan and Priscilla knew that discussing the purpose of their meeting with "the force" was off limits.

In any event, their meeting had essentially removed any remaining doubt as to Priscilla's future in the Ohio Senate or anywhere else, for that matter.

As one Statehouse observer put it, "Damn it man, she met with all three of those guys, and they came to *her*. Go figure."

And Leland Stanton? Should he not have known all the answers?

Not necessarily, that, in spite of the fact he had compiled an LBO dossier on Priscilla which contained the type of data that any executive-search firm could have discovered.

But Leland, although Priscilla never knew it, was perhaps the one who had set the perimeters in the final outcome.

In fact, Leland had spoken directly to the unlikely linchpin in the affair. For Leland had called the Prendergast Rotary and spoke with a man named Bob Shamansky. But before the secretary put his call through, she had asked, "And the nature of your call, Mr. Stanton?"

"We're doing a background check on Priscilla J. Austin because she's being considered for an executive-level position in the Ohio Senate," Leland had said.

An instant later: "Bob Shamansky, here, how may I help you?"

"Hello Bob. I'm Leland Stanton with the Legislative Budget Office in Ohio. We have an applicant, Priscilla J. Austin, who's under consideration for an executive-level post in the Ohio Senate, and we need some information about her character. It is our understanding that her father used to be a member of your organization."

"OK." Bob Shamansky had cleared his throat. "For starters, young Ms. Austin is a very bright and talented individual. An excellent speaker, too. You know her old man—our Nelson—was so proud of her that he *made* us bring her in as a guest speaker once."

"That's all well and good, but can you shed some light on her char—?" Leland had tried to insist.

With that, Bob had spoken with more candor. "Young man, Prendergast might be small, but we're not off the radar screen. We have newspapers, radio and television, too, and so we're quite familiar with the Madison defection. And don't forget that Theo Madison was raised here, too. And so I hate to break it to you, but you'll get no bad words from me or anybody else on the Austins."

And that, effectively, had been that—at least in Leland Stanton's perception.

But Bob Shamansky had been miffed. He had liked Nelson Austin. So he acted in behalf of his old friend's child. Bob thought a moment and then instructed his secretary to "track down Joseph Jordan's son, Bart. I don't care how long it takes," he had said. "Just find him."

A short while later, the secretary had succeeded in contacting Bart, and soon the two Prendergast natives had reconnected.

"Bart," Bob had said, "I understand one of our own is in a bit of a pickle. It's Nelson Austin's daughter Priscilla. You remember her, yes? You probably saw her name connected in the media with that debacle connected with old Theo Madison." The two men commiserated about the affair of their native son. And then Bob continued: "Unless the news reports have intentionally left certain facts out, are we in agreement that Priscilla has done nothing wrong?"

"Yes," Bart had said. "We're in absolute agreement that she's done nothing wrong."

"Okay, then," Bob said. "Can we fix her up with an impressive job somewhere? I mean, that kind of loyalty and steadfastness ought to be rewarded. Don't you agree?"

"Yes," Bart had said. "Let me run this past the fellows. I'm sure we can make something happen to your liking, Bob."

But then Bart had said, "For goodness sakes, Bob, I'd almost forgotten!"

"Yes, yes," Bob had said. "I'm sure you did, but our guys have contracts with the state of Ohio, too. Added to that, I kind of owe the good Reverend a favor or two."

"Consider it done, Bob," Bart had said. "Consider it done. And let's keep in touch." Then Bart hung up the telephone.

Bob had grinned at the phone. Perhaps, he thought, the highly esteemed House Speaker Tip O'Neil had been correct after all when he had said, "All politics is local."

That night, because she was still a little paranoid behind the Madison defection, Priscilla invited Julia over to discuss the Delgato offer. After relating the day's events, she cut to the chase. "Do you think this is a convenient way to wrap things up?"

"It's your call," Julia said. "Sometimes good breaks come your way when you least expect them. At least you have some great new options, girlfriend. The issue is whether you want to join the ranks of corporate America or go it alone. Either way, you can handle it. One thing's for sure: You might talk about making more money than you can count, but for the Priscilla I know, that's all that is—talk." She laughed. "Otherwise, you wouldn't be asking my opinion about the Delgato offer. You'd be informing me about taking it."

Priscilla nodded and smiled. "If I accept, it might appear as if I've indeed been party to some well-orchestrated scheme. If not, even the big-wigs will know, 'This girl ain't for sale'—at least not exclusively."

Priscilla continued to mull over her decision. As alluring as the new financial and social prospects were, she detested that she would be doing exactly what had consumed so much of her father's life. She did not want to be a political animal for hire—at least in an exclusive contract. Besides, she thought: *Just because a person is good at something doesn't mean that's what the person ought to do.*

And so she decided not to accept the Delgato offer.

Instead, without fanfare, she quietly resumed her academic pursuits.

For Priscilla, that decision had been brewing since her uncomfortable conversation with Liza on their cross-country trip to Sills Creek. As soon as she realized she was sick of politics, she had begun to lay her plans to return to the academic arena. Since then, the only soul she had shared this with was her old college friend Cathy. Priscilla had wanted her to know that she had met her bluff head-on.

Priscilla took heart that as an exit strategy, a backup plan or whatever one might call it, her decision had also fitted Nelson's caution: "What else can you do if the chips fall unexpectedly?"

Epilogue

For the rest of the spring of 1983, Priscilla worked hard and enjoyed, along with Senator Callahan, the fruits of majority-party control of the Ohio Senate. But it did not take long before the thrill lost its flair. For a long time now, her interests had extended beyond the workplace of the Ohio Senate. Priscilla was no longer satisfied with "that darned desk job." What she zealously wanted was to solidify her consulting business and get on with other aspects of her life.

As she groped her way toward a new definition of her future, Priscilla said to Julia: "You know, I've been propping up and promoting someone other than my own choosing for quite some time now. And I've been wondering that, if I'm half as good at this game as some people say I am, then why not go out and do it exclusively for myself?"

"You *are* 'as good' as people say you are," Julia assured her. "But I'm curious whether you've come to terms with another, though less pleasant, issue."

Not the least prepared for what was coming, Priscilla put down her cup of coffee. "Julia, what *are* you going on about?"

Sensing there would never be a time as suitable as this moment, Julia put the matter bluntly: "Priscilla, have you even reconciled to the fact that your vehemence against Senator Madison was your way of beating up on yourself? And that—?"

Priscilla tried to cut her off by letting loose an incredulous laugh.

"Stop it, Prissy. This time I'm not letting you change the subject and act like the matter is closed."

Priscilla squirmed in her seat, but for once she remained quiet and simply listened.

"Don't you remember when you told me how much Senator Madison reminded you of your father? Then, suddenly, when he defected, for you he was off the pedestal. You lost all admiration and respect for the man."

"My Daddy would *never* have done what Theo Madison did."

"Perhaps, perhaps not. But my point still holds. When Senator Madison stepped outside of the perfect image that you'd framed him to be—of your daddy, you cursed the ground that he walked on. And in public, of all places. Your letter skinned him every which way possible. You were distraught, Priscilla. Senator Madison was supposed to have stayed in his proper place, to maintain proper comportment; only he didn't. He showed you and the rest of the world that he had human needs and desires—and he stepped outside of the box. But you despised him for that. Once again, Priscilla, I'm asking whether you've come to terms with any of that. Until you do, it'll happen to you again. But the next time, you might not have the type of backup that was there this time."

Priscilla fidgeted with her coffee cup. "I suppose, as much as I hate hearing it, there is a tinge of truth in what you say." Priscilla squashed her umpteenth half-smoked cigarette. "Momma and my sister Ellen often criticize my 'rosy' and 'overly simplistic take on life in the South'—and especially my views about Daddy. But it never occurred to me that might be the reason I'd gone after Senator Madison with such vengeance." She sighed but then she smiled at her friend. "Lord knows, I hate it when you speak the truth so plainly."

"And what about your boss?" Julia asked. "Does he still have the audacity to think that you did all of that for him?"

"One thing's for sure, he definitely knows now that there's a part of me he doesn't know about. And he's smart enough to leave it alone, just as I've done with so much of his life and politics. Even so, I kind of think he knows that he's not the gravity in my universe. Well, *whatever.* I'll leave him to his glory."

"And your animosity towards Brad and the Greek's team?" Julia asked. "Have you reconciled with the truth that you went all out to show there's no end that you'll go to make your point? It's as if you'll do anything to win."

Priscilla firmly shook her head. "Now you go *too* far. I'll not 'fess up to that point."

"Well, this is better than I'd expected of you." Julia had waited a long time for her friend to come to terms with her actions. At least this was a step in the right direction. "Missy, I know it's been difficult for you, but I'll be here to help you, as usual, *if* this is your decision. Have you told Senator Callahan yet that you're leaving?"

"Not yet. But soon. My decision is not open for discussion. But the senator does deserve fair notice."

The afternoon when Priscilla did finally tender her resignation, the senator just nodded.

"I've been expecting this. Was there something in particular that brought it on and at this time? And I guess I'm a little curious that you're leaving while we're on top. Why is that, Priscilla? In a way, I guess I thought you might never leave after you weathered the Madison defection, and certainly after you turned down that lucrative Delgato offer. So, what gives? Why leave when everything's going our way?"

Priscilla spoke her mind: "Well, Senator, things around here happen in cycles, and I'm no longer impressed or excited by the fallout. Two years from now, you guys could be right back in minority-party status *again*, and I've already played my best hand. So maybe it's time for me to move on and out. That's all. It's just time for me to find my own way."

Although Senator Callahan did his best to persuade her to stay, she was resolute. Just as her father had pressed her, she had finally begun to make decisions *for* herself and *by* herself.

Later that day, she rode the bus home as happy as she had been in quite some time. At her front door, she stared at the brass plaque that she had affixed to the wall next to the doorbell: "P. J. Austin and Associates, Incorporated".

She remembered something her eldest sister Ellen had said to her years ago: "You'll know when it's time to get up, get off the merry-go-round and move on with your life. You'll feel it deep down within. That's when it's time to act, Priscilla, even if you don't know how you'll feed yourself. That's your natural instinct talking to you, one of God's ways of guiding you. Follow it, Priscilla, follow your natural instinct."

Priscilla reflected, as she turned the key in the lock, that she had felt it and had finally followed it. She threw her head back and smiled.

"Thanks, Ellen, for teaching me to know when it's time to get on with my life. This time, even Daddy'd be proud of me. Yes Sirree Bob, 'cause this time, Daddy, I'm doing it for myself."

There was that smirk again.

About the Author

Dr. M. J. Simms-Maddox is a tenured-professor of political science at Livingstone College in Salisbury, North Carolina, where she is a founding member of the Faculty Writers' Club. She earned her Ph.D. in political science from The Ohio State University, served as a legislative aide in the Ohio Senate, has operated her own public relations agency and has published in various academic, community and religious publications for over thirty years. She is affiliated with the North Carolina Writers' Network and the Women's National Book Association.

She enjoys reading, traveling, watching culinary and travel shows, and writing; and, she enjoys getting her hands dirty pulling weeds in the landscapes of her yard.

Contact Dr. Simms-Maddox for book signings and keynote speaking about her book at *www.mjsimmsmaddoxinc.com*.